SABREHILT

To Patrick and Noeleen

with very best wishes,

Max

SABREHILT

Maxwell McCann

Maxwell McCann

ISBN: 1461017203
ISBN-13: 9781461017202

To my mother

— Prologue —

Many an era has had its dark age, snags in the warp and weft of history. The world has been beset by them since the beginnings of time. Such lapses have largely remained unrecorded. Not surprisingly. Why dredge deep when you know what lies beneath the veneer of civilization?

Dark ages lurk at the very roots of Time itself. Their shoots pierce the earth when their season comes, taking unfortunate humanity by storm. Pestilence, blight, murder and mayhem engulf society and drag it down to murky depths where few things thrive. Those who *do* thrive are beacons of despair and loathing.

Don't be fooled into believing that they are a thing of the past. Who knows what awaits us around the next corner...

This tale is an exception to the rule. Not merely because a dark age has been recorded for posterity, and recorded in a most unusual manner. It is extraordinary because it was confined to a small circumscribed area, a narrow peninsula in the Province of Fingal. In addition, this is the very first dark age ever to be…

But that's the story about to unfold.

Let the manuscript speak for itself.

Gerty Mallock sighs as she unlocks the clasp of the enormous book on the table before her.

'I'm going to have to face up to this,' she murmurs while raising the cover. 'Once more am I duty-bound to see what these ruffians are up to and delve into their scurrilous hearts. Woe is me... And who... who, oh, who, will help us?...

'But wait!

'Who is this I see emerging?...

'Could it be...?

'Dare I hope...?...

'Three of them!...I will do all I can for you, my brave little soldiers.

'I swear it on the Book...'

The sword with no name
Shall cleave to
The son of a son
Of a son,
And he shall be called
Sabrehilt.

Anon

—PART I—

FIRST TIDINGS

— 1. Eye of the Storm —

Edgar "Sabrehilt" stood before the huge brick fireplace listening to the storm outside. Flames spluttered and hissed at intervals when raindrops pitched down the chimney. The logs collapsed with a muffled 'whumph' and startled him. Bending down, he took another from the scuttle and threw it on the fire. It sent up a shower of sparks, stars to be sucked up the chimney into the night sky. His eyes strayed above the broad mantel with its pewter mugs and plates to the sword propped between rusty nails - his grandfather's sword, hero of the Battle of Bayersbrook. How Edgar wished he was still alive to regale him with tales of honour and heroism. He'd loved nothing more than to sit on the hearth-rug and listen to him, watching his smoke-rings drift lazily upwards to the heavy oak beams of the ceiling. He had died three years earlier, a month after Edgar's tenth birthday. All that was left to remember him by was his sword, the selfsame sword that had favoured him with his nickname.

One midsummer evening, while his mother was milking the cows, he and his friends had taken the sword and sneaked out to the woodshed. There they had thrust and parried to their heart's content.

'Is it sharp?' one of them asked, Nico Smallbottom by name.

Edgar shook his head while testing the blade with his thumb. For some unaccountable reason, he stabbed one of the uprights of the shed. In shock, he let go of the sword and took a step backwards. It was buried up to its hilt in the post. The rest of the boys stared at the corrugated handle in amazement.

Lee Chetwood, Edgar's best friend, smirked and broke the spell. 'Must have been rotten,' he said, stepping forward and tugging at the handle.

It refused to budge. With a puzzled frown he tried again, feet wedged against the base of the pole. The sword was stuck fast.

'Edgar, you try. You put it there in the first place.'

Finger by finger, he clasped the hilt of the sword and braced himself. There was no need to. A gasp escaped them all when he drew it out with ease.

'Try stabbing it a second time.'

It pierced the wood as if it were butter.

'Here, let *me* do that.'

Lee grabbed the sword and went at the upright. With a cry of pain he dropped the quivering blade and gripped his wrist. 'Holy Bayersbrook... What the hell is going on here? How were you able to *do* that?!'

Edgar just shrugged his shoulders and grimaced. He was as mystified as they were.

In awe they watched him replace the sword above the mantelpiece.

1. Eye of the Storm

'Well, Sabrehilt,' Lee quipped, 'there's something mighty strange going on here.'

The name had stuck.

Gazing dreamily into the fire, he smiled to himself. He and Lee had got into many scrapes together, and got out of them again unscathed. Lee had once saved him from drowning. He owed him his life. He was a week older than Edgar and constantly harped on the fact. Black-haired and swarthy, he was his exact opposite, for Edgar had fair skin and strawberry blond hair. Sabrehilt was preferable to "Paleface" anyday.

Thoughts of that evening still filled him with wonder. Why him?... What for?... It was expected that he would follow his father into the milling business but he had other ideas, spawned by his grandpa's example; romantic ideas of adventures far away, in lands never heard of. He had no intention of remaining in this scut of a village covered in flour dust.

Stretching up, he took down the sword, turning it this way and that in the glare of the fire.

'How many times have I told you to leave that thing where it belongs?' barked his mother as she came through the door from the kitchen, wiping her hands on her apron.

He winced. 'I'm only looking at it.'

'Still... Swords bring nothing but trouble.'

'Not to Grandpa, it didn't.'

She smiled, rubbing his back. 'You still miss him, don't you?'

Edgar nodded, biting his lower lip. They couldn't imagine how much he missed him. He had been more than a friend to him, a second father. But why had he never said anything about the sword's magical properties? *Why*?...

'Supper will be ready soon.'

Once his mother returned to the kitchen, he recommenced turning the puzzle over. Why keep such an important secret to himself? Unless... It can't just be magic for *me*, can it?

The house heaved with the force of the wind. It was screeching about the eaves and rattling the windows, like somebody battling to get in at them. The heavy drapes stirred. A vague feeling of dread ballooned inside him. Something was wrong. Out there. The howling and shrieking sounded more like a hideous monster than the wind.

'Ed!' came his mother's muffled voice from the kitchen.

'Yeah?'

'It sounds as if the barn-door's come unbolted. It'll be blown off its hinges.'

'I'll go.'

'Good lad. Mind you wrap yourself up.'

He did, but he felt that all warmth and peace would be destroyed any moment. And he wouldn't have been the least bit surprised if it all had to do with the village and its ruined tower. Any village with place names like Hangman's Arch, Blindman's Alley, Coffin Street and Witch Square where innocent spinsters were burnt at the stake, was asking for trouble. Thoughts of the tower and its gargoyles standing over them made him shiver. The people of Garten had a lot to answer for.

1. Eye of the Storm

Winter had come upon them unexpectedly that year, as if she'd crouched and sprung out of the nowhere. October wasn't yet over and already it was bitterly cold. They were in for a long haul, before spring charmed the shoots from the soil, unsheathed the buds on the branches. He shivered involuntarily as he raised the latch and gripped the edges of his hood, slamming the door behind him. The rain was torrential, the wind unimaginable, a solid force to be reckoned with. White smoke fled from the chimney, flustered in all directions. Rain slashed his face and stung like hail, drenching him in seconds.

The barn-door was banging dangerously, he heard the cows lowing inside. They too were frightened. He slipped through the mud and slid the bolt home. On second thoughts, he opened the door and searched for a piece of cord to knot it in place. The atmosphere was warm with the smell of cows and milk and musky straw. The cart-horse next-door snorted and whinnied, nervously stamping its hooves. A ghostly barn owl perched in the opening communicating with the stable. It was no night to be hunting outdoors. Hunger was preferable to being chased down the wind, smashed out of the sky. The stone walls deadened the rage of the storm, but not the vague, niggling sense of foreboding that had settled in his breast.

Edgar felt as if something huge and malevolent were hovering directly over his home. Securing the bolt in place, he sprinted back to the house, keeping his eyes fixed firmly on the ground. Light spilled out of the opened door and engulfed him, bejewelling a curtain of raindrops.

'Mam?... Where's Dad?'

'Where do you think? Over at the mill. He's afraid the swollen river will damage the wheel.'

'I'll go help him.'

'There's no point you *both* getting soaked to the skin.'

'I'm soaked already.'

'Tell him to hurry on in before his supper gets cold.'

A ferocious gust goaded him into action. He was scared to think of his dad out there alone. Anything could happen. A bough might fall and crush him. He could tumble into the river and drown. But if a bough fell on *him*?... That might never happen. Not if he were meant to wield that sword. A strained voice, buried deep inside him and scarcely audible, said he would. He'd heard that voice before. It always told the truth.

He opened the door and flung himself out before he could change his mind. The storm raged worse than ever. At a slant he made for the millhouse. Partially sheltered by the evergreen hedge, he stumbled towards the rickety bridge, shocked by how swollen the river had become. A veritable torrent boiled and frothed beneath him. He had to grip the railings so as not to slip on the sodden planks.

Edgar slid to a halt and stared in disbelief at the sight that accosted him. It wasn't that the mill-wheel was about to be ripped from its moorings. It wasn't that the weltering water was about to swamp and drown them all. No. It was worse than that. He crept forward for a better look, just to make sure he wasn't seeing things. The very fabric of the wheel had come to life. On every paddle were heaped great, big, ugly toads. There must have been thousands of them. They crawled over one another. They slipped and fell into the river only to leap back out again. And some of them eyed him with fixed, malevolent orbs. A shudder sprang down his spine. He almost gagged for fear.

'Dad!' he roared above the mayhem. *'Dad!'*

'Yeah?!'

The mill door shot open. There was his father framed in the doorway, big and sturdy and secure. He felt the urge to run into his thickset arms, to breathe in his warmth and tobacco. He didn't want to be a swordsman any more. He wanted to stay at home, a miller like his father. But that voice, that voice kept hinting...

Spike, the shaggy terrier, barked and wagged his tail on seeing him.

'Get in here before you catch your death,' his father ordered, shutting out the storm and the toads. 'What have you in mind out here on a night like this?'

'I thought you might need help,' he answered rather sulkily.

'Good lad,' said his dad to console him, tousling his hair. 'We're in for a rum night, Ed, I don't mind telling you. Whether we'll be able to save the wheel is another matter entirely.'

'What if we just let it go round?' He was secretly hoping to spin those loathsome toads into kingdom come.

His dad shook his head. 'It'd fair spin off quick as lightning.' He sniffed and put a bare brawny forearm to his nose.

Ed loved the sight of his bulging muscles, the hairs that sprouted from his skin. He longed to resemble him. Yes, there was a hint of down on his upper lip but when, oh, when, would he sport a chest of thick fur like his father's?

'What if you don't, Dad?'

'Hmm?' Another sniff. He glanced at his son and smiled a rueful smile. 'It might hold. It might not. No point breaking our hearts over it... Come on. Let's go in to supper.'

'Did you see the toads?' Edgar asked with a shudder.

'Aye. There's many a rum thing happening out there tonight, my boy, things I've never seen the likes of before.'

'What should we do?'

'Nowt. What *can* we do?'

They stood there in the warm floury atmosphere and looked at one another. He was proud of his son, damn proud. He was a tough man but a kind one, fair-minded and true, and Edgar took after him. He'd do anything to protect his wife and his son, and he knew his son would do the same for them.

Without another word, Miller Falchion opened the door, put a protective arm round Edgar's shoulders and hurried him across the yard.

'She'll have our heads if it's burnt,' he roared above the wind before opening the door and pushing him in.

The smell of cooking assailed their nostrils, setting up a famished pang in their stomachs. *She* stood the other side of the door, hands firmly on her hips.

'Look at the pair of you,' she declared with a rueful shake of her head. 'Get up and change into dry clothes and be quick about it. Here are warm towels to rub some life back into you.'

'Thanks, Moll.'

'What did you let that mutt out for?' she shouted after them. 'He stinks now he's wet and his muddy pawprints are everywhere. Get away from me, you filthy bowler,' they heard her cry as Spike tried to dry himself on her skirt.

Edgar went to his room and closed the door. Fingers chilled to the bone, he could hardly undo his buttons. Slowly a heap of soggy clothing gathered at his feet. He dragged the warm towel down his chest and belly before vigorously rubbing some life into his arms and legs. His toes and fingers tingled uncomfortably as hot blood surged into his veins. Ignoring the pain, he donned dry clothes and skipped down the steps, knowing which would creak, which complain.

†

— 2. Harbinger Felled —

His dad was already ensconced in the kitchen. With his pipe he pointed at Edgar's chair. A mightier gust than normal had them all staring at the window, imagining the confusion if it burst in on them. The miller laid their fears to rest.

'It'll take more than *that* to blow this house down.'

'I hope you're right,' said his wife.

Edgar turned to watch his mother. Fragrant, fatty steam billowed from the oven and engulfed her. The scent of lamb and rosemary and garlic had his gastric juices flowing. Yet they could do nothing to dispel his foreboding. It had settled on his heart like ice, thickening by the minute.

A fat, noisy bluebottle flew dangerously close to the oil lamp. Buzzing furiously inside the glass globe, it darted into the flame to be snuffed out in seconds. Edgar couldn't help wondering if it might have escaped greater terrors yet to come.

A heaped plate of lamb and roast-parsnips and potatoes was placed before him. They passed round the butter, fresh from the churn, the mint-jelly made with windfalls. Then there came upside-down plum-cake topped with cream.

Stuffed to the gills, he sat back with a satisfied groan, patting his tummy.

'Now for a smoke,' he joked, eliciting a sham frown of disapproval from his mother.

'It's time for bed, young man,' she said. 'There'll be plenty of clearing up to do tomorrow. If there *is* a tomorrow.'

'Don't be like that, Moll,' his father interjected. 'Why make it worse than it is?'

'It's bedtime for you too, while we're at it.'

'And you, my pretty.'

They retired early. There wasn't much point in staying up when nerves were run ragged by the storm. It continued relentless. As if the world had lost all reason.

Edgar lay in the dark, rubbing his feet together in a bid to warm them. The heavy meal made him drowsy, but just as he was about to nod off a ferocious gust would rouse him again. He tried to concentrate on Rhoda Barrows to calm his fears, knowing full well what the Reverend Prickleback would say. Old misery guts, he scoffed. Sport for him was to scour the hedgerows, ambushing young lovers with his blackthorn stick. But he could turn a blind eye to things when it suited him, far more serious things at that. Nothing but a Pharisee, his father was wont to say. He smiled and murmured in agreement. Gradually he drifted away, but not to a land of peace and puzzlement. Strange creatures lurked in the corners of his dreams and sat under his window looking up at him. The village belonged to them now.

He woke again, bathed in sweat. The sheets were knotted all about him. He lay there, frustrated, wishing he could sleep, preferring not to because of the dreams that awaited him. Tarry not in the land of nod, he remembered his grandpa warning him. Now he understood. Reminded of the sword, he wished he were clutching it there in the bed to defend himself with.

The wind died a death of a sudden. A frightful shriek echoed off the firmament and rent the night, freezing the blood in his veins. His mind seemed to shudder and grow blank as a black pall dropped before his eyes. His lips quivered. How he wished he were in bed with his mam and dad. An horrendous gust smote the house like a battering-ram. There was a creaking and a splintering and an enormous muffled thud which shook the wall behind his head - as if a giant had struck his home a monstrous blow.

'Edgar? You all right in there?'

Was he glad to hear his father's voice. He could have wept for joy.

'Yeah… I'm all right, Dad.'

'Don't worry about a thing. That's the old elm down, it was bound to happen. We'll deal with it in the morning.'

'Sure thing, Dad.'

He smiled to himself and snuggled down under the covers. At times like these it was nice to be a boy again, with a strong father to protect him.

The ancient elm by the gate had been a landmark for centuries. He felt a twinge of sadness. He'd lost a friend, so to speak. Now it lay prone next the house, arthritic fingers scratching the diamond panes of his window as if trying to tell him something.

A howl, half-human, half-animal, drawled harshly on the edge of the wind and stopped his breathing. He muzzled his overactive imagination. If he didn't, he'd go off his head. Screwing up his eyes, he willed himself to sleep.

He wandered in and out of a labyrinth of dreams – dismembered dreams repeated and partially known till day dawned, leaden and silent. No chorus of birds serenaded the rising sun. If it weren't for the stricken elm, last night might well have been a nightmare. But real things were broken this time, living things. Part of the world seemed to have been palsied by a stroke, the better part, and getting up meant facing the truth.

— 3. Morning Broken —

Reluctantly, Edgar crawled from the covers. He poured icy water from the earthenware jug and splashed his face. Testing his jawline for bristles, he sighed to himself. What a pity he couldn't lather his face and shave like his father. It seemed so far away still.

The smell of toast rose to greet him. Still in his nightshirt he descended the stairs barefoot, vigorously scratching his scalp. His dad came through the door from the yard and smiled up at him.

'Keep that up and you'll be bald in no time.'

Edgar smiled back at him, stretching his neck muscles.

'You'll be glad to hear the mill-wheel held out.'

'Did it?' He was surprised to hear it. 'And the toads?'

'All gone.'

What a relief. The miller tousled Edgar's hair and steered him into the kitchen. His mother had her back to them, stooping over the range. His clothes of yesternight were drying on the line overhead; russet breeches, a white shirt and a tanned leather waistcoat. She took up the kettle and made the tea. Facing about with the pot of porridge, she glanced at her son.

'Could you not have combed your hair or is that a haystack on your head?'

'I *did* comb it. *Dad* messed it.'

His mother sniffed and purled a stray hair behind her ear. Hers was the colour of Edgar's, tied neatly in a bob at the nape of her neck.

'The milk was sour straight from the cows,' she informed her husband.

'Not surprising after last night, Moll. Fear must have turned it.'

'There were mice in the flour, I've never seen as many.'

'It's only to be expected... We'd better get on. We've a lot to do today. Have you finished, son? You fetch the saw and the axe while I feed the animals.'

Edgar stepped through the door into a pale imitation of morning. The steam off his breath had a peculiar green tinge to it. The sun was a sickly colour, he could stare into its face without hurting his eyes. As for the stringy clouds in the East, they were wool stained by blood.

A menacing breeze stirred. It seemed to his ears to be whispering threats at him. The beasts heard it too. Stamping and snorting, whinnyiny and lowing, came worryingly from the outhouses. The short hairs on the back of his neck bristled and a vague sense of dread settled on his mind. Leaden. Disturbing.

No cocks crowed in the neighbourhood that morning. No dogs barked. Spike was obvious by his absence. He heard his father swearing because neither the cows nor the horse showed any interest in feeding. He frowned and shook his head to see the geese so forlorn. They were hanging their heads, didn't dare look up into the stricken sky. The gander had mislaid his arrogance. He skulked behind his women.

With a sigh, Edgar strolled to the woodshed for the saw and the axe. At least there would be forgetfulness in activity. It was sad to think they were going to saw up this Goliath of a tree that had stood so long, a tree he and his father, and his grandfather before him, had climbed and swung from. A wedge of history had tumbled down about their ears, fit for the fire.

They felt they were slicing into their own flesh and sawing their bones once they started on the tree. Edgar winced and sucked air through his teeth. His dad nodded in agreement and gave a sad shake of his head.

'End of an era, son... End of an era.'

Wooden fingers flopped to the grass at their feet, gnarled and contorted with age. Brittle twigs snapped off to be walked into the turf.

The miller stopped to wave at someone. Edgar turned and grinned. Coming through the gate were Lee, Sam Belwether, Piper Whittle and Brad Hollyspike, all close friends of his. Spike, who had finally made an appearance and was snuffling under their feet, barked at the boys, tail wagging furiously.

'Hey!' Edgar shouted in greeting.

'Hey to you too,' quipped Lee.

'Hallo, Mr. Falchion,' they said with a courteous nod, standing in a semi-circle and studying the tree.

'Wasn't it an awful night?' Lee stated, eyes widening. 'I don't mind admitting I was scared.'

'So were we, lad.'

'Can we help, at all?'

'Don't you have work of your own to do at home?'

They grimaced and shook their heads.

'No damage in the village, then?'

'Not much.'

'Sheltered by the woods, no doubt.'

Lee avoided the miller's gaze and shuffled his feet. Edgar wondered what was the matter with him. He seemed almost guilty.

'Everybody safe, then? Nobody hurt?'

'Not yet,' Lee muttered.

'Not *yet*? What's that supposed to mean?'

'Oh, nothing. I mean, I don't think it's over yet.'

'You could be right there... Now, if you want to help, fetch the saws from the woodshed, they're hanging inside the door. Be careful, mind you. They're sharp.'

All four of them returned with a bow-saw each. He instructed them to work on the lesser branches while he and Edgar tackled the thicker boughs closer to the trunk. Soon afterwards he stopped Edgar with a smirk and a nod. Sam was actually sawing the branch he was sitting on. There was a sudden crack, a roar, and he hit the ground with a thud. Everybody laughed while he got to his feet and wiped mud from the seat of his pants.

'I haven't seen the likes of that in a long, long time,' guffawed the miller. 'Where did we get you from?... You're not hurt, are you, son?'

'No. I'm all right.'

They knew he was saving face. There was pain in his eyes when he began again, both feet firmly planted on the ground this time.

After an hour and a half of strenuous work, the miller stopped them.

'Right, lads, that's enough for the present. Time for a bite to eat, wouldn't you say?'

They eagerly nodded in agreement. All of them had first-hand knowledge of Mrs. Falchion's culinary prowess.

'There are spiders everywhere,' she complained in the kitchen, waving away a streamer. 'It's not the end of the world, I suppose?'

'Felt like it last night,' rejoined the miller, 'but we're still here, aren't we, lads?'

'And how are all your folks?' she directed with a smile at the boys.

'All right,' they muttered uneasily, shuffling again and clearing their throats in embarrassment.

Something was definitely wrong. They weren't normally shy and awkward like this. Edgar was dying to ask what was up.

Hunger banished their awkwardness. There was a feast fit for a king and it wasn't long before they were groaning in discomfort. Not much work was done that afternoon. They sat about and dozed till the fear of approaching dusk had them all scurrying home. Lee remained until it was too dark to leave, waiting for Edgar's mam to insist that he stay the night.

'You'll have to share Ed's bed, Lee, there's nowhere else. What will your folks think? Won't they be worried?'

'I told them I might stay the night.'

'Did you, now?'

She was surprised they had let him. I wouldn't allow Ed out on a night like this, she said to herself. As for staying over… Parents these days, she thought, tut-tutting to herself and wryly shaking her head.

†

— 4. Midnight Cloaked —

Both boys lay under the covers, staring up at the ceiling. Though neither voiced the fact, they were mighty glad of the company. They weren't the better of the storm yet.

'What's going on?' Edgar asked, unable to contain himself any longer.

'Nothing,' replied Lee, lying through his teeth.

Twiggy fingers scratched at the window-panes. Like chalk on slate.

'Sad about the tree,' Lee said.

Edgar got up on one elbow and looked down at his friend.

'The funny thing is...'

'What?' Lee was all anticipation.

'Well... I could have sworn last night that it was trying to tell me something.'

'It?'

'The tree.'

'The *tree*?... You're having me on.'

'No, I'm serious... I mean, why did it fall against my window?'

'Because that's the way the wind was blowing.'

'Listen, would you… It fell against my window and it kept tapping at it as if it was trying to tell me something.'

'What? Help, I've fallen down? Would somebody please push me back up?'

Edgar clicked his tongue with impatience. 'Be serious.'

'Oh, and *you* are? *You're* the one trying to tell me a tree was talking to you.'

Edgar lay down and turned his back on Lee.

'No. I didn't mean…'

Lee sat up this time, clutching Edgar's shoulder and trying to tug him over. He chucked him off.

'I want to hear more!… I promise not to laugh. Cross my belly and hope to die.'

Mollified, Edgar lay on his back and continued.

'It fell for a reason, I feel it deep inside me.'

'But *what's* the reason?'

'That's the annoying thing… I haven't a clue.'

'Do you think it has something to do with the sword?'

Lee could have kicked himself. The last thing he wanted to bring up was that sword.

'Em… I don't know. It's just a hunch. Like something bad is happening out there.'

A thoughtful frown furrowed Lee's brow.

'They're real feelings... So the tree *has* to be telling you something!'

'Yes, but *what*?'

'Someone could have buried something underneath it.'

'Yeah. That could be it.'

'Did you look?'

4. Midnight Cloaked

'Never even thought of it. Too busy helping Dad saw the branches.'

'Let's look now!'

'What? In the middle of the *night*?'

'Why not? There's no storm... Come on. Get up.'

He nudged Edgar who immediately threw back the covers. He put a warning finger to his lips.

'Don't let them hear what we're up to,' he whispered. 'We'll get a lamp from downstairs and creep outside. I'll go into the kitchen first and let Spike out or he'll bark the house down. Follow me, and mind you step where I step.'

As carefully as can be, Edgar raised the latch of the door. He stepped into the halo of light cast by the lamp Lee was holding. Spike kept close to his legs, as reluctant as they were to face the night. A sullen, morbid silence weighed them down. Myriads of stars shone fiercely in a piercingly clear sky. The aurora borealis margined the horizon, more vivid than they ever remembered. Translucent veils of colour wavered and shimmered in a non-existent breeze.

The ghost of the stricken elm glimmered in the lamplight, tortuous branches clawing hopelessly at the sky. They hurried to the crater where the tree had once stood and gazed into its yawning throat. Reluctantly, they slid down the muddy bank. It all seemed such nonsense now. As if a tree could tell you anything. Edgar felt a fool for suggesting it.

Then it was that it caught his eye. It wasn't something really startling. It just struck him as odd. Instead of spreading outwards from the base of the tree, the roots were joined.

As if the tree was clutching something close to its body for safe-keeping. As if it had grabbed it immediately it began to fall.

Edgar nodded at the strange phenomonen. 'Look at that.'

They scrambled out of the pit and went to investigate. These were the main roots, those that anchored the tree in the ground. It had fallen in a fruitless attempt to guard its secret, a secret that had endured for centuries. Perhaps it had lived solely for this purpose, waiting for the night it had to fall, willing the wind to strike it down. Not one root-hair was broken. The tree seemed to have let go of the soil all at once and keeled over.

Both boys gripped the earth-encrusted limbs and tugged for all they were worth.

'It's no good,' Edgar panted. 'They won't budge.'

'How about the sword?' Lee suggested. 'It could cut through them like butter.'

'I never thought of that!'

Edgar ran to the house and returned immediately. Now the time had come, for which the elm had been planted in the first place. What was his surprise when the moment he touched the roots with the blade, they began to separate. Both he and Lee almost toppled into the crater with astonishment. The mighty limbs stretched out towards him. Like hands, they held out a ring of black iron, an inch thick, four inches in diameter. They stood there staring at it, unsure what to do. The elm was literally offering it to Edgar.

'Go on,' Lee croaked. 'Take it.'

'I suppose I should,' Edgar faltered, hoping it wasn't a trap.

He stretched out a trembling hand and touched the ring with the tips of his fingers. Nothing untoward happened so he accepted the gift, if gift it was. Next minute, he started and almost dropped it. The whole tree shuddered and groaned and began to sink into the ground, disappearing from sight as the turf closed over it.

'God Almighty,' whispered Lee. 'You were right. It *was* trying to tell you something! You really *are* special, Ed.'

Edgar cradled the iron ring in his palm. At one point a minute, perfectly-formed hand, wrought in silver, grasped the ring.

A hollow sound rippled through the breeze and made their flesh crawl. Something resented the discovery they had made. A sudden drop in temperature pinched their flesh. They shivered, exhaling steam through chattering teeth.

'Quick,' Lee urged, rubbing his hands and blowing on them. 'Let's...'

The words faltered and evaporated from his lips. They gaped at the horizon in disbelief. The northern lights were fast disappearing before their very eyes. And, one by one, the stars were being doused, as if plunged into cold water. A black shroud was being drawn over the firmament. Soft muffled sounds reached their ears, interspersed with high-pitched semitones. All they could think of was that a cloak was being thrown over Garten and that they would soon be under it.

'What now?' whined Edgar in a despairing voice.

'Why wait to find out? Come on!'

They both rushed indoors and barred themselves in.

Spike burrowed beneath the covers and cowered at their feet. The sword lay on the rug by the bed - in case it were needed. Edgar held up the ring and the two boys gazed at it. Lee regarded him in a different light now. Ed would be great one day, was having greatness thrust on him. But what price greatness, that's what he would have liked to have known. He didn't feel guilty any more. This was Sabrehilt and he decided it was time to come clean.

'Ed... There's something I have to tell you… Remember that time in the woodshed with the sword? Well, afterwards, we blabbed to our folks.'

'And?'

'They didn't believe us. Until now.'

'*Now?*' Edgar sat up, scrutinizing Lee's face. 'Why now?'

Lee looked away. An uncomfortable heat was rising from under the bedclothes.

'They started going on about it this morning,' he confessed. 'Last night put the willies up them.'

'You mean they're blaming *me?!*'

'No-o. It's just that… They've being going on about it ever since the storm. They're having a meeting tomorrow.'

'About me?'

'I can't say for sure. All I know is that they're all talking about you and it's all our fault.'

Lee glumly shook his head. Tears pricked the corners of his eyes. He felt he'd betrayed his best friend. He'd never seen the villagers so angry and afraid before. Anger and fear were dangerous company in Garten. He knew what that led to.

'Forget it. Nothing's going to happen,' Edgar declared with conviction.

'I wish I could be so sure.'

†

— 5. They Burn Witches in Garten —

Pale, weak flames fired the sun that god-forsaken morning. The bell of the church seemed cracked as it tolled, sounding a death-rattle in the belfry. There was a sickly sweet smell in the air and the River Mead was frozen solid. Fish and frogs and newts and weeds were held fast in suspended animation. Ducks and moorhens, taken by surprise, were trapped by their feet. A fox that had been lapping at the water had its tongue caught in the ice. It dug in its paws and tugged and whined with pain.

The village was surrounded by trees, all that remained of the ancient forest of Werwyvern. It didn't nestle behind these trees. It skulked. Garten was a narrow peninsula resembling a thumb jutting into the sea. Jagged cliffs and treacherous rocks scowled out to sea night and day. The shingle protested its harsh treatment by the waves, slave of the ebb and the flow, chained to an indifferent moon. There, terrible secrets lay silenced by the roar of angry surf, and buried by shifting sands. All was not well in Garten.

Shipwreckers for a generation and more, they were aided and abetted by the Reverend Prickleback, a wolf in sheep's clothing if ever there was one. They would make for the cliffs on storm-tossed nights, hoping to chance upon a vessel in distress. A man would stand on the beach waving a lantern, giving the impression that it belonged to a ship in a safe haven, luring the beleaguered helmsman onto the rocks. And while the ship foundered and broke to pieces, they gathered as much of its cargo as they could. At first they had stared in horror while their ringleader clubbed to death those few stragglers who had dragged themselves ashore. 'We can't have witnesses!' he'd roared above the squall. Murder came easy once they felt the hangman's noose tighten round their necks. Blood had turned the surf red and cried aloud for vengeance.

"Snake" was their ringleader's nickname. Elmer Broadbent struck like an adder and asked questions later. Anybody whose conscience got the better of him died by his knife. But Snake himself came to a sticky end too, dashed to pieces on the rocks while wading out to a chest full of gold. In his greed, it never occurred to him that gold would have sunk to the bottom. All the chest contained was ladies' underwear. He had forfeited his life for a froth of lace.

His son, Mort, took his place. A sly, scheming psycopath, he ruled the mob but briefly. He married a timid, mousey creature from the village. Deep down he was afraid of women and vented his hatred on his helpless spouse. Underhand, persistently surly, he never looked anyone in the eye, ground down by the blows of his own violent father. Power, he worshipped, holding children beneath the waves till they ceased to struggle. Any who were repelled by their own filthy crimes were too terrified to step back from them. Mort was more vicious than his father had ever been.

But Mort had become too big for his boots. The Reverend Josiah Prickleback had no choice but to strike him down in the name of the Almighty. There could be but one supreme family in Garten and Prickleback was their name. Poison, the coward's recourse, that's what he resorted to, persuading Mort's wife to administer the lethal concoction. Subtly he schemed, convincing her that it was her beholden duty to rid the village of such a demon. She did as bidden, only to be coerced into wedlock with the man himself, threatened with burning at the stake should she open her mouth.

For more than a century the villagers had religiously guarded their secret. More "witches" have been put to death in Garten than anywhere else in Europe. Obviously a community who hunted down and immolated witches with such fervour, was a good and a holy one. Their reverend leader of the time, Prickleback's grandfather, honed their religiosity with witch hunts, as did his son after him. So zealous a man was *he*, that he became archbishop and chose the medieval castle in Garten for his palace. The shepherd remained among his flock, bringing great bounty to his faithful.

The man had sold his soul to the devil, his son and heir along with it. Josiah Prickleback dwelt in his father's palace and hoped, one day, to receive the mitre and crozier himself. Grown wily in the ways of his forebears, he used God to keep his minions in their place. He did not fear the innocent in their midst for he could soon turn their innocence against them.

When Edgar was but a babe-in-arms, the last of the witches had been burned at the stake in Garten. Ellen Barchester was her name. Her glaring fault had been the sheer, unspeakable effrontery to have inherited more land and property than Prickleback. She had proved an easy target for her love of animals had always attracted suspicion.

He paid her a visit in the dead of night and accused her to her face.

'You have associated yourself with the beasts of the field! You have cavorted with the denizens of *hell!* Witches and *warlocks* have been your companions! You shall be burnt at the *stake!*'

'No!' she shrieked and fell to babbling incoherently.

'Yet, even now, my daughter, I can save you,' he breathed.

'Save me! *Save* me!' she sobbed. 'I will do anything you say.'

'You have no progeny of your own. You are an orphan in this world on the final league of your journey to our Creator, may he be praised and blessed forever.'

She nodded eagerly, her hands clutching his knees.

'I don't want to burn, I don't want to burn,' she whimpered.

'Nor shall you, my child... Have you written your last will and testament?'

She shook her head. Her only worry had been who would take care of her animals. Gladly would she have bequeathed all her belongings to such a soul.

'Do so now, my daughter. I shall look after you. *And* them.'

He had her burned anyway.

From the pulpit that following Sabbath he denounced her. The horror of his betrayal enfeebled her brain. She twitched and muttered and cackled to herself while they dragged her to the village square with glee, tying her to the stake, heaping straw and faggots at her feet and setting her alight.

The screams of Ellen Barchester still rang in their ears.

†

— 6. The Slaughtered Ox —

On a roughly carved board over the inn door it read in faded red and gold lettering:

Sole proprietor, Turlough Grindlewick
Purveyor of fine wines and spirits to the gentry

The only member of the gentry ever to have darkened its doors was a certain Annas Trefoil, and he was dead at the time, thrown from the window of his coach when it overturned. They'd laid out his corpse on a table in the parlour before his family came to reclaim him.

The inn was no place for civilized folk or their horses. The water was foul, the straw damp, the hay mildewed and inedible. Above the double door, hanging from a spike and creaking rustily in the wind, was the inn's sign: a painting of an ox with its throat cut, strung up by a rope with a pool of blood under its dripping muzzle. It certainly left wayward patrons under no misconception that a ruddy, beaming landlord was ready to welcome them with open arms.

The Slaughtered Ox was the first building encountered on entering the village, the other side of the bridge over the River Mead, at the bottom of a short, but steep, incline. To the right stood a gnarled, arthritic oak-tree of ancient pedigree. The inn itself was long and low. A frowning facade of uncut stone was studded with squat and grimy windows. Dwarfish outhouses huddled together in the rear, doors rotting off their hinges. This was the domain of the innkeeper's son, a lad soft in the head who answered to the name of Oaf. Behind Oaf's world, literally backscratching the stable walls, rose a low hill crowned by a copse of hazel.

This devilish haunt was the only inn in Garten. A foolhardy blow-in had once tried to establish a rival watering-hole. It burned down the very first night it opened. The ashes of his owner mingled with those of his premises. Indoors, it was a dreadful place, infested with mice. They ran along the counter. They tripped over your shoes. They scratched behind the wainscotting. They were the cause of the sweet and sickly smell pervading the atmosphere. If one chanced upon the counter whilst Grindlewick was serving a customer, he smashed his fist down on it, smearing the tankard of ale with its blood. Woe betide anyone who dared to complain.

Turlough was a burly, greasy individual, oozing oil and sweat from every pore. Pimples mottled his cheeks. Boils bulged on the back of his neck. His wife was a buxom, oily creature too, a veritable blubber-queen. She would sit in the parlour, a stained white cap on her head, framing a face raddled by alcohol. There were gaps in her teeth which only added to her charms. Her husband had knocked them out for her. As vicious and hot-tempered as he, she gave as good as she got.

6. The Slaughtered Ox

They were misers, the pair of them. Money and land were their gods and they had an ample supply of both. Eagerly they watched the local drunkards drink themselves dry, appropriating their farms to settle their debts. As for gold, they hid it in every conceivable place they could think of. What a shock poor Oaf got the morning he wandered in holding a coin between finger and thumb. 'Give it 'ere,' his father had snarled before giving him such a clout on the head that it knocked him unconscious and damaged his eye for life.

When a guileless jackdaw, merely following its instincts, made off with a sixpence, the innkeeper swore enmity on its kind. He caught it eventually and day by day, quill by quill, he plucked its feathers. Its pale blue eyes started from its head when it heard the sadist's steps approaching. Great was his disappointment to discover it dead at his feet one morning.

To the inn the shipwreckers wended their way for meetings. To the inn they directed their steps that morning while Lee and Edgar were still abed. The Reverend Josiah Prickleback had convened the assembly and was there to greet them. They arrived in dribs and drabs, stamping their feet to enliven their toes, chafing their frost-bitten hands, whistling through their teeth to give weight to their remarks on the doorstep.

'Come in, come in,' crooned Prickleback in a jovial singsong, gesturing them towards the fire in the parlour.

Gladly did they outstretch their open palms towards the muffling flames, nodding to one another and commenting on how incredibly cold it was.

'Mead frozen solid.'

'Aye. Fowl and beast trapped.'

'An axe wouldn't crack it.'

''Tis devil's work, so it be.'

'You could be right there, Col Lickspittle. I've never seen the like.'

'That's what comes o' turnin' a blind eye to some folks not a stone's-throw from here.'

Many murmured their assent. They would have been glad to see the miller and his cronies hang. They hated them for refusing to help with the shipwrecking.

Soon the parlour was jam-packed. A fit of sneezing near the centre had the mass sidling away as best it could. Some muttered angrily over their shoulders, as if the poor man were responsible for catching a cold.

'Men, men, men,' repeated the reverend, lowering his voice to attract their attention. 'Not forgetting your good womenfolk,' he added with a courteous smile.

His tone grew solemn.

'We all know why we're here... Things are not as they should be, as the Almighty intended.'

Here a murmur rose, a bucolic hear, hear. He leaned forward with a scowl fit for the pulpit and they held their breath expectantly.

'There are demons abroad,' he hissed.

'It's the end of the world!' roared a man from the back.

A murmur and shiver rippled through the crowd. For what had they toiled so hard all their lives? To have their bones bleached by a treacherous sun? The thought of their wickedness smote them. The fear of hell gripped their vitals. Screams of the dead rang in their ears. Blood seemed to seep through the cracks in the floorboards. It was all *Prickleback's* fault. If it hadn't been for him and the rest of his family...

He was aware that once he lost control he would never regain it again. He had to remain in charge or else all his plans would fail. Masterfully, he defused the tension.

'Not quite the end of the world, Sim Bladderwrack, though something akin to it, my man,' he rejoined with a friendly leer. 'Not quite, I say. But demons are demons, end of the world or not. And demons have to be outed and banished to the realms of fire and brimstone whence they issued.'

Shock waves of relief thrilled through the mob. Sheer madness, on their part, for the reverend had no intention of offering his services. He read their thoughts but, cunning fiend that he was, he knew with surety how to fob them off. He would strum their own fears, the ignorant cowards. He pounded the counter with his fist.

'Men of Garten…' They went rigid at the sound of his voice. 'Am I about to commandeer your brave hearts, armed with pithforks and sickles against demons?… No, I am not.'

One woman spat out of the side of her mouth. He saw her because he expected to see her.

Gerty Mallock.

She was there. She was everywhere. Weaving in and out of the crowd like an avenging spectre, his dead conscience resurrected in female form. And nobody, the reverend included, dared expel her - despite the mockery in her fiery eyes, the sneer on her lips, the defiant hands thrust deep into her pockets. Unnatural, they called her. The get-up of her, the way she stood, it was all flying in God's face. Barbed comments she had for everyone at the end of a forked tongue, Prickleback amongst them. She definitely held some sway over the man. How else could she poke her nose wherever she chose and get away with it? More man than woman, more witch than angel, now, *there* was one who had dealings with those who had passed over to the other side. *They* would come to her rallying-call and defend her, no bones about it.

Prickleback raised his voice for effect, to tighten the noose further, ignoring the scorn on Gerty's face.

'Am I about to send forth your very children into the jaws of *Hell*?!... No, I am not.'

A wit was tempted to shout, What *are* you going to do, Prickleback, but knew he'd never leave the inn alive, torn limb from limb by a frenzied mob in the hands of a wily mobster. Hanging on his every word, they all waited to hear what he was about to propose.

The innkeeper and his spouse exchanged glances. Turlough was cynical about the whole affair. He didn't know that he really believed in the existence of demons. With the exception of Old Nick, he said to himself, surreptitiously squinting at Prickleback. What a lot of old hullabaloo over a blinkin' storm, he thought.

Prickleback asked another question.

'Can this work of the devil be vanquished by...'

Oaf had crept to the door to see what was going on. At the word devil, he broke into fearful roars of despair. The entire assembly, Prickleback included, leapt six feet into the air.

'Would someone kick that fool out where he belongs!'

Grindlewick ground his teeth and cursed the boy under his breath, swearing he'd clobber him at the first opportunity. The commotion subsided as the lad was dragged off, his roars fading past the window to the rear of the inn. It left them jittery. They desperately needed a scapegoat and Prickleback was about to provide one.

He'd set his sights on the mill. Folk needed bread, and for bread they needed flour. If desperate, they would pay double the market price, as desperately as they would soon latch onto their victim.

The time had come. Patience had rewarded him. They might as well have danced to his tune at will. If he had known, if he had merely suspected, he would never have spoken that name.

†

— 7. Thrown to the Jackals —

'What of this boy, Sabrehilt?' he shouted.

'What *of* him? Is *he* the one?!'

'No, no, no… But there are forces swirling about him. *Inhuman* forces.'

'Aye,' they murmured in unison and began whispering among themselves, nodding and grimacing.

The reverend held up his hands, beseeching quiet.

'Can he free us?' he pondered aloud. 'Does he not possess a sword of supernatural powers?'

'Aye, that he does.'

'Can he not wield it as nobody else can?'

'Sure enough he can, from what we've heard.'

Edgar's mates would have been horrified to see how their words were being twisted to suit this king of hypocrites. Gerty glared into his eyes, slowly shaking her head. He knew her meaning.

Mustering courage and defiance, he stood tall and stared back at her. What can a mere woman do to me, he asked himself with an inward snort of scorn. I am a man of *God*, set apart from other men. What can that hellhag do to me?… He amost laughed aloud, so exhilarated did he feel by his own invincibility.

His empty triumph was short-lived, however. He knew the power she held over him, the power of knowledge and proof. She was fearless. She would use it if he provoked her.

'What will we do with the Falchion brat?' piped up Racker Booth, a scraggy individual always thirsty for blood.

Prickleback shook himself free of Gerty's spell and nodded to the questioner with an admiring smile.

'Always on the ball, Rack, my lad. Well said.'

Emboldened, he darted a glare of contempt at Gerty. She laughed it off in silence.

'Well said,' he repeated, grinding his teeth.

'Aye,' agreed Racker with a self-satisfied simper.

Those next to him shuddered. Racker was another Mort Broadbent in the making. The reverend would groom him to that end, no doubt. Maybe that wasn't a bad thing, though - those who were useful to the Pricklebacks died eventually.

'Well?' Racker barked impatiently. 'What *are* we going to do to him?'

The circular space around him widened, a makeshift no-man's-land. Racker sensed the movement and looked about him, grinning maliciously. He liked to frighten people. Josiah Prickleback slowly shook his head, approbation beaming from his eyes.

'You're one after my own heart, Racker Booth,' he crooned, more forthcoming than usual, pondering the use he could make of him. 'But!' he shouted, to snap their attention back to what he was about to say. 'The more important question is... What use can the boy be to us *before* we let Racker at him?'

Racker smirked and nodded appreciatively. The rest murmured in agreement.

'What if he don't want to?' Turlough asked, both arms resting squarely on the counter, a tumbler of brandy in his fists.

'Oh, I wouldn't worry about that, Gindlewick. We have ways and means of convincing him…'

'What ways?' a riled Turlough shot back at him.

'Let's leave it at that for the present, shall we?'

'Humph.'

Grindlewick felt nothing but contempt for the man. He threw back a tumbler of cognac and smacked his lips. The golden warmth flowed down his gullet into the pit of his stomach, fanning the embers aflame. No damnation reverend is goin' to get the better o' *me,* he thought to himself. Sanctimonious fool… Pity that boy wouldn't run *him* through with his sword. Now, wouldn't *that* be a blessin' we could all celebrate?

A sly glance scrutinized Racker for a moment. Then all I'd have to do is get rid o' that rat into the bargain… A few drinks on the house an' they'd be eatin' out o' my hands, Racker wouldn't have a chance in hell. And *Hell's* where Racker's headed. *And* Prickleback with him. He smiled to himself, chipping his glass with the neck of the bottle while filling it.

While he was busy with his thoughts, the reverend noticed an aisle forming out of the corner of his eye. There was Gerty making for the door and the fools separating like the Red Sea before Moses. Before she crossed the threshold he shouted, forcing her to turn her head and listen.

'So! Are you *with me?*'

They murmured their assent. Gerty turned about and waited. Good, he thought, smiling smugly to himself. When I pipe, my dear, you *will* dance. *Or*... I'll kindle flames beneath your feet. You'll skip to a different tune *then!*

But flames reminded him and he ground his teeth in frustration, a wasp nibbling painfully at the edge of his memory. He had sent so many to their deaths unlawfully and Gerty knew it. She had proof... proof of everything. There must be some way to get at her, he thought... There *has to be!*

The mob began to cough and shuffle their feet. He shook himself free of anxiety and prepared to dismiss them.

'Shall I leave you to it?'

'But what's to be *done?*'

'Go get the boy, isn't it obvious?'

'*Then* what?'

He turned away from them for a second, inwardly lambasting their stupidity.

'The boy must...' He had a better idea. Inspired, he was, from on high. Of course! They're *terrified* of that damn tower. Nothing could be better... Out of fear, the boy will refuse to go to the tower and then they will kill him. His voice rose to fever-pitch. 'Don't you realize what happened the other night?'

They shook their heads.

'Why the tower, you fools. *That's* where he must go. All that is evil is spilling from that *tower!*'

A cacophony of voices erupted in the inn. Prickleback raised his hands for silence. He leaned forward, triumphant.

In a low voice he said, 'I'll leave you to it... I can count on you all. I know my men… *and* my women.'

He saw Gerty turn and exit abruptly. Off to the meddler Buckrake with your tales, no doubt. That witless fool, what can *he* do? I know all about him. A raker of dirt cannot stand in the way of the son of a bishop. He glowered after her disappearing figure. I have you in my sights, Gerty Mallock. You won't escape me this time. I'll find your Achilles' heel…

'To the *mill*. And then to the *tower*!' he hollered.

They stormed from the inn, a welter of anger roused and focused, grabbing sticks and stones as they went – the miller was far too burly to tackle unarmed.

Grindlewick and the reverend looked at one another across the empty parlour. They said nothing. The rabble-rouser was thinking deeply. What if the Falchion brat *does* go, what then?… I'll think of something. Perhaps I'll let Racker at him. With a smirk Prickleback withdrew, coat tails flapping in his wake. The innkeeper let out a low growl and flung his glass at where he'd been standing. It smashed, a brittle decrescendo engulfed by silence. His wife shot a sly glance at him and crept away, sashaying her hips when out of sight.

†

— 8. Unhallowed Ground —

Prickleback sauntered home, humming a tune to himself and lopping the heads off weeds with his cane. He swung round and looked up the road whence he'd come. His eyes strayed upwards to the lowering clouds. The "atmosphere" he didn't fear. As for the tower, it was all hocus-pocus. His flock were nothing more than superstitious fools. But the tower had turned useful for bending their wills to his own.

'The boy won't go. He'll be too afraid to. Let them kill him and be done with it. And… if I am very fortunate, they'll have to kill his father as well.'

He laughed aloud. A donkey in an adjoining field brayed harshly and silenced him. A prickle of annoyance crept over his neck and shoulders. Was it laughing *at* him or with him? He gripped his cane, desirous of bringing it down smartly on its haunches.

He smirked. His reverie faded and he strode purposely forward, making for the church. An idea was taking shape and he knew who best to assist him.

'I'll just make doubly sure beforehand.'

He struck the road with his cane and skipped to a canter, in ebullient spirits. They flagged in the vicinity of the churchyard. A dark cloud cast a shadow across his narrow patrician features and furrowed his brow. Tumbledown cottages leaned towards one another opposite the perimeter wall. The reek of smouldering turf and poverty assailed his nostrils. A ragged woman stood in a doorway watching him, a filthy, naked child clutching her knee. The hacking cough of her consumptive husband came through the broken window, unceasing, maddening - so maddening he wanted to beat his brains out to silence him. The likes of that should be evicted, he thought. God has no time for wastrels and vagabonds. He favours those who help themselves.

Ignoring the woman, he took out a ring of keys and unlocked the church gate. Securing it behind him, he looked up at the imperious oak standing next to the walkway. It was one of the mightiest trees on the peninsula, almost a rival to that of the inn. Which reminded him of its proprietor.

'Grindlewick,' he grumbled sotto voce. 'Someday soon, I hope, I shall see *you* pushing up the daisies. I look forward to burying you.'

Lichened tombstones leaned this way and that. Living stalagmites of Irish yew rose upwards at intervals, solemnizing the cemetery with sombre shadow. The church itself was well-situated on a knoll overlooking the parish. The stiffened limbs of ancient sycamores sheltered it at the rear, leaning over a high stone wall and wagging arthritic fingers at the burgeoning population underground. I told you so, I told you so...

An ornate sundial, temporarily redundant, was set into the wall above the studded door. Its motto, *Tempus fugit,* was ignored by the reverend. Death and judgement never entered his head, not even while he wandered between those grim reminders all about him. He may have advised his congregation to lay up treasure in heaven, but he himself was hell-bent on amassing as great a fortune as he could down here.

Choosing another key on the weighty loop, he opened the door and entered his domain. Cool, sepulchral silence enveloped him. His footfalls rang loudly on the flagstones. He swerved and drifted by the tomb of his grandfather, buried in the aisle. With a fulsome sigh he stopped before the baroque monument sacred to the name of his father. Elbereth Jehosaphat Prickleback had been christened for a bishop. His coat of arms, carved in granite, stood out above a prone and griefstricken figure. At the top could be seen a bust of the bishop himself, hair combed forward over sloping brows knitted together by ponderous thought. The great man was interred in his cathedral in Dublin. Prickleback prayed that *his* day would come.

With a scowl of hatred he glanced at the pew where his wife cowered on Sundays. She was a millstone around his neck. What a blunder he had made in marrying her.

'I should bury her with her husband,' he snarled, 'in the hope that he'll harry her for all eternity.'

He went to the sacristy, took a key off a nail behind the door and attached it to the ring. Once outside, he made for the rear of the church, weaving between the headstones, reading an epitaph here and there, as if burying them had conferred power over life and death upon him. He came to a halt and chuckled merrily at one in particular.

Herein lie the
Mortal remains
Of
Elmer Broadbent,
Devoted husband and loving father.
Requiescat in pace.

'Hah!... Devoted husband and loving father... The man was nothing short of a brute.'

Looking about him to ensure there were no witnesses, he skipped a jig on his grave.

'And where is...?' He swung round hastily. 'Aahh... Dear old Mort of loving memory. The beloved son... Pity my scrag-end of a wife isn't down there *with you!*'

As a dutiful minister by Mort's bedside, he had watched Death stealing upwards, inch by inch, until Mort was no more. Hemlock had worked its charms on him.

'If only it were possible to prove that *she* had poisoned him. I'd be rid of her, then, swinging on a gibbet till kingdom come. But nobody would believe such a timid creature would do it.'

He turned on his heels and strode purposely to the entrance of the crypt behind the church. A huge limestone cross was fenced off by ornamental railings, embellished by fleur-de-lis and trailing ivy. He cursed the squires and their pretensions, consigning them to dungeons with rats for companions. He shook the barred gate before opening it with the key from the sacristy and descended the steps. Below, he tested the strength of the wrought-iron gate and checked that the key still turned in the lock. Deep in thought, a finger wandered distractedly over the trailing vines, the coats of arms, the furled leaves green with age.

'Good... *Good.* This should do admirably,' he muttered before vaulting up the steps and locking the gate behind him. 'How everything begins to fit neatly into place,' he purred with a winsome smile while he walked towards the front of the church. 'All that mumbo-jumbo about the sword... Providential, yet again... Miller Falchion, all you possess is mine or soon will be. I'll have you all burnt and throw my wife on as kindling.'

Brushing the rust from his hands, he turned for home, a sight which never failed to please him. Fields margined by kempt hedgerows gently sloped away from him. Dew glistened in the tussocky grass. Normally the air was full of birdsong but they were strangely quiet that sullen morning. A pride of mighty elms jostled together in the largest field. Behind them could be seen the bishop's palace surrounded by a haze of naked branches. Lofty, castellated, with portcullis and drawbridge, it was all he could have wished for...

He cursed and stamped a foot. If only he had a *son!*

A familiar pain darted through his chest, lance-like. He drove his fist against it and stumbled to a stile for support, gasping for air. The pain lingered briefly before waning to a memory. Recovered, he ambled homewards across the fields, swinging his cane. Seeing the castle struck a raw nerve, rubbing salt into an old wound. With him the Prickleback line would come to an end. That barren jinnet was to blame.

'Damn her!'

The shout had the rooks leave their nests, cawing and loping slantways across the fields.

Part of his heart craved to run fingers through soft curls atop a tiny tot head, to set a child of his own upon his knee – not merely the human desire for continuity, but the deep-rooted ache of a heart with no one to love.

As he stood in the hall with its high mullioned windows, its blackened oak panelling and dreary old furniture, he breathed in the scent of his own home and hummed a merry tune, forgetting the thorn in his side.

A man-servant appeared from a recess.

'Ah, Gannet. Is my breakfast ready?'

'Yes, Your Worship.'

'And Madam?'

'Madam has already breakfasted.'

His master nodded and smiled to himself. Back to the fire in the dining-room, the musical tick of the clock on the mantelpiece harmonised with his thoughts.

'What do you want?' he growled when his wife came in.

'I only came to see if you lacked anything.'

'Nothing *you* can provide.'

'I…' She stalled.

'You what?'

No answer was forthcoming. She was terrified of him. He didn't need to lay a finger on her. His cutting remarks and hate-filled eyes more than sufficed. The depths of the moat kindly beckoned to her, but she recoiled in horror. Anything was better than that. Unhallowed ground, the very thought of it sent shivers down her spine. Unhallowed ground here and hell beyond.

'Get me more toast,' he ordered just to be rid of her.

But her presence lingered, a nasty taste in his mouth to spoil his breakfast. His temper rose. He imagined her falling from a turret window, her despairing wail cut short indefinitely. That brought a smile to his lips. And meanwhile, his burly henchmen made their way to the mill.

Tick tock... tick tock...

†

— 9. Sticks and Stones and Straw —

Lee remained at the mill, reluctant to wend his way homewards. Miller Falchion could not explain the disappearance of the tree and neither boy cared to enlighten him. It was another rum incident in a topsy-turvy world. They were cleaning out the stable when he gripped Edgar's shoulder and stopped him in his tracks.

'Best get inside, lads,' he cautioned.

The boys went to the door and followed the miller's gaze out the gate. Half the village seemed to thronging the laneway.

'What do *they* want?' Lee asked.

'Whatever it is, it ain't friendly.'

It was obvious, even from a distance, that an angry mob was approaching the mill. Their gait, the inimical deliberation in their steps, the few harsh words that reached their ears on the wind, said it all. Benjamin Falchion grew apprehensive, impatient to have the boys safe indoors.

'Get inside, I tell you.'

Lee groaned aloud with shame. His father was in the vanguard, their elected spokesman. This comes of shouting your mouth off about the sword, you fool. I *knew* they were up to something last night. Curse me for an idiot, as dumb and stupid as Tomothy Brindleshanks. Tomothy Brindleshanks was the village idiot.

Lee skipped to a canter when the unruly mob jostled its way through the gate and made for the three of them.

'Dad, what are you *doing?!*'

The urgent pleading in his voice fell on deaf ears.

'Get you home, boy,' was the sullen response he elicited.

'But what do you *want* here?'

'Nothing to do with you. It's him yonder we're after.'

'Leave him alone!'

Brough Chetwood raised his hand but Lee was too quick for him. His father blew a fuse at that.

'He's my friend, my *best friend*,' Lee cried in his face.

'Fool!... Get home and do as I say or I'll leather you when I follow in your footsteps.'

'I'm not leaving him.'

'To the devil with both of you!' Chetwood roared at his son, features distorted by hatred.

The miller came up behind Lee and placed a sympathetic hand on his shoulder. This was nothing short of a hanging assembly, he knew. He looked into the eyes of his drinking companions of yesteryear and nodded cooly. Brough Chetwood. Hosea Lamplight. Samuel Clegg. Ezekiel Hardfrost. None returned his greeting. Some lowered their gaze with burgeoning confusion.

The miller's voice rose clear into the air.

'What can I do for you?' His eyes scrutinized the crowd purposely.

Those in the rear shifted uncomfortably. Those to the fore didn't like the look of his tight fists and bare, muscled forearms. What could sticks and stones achieve at close quarters? They looked over his shoulder, distracted by the emergence of his wife.

'Be-enj… what's the matter?' she nervously called.

'Get back inside, Moll, and take the lads with you.'

'Why? What's wrong? What are they here for?'

'Do as your husband bids you!' shouted an angry Brough Chetwood.

She started back in surprise and stared at him. 'What's come over you, Brough Chetwood?'

He clicked his tongue in annoyance and stamped his foot. 'No woman of mine would answer back in such a fashion,' he growled.

'Because you're not man enough to treat a woman proper,' rejoined the miller, taking her arm and holding her tight.

'Get along, you strumpet!' Brough shouted.

'I'll fell you to kingdom come for that,' growled her husband, taking a step forward.

His right fist caught Chetwood on the side of the head and flung him into the mud. Muttering angrily, the mob edged forward, still careful to keep a safe distance. Brough rubbed his jaw and spat blood before rising to his feet. Murder blazed in his eyes but the craven fool depended on the mob for courage and, since theirs was flagging, his waned too.

'I'll get you for that, Falchion, if it's the last thing I do.'

'It will be, if it ever happens.'

They stood glaring at one other like two fighting cockerels, breath misting through their flaring nostrils. Nobody dared break the silence until Chetwood got his wits back. Vengeance was far sweeter taken out on the boy. Grinning maliciously, he pointed at Edgar.

'It's him we're after.'

'Wha'?... What have you got to do with the boy?' Fear had crept into the miller's voice and Chetwood relished it.

'Aye, he's the one we're after... Sabrehilt.'

'Sabrehilt?' faltered Edgar's dad, putting an arm round his son. 'Who's this Sabrehilt?'

'*He* is,' Chetwood replied, nodding at Edgar.

Both his mother and father stared in puzzled wonder at their son while Lee hung his head and sobbed. Edgar felt a blush rising up his neck and suffusing his cheeks.

'E-ed?... What's he on about?'

'I, eh... Em... It's my nickname.'

''Tis the first I've heard of it... What does it mean, Ed?'

'It's the name they gave me because of the sword.'

The boy blushed more than ever. He hated speaking about himself before this feral audience. This was something he wished he had explained in private.

'The *sword*, you say?'

'It's all my fault,' groaned Lee, covering his face with his hands.

'No, it isn't,' Edgar declared to quell his guilt.

'What's going on here?' the miller probed with a hint of impatience. His nerves were fraying.

'He's taking that sword and he's going to the tower,' interrupted Lee's father.

'He's only a lad, what can he do? Stay. son,' he murmured, putting a restraining hand on his shoulder. 'You're going nowhere.'

'He's getting the sword and he's going to the *tower!*' roared an incensed Chetwood, drawing a dagger from beneath his jerkin.

Edgar stepped forward.

'No, Ed. Stay where you are,' his father ordered.

But Edgar ignored him, walked directly up to Lee's father and stared him straight in the eye. 'Put that knife away... If you don't, I'll take that sword and make mincemeat of you.'

Brough knew he could and quailed before him. As if in a trance, he replaced the dagger under his jerkin and withdrew an empty hand.

'Now,' Edgar continued, 'what do you want with me?'

'You must fetch that spellbound sword of yours and take it to the tower and rid us of whatever is out there.'

'There's nothing out there,' growled the miller. 'You've all gone mad.'

'There *is*! Reverend said so.'

'Reverend... I should have known he was behind this. Didn't come himself, though, the filthy coward.'

'He shall hear of your words.'

'Let him. I'm not afraid of that dastardly hypocrite.'

'I'll get the sword, Dad,' Edgar directed at him before turning for the house.

'No!' cried his mother. 'You'll be hurt, maybe killed.'

'We'll all be hurt, Mam, if I don't.'

His father watched him go. 'He's braver than the whole lot of you put together,' he shot at the hotchpotch assembly before him.

Lee ran after his friend into the house. Spike was barking wildly in the kitchen, jumping up and down to get a view through the glass.

'Sneak out a back window!' Lee loudly whispered.

'And what'll they do with *them*?' Edgar asked, nodding towards his parents.

'I'm coming with you,' Lee declared after a pause. 'I got you into this mess so I'm coming with you, like it or not.'

Edgar nodded and smiled at him. Lee watched while he went to the fireplace and stretched up for the sword. Thoughts of the tower gave him the creeps. He recalled the blackness of the night before, the cloak overhead. A shiver crawled down his spine and up it again. Once they reappeared in the doorway his father mocked him for siding with Edgar.

'At least I know what friendship means,' he shouted back, slamming the door in his face. 'They don't care what happens to you as long as they're safe,' he said to Edgar. 'He doesn't even care what happens to me,' he admitted with sadness

'No,' Edgar whispered, watching the tears gather in his friend's eyes. He couldn't think of anything to say but, 'You'll always be my friend, Lee Chetwood, I can swear to that. On the Bible.'

'Come out, the pair of you!' came Brough's gruff voice the other side of the door. 'And be quick about it.'

'Or what?' growled Lee under his breath with murder in his eyes.

'Are you *there*? Can you *hear* me?'

'Yeah, we can hear you, you old fool,' he murmured. 'I'm glad your dad punched him, Ed. It's all he deserves.'

Spike began to bark wildly when he saw Edgar reach for the latch. Dashing through the door, he skidded across the yard. A frenzy of barking erupted as he pranced and skirted the group. He sniffed their ankles, growling all the while. As they warily shifted their legs and grunted at him to be off, the scent of fear hanging about them had him barking all the louder.

A shout went up from Lee's father for Spike had nipped his heel. He made to kick the dog but Spike was far too fast for him. He tugged at his trouser-leg while Chetwood hobbled after him, cursing him at the top of his voice. A final tug had him floundering once more in the mud.

'Even the dog knows you for what you are,' growled the miller. 'Has you worsted, so he has.'

'You shut your mouth, Falchion. I'll slit his throat for him once I get a grip on him.'

'That you never will, Chetwood,' came a voice from behind them. 'I'll carve you up like a roast joint if you harm a hair of his head.'

All eyes darted to the speaker, the almost unrecognizable boy gripping his sword. *The* sword. He meant every word.

'Get you to the tower, boy,' spat Chetwood, 'else we'll do to you and yourn things you never dreamt of in your worst nightmares.'

Edgar walked straight through the mob who leapt back out of his way. Lee and Spike followed as fast as they could. He heard his mother sobbing behind him but didn't turn to look at her. His dad would have to comfort her. He couldn't.

'Ed!' his father called.

He turned his head to look at him.

'Go safely, lad. Good goes with you. You'll be fine, son.'

Edgar nodded.

There were some in the crowd who sniggered. Relief at having someone else to face the danger blinded them to the truth.

Both boys strode manfully through the gate with Spike at their heels. The downtrodden mob came blundering in their wake, the miller behind them, supporting his wife in his arms.

'I won't stand by and see him come to harm,' he promised her.

She gripped his arm and resolutely followed her son, to death if necessary.

The boys crossed the mill river at its narrowest and made for the woods hiding the tower from view. Spike ran ahead, waiting for them to catch up before bounding off once more.

'What do you think we'll find there?' Lee whispered.

'Dunno. Maybe nothing at all.'

'You hope.'

'And if we *do* find something?'

'Oh…' Lee exhaled, shoulders sagging, 'I don't know what we'll do or whether we'll get out of this alive.'

9. Sticks and Stones and Straw

'Mind you don't make a run for it,' warned Lee's father behind them.

'As if we would,' sneered his son. 'We're not the cowards round here.'

'Come back and say that to my face, you cur.'

'I will when we're finished at the tower.'

His flush of bravery died instantly. They reached the perimeter of the woods, stalled momentarily and plunged in. They stumbled on through a tangle of briars and dead branches. Spike foraged ahead, sniffing furiously, racing down the bald pathway of a fox or a badger. It was dank and miserable. The boughs and trunks were stained black by torrential rain. Sunlight was extinguished by a thick pall of cloud overhead. They slipped and skidded in muddy ooze, felt it penetrating the cracks in their boots. The edge of the woodland approached too quickly. Stooping beneath the branches curving down to the ground, they lurched into the open air and stood up straight. There it was before them, silhouetted on the brow of a hill, stark and ominous.

As they passed through the few intervening fields, Edgar walked backwards for a few paces. He hated scarecrows at the best of times, but these seemed to be watching him. He had never seen a budge out of one of them but, wherever he stood, their eyes were on him. Nor did he like the look of the hooded crows perched on their shoulders. The "hoodies" also had their eyes peeled on Edgar, muttering into the ears of the scarecrows. They flew from one to the other, spreading the news.

Spike growled, the hairs down his back standing up like a porcupine's.

'What are you looking at?' asked Lee before stumbling into a row of turnips and swearing loudly.

'Have you ever noticed how they keep watching you?' asked Edgar, grabbing his arm and helping him up.

'The *scarecrows*? Sure, they're only straw and stuff.'

'But look,' Edgar ordered, gripping his friend's elbow and turning him round. 'They're looking at us now.'

'That's just the way they're facing.'

'But they were facing the other way when we came out of the woods, weren't they?'

Lee stopped in his tracks. The mob edged closer and shouted at them to hurry it up. They wanted to be away from the vicinity of the tower as soon as possible. Some of them were beginning to wish they'd never come, muttering imprecations on Prickleback's head. He knew when to keep away, did the reverend.

'Now that you mention it...' Lee breathlessly began. He clicked his tongue. 'You always expect them to be looking at you.'

'That's because they always *are*.'

'But they're not *alive* or anything.'

'Aren't they?... Why are they moving, then? And why does each one of them have a hoodie on his shoulder, aren't they supposed to scare them off?'

Lee halted again and nodded. The tramping of the mob behind had him skip into action, running to catch up with Edgar.

'Do *you* think they're alive, Ed?'

'I don't know if they're alive, but there's something very strange about them. They've always given me the willies, ever since I was a little boy.'

'I never was much fond of them myself. Ha, ha!' he roared and pointed.

Spike was cocking his leg on one of them. But his laughter subsided when the dog let out a howl of anguish. The hoodie had swooped down off its scarecrow's shoulder to peck at his eye. He came skidding back and, after a fit of nervous sneezing, shook himself and gave a feeble woof from between his master's legs. Edgar bent down and checked his eye.

'He meant business,' he said with a shake of his head.

He picked up a stone to pitch at the offending hoodie but Lee laid a hand on his wrist.

'Don't, Ed.'

Edgar dropped the missile in the muck between the drills.

'Now you know what I'm saying.'

Lee nodded.

They came to the end of the turnip field and climbed over the gate into the next. Feet caked in mud grew heavier and heavier. The tower rose higher and darker the closer they got to it. All eyes were fixed on it now, the other side of a last tangle of hawthorns.

†

— 10. Totem —

Emblem of previous dark ages that had beset the village, the tower had stood there since time immemorial. Huge, uneven boulders were held together by mortar made with bull's blood. The stones were stained black, as if there had been a fire at one time. Remnants of an arched door hung from rusty hinges, yawning mouth of a fractured skull. One crumbling window was an evil eye observing the village crouching with fear.

A desolate spot, it was avoided by man and beast. No animals grazed near its darkling walls. No birds nested on its ledges. Few, if any, flew over it. Rank tussocks of grass and nettles were all that grew beneath the tower, interspersed between the boulders strewn about the field - as if an explosion had burst it asunder. Weeds wilted and withered where its shadow was cast. A pall of silence enveloped the place. It was cursed, the ghost of a castle with feet of clay.

There, on the brow of the hill, it brooded over the entire peninsula, a silent sentinel intent on wickedness. The first floor was still intact, exposed to the elements. The floor above it had collapsed long ago. The jagged walls ended thirty feet or so above the window. Elderberries had taken root in the litter on the floor. They grew towards the light above and thrust branches through the window. A spiral stone stair-well ascended to the first floor in one corner.

The field belonged to Obadiah Buckrake, had been in his family for generations. A local farmer, he was hated by the shipwreckers for not rowing in with them. It was rumoured that his ancestors had built the tower, astrologers and necromancers who called down evil on all their enemies. An associate of that foul fiend, Gerty Mallock, they didn't dare harm him. They ground their teeth but they kept their distance.

Buckrake feared no man living. He would sit in the snug of The Slaughtered Ox of a Friday evening, scowling at all about him and listening intently. A mane of white hair fell to shoulders unbowed by age. The only one who was up to the likes of him was their reverend leader but he seemed none too eager. All they could do was growl into their mugs when he passed behind them on his way out the door.

The two boys and their dog scrambled up the last few yards of the hill and stood before the door of the tower. It was as silent and as empty as a tomb. They felt dwarfed by its massive walls. Each block of stone seemed to seethe with anger. Hideous gargoyles sprouted from every corner, over the window and above the door. They were demons of every description, uttering evil, vomiting war on all men of good-will. A sharp breeze whistled through them and gave them voice, sneering at two foolhardy boys who had the audacity to approach them.

A raucous cawing began overhead. A hooded crow circled before perching on the sill of the window, black eyes staring fixedly into theirs, willing them to become carrion to feast on. They quailed beneath its gaze.

The mob stood at a safe distance behind them, refusing to allow the miller and his wife to go to their son. Three men held him in a clinch and whispered threats in his ear.

'What ye waitin' for? Go to it!' shouted a nameless voice in the crowd.

Neither one of them turned but both of them sighed. Their shoulders were seen to sag.

'You're a disgrace to all fathers, Brough Chetwood,' croaked Molly with a sob. 'Letting your son walk in there.'

'Shut your mouth, harlot. He chose for himself, let him be hanged for it.'

Spike leaned towards the doorway, paws firmly planted on the ground so he could leap back if necessary. He whined and looked up at them.

'What can we do?' Lee whimpered.

'Nothing for it.' Edgar said, making a move. 'You can stay here, if you like. I'll go in alone.'

Though he said it out of kindness, he didn't mean a word of it. Even if the sword did work, he was sure he was too frightened to wield it. Walking through that door probably spelt certain death. Lee dashed tears from his cheeks and stared after his friend. A sob escaped him and he ground his teeth in fury at his father and his cohorts. He wished he had the strength to force them all inside, to barricade them in as punishment for sending two young boys to their deaths in this way. He hated them so much. But he hated himself still more for not following his friend.

'No, Ed!... Wait for me.'

Edgar turned his head and smiled at him over his shoulder - such a bright smile of love, for a friend willing to stride into the jaws of hell alongside him. Now he knew he had chosen wisely. Fate had brought them together. Perhaps they *were* going to their deaths, but of one thing he was certain - he would fight to the last drop to save Lee.

The once cold blood in his veins was simmering. Giddy elation stormed his battlements, his fingers itched to use the sword. He didn't seem to care what happened to him, willing to brave any danger, to be himself and let no man or creature rob him of that. Lee began to see the change coming over him. He felt his own blood thawing, hope returning and courage enkindling within him. He wanted to shout, to cheer, to turn and mock the cowards behind him.

'Come on, then,' Edgar said in a low, confident tone.

Lee nodded and smiled. Flames of joy coursed through his arteries. They lunged forward and rushed in together, followed by Spike providing battle-cries for all of them.

All three disappeared through that door to be engulfed by darkness.

†

— 11. A Joust of Sorts —

'Ah, there you are,' exclaimed the Reverend Prickleback, opening the door with a wan smile.

He'd been expecting him. He watched him now as he ascended the last few steps. Was there a slight puffiness about his breathing? Information like that could be stored and retrieved.

'Come in, Mr. Booth. Pray enter my humble abode.'

Racker Booth nodded before taking his hat off and crossing the threshold. The reverend scanned the avenue for spies before closing the door.

Quickly he led his guest towards the library, throwing over his shoulder, 'I've sent her to the back of the house. The servants are all in the kitchen and ordered to stay there.'

'Is that so, Prickleback?'

He didn't like his surly tone. As for addressing him by his surname, such disrespect piqued him dreadfully. An army of ants marched down his spine. But Racker might prove useful. He swallowed his pride and managed a smile of sorts.

Booth sensed his thinly disguised irritation and leered broadly to prove it. 'My, ye were a bag o' hot air back at the inn, weren't ye, Prickleback?'

'I convinced them.'

'Aye, that ye did... Easy to convince such fools.'

'That's what separates us from them, don't you think?'

'I suppose...'

Racker looked him up and down, scrutinizing every feature, letting him know he could see right through him. The urge to smite Prickleback was difficult to curb, to hit him and keep hitting him till his skull cracked and his jellied brains smeared the flagstones.

'Shall we?' intervened the reverend to dissipate the tension, gesturing towards the library door.

Booth glanced up at the shelves upon shelves of books. He could barely read himself but he wasn't cowed by learning. Rather, he held it in scorn.

'What did ye ask me here for?' he growled.

'Ah, but you wouldn't have come if not driven by gain, am I right?'

Thus did Prickleback try to master the situation. His adversary wasn't so easily tamed.

'Think what ye like, Prickleback, but don't put words in me mouth.'

'I wouldn't dream of such a thing, Mr. Booth.' Try placating him, he told himself. Igniting a bonfire won't benefit either of us.

Sensing that he now had the upper hand, Racker became less insolent. As a last gesture of defiance he seated himself before the fire in what was obviously Prickleback's armchair and held up an empty pipe to be filled.

'Any baccy about the place?'

'I'm afraid I don't smoke, Mr. Booth.'

11. A Joust of Sorts

The "Mr. Booth" was becoming a taunt. There was mockery behind it. A mute duel ensued, brief but unsettling for both. Leaning forward, Racker placed his elbows on his knees and jutted his unshaven chin at his opponent. Overtly nonchalant, Prickleback leaned back in his chair, crossed his legs and brought the tips of his fingers together. But beneath his hooded eyes thoughts were simmering. This is no clash of Titans, you ruffian. If you think you can intimidate *me,* think again… If I wasn't quelled by the likes of Mort Broadbent, I certainly won't be by a pale imitation. Mort had his uses. So shall you. And then you'll follow in Mort's footsteps, my man.

Booth held his peace. He had ulterior motives and he didn't wish to scupper his chances.

'Ye asked me to come…?' he grumbled half civilly.

'Ah, yes,' cried Prickleback, visibly brightening. He leaned forward and lowered his voice. 'I want you…' he stalled, rewording the phrase to avoid further friction. 'How about you follow that mob out to the Falchion place, hmm?' His smile was unctuous.

'To do what?'

Rack was suspicious. His eyes were mere slits in his head. He wasn't doing anybody any favours unless he was well rewarded. He knew the prize he was after, but was the other after it too?

'Here we come to it... As you yourself rightly said only a moment ago, they're fools. So, you see, I cannot trust them to complete the simplest of tasks… What they need is a goad and you'll make a fine goad, my man.'

Here he gave a complicit chuckle which wasn't reciprocated.

'What to do?' Rack reiterated.

Prickleback took a deep breath and dived. He knew he was compromising himself by associating with this neanderthal. Where there were rich pickings to be got, risks had to be taken. Furthermore, he felt fully in control of his destiny.

'I've thought of seizing the boy's parents and incarcerating them in the vault beneath the church.'

'Incarceratin' be damned. I'll kill the pair o' them.'

'No!… Not so fast… They're the leverage to convince the boy.'

'Of what?' Light dawned quickly in Booth's eyes, glad tidings to his twisted soul. 'Ye believe, don't ye, Prickleback?'

'Believe?'

'Aye… That there's something out there.'

'Pooh-pooh.'

'Yes, ye do. I see it in yer eyes, man!'

Prickleback flushed despite himself. *Did* he believe?… He wasn't sure what he believed but it was better to be safe than sorry. If there *was* something, and if they chose to believe in the magical properties of the sword, why should he stop them? And if the lad got eaten or slaughtered, better still.

Having regained his composure, he felt able to fence once again with this curmudgeonly fool. You're that close, Rack… A hair's breadth… The abyss yawns beneath your feet and you see it not. But soon, very soon, I will open your eyes for you and push you in.

'Admit it, man!' shouted Racker, nettled by silence he mistook for insolence.

'Admit what, pray?'

'Ach, yer not man enough to own up to the truth.'

'The Truth is my profession, is it not?'

Racker guffawed, long and heartily. He had no intention of curbing his mockery. But he was unaware of what his mockery stirred beneath the collected exterior of his opponent. Had he been, he wouldn't have wallowed so ostensibly.

The laughter halted mid-breath. The eyes became sly and hostile. There was an edge to his voice.

'Ye want the mill.' It was more an accusation than a statement of fact.

Prickleback feigned surprise. 'I?'

'Yes. You!'

'What on earth would I want with a mill? What good is it to me?'

'Money, Prickleback. Money... *You* worship it as much as I do.'

He held up his hands in dismay, making believe he was offended. 'Layeth up treasure in heaven where neither rust nor decay...'

'Don't give me that.'

'You cannot serve God and mammon.'

'Ach.' Rack spat into the fire, the sudden sizzling a fitting background to his response. 'Rhymes and fairy tales for children, Prickleback, not for me. And since when did *you* serve God?'

He might as well have struck the man a blow with the fire-irons. Hatred smouldered in the reverend's eyes. Fury tingled in every muscle fibre. The blackguard's words were gall to him. He was on the verge of pitching Booth into the fire with his own bare hands. Refusing to rise to the bait, he swallowed the bitter draught and muzzled his indignation. Tension seeped from his body. He relaxed and smiled in surrender.

'Have it your own way, Rack.'

'Hmm.' He was disappointed, looking forward to a flaring row. 'I want the mill,' he snarled.

Dismay flitted across Prickleback's features. What could he do, having claimed in no uncertain terms that the mill held no attraction for him. Then again, he could always dissemble. Greed would keep Racker keen on the scent. And once the ruffian was disposed of… he would appropriate the mill to himself without fuss.

'Take it, Booth.'

'Oh, I *will* take it, Prickleback.'

'And welcome. Just lock those two in the church vault first, will you?'

'And kill them later…'

'Once our work is done.'

'While you keep your hands squeaky clean.'

What a ghastly leer he made at him. He felt the heat rising under his collar.

'I alone am the one who can convince the Law that we are a holy people.'

'Is that so?'

'I am all that comes between you and the hangman's noose, forget that at your peril.'

'I'll remember, Prickleback. Much obliged.'

With a sneer he got to his feet. He turned on his heels and gripped Prickleback's arm. 'I *will* have the mill,' he growled through gritted teeth.

Prickleback just nodded, a curt nod at that. He was beyond bandying words with the ruffian. Opening the door, he ushered him out as if he were ridding the house of a repulsive blowfly.

'Inveterate fool,' he mumbled under his breath while he watched the man lope down the avenue. 'I should have dropped the portcullis on you and split you in half. I will yet... Grist to the mill... If only the boy *did* have an enchanted sword... I would borrow it from him.'

Cold fear trickled sickeningly beneath his skin. Would Booth turn out to be a greater nuisance than Mort had? Trepidation lurked in hidden depths. He was angry with himself. Instinctively he turned on his wife, heat spreading and melting the icicles. He sped upstairs, shouting her name.

— 12. Orphans Perforce —

Two boys and a dog stopped dead in the gloom, dazzled by the light outdoors. Dark, dank air was cool on their faces. Not a sound could they hear, nothing but absolute, portentious silence.

Dim light haloed the top few steps opening onto the first floor. Edgar edged to the bottom stair. He was afraid the lull would dissolve his recently acquired courage. Gripping the hilt of his sword with both hands, he swung up the stairs only to come to a standstill.

He thought he had heard something.

There it was again. Down *below!*

Lee heard it too.

But Spike wasn't growling. His tail was wagging. The next moment they were startled by a voice and stepped back into the shadows.

'Good boy.' A whisper, nothing more than a whisper. 'Who's a lovely doggie?'

A small voice. A gentle voice. More a boy's than a girl's. But whose?… It couldn't possibly belong to the monster they were expecting. *It* would have growled and torn Spike to pieces. But how could a young boy be at the root of such evil? How could a mere chit of a lad summon such a storm?

By now Spike was in the throes of delight, with the young fellow's arms thrown about him. The two of them seemed to be in some sort of enormous fireplace, revealed by the faint glimmer of light coming down the chimney. Trusting to providence, both Edgar and Lee approached him and got down on their hunkers.

'Hello,' came a timid greeting from behind Spike's shoulders.

Edgar gasped. He recognized the voice.

'You're Berry Blakelock!' he breathlessly exclaimed.

The dark head nodded. The sweet, unpleasant smell of neglect reached their nostrils.

'You're not going to hurt me, are you?'

His voice trembled. The poor boy pressed up against the wall of the fireplace, unable to trust anyone but the dog.

'I thought you were *dead!*' Lee voiced in disbelief.

'Everybody thinks I'm dead. They're *supposed* to think I'm dead... You won't tell them I'm alive, will you?'

Both boys vividly pictured him in their mind's eye, clearly recalling the uneven gait, the club-foot, the withered hand with its rigid thumb and fingers curled tightly against his wrist. Painfully they remembered the angry sideways glances made in his wake in the village, the cruel words voiced aloud in company. Devil's kin. Bastard changeling. Bringing nowt but bad luck on us all. They felt huge pity for the poor mite.

'The whole idea was to make them think I was dead,' Berry explained.

'And you've been hiding here ever since?'

He nodded at Edgar. The two companions looked around his enforced dwelling-place, more a dungeon than a home. They both shivered at the thought of living there.

'How could your folks let you?' asked Lee before a sickening lump bulged in the pit of his stomach at the thought of his own father.

'They had to...' Berry answered. 'The villagers threatened to stone me if they didn't get rid of me. They said they'd burn my mother at the stake because only a witch could have a child like me.'

'And they hid you here,' Edgar murmured.

Berry looked up and studied both their faces before replying. They were kind faces, not cruel like the other boys of the village who'd called him Hobbedly, Cripple, Claw. Spike licked his face. He smiled, gently patting the dog's head.

'After pretending that I'd fallen over the cliffs and drowned.'

'So there was no body.'

'That's right. They said the waves took me out to sea.'

'God, but I hate these people more every minute,' growled Lee.

Edgar nodded dumbly, his mouth a grim line of censure.

'And they hid you here because they knew they were cowards and that not one of them would come through that door.'

'Yes.'

'But what do you eat?'

'My mother and father bring me food late at night when they won't be seen.'

'You're not afraid?' asked Lee.

'I was more afraid of them out there than anything in here.'

'So that means...' Lee gaped in wonder, brightening to euphoria. 'This whole business up here was a wild-goose chase!'

Edgar wryly shook his head. So did Berry.

'He said *was*, Lee.'

'But,' Lee began, faltering, '*you* didn't cause the storm... So why are they saying there's something up here?'

'Because there is...' Berry nodded apprehensively.

'Wha-at?' Lee stammered.

Berry raised his eyes roofwards. Edgar and Lee did likewise.

†

— 13. Denizens of the Night —

A cold wave of panic washed over Edgar. It was the mill-wheel all over again. Stirring, muttering and squeaking, the roof came to life.

'When did *they* arrive?' Edgar croaked, the words lodging in his throat.

'Last night,' Berry answered with a shiver.

Lee tried to say something and failed. He didn't know what "they" referred to, he didn't want to know. Against his wishes, Edgar enlightened him. The word was enough to make his flesh crawl.

'Bats.'

Hundreds of thousands of bats. There, a mere six feet above them, clinging to every crack and margin of cut stone. Leathery wings twitched and stretched. Heads swivelled on necks to get a proper look at them. They could feel black, beady eyes boring into their skulls. Malice echoed in the sonar squeaks suddenly raining down on their ears. Any moment, they thought, and the whole seething mass will fall upon us - bats bloated on our blood...

'They never touched *you*, Berry,' Lee remarked, clutching at straws.

'They've only started getting restless since *you* turned up,' Berry stated, dashing his hopes. 'You'd better go,' he suggested in a hoarse whisper.

Lee sighed forlornly. They would be forced back inside if they emerged. Worse still, there was the risk of the villagers finding out about Berry and blaming him for everything. They'd string him up from the nearest tree.

'That's what we saw last night,' he commented. 'That's what made the sky go black. But why *here*?'

'I don't know,' Edgar replied. He peered at Berry, hair stirring at the probable answer to his forthcoming question. 'Berry...' He licked dry lips and cleared the plug of mucus in his throat. 'Nothing *else* arrived last night, did it?'

'No... I don't think so.'

'There's nothing upstairs, is there?'

Eons passed before he answered.

'*I* didn't hear anything. But I can't be sure. All I can say is that nothing came down here from up there.'

'We'd better go check.'

Lee shook his head in exasperation. 'You've got to be kidding.'

'What *else* can we do?' asked a rattled Edgar, moving towards the stairwell.

'Wait... I'll come with you,' sighed a resigned Lee.

Berry clasped Spike around the neck. If Edgar had expected the dog to go mad, barking and struggling to free himself in order to follow him, he was sadly mistaken. With a nod of his head, he beckoned to Lee and they began to creep up the stone stairs together.

13. Denizens of the Night

Edgar had a horrible feeling that once he poked his head through to the floor above, he'd be decapitated. He tried to muster the necessary courage - alone, with no one to make his decision for him. It was not knowing that was scary, that and anticipating the worst.

Lee's breath was warm on the back of his neck. He braced himself and poked his head into the room.

All clear.

Blessed bladder-tightening, brain-clearing relief. A smile dawned and spread over his features. Manfully, a little sheepishly after all his empty fears, he rose into the second floor room and waited for Lee to follow. They both stood erect, necks craned, staring up at the sheer walls framing the rectangle of cloud overhead. Rapidly they took in the craggy elderberries, the soup-plate fungi, the tumbled boulders strewn about the floor, and the gaping window. The two of them approached it to get a peep at the crowd down below.

They never did.

Instinctively, before their brains could register, they ducked and hit the floor.

†

— 14. Domestic Bliss —

Sebastian Trefoil descended a fittingly magnificent staircase on his way to breakfast. His face shone like the varnished portraits of his ancestors. Lathered, shaved, powdered and dressed by his valet, he was ready for a new day - what was left of it. A footman opened the breakfast-room door, reminding him of his lofty station in a pampered existence. His butler stood to attention at the sideboard, ready to serve him. He acknowledged neither. He had no intention of being badgered by his own servants in his own household, he had enough of that from his wife. The squire of Garten was a faint-hearted knave. He wobbled upon his forebears' shoulders and cowered behind his wife's petticoats - when he wasn't being shooed from under them.

'Ah, there you are, m'dear.'

He greeted his better half as she came through the door and popped another morsel of toast in his mouth. Waving his pudgy fingers, he dismissed his servants. He studied his hands while they took their leave. The redness of his skin was a constant mortification. Recalling his wife's presence, he quickly hid them under the table.

Isolda Trefoil, née Furnival, tried her very best to ignore his foppish ways. She couldn't quite quench the feelings of anger and contempt that welled up inside her. Hailing from a family of wealthy cattle-breeders, she preferred her men to be men, not mincing ballet-dancers with dainty feet. Once, when he'd held out a shapely leg to be admired, she'd kicked his ankle and left the room, her rustling dress a growling thunder-cloud in her train.

Hers was an arranged marriage. She had never forgiven either of her parents for lumbering her with such an 'old maid.' She would have been far, far happier coupled with a highwayman, a swashbuckling, womanising Goliath who had swept her off her feet and thrown her over his shoulder. There wouldn't have been the same sensation of a noose around her neck that she experienced while she watched her dearly beloved waltz into a room, flail his belaced wrists and heard that falsetto laugh of his explode on her eardrums.

He, on the other hand, was delighted with his conquest. She was the most beautiful woman in the county; his appreciation of her attributes was analogous to that of a farmer for a fine Friesian cow. Certainly he could have done without her 'bullish' character, but it was a small price to pay.

Squire Trefoil crinkled his nose and sniffed the air. With a feathery sigh he placed his knife on his side plate and frowned at his spouse.

'I do wish, m'dear, you wouldn't visit them so often.'

'I take it *them* refers to your tenants?'

'Smelly, nasty people living in lairs.'

'Lairs you provide for them... You should be ashamed of yourself.'

'Should I?'

'Poverty confers a type of heroic dignity, you know.'

'Leave them poor, then.'

She ignored his riposte.

'Prickleback also despises the poor,' she said, hoping to shame him.

'They remind him of his origins,' he shot back, congratulating himself on his wit.

It was pointless berating him. He was too shallow to recognize his own failings.

'Speaking of Prickleback... I saw our Highpriest skulking round the graveyard this morning. And, the most extraordinary thing... If my eyes weren't deceiving me, he was actually dancing on one of the graves.'

'Which one?'

'Does it matter?' she asked, voice thick with sarcasm.

Sebastian clicked his tongue in annoyance. 'Nothing about that upstart would surprise me.'

'Our opinions do converge occasionaly. Obviously the outcome of this morning's meeting was to his satisfaction.'

'Meeting? What meeting?'

'At the inn.'

'Another one?! What in heaven's name are they up to this time?'

'Oh, I'm sure it had to do with the freakish weather of late.'

'Oh, that. The least thing has them quaking in their breeches, the fools.'

'I'm not so sure... There's a certain undeniable expectation in the air, unsavoury at that.'

'You think we're in for it, do you?'

'I fear the worst.'

'Tut-tut. You're becoming as superstitious as they are. You…'

'When you've quite finished your diatribe… You *will* leave them under the reverend's sway. In the recent past your family has done nothing, never raised one finger. Left the demagogues to their devices and the populace at large in their wily hands. If you and yours had excercised true leadership, as you were born to do, none of these unfortunate incidents would ever have seen the light of day. To think you have in your possession…'

'Don't you dare breathe a syllable.'

'I wonder how people would react if they knew you had it.'

'Pshaw! People know nothing.'

'Nevertheless… If they *did* know…'

'Are you threatening me?'

'Men!' she cried with exasperation, stamping her foot. 'What on earth happened to the real men I used to know?'

'We've heard all this before, m'dear… These are different times. We have progressed from all that muscle-bristling, chest-heaving, sweat-smelling tomfoolery. None of that proves anything nowadays.'

'When the cards are down, Sebastian, I'd much rather depend on one such *real* man than a score of lily-livered popinjays.'

'And what, pray, do you imply by that?'

'You know damn well... Small wonder Daniel had to be sent away.'

'Don't be unkind. And remember… *You* were the one who sent him away. I quite liked the boy.'

'That boy happens to be your *son!*'

'Ah, yes, so he is.' He smiled wickedly to himself at that. 'Which is more than can be said for Prickleback, for all his fine airs and graces,' he declared while scratching butter onto a piece of toast. 'When have a scattering of turrets and a moat ever conferred pedigree on anyone, pray? Fiddlesticks to him, say I.'

'I'm sure he'd quake in his boots if he could hear you. And, fiddlesticks or no fiddlesticks, I'm almost certain he has his eye on this place.'

'Why, the absolute scoundrel! The damn *cheek* of the renegade!' blustered the squire. 'He wouldn't dare.'

'He's dared before now.'

Sebastian's expression brightened. 'Ah yes... But I have...' With a sly glance at his wife he stopped himself in the nick of time.

'Aha!' she cried, smiling in her turn. 'So you *haven't* forgotten.'

'I refuse to speak about it.'

'Some day soon you may not be able to refuse so lightly.'

'Let us cross that bridge when we come to it.'

'By all means. But... *You* won't want to cross it... You will run as fast as you can in the other direction.'

'And abandon *you*, m'dear?'

'Possibly... Quite possibly... Your ancestors fought, a long time ago.'

'Surely to God you don't think such a time is upon us again?'

He sat up and stared at her in disbelief. All she did was slowly nod her head.

'But...' He was becoming alarmed, glancing this way and that as if he were already seeking an escape route. 'Stuff and nonsense.'

'It is your duty.'

'*Duty?!* Don't talk to me of duty.' He scoffed at the idea.

'Yours or your son's.'

'You won't shame me that easily.'

'No, I suppose not,' she sighed resignedly. 'I'm only thankful your son is not here to hear you. You expect others to do your fighting for you.'

'*For* me? What on earth has it got to do with *me?!*'

'In heaven's name, what do you think it's *here* for?!' she cried, furious with him. 'I'm certain such a wondrous possession has the power to do good. You *must* use it. It's your responsibility as Squire of Garten.'

'I said I refused to discuss it and I meant what I said...'

'You'll rue the day, it stands to reason.'

'Tommyrot.' He sighed and shook his head despondently. 'You've quite ruined my breakfast, do you realize that?'

'There are some out there, poor as they are, who *will* fight.'

'If you are referring to those thieving wretches... The sooner they're swept away in combat, the better. They breed like rabbits, they should be culled like rabbits.'

'They're human *beings!*... Perhaps *I* should fight.'

'You?! What can a woman do?'

Isolda dug her fingernails into the palms of her hands. Scowling darkly, she turned to leave him.

'Before you go, m'dear.'

'Yes?' she barked, her rigid back towards him.

'Have you discussed the particulars of lunch and dinner with Cook?'

'Of course.'

'Excellent. Oh, don't let me detain you.'

After she had slammed the door he smiled to himself.

'I think I wrapped that up rather neatly,' he purred. 'Well done, Sebastian!'

†

— 15. Flight for Some, Flight for None —

Edgar finally understood the meaning of the phrase 'blood running cold'. Bats shot out of every crevice and exploded through the window. A dark cloud of them instantaneoulsy emerged through the door below. The noise of their wings was breathtaking. The tower was vomiting black filth. It soared into the air and swooped on the unsuspecting crowd outside. Uproar broke out. A stampede ensued. The mob fled in the direction of the village pursued by their leather-winged adversaries. The miller and his wife were driven away with them.

Edgar and Lee crouched below the window-frame, expecting the bats to return. When that didn't happen they cautiously got to their feet and squinted through the opening. Not a soul remained. All had fled.

Lee broke the silence.

'I wonder did they even realize they were bats.'

'Probably not. They were so scared, I wouldn't be surprised if they imagined it was a dragon.'

'Well, we have to thank the bats for getting rid of them.'

'Mmm... Come on, we'd better check Berry's all right.'

They skipped down the stairs. With the bats gone, they had nothing to worry about. Berry was still where they'd left him, with Spike in his arms.

'We'd better get you out of here,' Edgar said.

'Wha-at?' Berry stammered in surprise. 'You know I can't leave this place.'

'You can't stay... Hide out at my place, nobody will know.'

They helped him up. He followed them to the door.

His two companions gasped and staggered backwards. They blinked and gaped in horror. The cry of despair which passed their lips trailed off to a hollow moan.

'What is it?' Berry asked, limping up and looking over their shoulders.

Words failed him.

As yet oblivious, Spike playfully thrust his head through his master's legs. He yelped at the sight before him. His head shot back and a low growl was all that reached their ears from the gloom inside. Edgar looked over his shoulder. Everything had suddenly acquired a dream-like quality. He didn't want to, but he had to turn round again and face what he knew was still there. His spirits sank into a dark murky pool of stagnant water, never to resurface again.

Scarecrows.

Countless battalions of scarecrows surrounded the tower. They stretched to the horizon, as far as the eye could see. If Edgar had mistrusted them before, he had every reason to fear them now. These scarecrows were different. They didn't follow you disjointedly with their heads or have crows on their shoulders whispering in their ears. They were mobile. The supporting sticks had taken root. They had grown limbs and joints. Long, tapering twigs poked out of their sleeves and trouser-legs. Black, ghoulish eyes stared out between tangled webs of straw. There was a hole for a mouth, no tongue or teeth to speak of. Slavering black wolves stood next to them, fierce eyes fixed on the boys.

They had a leader who stood to the fore. He wore a tall black hat and a long black coat reaching to the ground. His wolf was half a shoulder taller than theirs. His subordinates were meanly clothed in comparison. Ragged coats hung off spindly shoulders. Torn trousers were hoiked up at an angle. Battered hats sloped over tattered brows. They were a beggarly bunch, a sight for sore eyes.

Not a filament of straw stirred in the air. The scarecrows stood still, mute as corpses. A sudden eruption of caws announced the presence of the crows. They lined the tops of the walls and the window-sill. They perched on the heads of the gargoyles, calling for blood.

Every hair on the boys' heads stood on end. Spike had a tuft of fur standing high between his shoulder-blades. And still the scarecrows moved not a millimetre, uttered not a sound. Innumerable eyes bored into their victims trapped in a dead-end. Edgar licked his dry lips, moistened his parched throat and willed his paralysed limbs to respond. He took a step backwards, in a bid to draw a veil of darkness between him and the multitude outside. Spurred into action, his companions did likewise.

A hollow, unearthly moan issued from the empty mouths, amplifying gradually till the boys had to cover their ears and Spike howled in misery. Seeming to resonate in bottomless lungs, it was worse than curses or threats. Was it madness reverberating in empty skulls? Was it anger welling up from the despairing void and sucking them in? On and on it went, rising into the air, causing the walls of the tower to resonate.

As suddenly as it began, it ceased.

The chief scarecrow twisted his neck and nodded at a minion. It stepped forward and stood on the threshold. Edgar, Lee and Berry edged further into the gloom till they met with resistence from the cold, jagged stones of the wall. The ghastly silhouette in the doorway wobbled and entered the tower.

With a cry of desperation, Edgar launched himself forward. He hacked wildly at the creature, lopping off both its arms, beheading it and cleaving its body in two. Panting, heart in his mouth, he stared down at the ragged remains in a stupor.

'Well done, *you!*' Lee cried exultantly.

But Edgar's sword hung limply by his side.

'I can't keep this up,' he sobbed. 'Not one after the other. There are far too many of them.'

Those scarecrows nearest to the door stepped back three paces. Their leader lowered his head and stared fixedly at the relics of one of his cohorts. In silence he raised a hand to his waist and beckoned. The tortuous claws of the felled creature began to drag themselves towards him. One hand gripped the severed head and battered hat, leaving a trail of straw. At a summons from their leader, a group of five stepped forward and took up the pieces before disappearing into the sea of staring faces. This was an invincible army, able to replenish itself. What could a single sword achieve against so formidable a foe?

Once again the leader chose a volunteer, disapproval evident in every gesture. The creature that broke the ranks this time stuck out like a sore thumb. His clothes fit snugly. His eyes didn't stare. His mouth was closed. Even his wolf was different, with a pelt of silver and soft blue eyes. This scarecrow tottered forward and came into the tower.

Edgar clutched his sword but stayed his hand. The scarecrow gestured for them to go to the fireplace where they couldn't be seen. Then he spoke to them. It was the wind in a field of barley, a whistling, whispering rustle that came and went in waves.

'Do me no harm. I mean you none.'

'Why shouldn't we?' Lee growled, unconvinced.

'My name is Bert Windlestraw. I wish to help you.'

'What can you do to help us? How do we know we can trust you?'

'Shush,' Edgar ordered. 'How can you help us?' he asked the scarecrow with a timid smile.

'Ed! Don't be such a fool. For all we know, this could be a *trap*.'

'Let him speak first, Lee. What choice have we got?'

The scarecrow nodded his head in agreement. He tried to draw the corners of his mouth upwards in a smile but failed. 'You can trust me,' he claimed. 'I will prove it to you.'

'Go on,' Edgar gently directed at the creature.

'Make use of the ring.'

'The ring?... What ring?'

'The ring given to you by Old Lem.'

'Old Lem? I don't know any Old Lem.'

'Old Lem, the ancient, the venerable scion.'

Edgar bowed his head and groaned aloud. It was hopeless. What else could you expect from something with chaff for a brain?

'The Ancient Elm of Garten.'

Edgar's head shot up. At last he understood.

'You mean *this*?'

He fumbled impatiently and withdrew the iron ring from his pocket, holding it out to the scarecrow who let out a low gurgling chuckle and tangled his fingers in glee.

'Place it on the ground. *Then* will you understand.'

Edgar got down on his haunches and did as bidden. He couldn't believe his eyes. The silver hand attached to the ring came to life. The fingers stretched out and dug into the dry earth of the floor. Edgar looked up, waiting for further instructions.

'Grip the ring and pull.'

He did so. To his amazement, a trap-door appeared out of nowhere. He struggled to lift it, Lee skipped forward to help him. They both looked down into a rectangular chamber.

'Get in. All of you,' urged Windlestraw.

'How do we get out?'

'Use the ring.'

Edgar clambered in, clicked his tongue and climbed out again.

'What?' asked Lee, confused.

'We have to help Berry get in first,' he whispered.

Lee looked up to heaven and nodded. They gripped his arms and lowered him into the hole, handing Spike to him before getting in themselves.

'Pull down the door,' their deliverer instructed.

'But what about you?'

'I must go back. If I do not, they will suspect.'

'Won't they suspect when they find out we're missing?'

He ignored the question. 'Do not emerge till all is quiet some time. Hurry. He comes.'

Edgar pulled on the ring, which had sunk through to the inner side of the trap-door, and together they lowered it into place.

'Goodbye, Sabrehilt,' was the last thing they heard, a murmur on the wind.

They crouched in the dark, listening intently. The word had gone out. There was a sudden onset of stamping feet overhead. The scarecrows were examining every nook and cranny. Angry moans echoed inside the tower, setting their teeth on edge. Hearing a wolf growl directly above them, they held their breath. But they had nothing to fear. No creature's nose could track their scent, just as no eyes could see them. They were safe. All they had to do was wait for the muffled groans of the scarecrows to die away.

— 16. Homeward Bound —

Edgar curled his fingers around the ring and raised the trap-door. Not a scarecrow or a wolf was to be seen. They climbed out of their secret chamber and stretched their aching limbs. When he lowered the trap-door into place the silver fingers loosened their grip in the earth and curled themselves tightly round the ring. He stooped to pick it up and stood there cradling it in his palm, deep in thought.

'I've never seen magic like that before,' Berry breathed in awe.

'Just wait till you see what he can do with that *sword,*' Lee exclaimed with a chuckle.

Edgar shook his head, still staring at the ring. Putting it back in his pocket he searched their faces.

'How did he know I had it?'

'There are lots of things we don't know,' Lee answered. The tree... The ring... The sword... It's all a mystery.'

'What's going on, Lee? Is it by accident or is it meant to happen this way?'

'I dunno,' he replied with a deprecating grimace. 'Don't ask me. Maybe we're not supposed to know... Maybe it's better *not* to know... Maybe we'll know in the end.'

'It's as if someone is watching our every step. That's why everything fits into place so well… Old Lem falling down… Bert here to show us what to do with the ring. He knew me because he was sent. But *who* sent him?…

'Well, all I can say is… I just hope there's always someone to help us and tell us what to do.'

With that, they all edged towards the doorway. The field was empty, the landscape bare.

'Come along, Berry. I don't fancy being out here at night.'

Spike sniffed the pitted sward like a bloodhound, then bounded off homewards, the boys in quick pursuit till memory served them and drew them back - a limping boy couldn't hope to keep up such a pace. They beckoned him to loop an arm around their necks and half carried him home.

'We'll have to get you a wheelbarrow,' joked Edgar as they jogged along. 'Look!' he cried when they'd reached the cabbage field. 'They're gone. The scarecrows are *gone!*… My guess is that the one in charge somehow summoned them all.'

Berry looked from one to the other with a melancholy expression. 'I have a funny feeling we'll meet him again,' he said.

Lee and Edgar stopped, ducked from under his arms and tried to read his mind. Lee cleared his throat before speaking.

'What makes you say that?' he asked.

'Can't you feel it?'

'*I* can,' said Edgar with a nod.

'Feel *what?*' asked Lee with exasperation.

'Can't you feel it in the air?... Something is hanging over us... Something bad... Something that means us harm.'

'Oh, that.'

'I feel it in my bones. Those bats and scarecrows are here for a reason. So are we and that's the most frightening part of all. We're all mixed up in this together.'

Briars grew in profusion. Grunting with the effort, they carried Berry over thorny trip-wires. At long last, sweating profusely, panting for air, they emerged from the rank woodlands. It was easy-going now, just the beaten pathway to navigate before they reached the road.

A stifled cry escaped Edgar. He ran forward with a groan.

†

— 17. Doomed to Greatness —

The sight in front of him would haunt him for years. The three of them stood in venerable silence. Edgar pulled Spike back by the scruff of the neck when he moved in snuffling.

Bert lay there. What was left of him. And what was left of his wolf.

Edgar crouched down beside the crushed straw head. His mouth was twisted, as if he had died an agonising death. Wisps of brain-chaff mingled with the grass and clung to the twigs of the boundary hedge. Each toe and finger had been snapped off at the roots. His limbs were splintered and hacked to pieces. His clothes were torn and trampled in the mud. His hat had been flung into the fork of a tree. His wolf lay dead by his side. A huge gash gaped in its belly.

'Poor Bert,' Edgar whispered.

'How could anyone *do* such a wicked thing?' asked Berry, trembling with fear and rage.

'*Not* anyone,' Lee mused aloud. 'Them. The scarecrows. They're not *anyone*... They're things.'

'They knew he'd helped us escape,' moaned Edgar, blaming himself for not forcing Bert and his wolf through the trap-door. 'He knew this was going to happen,' he sobbed. 'That's why he said goodbye to me.' His expression grew stern. He gritted his teeth. 'If I ever see their leader again, I'll do the same to him... So help me God, I'll break him into pieces so small there won't be anything left of him.'

'Bert was different to the others,' Berry interjected. 'He stood out. The one in charge never liked him, did he?'

'Hey!' Edgar ejaculated, turning his head sharply to look up at his companions. 'What if... Maybe we can bring *him* back to life!'

The boys stooped to gather Bert's remains and take them with them. The instant they did, a cloud of hooded crows swooped upon them. They flew at the boys and drove them back. Taking every trace of Bert with them, they disappeared into the depths of the wood. One straggler spat out a filament of straw to taunt them before speeding after his companions. How the boys wished they had a catapult to shoot him with. They watched the straw fall, veering to right and to left before disappearing into a ditch - all that remained of Bert Windlestraw.

Sad eyes stared down at the wolf the crows had left undisturbed.

'Should we bury him?' Berry asked.

'There isn't time,' Edgar answered, looking up at the sky. 'It'll be dark soon and this is no time to be out in the dark.'

Mechanically, in a daze, they plodded towards the mill.

17. Doomed to Greatness

As they walked listlessly through the mill gate, four of their friends came scrambling out of the barn, straw clinging to their clothes and hair. Sam, Piper, Brad and Nico stood with their eyes out on stalks. An inquisition erupted, question after eager question. Edgar was glad to see them but he dearly wished to run into the house and see his mam and dad. Once his four friends recognized Berry, a cacophony of awestruck comments ensued.

'Why *you're...*'

'It's Berry Blakelock!'

'My God! I thought he was *dead*.'

'He *was* dead!'

'Why *aren't* you dead?'

'Where have you *been* all this time?'

'Ed! Did you hear what they did to your folks?'

Edgar was about to tell them to shut up. That last question smote him in the heart.

'What have they done to them? They're not *dead*, are they? Answer me!'

Another barrage of information rang shrilly in his ears. They all wanted to be the one to tell him, words tripping over their tongues with excitement.

'They came back here dragging them with them.'

'Then Racker Booth came out of the mill. Sort of sauntered round as if he owned the place.'

'Said they were to take them to the vault straight away and lock them in there. Said...'

'The *vault*?!' Edgar loudly interposed, unwilling to put up with any more noise.

'They've locked them in there with all the dead bodies.'

'It's me against all of them now,' Edgar murmured.

Nobody heard him, too intent on satisfying their curiosity.

'Are you going to rescue them now?'

'Will you kill Racker with the sword?'

'SHUSH!... Shush... Is Racker there with them?'

'No. He went off.'

'But he left two men to guard them!'

'One of them's my dad,' claimed a dejected Sam, blushing for shame.

'You think *your* dad's bad, Sam. What about *mine*?' Lee asked to console him.

'Thank God none of us has Racker Booth for a father.'

'I'll have to go to them.' Edgar was resolute.

'Nooo!!!' they all shouted at once.

'No, Ed,' Brad declared, introducing a note of stern calmness. 'Your dad said not to.'

'But *why*?'

'Not tonight... He's afraid something will happen to you.'

'And it'll all be over after tonight, is that what he thinks? Because if he does...'

'Maybe he means they'll have calmed down by tomorrow, they won't be acting like madmen.' Brad was two years older than the rest of them. It showed. They listened to him. 'Anyway, they have food to eat and water to drink.'

'Hey!' Sam interjected in high dudgeon. 'That's for *me* to tell.'

Brad gave in and Sam visibly perked up, swelling as he listened to his own words extolling himself.

17. Doomed to Greatness

'I *knew* they'd be hungry, what with being out all day without a hope of dinner or tea. I knew they wouldn't get anything off them lot so I grabbed what I could in the kitchen at home, filled an empty flagon with water – it didn't half weigh a ton – and took it all round to them…

'As I came along I was wondering to myself how I was going to get past the two guards. I knew for sure they wouldn't let me give anything to them… So Brad here… My chum Brad.' He patted him on the shoulder. '*He* had this grand idea. He and Piper here, they both hid behind one of the big tombstones and threw rocks into the bushes. They went to have a look and that was my chance. I crept up and climbed over the gate and went down them steps and handed the food to your folks.'

'How were they?' Edgar asked.

Sam made a glum face before he answered. 'They seemed fine to me. I don't even think your mam was crying, which is amazing for a woman. *She* took the food. Of course the flagon wouldn't fit between the bars, I never thought of that. Your dad looked round for something to drink out of. I was dreading it. In case he used a skull. In the end I had to pour water into their hands for them…

'Your dad told me to hide it in the corner and put loads of dead leaves over it. Then he told *me*,' another glance Bradwards, 'to tell *you* not to come tonight. By then the guards were back and I was stuck. That gave me the willies. I thought I'd be there for the night as well. But Brad here, Brad the genius, he had another great idea. He came out from behind the tombstone and asked the guards if they were hungry. I heard him say it. I crept up them stairs and looked through the railings at them. It's obvious they got a fright because they were really cross with him. But they stayed put where they were which was no use to me. So Brad, he began to call them names and laugh at them. That made them boil and they ran after him, giving me my chance to get away. And here we are.'

'What about *me*?' Nico wailed.

'You did nothing,' Sam shot at him with a sneer.

Edgar ignored their bickering. 'Thanks for your help, Sam. Thanks to all of you... You'd better go home now. Before it gets dark... There are things out there, I'll tell you about them another time. But there's worse to come, so the sooner you get home, the better.'

'Why can't we stay here with *you* three?'

'There's no point in us all getting into trouble. Besides, we don't want to call attention to Berry. We're bound to if all of you go missing and they come here to ransack the place looking for you.'

With slumped shoulders, Sam, Nico, Brad and Piper wended their way home.

'Just when it was beginning to get exciting,' Sam mumbled disconsolately, kicking a stone into the ditch.

'You never let me get a word in edgeways,' complained Nico.

'Oh, belt up. You need your nappy changing, is all.'

†

— 18. A Cold and Empty Hearth —

Edgar stood in the middle of the room staring about him. Nothing had been disturbed since they had left that morning, a morning that seemed whole lifetimes away. He peered through the door into the empty kitchen. Everything was the same yet nothing was the same. The fire in the range was out, he felt that unmistakable chill in the air - the heart of his home had been extinguished. No friendly shout of greeting reached his ears above the rattling of pans and plates. No heady scent of sizzling fat filled his nostrils to churn an empty stomach. No burly miller stamped his feet before raising the latch and entering, hair grizzled by flour. The vacant armchairs trumpeted their absence. The ash in the grate weighed heavily on his heart. A dull pang of emptiness ballooned inside him.

With a sigh he walked hesitantly into the kitchen, ran a finger along the edge of the table and gripped the back of his father's chair. One by one he looked at the empty places. Would they ever sit round this table again? Porridge had congealed in the saucepan on the hob. The kettle and teapot were cold. He opened the oven door and peered in. Rashers of bacon were curled and brittle. How sad he felt, sad and forlorn and desperately alone.

Back at the table he scooped sugar from the sugar bowl and let it pour from the spoon, a peaked heap of white crystals on a snowy incline. He dipped a finger into the pitcher of milk and sucked it.

'You okay?' Lee asked with concern.

Both he and Berry had been watching him in silence, reluctant to invade his grief.

'Aye', he replied with a wry nod of the head.

Spike whined and scratched the back of a chair. He jumped up, insistently. The glaze gradually cleared from his master's eyes.

'I know what's wrong with you. You're hungry!'

Spike did a dance, twirling in a circle after his tail.

'Well, I suppose you can have some of this for starters.'

Edgar poured milk from the pitcher into his bowl. Spike lapped it up. The quick sloppy sounds of a sliver of pink tongue drew Edgar from his reverie. The lowing of the cows penetrated the panes of the kitchen window, he turned his ear towards them.

'They need milking,' he stated matter-of-factly. 'I'd better do it now. They must be bursting.'

'We'll help,' Lee offered.

'Can *I* try?' Berry asked. 'I'd love to give it a go.'

'Sure,' Edgar returned with a smile of appreciation.

Farmyard chores were good for him. They nailed him down to reality, forbidding flights of fancy over the horizon of despair. Once the cows were milked and fed, the horse and hens and geese had to be attended to. Having seen to them all, hunger pangs returned with a vengeance. They sat themselves down to a very late breakfast. The mill was home to all three of them now. Indefinitely.

†

— 19. Who Goes There? —

Full as ticks, they sat before a roaring fire they had finally coaxed to life. Darkness had fallen and the cosy flames helped to dispel the gloom. There had been a wrathful sunset that evening. Deep purple clouds had been furrowed with frowns, slashed here and there and bleeding profusely. The setting sun had unveiled the skeleton of a dead day.

The fire kept their worries at bay, a vestige of home to cling to. Edgar fought hard to keep his mind from reverting to his parents. How glad he was that Lee and Berry were with him. He told them so.

'There's no need to thank *me*,' Berry retorted. 'I did nothing at all. I should be the one thanking *you two* for rescuing me from the tower.'

His voice faltered. Tears glistened in his eyes and he averted his face, staring into the flames in a bid to compose himself. Edgar fixed his gaze on him, noting with sadness the deformed foot, the withered hand. It just didn't seem fair. Why pick on someone like Berry, he wondered, when so many bad people get off scot-free? They pillage and cheat and murder, but nothing bad happens to them. Where's the justice in that? Why doesn't somebody *stop* them…?

His grandpa had always said that their evil ways would catch up with them one day. He hoped they would. As for Berry, at least they had taken him out of that filthy hole which had been his prison-house for ages.

'Fancy anything else to eat?' he asked him to snap him out of it.

'No-o,' he replied, wide-eyed with disbelief, whimpering at the thought of another morsel. 'Oh, my God!' he cried. 'My mam and dad! They'll have brought me dinner by now. They won't know where I am. They'll think the villagers *found* me!… I must go to them. They'll be worried sick.'

'It's too dangerous, Berry. Better to leave them worrying than find out you're dead tomorrow.'

'I…'

Spike broke wind and sniffed the air.

'Just as well we don't do that,' joked Lee.

They all laughed, Berry the longest and heartiest. It had been many, many moons since he had heard anything so funny.

Spike stirred and growled and they cocked their ears. A loud rap came from the door. For a moment of pure ecstasy, Edgar imagined it was his folks returned. But they would never have knocked. Disappointment brought all his sorrow rushing home to inundate him.

'I'd better go,' he sighed, gripping his sword.

'Don't be stupid. *I'll* go.'

Lee gingerly opened the door a sliver, inspected who it was and widened the gap a little. Muffled voices could be heard before he closed it and came back.

'It's for you,' he said to Edgar, jerking his head towards the door with a shiver of aversion.

'Who is it?'

'The Eelman.'

'The *Eelman*? What does *he* want?'

'Blest if I know.'

With a click of his tongue Edgar went to the door, frowning with annoyance. He jerked it open and looked sternly out at the man, distilling the tension in the room.

The Eelman simpered, as was his wont. Pius Hornswoggle, the local schoolmaster, *was* as slippery as an eel. Yet many adults were fooled by his unctious charm, disarmed by his witty banter. As for his victims, he mesmerised them like a snake .

Pius only had eyes for good-looking boys. It was Edgar's turn to bear the brunt of his importunate attentions. The Eelman tended to pick you up and then grow tired of you, to throw you back down and set his sights on another. It was an endless cycle and Edgar couldn't wait to be dropped.

If the flavour of the month gave lip, perchance, Hornswoggle shrivelled up inside himself, as if he'd been mortally wounded. He looked physically ill, almost panic-stricken. His hands trembled. He stuttered his words. Recovered sufficiently the following day, he took it out on lesser mortals, flying into a rage at a spelling mistake, a poor subtraction, drawing blood from innocent palms with his cane. He was a ruthless bully when roused, and Edgar did his best not to provoke him.

Hornswoggle wished to possess Edgar, body and soul. He was suspicious of the man's advances without being able to put a finger on it. He couldn't talk of it to his parents - he didn't know how. All he felt was creeping revulsion. He absolutely refused to tarry after school and get "help with his homework". If others suffered subsequently, he was sorry for it. There was only so much he could do to spare them. All the schoolmaster offered was thraldom disguised as friendship, and subsequent self-loathing.

'Hullo, Edgar,' purred the Eelman with his familiar simper. His voice had a-drip-at-the-end-of-his-nose about it.

Edgar nodded curtly, refusing to speak. It would only encourage the fool.

Hornswoggle began to wilt before his eyes. He felt the coolness but desperately needed reassurance. Any sign of affection would do. He willed it like a drowning man craving oxygen. Edgar had become his life's blood and he urgently needed a transfusion. The boy sensed the edge of his desperation and yearned to slam the door in his face.

'I see you have the Chetwood boy with you.'

All Edgar did was nod. Calling him the Chetwood boy didn't fool him. Lee'd be his favourite soon enough. Lee was a very handsome chap, a mischievous, loveable rogue, it was bound to happen before long.

'What? The cat got your tongue, did he?'

It was a feeble attempt at wit. A faint blush suffused the master's cheeks, he deflated immediately. He let on to cough and cleared his throat.

'I think it's dreadful what they have done to your parents. I...'

His voice faltered, he cleared his throat once more. Edgar gave him no help whatsoever. The man seemed to steel himself. He continued where he'd left off.

'I came to see whether there was anything I could do…'

Edgar shook his head. Uncomfortable, he lowered his gaze and stared at the schoolmaster's boots.

'I didn't like to think of you out here alone after the ugly scenes you have witnessed. I…'

'I'm not alone,' he brusquely interrupted.

'Yes, I see that. I see you have the… Lee for company. But I'm nervous about two young boys without… defenceless… Perhaps I should stay to…'

'No!' Edgar exclaimed. 'We do have somebody here.'

'Oh… Who?'

'An uncle of mine, from out of town.'

'An uncle? On your mother's side or your father's?'

While he asked he edged closer to the door to get a better look into the parlour. Edgar moved to block his view and kept a tight grip on the latch. The man was beginning to irritate him intensely.

'My mother's,' he finally declared with resolution in every syllable.

'Well, if you're sure you'll be all right… I'd hate anything to happen to you, to my best pupil… the pupil I'm most fond of.'

His smile belied how he really felt. He was no master but a slave of his own desires, a vacuum sucking youth into his soulless body. He was a vampire of sorts, a frightened boy in the shell of a man.

'If you're sure… I'll leave you, then.'

He seemed to be trying with all his might to tear himself away. His eyes wandered to the light from the windows, yearing to gain access, acceptance, friendship, but a friendship that devoured so that all that remained was a husk, an ulcerous sore unable to heal.

'Is there nothing I can do for you?'

'Well...'

The idea had come to him to ask the master to go to Berry's parents and inform them he was safe at the mill. He couldn't trust the man. Besides, to trust him was to place himself in his hands and empower him. Edgar had no intention of doing that.

'Yes? What is it?'

'Nothing. I made a mistake.'

'A mistake? I don't understand.'

'Nothing,' came as a stern rejoinder and Pius knew he was defeated.

'I'll be on my way, then.'

'Yes.'

'Goodnight.'

'Yes.'

Edgar firmly closed the door and leaned against it.

'What did he *want*?' Lee loudly questioned with a grimace of disgust.

'He wanted to stay the night with us.'

'That doesn't surprise me. He's a weirdo, if ever there was one. He should do us all a favour and dig his own grave and drop into it.'

Edgar came and flopped down in an armchair, massaging the skin of his face. He was worn out battling man and beast. They just refused to go away. What was his shock and anger when he heard footsteps outside and another rap at the door. His blood boiled. He shot out of the chair, grabbing his sword.

'This better not be him back again,' he growled through gritted teeth. 'I'll chop his head off if it is.'

'This I've got to see,' said Lee, going with him.

'Whoa!' came a shout from outside. The man backed away, arms raised in surrender. 'If I'd known this was the sort of reception I'd get, I wouldn't have bothered me barney.'

It was said with humour and the figure came forward again. The rectangular beam of light from the door illuminated their visitor.

'Why, it's the Billy-can Man!' exclaimed Lee in surprise.

'Aye, it is, indeed. May I come in?'

Edgar opened the door to its widest and in walked the billy-can man with a nod to the two boys. He was about to speak when his eye caught sight of Berry by the fire.

'I was a-wonderin' when you'd fetch up here.'

'You *know* about him?' both boys asked in amazement.

'Aye, that I do… For quite some time now. I used to frighten them away, those stragglers who came a-huntin' his folks of an evenin', the yellow-bellied cowards. Thought they'd catch two devil-worshippers, so they did. Would have been worse for him if they'd caught poor Berry Blakelock here. *And* for them… Would have had to silence them for good, so I would, and no regrets on that score either.'

Berry rose to his feet and took his proffered hand.

'Now, my boyos, can't a body warm himself by that fine fire you have a-roarin' up the chimbley?'

They followed him to the hearth, Spike sniffing at the hems of his trouser-legs. Edgar prayed he wouldn't cock his leg against one of them. Their visitor sat down in the widest armchair and held out his hands to the flames, splaying his fingers to warm them.

'He smells my mutt, I'll be bound,' he remarked, nodding at Spike. 'I left him at home. 'Tis no night for a man's best friend to be out and about.' His expression grew grave as he pondered the context of his words. Brightening, he added with a smile, 'Be the Holy, you've got a fine blaze goin' here, my lads. You'll get by... *You'll* get by.'

The Billy-can Man – they didn't know his proper name – was a venerable veteran of the village. A doughty soldier was the Gaffer. He had fought alongside Edgar's grandpa, who had often remarked that he was the bravest, loyalest campaigner in Christendom. He lived alone on the outskirts of Garten, in a wooden shanty hidden behind overgrown hedges. He had forsworn the ways of men after his experiences in battle, despairing of their greed and violence. He eked out an existence on the roads, maintaining the verges and keeping the ditches clear to avoid flooding. He needed little and kept his peace. His black and white collie was his constant companion, sitting panting on the banks during the hot summer months and sharing his frugal lunch of wholemeal bread and tea. One o'clock on the dot, he knocked on certain doors, handing in his billy-can, receiving it back brimming with boiling water. Theirs were the best kept verges, the neatest gateways and the tidiest hedges on the peninsula. It was a sobering thought to realize that there were those who refused him such a simple act of kindness. He never spoke a harsh word against them, but he never darkened their doors again.

The inhabitants of his favourite haunts often came upon medicinal herbs, mouthwatering mushrooms and succulent berries on their doorsteps. That wasn't all. Unbeknownst to them, he watched over their families as well. He had his allies in Garten, people he visited of an evening. They shared their thoughts and misgivings and pondered the mood of the village. Thus had he heard of the plight of Edgar and his parents. Thus had he bided his time and chosen the apt moment to call, hiding in the shadows of the barn till the schoolmaster had left the premises. A watcher he was, an anonymous guardian, an unexpected hero never taken by surprise. "Gaffer Hedgerow" was considered too dimwitted to be a threat by some. How wrong they were.

'So, me laddies… You've been at the sharp end of it today, haven't you?'

'You can say that again,' Edgar replied in earnest.

'Thought my end was up a few times, I don't mind saying,' admitted a grim-faced Lee.

'And what about you, young fellow?'

'*Me*?… I'm just glad to be here,' Berry solidly declared, stretching his legs towards the fire.

For the first time in ages Berry felt self-conscious about his club-foot and drew it back. The billy-can man remarked it to himself but wasn't unduly saddened. He knew a thing or two. He would have smiled to himself if it wouldn't have given him away. They must grow all by themselves, he knew. The die is cast.

'Your folks supped well, I hear.' He wanted to keep the mood upbeat.

'Thanks to my friends,' Edgar stated with pride.

'Aye. You young 'uns'll be the makin' of this place yet, mark my words... I see you got rid of that schoolmaster quick as a flash, the fell vagabond.'

Edgar nodded his head, then shook it in slow-motion to show his disapproval.

'Don't you worry, lad,' he advised him, heaving himself up to get his pipe and tobacco-pouch from his pocket. 'I doubt you'll mind if I smoke. The place reeks of tobacco.'

'My dad.'

'Miller Falchion, there's a brave and honest man for you. As brave and honest as his father before him.'

Edgar stared into the fire, trying vainly to stifle a sob.

'They'll be fine,' the billy-can man said, squeezing his shoulder. 'They're tough folk. As tough as the fine lad they have for a son...

'Which... brings me... to why I'm here,' he staggered between pulls at his pipe, holding a burning faggot to the bowl with a tongs.

Before explaining he exhaled a wreath of smoke into the air, sweet-smelling tobacco they all inhaled, a homely feeling to banish the phantoms outside from their minds.

Portent amplified the flames to tongues of fire licking up the chimney. They waited with bated breath. This unexpected visit wasn't a social occasion. Their guest was here for a purpose, pivotal at that, they could read it in his eyes.

He had a mission of his own to fulfil and, until he did, he could not leave.

He kept his eyes fixed on the sword at Edgar's feet. Finally, summoning the courage, he jabbed the stem of his pipe at it, smoke curling from his barely parted lips.

'Is that what I think it is?'

Edgar looked down at it. 'Grandpa's sword, you mean?'

'Not grandpa's nor yours... He wondered whether you would be the one...'

'*Grandpa* did? Then he *knew* about the sword!' Edgar exclaimed with a surge of emotion.

'Aye, he knew... He knew what it was capable of in the right hands. What he didn't know was whose those hands were to be.'

'But why didn't he ask me to try it out and see?'

'He couldn't have done that. He who is to wield the sword must discover that for himself.'

'Did it work for him?'

'Never the once.'

'So how did he know about it, then?'

'As certain as his name was Falchion.'

'In other words...'

'Go on,' he cajoled with a smile.

'I'm... not... the first.'

'Oh, be the Holy, there you have it. It has been in your family for generations. And many's the eclipse that has passed overhead since a Falchion last had the advantage of its powers.'

Edgar began to see. But it was a cold, dreary, haggard dawn that glimmered faintly before him. He shivered. 'Did… that Falchion get to use it?'

'He did.'

'Did he…? Was he…?'

The billy-can man caught his drift and shook his head, lips a taut line of reluctance. He had hoped to avoid the question but the lad was too quick for him.

Edgar's voice fell to a solemn murmur. 'He died, didn't he?'

'Yes… He died… But not before doin' his duty. What he had been brought into this world to do, and the world was a better place for him.'

'And what did he have to do?'

'What difference does that make? He did his duty, that's all you need to know. A dark age descended upon our world. He, it was, who rekindled the light.'

'So… if the sword works for *me…* we're in another dark age.'

'We're on the brink of one.'

'Why now?'

'There's someone who knows more of these things than I do. Him you must speak to. A neighbour of yours… Old Buckrake.'

'*Farmer* Buckrake?'

'None other. Go speak with him tomorrow. He will be expectin' you. DO NOT go there tonight… Do not cross this threshold until morning, your lives depend on it. To venture forth tonight would be the ruination of all our hopes.'

'What about us?' Lee croaked, gesturing at himself and Berry.

The billy-can man nodded and smiled. 'You two are involved as well, so it seems.'

'Are we going to die?' Berry's timid voice quavered, a chill draught in the warm atmosphere.

'I cannot say, young man. I do not know what will befall you. You may die. You may live.'

'But we must do what we have to,' Edgar firmly stated.

'If you don't, it won't *be* worth living.'

'So, we have no choice.'

'You always have a choice, everyone does.'

'Not one worth making.'

'You are blessed to understand that. Such a blessing comes with the sword, so I'm told.'

'And my mam and dad?' He suddenly felt a small boy again, insecure and vulnerable.

'Life won't welcome them either if you fail.'

'I knew you were going to say something like that.'

'... One day they'll sing ballads in your honour.'

'I don't care about ballads.'

'I am glad to hear it. You are one in a million, worth your weight in gold. Your grandad always said so. That was why he had his suspicions about the sword... He was a great man, your grandad. But you will be greater still, Edgar Sabrehilt.'

'You hope so.'

'I *know* so.'

'Well, I just hope you're right and won't be disappointed.'

''Tis a heavy load to carry on young shoulders.'

'If everything goes wrong, I am to blame forever.'

'The head on them shoulders matches the load, so I see. You will not be to blame for anything that arises. Success or failure is yours and yours alone. And no sad reflection on you, son, if you do the deed... Time crept up in ambush on you. The last Sabrehilt, he was in full manhood.'

'Maybe they learnt from the last time.'

'They?'

'Whoever we're up against.'

'Aye. Is it they, though...?'

He got to his feet and stretched his legs. 'They're stiffenin' up, I'm not as young as I used to be... Well, I must be gettin' back. Can't leave the poor mutt alone on a night like this. And remember – do not stray beyond this door, no matter what. No matter *what*...

'So long now. Good fortune to you. You're your grandad's grandson, so help me God.'

At the door he placed a hand on Edgar's shoulder.

'There's something your grandpa always used to say on the battlefield. I can see him now, sword in hand, doing all he could to keep our spirits up. Perhaps he often said the same to you as a boy. I'll tell you anyway, it's worth repeatin'... Cowardice, men, he used to say, is a devilish miner hacking his way, shaft by shaft, to the core where courage lurks unseen. That's worth rememberin' in times like these that are upon us.'

Before leaving he offered the boy his hand.

'I'm proud to shake it, lad. Proud to know you and yours. Proud to have fought with your grandad. Goodnight now and God bless. I'll let the young fellow's folks know his whereabouts first thing in the mornin'.'

His lumbering figure faded into the gloom. Edgar could still hear him long after he'd disappeared from sight. He was reluctant to close the door and break the ties between them, to shut out the one and only adult they would meet before morning.

— 20. Irrevocable Twilight —

Edgar returned to his armchair mulling these questions over. He sat down in silence and all three of them pondered the waning fire. It was getting late, too late to pile any more logs on. They were tired after a very long day and desperately needed their sleep, if sleep they would get that night. The bright yellow light faded from the diminishing flames. The logs collapsed when the one beneath them broke into charcoal wedges. Spike was curled up in Berry's lap, a luxury he hadn't been favoured with since he was a puppy. With groans of contentment he settled himself, tucking his tail round his snout

'I wonder what he meant by not going out, no matter what?' Lee murmured, dazed by the flickering light.

'I was wondering that too,' Berry echoed.

'I'm sure he meant that it was more than our life's worth,' Edgar voiced for them.

'But why?' Lee asked.

'Something's going to happen tonight. That's why he wanted to get home before it started.'

'I wonder what it is,' Berry droned sleepily, twirling one of Spike's ears.

Edgar got up and went to the window. The stars were shining, bright and sharp in a clear sky. He twisted his head to one side and frowned. It couldn't be... It was impossible... But it looked as if the Plough was upside down...

'Lee, come here.'

'What?'

'Look out there. What do you see?'

'The usual. What am I supposed to see?... What do *you* see?'

'Look at the stars.'

'What about them?' Lee leaned in closer, brushing against Edgar's shoulder. 'They look the same to me.'

'Berry, can you come here a minute?'

Gently but awkwardly, Berry lifted Spike from his knees and placed him on the cushion. He moaned in mild protest at the disturbance but nestled into the warm hollow and was soon fast asleep again. Berry limped over to the window and peered out for himself.

'Do you notice anything about the stars?'

'It's upside down.'

'*What's* upside down?' Lee craned his neck and rested his chin on Berry's shoulder. The human contact felt lovely after such a long time in the tower.

'The Plough,' he whispered in his ear.

'Oh, God,' Lee groaned. 'Something awful *is* going to happen tonight.'

As he said it the wind began to rise. They saw the twiggy tops of the distant woods sway and ripple. The open gate stirred and the wind curled around the house, beginning to find its voice.

20. Irrevocable Twilight

'It's starting,' Edgar whispered.

They edged back from the window. All that was between them and the outside were a few diamond panes of leaded glass that could burst in at any moment. They stood round the hearth, keenly aware that it was open to the elements. As the embers settled the wind grew angrier and the night prepared for war. With a whimper, Spike sat up, wide-awake. He shook himself and listened. Tail between his legs, he got down off the armchair and came and sat next to Edgar.

'I wonder will we get any sleep tonight…?'

'Can't we all sleep in the same room?' Lee pleaded.

'Is that all right with you, Berry?'

'Me? I don't mind where I sleep.'

'Aren't you afraid?' Lee asked in awe.

'I am a bit. But it's far better being here than in the tower.'

The door shook and the latch rattled furiously. They rushed and threw themselves against it, terrified something was about to break in.

'It's only the wind,' said Edgar. 'Help me to drag one of the chairs over here.'

They pushed and dragged the heaviest against the door, checked all the windows were fastened and bolted upstairs, throwing themselves under the covers, clothes and shoes and all, and Spike in among them. From there, hearts pummelling their tonsils, breath coming in gulps and gasps, they listened as the night unfolded.

'Damn and blast,' cried an exasperated Edgar.

'What?' Lee's voice was high-pitched with terror.

'I left the sword downstairs.'

'You idiot!'

'I'll go and get it.'

'We'll *all* go!'

They were up and down in a flash, panting and trembling beneath the blankets. Spike didn't know what to make of them. He sensed their fear and shivered between their legs, buried at the foot of the bed. If they got any sleep that night, it would be a miracle.

'Trust the billy-can man to frighten us out of our wits,' mourned Lee.

'Don't worry,' consoled Edgar. 'Me and you and Berry, we'll get through this all right.'

Brave words disguised his inner feelings. He missed his burly dad and soft-hearted mam more than he'd imagined possible. He half expected to hear reassuring words every time there was a harsher gust of wind. The silence only accentuated their absence. His thoughts turned to them imprisoned in that god-forsaken vault under the church. An insurmountable urge to go to them seized him by the scruff of the neck. He started up and tumbled out of the bed.

'What the hell is wrong now?' groaned Lee.

'I have to go to my mam and dad,' Edgar answered, half in a daze.

'You *what?!*' Lee shouted, sitting bolt upright. 'Are you out of your *mind?*'

'I've *got* to!' Edgar shrieked, beside himself with panic.

Lee leapt from the bed and grabbed him. 'You know what the billy-can man said!'

'They *need* me.'

'But you'll be *killed*, can't you get that into your *thick skull*?!'

Lee shook him mercilessly. Gradually consciousness returned to Edgar's glazed eyes and he looked about him.

'There…' Lee sighed with relief. 'Bloody hell, you had me frightened for a minute.'

'I don't know what came over me. One minute I was thinking of Mam and Dad, the next…'

'The next you were about to commit suicide.'

'I must have been dreaming… Let's all go and sleep in *their* bed, it's far roomier than this one.'

'Now you're talking. You've finally got your wits about you.'

It *was* much less cramped. Edgar got to inhale the scents of his mam and dad and feel closer to them. Reason regained, he scoffed at his folly. What could he have done that his dad couldn't do? Wasn't his mam far safer with *him* than here? Running out into the arms of death, whatever had come over him?

Something was trying to get him to go outside, he was sure of it - trying to force him to venture forth in a half-witted state, forgetting his sword. A trick was being played on him, a mind game of sorts. I must keep my wits about me, he determined. I mustn't let anything fool me.

The three of them lay abreast, like corpses in a row, hands clasped on their chests, feet together, staring fixedly at the ceiling.

Prickleback lay next to his wife. He had already lambasted her when she commented that it was no ordinary wind.

'Superstitious fool... You're as ignorant as those vagabonds in the village.'

He mocked her as he lay with his back to her. The wind did howl though, screeching round the castle. He shivered, putting it down to the chill night air, insisting he wasn't afraid. Yet he drew the sheet up to his chin and his nightcap down over his brows. Deep down, in a cavern he despised, a part of him was glad she was there beside him.

Far off, down some dusky corridor in a long-vacated bedroom, he distinctly made out the muted tinkle of breaking glass. Had the force of the storm blown in a window? Could Racker Booth have returned to the house unnoticed and hidden away in a room upstairs? As his fears escalated and his imagination condensed them, droplets of water ran down the walls of his mind. The cruel glint of steel reared up in his thoughts. Beads of perspiration broke out on his forehead and trickled down his spine.

She too had heard the lyrical breaking of glass, ears straining to catch any other sound. She too pretended not to hear, knowing full well she would be thumped from the bed and forced to investigate if she did. He was an abject coward in comparison with her psychopathic dead brute of a husband, dead at her own hands. What if…? Dear God above, what if HE had made the sound?!!!! What if *he* had finally returned to avenge himself for his untimely death? The ghost of Mort Broadbent silently, ghoulishly gliding along the corridor to pierce the wooden boards of the door and loom up at the foot of the *bed*!!!!!!!!!!!!!!! She shook uncontrollably, sobbing into her pillow until terror or exhaustion delivered her.

20. Irrevocable Twilight

Racker Booth raised his head from his pillow and listened to the yawling fury outdoors. Skulduggery was afoot and Nature herself consented. The noise was blood-curdling, ear-splitting. The curtains stirred in the draught, he almost cried out in fear. What if someone or something was hiding behind them? Waiting for him to fall asleep before beating his brains out with a length of lead piping, a sawn-off bough? What if it was the BOY??!!!! Goose-pimples erupted all over him, he whimpered a beseeching prayer.

'I'll do anything if you spare me… I'll be good, I promise…

'I-I-I'll let them gooo.'

The fury outside trebled and drowned out his feeble pleading, squeals of a cornered rat. Unable to stand it any longer, with a screech to drown out his terror, he leapt naked from the bed and tore open the curtains.

Nothing…
Nobody.

The relief of it had him close to tears. He scratched his groin and sniffed his fingers. Hawking loudly, he swallowed phlegm. A hard, evil smile played about his thin lips. He was alone and nobody knew of his momentary lapse. Nobody need ever know. If he'd had a wife, she would have died that night.

He squatted, drew the chamberpot from under the bed, slopped its contents and emptied his bladder. He rubbed the wetness off his fingers against his bony thigh, snorted, spat into the yellow froth and got back into bed. He scratched the brittle hairs on his chest, examined his wiry frame and drew the mouldy blankets over his head. The warm breath on his face reeked of stale alcohol. Rough, calloused palms rubbed heat into his skin.

A wife…

It troubled him deeply that women shrank from his amorous advances. The humiliation bored into him, a skewer tearing at his entrails. Still a virgin at his age, he belonged among the callow youth of the village, the boys with misty down on their lips, the Pius Hornswoggles of this world. It fairly drove him mad with shame. He ground his teeth, worn uneven by rampant emotion.

'I need a wife,' he growled into the darkness. 'Molly Falchion?… Any one of them will have me once the mill is mine…' Fear of embarrassing refusals decided him. 'I'll cut out the miller's heart and take his wife for my own. Warm… Well-fleshed… Pretty… She'll learn to love me, I'll beat it into her. I'll take what was his, his mill and his squaw. As for the brat… I'll spill his guts for him.'

With a coarse leer he turned on his side and punched his pillow, hauling the blankets up to cover his shoulder-blades. A shritch on the wind shrivelled the flesh on his bones.

Were the risks worth it?

He scoffed at his own timidity.

'The wind's up me this night,' he said, 'rattlin' me bones.'

To distract his wayward thoughts, he pictured Molly in the bed beside him. That brought a smile to his face, a shard of cruelty to his heart. To have her trembling and weeping next to him. Shaking like a leaf, begging him not to. It was well worth the risk.

''Tis a hellish night.'

His wife didn't answer him. Squire Trefoil tut-tutted and looked up to heaven. A dangler of a cobweb swayed in the decided draught. He made a mental note to read the Riot Act to the housekeeper next morning. He shivered and flung a second muffler round his neck.

'Devilish cold.'

Still no answer.

'My *dear,* aren't you listening to me?'

'I'm trying to read,' Isolda replied with a prolonged sigh. 'It's very difficult to read when a popinjay is wittering away in one's ear.'

'A popinjay? A *popinjay*?! Well, I never…'

He began muttering to himself. The very sight of her nonchalantly absorbed in her book was enough to make him blow a gasket.

'M'dear.'

'Mmm?'

'M'*dear!*'

She slammed the open book onto her lap.

'For crying out loud! What the hell is the *matter* with you?!'

'Haven't you noticed that the hounds of hell are abroad this night?'

'There's a little bit of a storm, that's all.'

'A *little* bit? Are you *deaf*? Have you gone out of your *mind*?'

'Is lying here listening to it like a half-wit going to stop it?'

'Well, no, m'dear.'

'*Well*, then?'

She resumed her book while he fidgeted beside her, settling his nightcap one minute, snagging the hem of his nightshirt with a heel to stretch it to its full length the next.

'Can't understand what you see in that book... Just listen to the wind... What terrors are being unleashed upon us tonight?'

'There may be more truth in your words than you care to admit.'

'Not all that again, I beg you.'

'It might be the very thing to calm your nerves.'

He held up a hand, forbidding her to continue, suspending the tiresome argument.

'I shan't get a wink tonight.' He sounded wistful, anxious at how wrinkled and old he'd appear in the morning. 'I shall be a fright.'

'Yes, you shall. But *I* shall sleep like a baby.'

With that, there was a more startling gust than ever and he flipped the sheet over his head.

Molly lay in her husband's arms, the locked gate a palisade of swirling leaves pale against the pitch-black steps. She trembled at the sudden gusts of wind.

''Tis all right, girl,' he murmured in her ear, putting his lips to her brow.

'I was thinking of Edgar.'

'So was I, lass.'

She raised her head and looked at him.

'Do you think he's safe, Benjamin?'

'That lad's a born survivor, Moll. I've lost count of the number o' times he's nearly killed himself as a little 'un and walked away scott-free. Luck hangs round his neck like a breastplate, he'll come to no harm.'

Nevertheless, he would have done anything to break his way out of there and hurry to the side of his son. The bars and lock were beyond his powers, he had nothing to force them with. He cursed those cowardly curs who couldn't fight but in packs. He swore to get even with them one day.

It was a horrible place to be incarcerated, especially for a woman, and how he felt for her. More horrible still with that thing in the corner. They had come across it when he'd begun to shift a few coffins to make some room for them. By pushing them to one end of the shelf he'd made a makeshift bench to sit on, a rock-hard bed to sleep on. Anything was preferable to lying on the damp floor churning to mud as rainwater cascaded down the stairwell. It was as damp and cold as any dungeon. There had been a horrible scrunching sound when he'd rammed a casket closer to the back wall. He'd stopped immediately and gone to investigate.

'Lord above,' he'd murmured, sucking in his breath.

'Oh, no,' Molly had said, drawing back with hand to her mouth.

A mummified skeleton was wedged between the lead coffin and the wall. They'd known her by the torn, mildewed dress clinging to her bones.

'Widow Staveacre,' he'd whispered. 'And us led to believe she had fallen foul of the witches, leaving all her earthly goods to...'

'The Reverend!' Molly had exclaimed sotto voce. 'Poor Lizzie. What a horrible way to die. God rest her soul.'

'She's out of his clutches now… Dad was right. That man's a demon, a fiend from hell. We're bigger mugs than I thought, hon.'

'Can he really be that bad, Benjamin?'

'Who else has a key to this unholy place?'

'Does that mean… You don't think he had poor Ellen Barchester burnt at the stake for nothing, do you?'

'Not for nothing. Remember... He got his grubby hands on all her property too.'

'Lord preserve us and keep us.'

'Amen to that.'

'I hate this place,' Molly said with a shiver, listening to the storm raging outside. 'I wish we were home with Edgar.'

'So do I, hon,' he agreed, hugging her tighter.

Molly broke down and sobbed into his shoulder.

'You lie in my arms now, I'll keep you safe. Try to forget where you are. Close your eyes and dream o' the mill.'

She nestled against his chest. He certainly didn't say so aloud but he wondered to himself how many other neighbours of theirs were stored in these caskets. So many had disappeared without trace over the years.

'Get some sleep,' he crooned soothingly into her hair. 'We'll be gone from this accursed place before you know it.'

Turlough Grindlewick and his ample spouse snored through the storm, the blood having rushed to their stomachs to aid digestion. Perspiration leaked from the crevices of their spare tyres. They had snuffled and chuckled at Oaf banging on the inn door and pleading for admittance. They had locked him out for the night. To amuse themselves.

He was curled up in a heap of mildewed straw, in a corner of one of the stables, ears still ringing with his shouts, fists still stinging after almost battering the door down. He was weeping bitterly.

'Why do they hate me, my own mam and dad?… Why are they so horrible to me?… I know I'm stupid and ugly but I'm still their son… I can't help the way I am, that's no reason to laugh at me and lock me out in the stinkin' storm for the night. I could get pneumonia or be dragged off by witches… An' I work so hard for them…'

He would have run away if every vestige of self-confidence hadn't been beaten out of him by his sadistic parents. As it was, he fell asleep, tears still coursing down his cheeks, sobs wracking his frame.

Lee's father cursed his own wife while she dabbed his split lip with spirit.

'Hold still, can't ye?' she growled, not put out the slightest. She was used to such treatment. A husband who wasn't in charge of his own household wasn't a man at all. 'It'll get infected if ye don't.'

'Be *done,* woman!… I swear I'll pay him back for this, if it's the last thing I do.'

'The cheek o' that good-for-nothin' holy Joe doin' that to ye. I'll have his guts for garters when yer done with him.'

'Aye, an' welcome to them, Sarey. Your're a woman after me own heart.'

'Isn't that why ye married me?' she said with a fond smile, wiggling the tip of his nose.

'Leave off, can't you?' he growled, brushing her aside with his arm.

Sarah frowned, then scowled with hatred. 'An' that little brat of ours to side with them against his own father. Unnatural, so it is.'

'He'll learn not to play games with me, don't you worry, girl. I'll flog the seat of his pants till he drops down afore me in a dead faint.'

'He deserves every lash of it.'

She swayed her broad hips and smiled a cajoling smile.

'Come to bed, Brough Chetwood. Come to bed and keep me warm, my man.'

A crooked grin overspread his features as he briskly got to his feet. He made to tickle her but she skipped back from him and nimbly scaled the stairs, laughing like a coy schoolgirl, emitting a shrill scream when she saw him following her. Lee was forgotten already.

Sam, Piper, Brad and Nico lay curled up under the blankets of their own respective beds. Their thoughts were with the three boys cooped up in the mill, the storm an abyss of malice between them. Without exception, they reproached themselves as craven imbeciles for being so readily talked into slinking home.

The wind moaned a hollow dirge, reminding them of the scarecrows, setting them rigid in the bed with apprehension. Clouds harried the moon, concealing it first, then pursuing it across the firmament. She fled before them, veiling herself in mist to shield herself from the dread developments below, a petrified child too curious not to peep through her fingers. A gust of mammoth force struck the mill. The wind went skreighing round the outhouses, roaring in the woods beyond. Intimidated, the boys felt very small and frail. They wondered what was happening to Garten. Nothing made sense any more. It was a nightmare come to life.

The barn door banged furiously, calling to Edgar to come outside. Thoughts of the mill-wheel spinning to destruction tempted him to brave the elements. He closed his mind to them, recognizing them for what they were – ruses to lure him to certain death.

A great calm descended in an instant. They lay there dreading what was to come next. A pattering started, faster and heavier. Rain lashed down on the roof, spat at the windows and doors, numberless pounding fists attempting to crush their refuge. It seemed like one vast sheet of water, a cataract from the skies. Tears were falling on stricken Garten. He thought of his parents and felt his heart being torn apart by talons. Lee and Berry knew he was crying. They lay there listening but there was nothing they could do. Edgar rubbed his sleeve across his eyes. Crying would get him nowhere. Whatever was out there wanted him to cry and feel afraid. Hatred and anger came to his aid and buoyed him up.

Lee wrapped his arms about himself and clutched his chest. Rage burned in his breast. He cursed himself more than ever for opening his mouth about Ed's sword. *My own mam and dad…* A great big tear rolled down the side of his nose, past the curve of his lip and chin to tickle his neck before soaking into the collar of his shirt. Manfully, he gritted his teeth and stifled a sob. One heartbroken boy was enough. His misery would only add to his friend's burdens.

Their sorrow communicated itself to Berry lying between them. No stranger to suffering, he felt for them both. His club-foot was a ball and chain tethered to his ankle as long as he could remember. His withered hand made a mockery of him. Once he'd gone to school, the whole gamut of taunts and insults were flung at him, echoing in his mind when he'd laid his weary head on his pillow. How often had he prayed to die during the night.

But now...

Now he was happy, glad his prayer hadn't been answered. Shoulder to shoulder with two great boys, the greatest he had ever known, basking in the warm companionship they had munificently conferred on him. He found it practically impossible to believe that they actually liked him... A comrade in arms, it was enough to make him giddy. He would prove himself to them. He would show them how loyal he was. Somehow, he'd think of something... He would give up his life for them, if it came to that. Willingly. Gladly. He had never felt as safe as he did then, lying between his two friends, the only friends he'd ever had. He snuggled down between them, warm and comfortable in a soft bed. It was hard to believe. Spike stirred at his feet. A contented groan came from beneath the blankets and Berry drifted off to sleep with a smile on his face.

The most awful racket began outside. They sprang from the bed and ran to the window.

'Oh, my God,' drawled Lee. 'It *is* the end of the world.'

The three of them stood staring out of the window. Their minds quailed at the sight. The might of Nature was unsheathed against them. The wind and the rain were working together, loosening the soil, tearing it up in clods and flinging them far afield. With cries of dismay the boys retreated from the window, transfixed. Old Lem, began to rise into the air, a corpse vacating its grave. Like a rag-doll, it was dashed against the ground, again and again. Boughs and branches were torn out of their sockets and sent spinning into the darkness. Splinters were flying in all directions, striking the window like hail before being sucked up into the sky. Lem had paid the price of his transgressions.

They had no time dwell on the fact. A familiar, shrill squeaking penetrated through to the bedroom.

They were back.

The bats were back, millions upon millions of them filling the sky. They all knew where they were headed.

To the tower, that beacon of night summoning evil from the four corners of the globe. Death lurked within its precincts... The Great Unknown.

†

— PART II —

NEMESIS

— 21. Axis of Evil —

Clouds of leathery wings wheeled and spun and tumbled from the sky, swerving to avoid one another. Their sonar echoes were shrill and deafening. It was a solid mass of sound rebounding off the outlying trees and hedgerows, concentrating in the confines of the tower. Tiny fingers clung to every nook and cranny like a swarm of bees. The inner surfaces of the walls were a seething mass of fur and claws and hairless ears. A dome of these creatures rose up on the second floor, like drones protecting their queen. Their work had merely begun.

Though the wind screamed curses and threats and swore revenge in the treetops, here, on the apex of the hill, dead calm prevailed. An active, deathly silence swallowed sound as night conquers day. Not a blade of grass stirred while all about it was blasted and torn up by the roots. No creature shuffled in the tangled undergrowth. All was dread expectation.

Round the circumference of the accursed field stood the battalions of scarecrows. Like priests before the altar of their lord and master, they eagerly awaited his rebirth. They crouched and tugged at the boulders strewn about the field, dragging and rolling them nearer the stump of the tower.

Though not a breath of wind bestirred it, the ivy began to rustle. Gnarled vines gradually detached themselves and slithered groundwards, fanning outwards in all directions. At this, the scarecrows ceased their toil and stood erect. They knew the procedure. They had done this before.

The fleshy green tips of ivy found out the nearest building-blocks and wound tightly round them. Slowly the boulders were dragged to the base of the tower and hauled into place on the dilapidated walls. A multitude of bats spat a mixture of soil and saliva into the crevices between the stones, packing it tight with their droppings. Nourished by their voidings, tender shoots sprang from the vines and fastened themselves to the newly-replaced blocks. Growing with the masonry, the tentacles of ivy reached further, lugging additional boulders into place before descending for more. Gradually, unopposed, the walls of the tower rose into the night sky, full five stories high. A window glared from each floor, facing North and South, East and West. A ring of jagged stones crowned the roof.

The tower was rebuilt.

It looked down on Garten and bared its teeth.

†

— 22. Totem Revivified —

On cue, a band of scarecrows separated themselves from the horde and radiated out into the adjoining fields. No one was abroad to defend their livestock. Shepherds and herdsmen were cowering behind barred doors, duty forsaken. Leggy shadows stalked across the fields, climbed into pens and paddocks, strode into barns and stables. A frightful din arose, sheer pandemonium. Defenceless beasts were driven by their unorthodox rustlers to the brow of the hill. The massive wooden door sprang open. Loops of ivy tumbled out, entangling the demented animals and pulling them inside. The door slammed shut.

The ensuing cacophony was horrendous. Bellowings and shriekings were muffled by slobbering and gulping sounds. Throaty, liquid rumblings started up, water in hollow pipes. Blood spewed from the mouth of every gargoyle on every corner of every floor. It dribbled down the face of the tower. It ran down the slope of the hill, polluting the earth. It filled the perimeter ditch and fouled the waterways. As suddenly as it had begun, it ceased. The last drops of blood congealed on the lower lips and protuding tongues of the fell guttersnipes. Thy licked their chops, muttered contentedly and closed their eyes.

The tower presented a hideous aspect in its pool of gore. The stone walls were smeared with blood and bat dung to the very roof. The stench of death was overpowering. And this repulsive monument to decay rose giddily into the air, towering above every building and knoll and tree on the peninsula. No eye could avoid seeing it. No mind could shut it out. Its presence could be felt in the deepest cave, at the foot of the tallest promontory, behind the heaviest of doors. A funereal silence descended upon the land like a black pall of mourning. Fear, like icy fingers, gripped the hearts and thoughts of every inhabitant of the village. Not one solitary soul could deny the presence of…

Something…

Something so evil, so terrifying, so unearthly, as to make death itself a welcome release.

— 23. Perfidious Fanfare —

One after the other, the sound of ponderous footfalls emerged from the empty windows and open mouths of the gargoyles. Up, up, up. Step by step. Floor by floor. The tower shook. The ground beneath it rumbled, echoes trailing away to issue forth from the mouths of smugglers' caves on the shingly shore. Waves, in reverse, bridled on the coast and swept out to sea, crashing against the cliffs of the nearby island, inundating unsuspecting craft beyond the horizon. A huge bulky shape appeared among the projecting spikes upon the roof. From corner to corner it prowled, scanning the horizon until it recovered its bearings. Massive fingers curled round a granite cusp. The silhouette of a colossal head on mammoth shoulders peered out between the granite teeth in the direction of the village. A gurgling sound vibrated in its throat. The head jutted out further and looked down the length of the polluted walls. Nostrils flared, it sniffed and snuffled the pungent reek of blood.

The scarecrows bowed low at the sight of it. A baleful moan escaped them, rising to a crescendo when it reached the roof. The wolves threw back their heads and bayed at the creature, an eerie wail of respect and despair. The crows awoke and tossed themselves into the air, a whirling cloud of cackling feathers. Mice and burrowing creatures froze in the undergrowth, beady eyes out on stalks. Herons and owls sped home to their nests. But the scarecrows stood to attention, wolves by their sides, crows perched on their shoulders, ready to do its bidding.

The shadowy form spread its legs and stood solidly in the centre of the roof. It looked up and snarled in the face of an affrighted moon. It growled at the light from the myriads of stars. Snub profile raised, it opened its mouth as wide as wide can be. A rumbling began in the pit of its cavernous chest, amplifying till a terrific roar detonated in its throat.

It was truly awesome, echoing off the firmament, engulfing everything in its dissonant boom; stalling the moon in its orbit, the clouds in their tracks. Showers of meteors bombarded the atmosphere, resplendent in their death-throes. Here, there and everywhere, stars went out like doused tapers till the sky was nothing more than a black shroud extending from horizon to horizon. A fissure distorted the moon's face. Its expression changed, from humorous wonder to a sullen leer. Bent low by the sound-waves, trees and shrubs leaned away from the tower and its occupant. The tide swept out beyond the island as if the oceans of all the world had been sucked dry. Fish floundered and beat themselves to death on the sea-floor.

And still the roar held sway. Through walls and windows and doors. Down burrows and setts and alleyways. In stables and barns and outhouses. Rupturing eardrums. Blinding eyes. Filling minds with its dread recoil.

23. Perfidious Fanfare

The Morgammeron Aetz has returned.

Let the Dark Age begin!

†

— 24. Reverberations —

Racker fell naked onto the floorboards and crawled under his bed. Upsetting his chamberpot, he lay quivering in his own voidings. A howl of agonized terror escaped his constricted throat. Damp and miserable, he shivered with cold, afraid he would die of exposure if not of fear.

'Lord preserve us and keep us!' he wailed. 'I won't touch a hair of her head, *I swear it!* I'll release the miller and his wife first thing in the morning if only you spare me from *ruin!*'

His hands went to his face and he wept inconsolably. Nose streaming, hair wringing with urine, he lay there alone.

'Oh dear God, I'm more lonesome than the devil himself… Lord, I swear, *I swear it, Lord!* Never will I turn my heart to his evil ways again. Lord, I swear it, if only you will snatch me from the jaws of hell!'

His wails of grief and his strident oaths were drowned by the roar of the Morgammeron Aetz.

Squire Trefoil shot up in the bed, eyes wild with terror. He dashed back the tassle of his nightcap bobbing before his face.

'What the blazes is that?' he cried in a strangulated voice, trembling in every limb. 'Aren't you awake?' he shrieked in disbelief at the sleeping form of his wife. 'Wake up!' he shouted while vigorously shaking her. 'I *command* you!'

Gripping her shoulder with both hands, he violently tossed her to and fro. A prolonged moan escaped her and she tried to shake him off. He redoubled his efforts. With a loud flump she rolled out of the bed and hit the floor. In an instant she was on her feet, fierce eyes glaring at him, purple in the face with rage.

'What do you mean? How *dare* you!'

She raised an arm and he leaned far away from her, shielding his face with his hand. A whimper escaped him.

'Can't you hear, woman?'

The roar entered her consciousness and struck her dumb.

'Ah,' he gloated, almost glad there was a hideous noise emanating from a fell throat somewhere on the peninsula.

Isolda sat on the edge of the bed, bowed down by grief.

'It has begun,' she whispered.

'*What* has begun? What on earth are you talking about? Are you quite mad?'

'Don't be such a fool,' she snapped, turning on him viciously.

'What have I done now?' he whined.

'You know full well. Don't play the idiot with me… It has returned. The funest beast has returned… After all these years.'

'You don't mean… No… It can't be. It simply can't be.'

'Don't try to delude yourself. You are the one who should be out there defending your people.'

'Me? *Me?!* Those *brutes*?'

'You have in your possession…'

'Don't you dare bring that up at the time like this.'

'This *is* the *time!*'

His eyes widened with fear and foreboding. He refused to countenance the truth, he just couldn't. I, I, I… I can't help it if I'm married to Lady Macbeth. I'm not strong enough. It's too much to ask. *I cannot!*

He pulled the cap down over his eyes and lay on his side.

'My God, just look at you… Sebastian Trefoil, *Squire* of Garten… Coward!… Your ancestors must be rolling in their graves. How I despise you.'

Her taunts fell on deaf ears, his mind too full of the ghastly roar and what it presaged. All he could dwell on was flight.

'Who will save us now?' she moaned, sinking back on her pillow.

Prickleback woke with a violent start. It took seconds to register it wasn't a dream that had wandered into his wakened state. The noise was real. The noise was hideous. It filled the bishop's palace and surrounding countryside. He felt the hairs of his head stand on end. A clammy perspiration broke out on his forehead. The acrid whiff of sweat rose from his armpits. His wife woke with a gasp beside him.

'What is it? Who can be making that horrible noise?'

'Don't let your imagination run away with you,' he growled. "Tis only a bull.'

'No earthly bull ever made such a sound.'

'Peace, woman!… Silence!'

Her natural reactions to the sound unnerved him. A chaotic medley of age-old superstitions reared up to confound him. He was powerless to renounce the fear they instilled, furious with himself for being such a weakling. The uproar seemed eternal. Shrill and discordant, it was a fanfare to hate and betrayal, slaughter and despair. He found himself wondering if the creature could be appeased in some way. He was prepared to do anything to save his skin.

Gerty Mallock, Famer Buckrake and the Billy-can Man ruefully shook their heads. They had been waiting for just such a manifestation. Forewarned, they had read the signs of its approach, dreading it with all their souls. They could not range themselves against the inevitable. Mere human beings, they were prisoners of time and history. Fear and hope mingled in their breasts, oil and water. It is upon us... There is no turning back... God help the lad. God give him strength for his unenviable task... Guide his hand. Make it steady and sure.

Molly cried out and buried her face in her husband's chest. Listening in awe, he stroked her head. It was folly to utter reassurances. This was no ordinary creature. This was treachery personified. He thought of his son and felt panic rising. A defenceless boy locked up alone in the mill, what on earth could he do to stave off such wickedness? All the foolish make-believe about the sword would spell certain ruin if he were mad enough to take account of it... If there was anything remotely special about that sword I would have known it. Damn me for not breaking it up or throwing it out years ago.

He wanted to leap off the shelf and shout his lungs up. He wanted to hurl himself against their prison gate and rip the bars asunder. He wanted to beat his own brains out and tear his own flesh for not being able to go to his son.

All the while, the boys slept soundly and peacefully. No noise disturbed their rest that night and they awoke refreshed.

— 25. Garten Bewitched —

Motes of dust pervaded the atmosphere, fall-out from the barrage of meteorites. The sunrise was lurid. Gaudy, aberrant colours pulsated through the firmament. The stricken moon rode high still, a churlish ghost of its former self. Accentuating the discordant atmosphere, ragged clouds reflected the garish hues of the sky. No bird dilated its throat to warble. No cock serenaded the dawn. The shadow of the tower loomed high over Garten.

The stench of mud and rotting seaweed hung heavy in the air. Foul exhalations rose from the fields and filled the dips and hollows. Mists curled round the boles of trees and choked the life from them. Slowly it wove its way round homes and outhouses. Foetid mire coated the beds of waterless rivers. Rank, rotting vegetation poked from its depths. Waterfowl and woodland creatures floundered, unable to escape its grip. Caked with mud, they sank below the surface.

It was warmer now, the stuffy warmth of a sick-room. Insects proliferated with the rise in temperature. Myriads of gnats filled the air, weaving rhythmically in the light. Clouds of mosquitos whined in their quest for blood. The buzzing of bluebottles and horseflies was incessant. Livestock snorted and stamped at their mercy, tethered in their barns and stables. The flick of a tail had black clouds rise above them only to descend again. They were fiendish in their onslaught. They penetrated the tiniest fissures in walls and windows. Swarms swept down the chimneys and crept under doors. Beetles poured from cracks in the floorboards and ceilings. Babies bawled in their cots, women screamed, men howled, slapping themselves raw to drive them away. They dashed from their homes, arms flailing, hair matted with bugs.

Headlong they rushed into shoals of mice. In their millions they poured into the village like a raging torrent, waves of them crashing against the walls and surging over thresholds and sills. The beleaguered inhabitants crushed them underfoot, slipping in their blood and guts. Driven to distraction, they fled from the village, crushing toddlers and the elderly beneath their feet. Their corpses littered the roadway, soon to be dispatched by ravening rodents.

With cries of dismay, they skidded to a halt and stood petrified at the sight before them. The tower was rebuilt, frightful to behold. A low growl emerged from the gargoyles' mouths and had the crazed villagers haring across the fields and through the hedges. They huddled at the foot of the cliffs, out of sight. But there were no boats - and no sea even if there had been – to take them away from there.

The sepulchral silence filled them with dread. The garish colours crushed their spirits. The stink assailing their nostrils sickened them. Some of them fainted, gashing themselves on the sharp stones where they fell. A few sank down on their knees and prayed for deliverance.

25. Garten Bewitched

One man, Brough Chetwood, pointed into the sky with a trembling finger. All eyes followed his and a groan of despair rose from all their throats. They quailed at the sight of the cruel mockery of a moon, the pallid, deformed features leering down at them with glee. Anxiously he looked about him, studying the faces of the crowd. He no longer wished to be their leader, but who was there to take his place? Prickleback was absent, Racker too. Fear and despair were rapidly turning on *him*. It was only a matter of time.

'Chetwood.'

He ignored them, pretending not to hear.

'Brough!'

Soon his name was on every tongue. He would have fled if he had't been hemmed in on all sides.

'What is it?' he barked in frustration.

'What are we to do?'

'How should *I* know?'

'Save us, Chetwood.'

An old toothless hag pleaded with him, lips trembling, tears in her bloodshot eyes. He hated her for her helplessness and struck her down. A gasp went up and they stepped back from him. Perhaps he could fight his way free. Reading his thoughts, the sturdier among them edged closer to intimidate him. Violence had undone him at last.

'Well, Mister-brave-enough-to-hit-an-old-woman, you can march right up to that tower and see what's going on for us. *That* should cool your ardour.'

They pushed and shoved him forward. Out of his mind with fear, he turned on the lot of them.

'Leave off, you varmints!' he roared.

'Get on with it. We're not afraid of the likes of you.'

'Back off, I say!... I'll see you in hell first.'

'Aye! That you will.'

They launched at him. He swung away and veered out to sea. With a surge, the vituperative mob were after him. Chetwood skidded on some loose stones. His feet began to sink into the wet sand, it resembled flight in a dream. With a final lurch he sank to his waist. He struggled to free himself and sank to his chest. The more he fought the quicksand, the deeper he foundered. Panic bubbled to the surface. Vividly he envisaged the slow and horrible death before him.

'Help me!' he shrieked. 'Help me, you fools!'

Wordlessly they shook their heads. No one could go to his aid without joining him.

The quicksand was skimming his throat.

'*Do* something... I *beg you!*'

The sediment passed his lips and poured into his mouth. He turned his head this way and that to breathe. His bloodshot eyes filled with despair, blinking to clear the filth. They too disappeared and his hair alone was visible, a scalp floating on the surface. It seemed to take forever to sink out of sight.

Nothing was left of Brough Chetwood. Were his last thoughts of his son? No one could tell. They had been sucked down into the morass, devoured by a trick of the sea.

No stone would mark his grave. He lay on the sea-floor, his bones mingling with those of his victims. His neighbours stood staring at the spot, aghast. Death had become personal. They had seen his features. He had come like a storm-trooper and it sent shivers down their spines.

'Let's get out of here,' growled one of their number.

They turned like sheep and followed.

The plague of gnats and mice may have infested the village but the reverend was beyond its bounds. He knew nothing of the torment inflicted on his flock, wouldn't have cared less if he had.

Rack, on the other hand, had been bitten and stung half to death. Gashing his head, almost dislocating a shoulder in a frantic bid to get out from under his bed, he fled hollering from his shack and flung himself into the stagnant pond at the foot of his garden. There he lay beneath the scum, out of harm's way.

He was a sorry sight when he emerged from the water. Puckered prune-skin was smeared with slime. Blood was congealed and matted in his hair. Hives drove him mad with itch and he scratched like a monkey. But he still had it in him to congratulate himself. Who would have thought of using a reed to breathe through but Racker Booth?

After a fierce onslaught, Pius Hornswoggle was left in peace. Those insects that did bite him fell dead to the schoolhouse floor. Instinctively, the mice never crossed the threshold. Did Pius exhult? No. He knew why he was spared and, deep down in the furthest cavern of his blacker than black soul, he hated himself.

As for the Grindlewicks, they were craftier still. A veritable warren of cellars burrowed beneath their inn and there had they hastened. Their brood they left behind them to challenge their fate as best they could. Oaf thundered on the door, begging admittance.

'Fall to your prayers, you idiot,' his father shouted back at him. 'If I were disposed to pray, which I ain't, I'd pray now, if *I* were you.'

Oaf slouched up the stairs to his waiting brothers and sisters, head bowed by grief. Inspired of a sudden, he bustled them into a stable where he set light to the damp straw. The thick smoke repelled the insects, he was astounded by his own inventiveness.

†

— 26. Hobson's Choice —

Berry stretched luxuriously beneath the blankets, careful not to rouse the others. Spike sensed his wakefulness and drawled a groan of pleasure which Berry understood full well. He hadn't slept so soundly for ever so long, longer than he cared to recall. He took a deep breath, exhaled deliriously and smiled to himself. From the depths of misery to this in less than twenty-four hours! Who would ever have thought it?... All was peace and quiet and prodigious contentment. He wanted to pinch himself to make sure he wasn't dreaming.

'You awake?' whispered Lee.

'Yeah.'

He nodded, turned and beamed. A smile gradually overspread Lee's features. Berry wanted to throw his arms around his neck and hug him. Spike crawled up and poked his head out between them, tail thumping the mattress.

'Is *he* still asleep?' Lee asked, nodding in Edgar's direction.

Berry nodded.

'Well, wake him up, then.'

'No,' he whispered.

'Poke your elbow into his ribs, that'll do the trick.'

'Ssshssshh.'

'I will if *you* won't,' grunted Lee, rising up in the bed and stretching across to tickle Edgar in the armpit.

Edgar jerked to life and groaned.

'What did you do that for? I was having such a lovely dream.'

'Yeah, I bet you were,' he answered with a dirty guffaw. ''Bout Rhoda Barrows, more than likely.'

Berry was shocked. He doused a florid blush, then giggled aloud. Edgar rolled onto his back, raised his head and smiled knowingly at Lee.

'Don't you mind him,' he said to Berry. 'He's got is a one-track mind.'

'As if you don't. And Berry too.'

Berry wished he had. He too placed his hands behind his head, the withered one that differentiated him from his friends tucked safely out of sight. He didn't really care about the bad things certain to unfold, not if it meant he was thrown together with these two wonderful fellows. He had died and gone to heaven.

He yawned, wide, long and luxuriatingly. Lee capped his open mouth with a warm, dry palm and Berry laughed into it. It was such a funny thing to do. Infected, they yawned on either side of him and that made him laugh all the more. In fact, everything made him want to burst out laughing. Never, ever, had he felt so happy. He suspected that if it weren't for the weight of the blankets on top of him, he would have floated away.

They lay for some time in silence, each wading through his own disturbing thoughts.

'E-ed,' Lee broached tentatively.

'Wha-at?'

'Do we have to… Why can't we just go away?'

'Go *away?*'

Lee sat up to gather momentum, his superior height an advantage.

'Why don't we just *skedaddle* out of here?'

'Turn our *backs,* you mean?'

Edgar sat up as well, frowning with surprise and misgivings. Lee just nodded back at him. He already sensed it was hopeless.

'How can we just up and go?'

Edgar's tone was accusatory. A compunctious Lee shrugged his shoulders. Berry felt so sorry for him. Lee was brave and strong and so, so loyal. He just said things without thinking.

'I was thinking the same, you know,' he said to console him.

'Were you?' The chirpiness had gone out of him, his voice was dull and spiritless.

Edgar was having none of it. 'It's all right for *you,* Berry, you've been through the *wars.* Nobody could blame *you* for wanting to get away from here.'

'I'm scared of dying,' Lee sobbed.

'So am I, Lee,' Edgar confessed.

'Death's not the worst thing in the world,' Berry unwittingly prophesied. 'There's a living death which is far, far worse…'

'God help us,' Edgar muttered.

'But we have to help ourselves, just as you helped me. It's better than running all the time, isn't it?'

Both Lee and Edgar nodded their agreement to that.

'Running and never really getting away,' Lee mused aloud.

'Exactly,' Berry declared. 'It'll be a bad world or a better world depending on whether we fight or not. I don't know how much fighting I can do, I don't know if I'll be any help at all, but you've got the sword, Ed, and that's for something. And more than anything else, you've got Lee here as your friend...

'I know I haven't much to lose...'

'Don't say that,' Lee firmly reprimanded him. 'You've got just as much to lose as we do. Even those dastardly fools in the village have something to lose, though they're making damn sure that Ed does their fighting for them.'

'And if I can't?' Edgar questioned.

'They'll pick on somebody else and go *on* picking somebody elses until there's nobody left but themselves. And then they'll turn on each other.'

'So, we're for it, then...'

Nobody answered.

'Come on, we'd better get up,' Edgar finally said after a lengthy pause. 'We've an awful lot to do today... The truth is... we can't just walk away because... We've got to do it to save... to save all that's important. Look at what's happening to our lovely village.'

'Was it ever lovely?' grumbled Lee with disgust.

Edgar looked at Berry. 'No... You're right.'

'So it's not worth fighting for, after all.' Lee concluded.

'Would you prefer to let it get worse than it already is?'

Lee shrugged the question off. 'Why should we care?'

'And what if it could have got a lot better years ago if only someone had stood up and been counted?' interjected Berry, once again hitting the nail on the head. Suffering had conferred premature wisdom on the boy.

'But what have they ever done for any of us?' Lee asked to support his argument.

'Nothing,' Edgar replied.

'Well, then?'

'It won't stop here if we do nothing,' interposed Berry.

Both boys marvelled at him. He seemed to have all the answers.

'Go on,' Edgar instructed him with a nod of his head.

'Well... What if... Maybe it will follow us wherever we go unless we put an end to it now.'

'But *can* we?' Lee asked in earnest.

'We won't know till we try, will we?'

'I suppose not.'

'We should at least....'

'Do our best,' Edgar concluded for him. 'What more can we do than our best? If it doesn't work out, at least we did all we could.'

'We won't *know* if we're dead,' Lee grumbled.

'Better be dead not knowing,' Berry affirmed, 'than alive and knowing we did nothing.'

'Let's do it, then,' Lee declared in desperation.

There was nothing more to say. Despite his obvious weaknesses, Berry had the upper hand. He was the brains behind their brawn, it seemed to them.

A death sentence swung over them like a noose. The animals were all indoors, the geese in the furthest corner of the byre. The udders of the cows were hard and shrunken. Their teats spat gobbets of blood and pus, the stink was woeful. The horse nibbled at the hay, then let the long wisps drop from its thick and velvety lips. Emerging from the stable, they caught sight of the barn owl swooping in the barren hayfield.

'Look at that!' exclaimed Edgar. 'It's a bad sign when an owl has to hunt in the daytime.'

'Anything with any sense is safe indoors,' Lee grumbled. 'And *we* have to go and find Farmer Buckrake.'

He felt his anger rising like steam. He wanted to shout and dig his fists into something. It seemed such madness. What would Buckrake know that they didn't know already? The billy-can man hadn't said all that much either. Stay indoors, that was about it. And who in their right mind would have gone out anyway? Did he think they were village *idiots*? Angrily he kicked a fair-sized stone which flew off at an awkward angle and struck Spike in the chest. He howled and skipped and whimpered.

'Watch what you're doing,' Edgar sternly admonished.

'I didn't *mean* it. God! No matter what I bloody well do it's wrong. I can't win, can I?'

'There's no need to take it out on an innocent dog.'

'It was an *accident!*'

'Yeah, well…'

'What about *him*?' Lee whispered to change the subject.

'Who? Berry?'

'Shush. Yeah.'

'What *about* him?'

'He'll need help, won't he? I can't imagine he can walk for miles like that. He'll be dead-beat in no time.'

Edgar stopped and turned swiftly.

'Do you want to come with us?' he asked.

Berry halted in his tracks.

'O-of course, I want to come. More than anything else.' Tears started to his eyes, he suddenly felt an outsider again. They were whispering about him. Were they sick of him already? 'Don't you *want* me to come?'

Both boys were stricken by the pain in his voice. They lunged back towards him.

'We didn't mean it like that.'

'We only meant to say...'

'What we...'

They hung their heads in shame.

Berry smiled, then chuckled. He understood. He had been guilty of misjudging them. It was time to douse that voice of self-pity always ready to rise to the occasion.

In high-pitched good humour he said, 'You're wondering if I can make it or not, aren't you?'

They nodded dumbly, refusing to raise their eyes to his. They only did so when his laughter eased their consciences.

'Look,' he said, 'I know I'm slower than you two, but I'm not *that* slow.'

'We're worried you'll get tired,' Edgar mumbled self-consciously.

'I *will* get tired, but I still want to go. More than anything.'

'We'll bring the wheelbarrow along,' Lee said, remembering Edgar's joke.

'That's a brilliant idea,' Berry responded, pretending that Lee had thought it up by himself. 'But I hope *you* won't get tired wheeling *me* around.'

'We'll take it in turns,' Edgar intervened.

Both boys were satisfied while Berry was over the moon. Spike sensed their jubilation and scampered ahead, one wary eye out for stones.

†

— 27. Vale of Woe —

Three boys, a dog and a wheelbarrow set out from the mill, a strange sight to behold under the best of circumstances. Out of the blue they noticed the changes that had occurred overnight. It was as if they had suddenly stepped into an alien world, brooding and ugly, a place they would rather not venture but couldn't go round. The only way forward was through it. The moment of no turning back was upon them.

The cowl of the Reaper cast its shadow over the land while his scythe sliced through it. The clinging, foetid stench of death and decay filled the air they breathed. The reek of seaweed and rotting fish clogged their nostrils. They gagged and buried their noses in the crooks of their elbows. A skein of offshore grey-lags separated and passed to either side of the stricken wilderness. No piercing warble of curlews, no boom of bittern rose from the barren wastelands. No mewling gulls flew inland. Out of sight, a raven barked. A crow cawed in mockery, its fellows taking up the throaty doggerel. Time and again they caught a low, sibillating whisper on the light breeze; angry, war-torn, expectant - the menacing calm before a thunderstorm. All earthly creatures awaited that first bolt of lightning to crack the sky asunder, the first low rumble to shake the planet.

Clouds scurried overhead, unwilling to tarry. Thick palls of mist clung like cobwebs to the trees and hung across low-lying fields, sour and unwholesome. Puddles of water reflecting the sky were pools of blood in their path. It was stultifying, this rampant distemper. Spike whined and kept close to them, afraid to poke his nose into bushes or hedges.

A hoodie sat on a fence cackling in their faces, yearning to feast on their flesh. They faltered at the sight, tempted to retrace their steps. But they pressed on regardless. They straggled through the laneway where Bert had come to grief and wisely skirted the woods. It was no place for humans or animals, a haunt of evil and burgeoning malice. Steadily, inexorably, hope withered within them. They felt as if the bats were flying overhead, clouding their minds, weakening their determination.

'We've got to keep going,' Edgar stated in a strained voice, more for himself than his companions. 'The farmer knows something, the billy-can man said so.'

'I hope he's right,' retorted Lee, 'because I can't keep this up much longer.' Turning, he spoke to Berry. 'How are you faring? Do you need the wheelbarrow yet?'

He did and they took it in turns to convey him.

Benevolence seemed to lighten their load. They were able to trudge on more easily. At that precise moment, Lee's father was sinking into the quicksand, but he tramped on oblivious.

27. Vale of Woe

Past the flank of the woods, Lee halted with a strangled cry of despair. He stood rooted to the spot, mouth working ineffectually. Edgar sprinted forward with the wheelbarrow.

'What is it?!'

There was no need for Lee to answer. He'd seen for himself. Berry joined them in horrified silence.

The tower thrust upwards from the brow of the hill, a rapier piercing the clouds. Thick trunks of ivy dug deep into the stonework like claws. Great splashes of blood glistened in the rarefied light. A dozen scarecrows stood at the base looking up while ravens wheeled in ever-increasing circles over the roof. The scarecrows turned to stare at them across the fields.

'It's… rebuilt…' Edgar eventually croaked, pronouncing each word with difficulty.

'But how can that be?' Lee asked in awe. 'It's impossible!'

Berry said nothing, his thoughts too full of what would have happened to him if his two friends hadn't come to his rescue. He had only just got out in time.

'What could have done this in a single night?' muttered Lee.

'It means something awful, doesn't it?' stated Berry. 'That's what the billy-can man was talking about.'

'What good is a sword against that?' Lee asked, his heart in his boots.

'I don't know, but Farmer Buckrake knows *something*,' Edgar replied, trying to dampen his own fears by clutching at straws.

'What the hell does it matter *what* he knows?!' Lee shouted in exasperation. 'A couple of old men, what *good* will they be?'

'Perhaps...' Berry began.

'Look at *that!*' Lee roared petulantly, stabbing his finger at the tower. 'Don't tell me that two old men can take on whatever rebuilt *that* in one night and win! Why don't we face up to the fact that we're, all of us, doomed?'

Lee forlornly shook his head before burying his face in his hands. Berry patted him on the shoulder but he shied away from contact.

'Don't worry, Lee. Something's bound to happen.'

'Something *bad*,' came his thick rejoinder.

'Something good, maybe. We have to go on and find out, don't we, Ed?'

Edgar nodded half-heartedly. He was inclined to agree with Lee. Why not just pack their bags, somehow rescue his folks, and get going as quickly as possible? All the high-falutin stuff he'd said last night and this morning was just drizzle on the wind. They were boys kidding themselves that they were heroes. The sword needed a man to wield it, not a mere thirteen-year-old with big ideas. We're fooling nobody but ourselves, Edgar groaned to himself.

Tearing his eyes away from the monstrosity before him, he said, 'Let's get going... We might as well go and see Buckrake since we're halfway there already. Come on.'

There were scarecrows in every field they passed through, all turning to keep them in view. Crows swooped from above the tower and perched on their shoulders, staring fixedly too. Wolves crouched at their feet and low intimidating growls reached their ears across the undulating terrain. Berry was glad they had to wheel him along in the barrow. When you were forced to think about others, you forgot about yourself, he'd learnt that tough lesson cooped up in the darkness of the tower. Perhaps he had been shown things for a reason. Perhaps he was just as important to this crusade as they were. He looked over his shoulder and grinned at Lee who just about managed a watery smile before looking away. He was so frightened that he no longer felt ashamed of his fear. No one could possibly feel brave and safe in a place like this.

— 28. Rendezvous —

Obadiah Buckrake caught sight of the motley group from his bedroom window. He stood and looked out, chuckling to himself.

'Who would ever have thought it?' he muttered. 'I've seen strange things in my time but this has got to be the strangest...'

His smile quickly faded, replaced by a frown. Fear had worn them down, he could recognize her trademark features in their drooping shoulders and weary footsteps.

'Struck low already and they haven't even begun yet.'

He shook his head and pitied them, clicking his tongue.

'God help the poor children. Aye, that's all they are... Fate can be cruel at times, cruelest to her favourites... Has she finally lost her bearings or is their innocence their strength?'

He pulled on his jerkin, stuck his pipe in his mouth and roughly raised the sash-window. The boys came to a halt and looked up at him.

'Well now, what have we here?' he barked good-humouredly.

'If you please,' Edgar began, on his best behaviour, 'the Billy-can Man sent us to talk with you.'

'Did he, indeed? I'll be down directly.'

They waited patiently till his face appeared in the glass panes of the garden door. Stooping, he unlocked it and invited them in, scowling momentarily at the lurid sky. Berry clambered out of the barrow and stumbled. He would have fallen if Lee hadn't reached out and caught him by the arm.

'Whoa!' shouted Buckrake with a chuckle. 'Steady there. We don't want any mishaps before we've had a chance to introduce ourselves. In you come, now. *And* the dog,' he added seeing Edgar hesitate and glance at Spike. 'A dog should be allowed to follow his master wherever he goes, isn't that so?'

As intended, his light banter and welcoming smile raised their spirits. They felt that if *he* could still be cheerful, they could afford to be as well.

'Make yourselves fully at home. I'll ask Grace to put some coffee on, shall I?'

They glanced at one another and shifted uncomfortably in their seats.

'Don't you like coffee?'

'We've never had it,' Edgar muttered, spokesman for all three of them.

'Well, then, we most definitely will have to brew a pot-ful, won't we?'

He roared for Grace at the top of his voice and fell to rubbing his hands before the fire.

A middle-aged, happy-looking soul came through the door, a woman they'd never seen in the village.

'Ah, Grace. A pot of coffee for the lot of us and... some of your delicious biscuits, there's a good girl.'

He held up a curved pipe with an ornately carved bowl, thrust it into his fulsome beard and lit a taper in the fire.

'Do any of you smoke?' he asked to break the ice.

Their eyes widened at an adult asking such a question. He shook with mirth.

'Come now... Be honest... You've sneaked a puff before now, haven't you?'

Edgar and Lee nodded in silence. Berry didn't. Buckrake knew of his existence from the billy-can man, but he was more than surprised to find he had joined forces with these two adventurers. It added a whole new dimension to his preconceptions.

'I have to admit I did as a boy,' Buckrake confessed. 'Was sick as a dog on both counts for my trouble.'

'So were we!' Lee exclaimed, delighted to meet such a forthright grown-up.

'I thought as much. Curiosity killed the cat.'

'But...'

'Ye-es?'

'Why is it that you still smoke now?'

A gravelly laugh escaped their host. He leaned back in his armchair, puffed away at his pipe and regarded them fondly. A pang constricted Edgar's heart. He was reminded of his grandpa.

'What do you think the answer to that is?' Buckrake asked Lee. 'Be honest, now.'

'Well... Maybe it tastes different when you're older,' he suggested diplomatically.

'You'd make a fine politician, lad... The truth is, we don't have the sagacity of youth on our side.'

'In other words?'

'We're stupid.'

All three faces lit up with awe and amusement. Spike stretched, prone on the hearth-rug, rigid legs almost in the flames. A whine of a yawn escaped him.

Obadiah fell silent and blew a few smoke-rings. He seemed reluctant to continue. The clatter of cups and saucers justified procrastination.

'Ah,' he said, sitting up with relief. 'That will be Grace and the coffee.'

He took up the steaming coffee-pot, poured the black liquid and handed it round. A bark of a guffaw erupted from him when they'd tasted it. Lips taut, eyes slits below furrowed brows, they looked as if someone had stuffed whole, peeled lemons into their mouths.

'I had forgotten what sweet tooths you young people have.'

He ladled sugar into their cups and offered them biscuits. They were delicious.

A cloud crossed the farmer's face and snuffed the light out in his eyes. It was time. He had put it off as long as he could.

'Now then… You spoke to Casey last night.'

'Casey?'

'Yes. Casey Renfall. The Billy-can Man to you. Fire ahead!' he shouted on noticing Lee's and Berry's eyes stray to the fruit-cake. 'Go on. Cut yourselves as big a hunk as you wish. And you?' he asked Edgar.

'No, I'm grand, thanks.'

'Sure?'

'Well, if you're offering...'

He slapped him on the back, waited till they all held large slabs in their hands and were chewing contentedly. He liked these boys. There was no nonsense about them. He began to have confidence in Fate's choice.

'Down to business!' he roared to flush himself into the open.

They waited while he leaned forward and held his hands before the fire. Briefly he studied the flames before lifting his face to theirs. He felt guilty now that he was about to turn their world upside-down.

Anger smouldered in his eyes of a sudden. His mouth was set in a grim line. Taking the stem of his pipe from his lips, he spat into the fire. A lingering sigh escaped him. Slowly he turned to them, sadness etched in his features.

'This has happened before,' he told them.

'You mean the bats and the tower and the scarecrows?' Edgar asked.

Buckrake nodded. 'What of the tower?'

'It's rebuilt,' Edgar told him.

'So soon?... 'Tis quicker than last time.'

'How do you know that?'

'I've read it in a book... A very important book you know nothing about yet,' he murmured with a doleful sigh. 'Vital for our survival.'

'Who rebuilt the tower? Was it the scarecrows?' Berry asked in a high-pitched voice.

'No... They helped. They and the bats... It partly rebuilt itself. To house...'

'What?' Edgar asked, knowing he was reluctant to explain any further.

Now the time had come.

'To house *It*. Their Master... The Morgammeron Aetz.'

'What is the Mor-whatever-it-is?' Lee asked with a quizzical look.

'Don't ask. Please don't ask. The very sound of those syllables fills me with dread... A conjurer drawing horror after horror from a smokescreen, that's what the creature amounts to.'

'The Morgammeron Aetz,' Edgar softly repeated.

'Aye. In the very mists of time it came.'

'Is that... Is that what I have to fight?'

Edgar had to force himself to ask. He couldn't get his predecessor out of his head.

'I cannot answer you that... Because I do not know... There is someone else you must speak to... You must protect yourselves, he will tell you how...'

The lines on his face deepened, there was a haunted look about him. He began to speak as if in a trance, a trailing litany of woe.

'A Dark Age is upon us... Who can tell what deeds shall be done in the name of God and religion?...

'The earth will rot. Plagues will waylay us. It will harry us half to death, a hideous visitator... Unspeakable terrors shall be unleashed at night.'

'At night?'

'Yea, at night. Daylight, it despises... moonlight... sunlight most of all. It was born to darkness. The light reaches to its innermost self and tortures it. That was the cause of the baleful cry last night. It saw the moon and hated it. It roared its defiance and the moon trembled…

'This will bring out the very worst in them, wait and see. You will not believe what depths those villagers can stoop to.'

'And you read all this in the book?' Lee asked with a hint of incredulity.

Buckrake nodded.

'No good can come of this.' He shook his head forlornly, devoid of all hope. 'The sap will never rise this Spring. Nature is in the grip of the Aetz… Damnation on them all!' he shouted in exasperation.

He looked at his pipe and placed it on the mantel.

'The empty worship of gold for gold's sake has been their undoing. The slain cry out for retribution. The land shall wash itself clean in blood. Blood for blood. Life for life. Death for death. All that is fair fell to earth and perished.'

Lee began to suspect he was a raving lunatic. He didn't understand half of what he was saying and he didn't want to hear any more. He leaned in close to Berry. They both were very scared.

Edgar too was scared. He was up against a formidable foe, and he only a child. It seemed ridiculous to go on.

Buckrake recollected himself. He gazed at them sympathetically. 'I've frightened you… Come, have some more cake.'

'We're not hungry.'

'Forgive me… Ignore the meanderings of an old fool. But there is something very important you must do.'

'*What* must we do?' Edgar asked, determined to know the worst.

Buckrake trained his eyes on him.

'There is a person you must see. It's vitally important that you speak with him. It may save your lives… This is a very dangerous business. I don't know what the outcome will be, I cannot see into the future. Nobody can. But there's always hope, else why are you here and why does that sword have magical properties in your grip?

'Believe in the sword and your destiny. My star is waning but yours have only emerged. They shine brightly now. They may shine brighter still if you speak with the hermit, a man wise in the lore of darkling days.'

'The hermit?'

'He dwells in the deepest part of the woods, away from all prying eyes. Go to him. Go by water. I have a boat moored outside expressly for you. Stay on this river. Never dare go near the River Mead. It is accursed. The River Rudd will lead you to him. He is expecting you.'

'You mean we have to go *now*?'

'Immediately. There's no time to lose.'

'But I was hoping to see my mam and dad.'

'No… No, no. Afterwards. Afterwards!… They are perfectly safe… You must go to the hermit first, I cannot stress that enough.'

Edgar looked none too pleased but nodded in agreement. His actions, his motives, his very will seemed in another's hands. He raised his eyebrows at Lee and Berry. They both nodded their consent and rose to their feet. Spike groaned when he prodded him to get up.

'I will show you to the boat,' Farmer Buckrake said, opening the garden door and gesturing them through it. He called to Grace who was busy packing lunch for them and followed. He placed a hand on Edgar's shoulder. 'If you like, young man, I will go and see your parents and tell them you are safe and well.'

'Yes, I would like that… Tell them I hope to be able to see them later on today… or tomorrow at the latest.'

'Certainly I shall.'

†

— 29. Embarkation —

'God speed,' Buckrake called with a raised hand, Grace smiling and waving beside him.

Lee pushed off with an oar and the current took them. He and Edgar rowed while Berry sat in the stern. They yearned to be with them on the river-bank rather than facing into the unknown.

Obadiah returned to his sitting-room with bowed shoulders. Things had not gone as he had planned. He had disgaced himself before Falchion's grandson, that was the worst of it. Taking up his pipe, he threw it down again.

'I sincerely hope the hermit has his wits about him and does more for them than I have,' he said to himself.

'They seemed nice boys,' Grace voiced, gathering up the cups and saucers.

'Yes… Very nice. Brave little soldiers.'

He sighed once she had closed the door after her.

'Much braver than I ever was,' he murmured to himself and fell to reminiscing.

Gritting his teeth, he struck his knee with his fist.

'I'll never forgive myself!'

The River Rudd sliced deeply into the land. The pinnacle of the tower sank out of sight. Berry had asked if he could take Edgar's place for a while – his oar was on his good side – and now Edgar sat in the stern, fingers trailing in the water. He wasn't thinking of the hermit or his parents. A gloomy sadness had settled upon him, hindering speculation.

'That fellow gave me the willies,' Lee eventually declared with irritation. 'So much for helping us. And what was all that about the Aetz? At one point I thought he was mad.'

Edgar sat up straight, drying his hand on his trousers. 'Mad with fear…'

'And trying to drive *us* mad as well.'

Edgar laughed despite himself.

'I don't see what's so funny. They keep telling us they're going to help us and all they do is shove us off to see somebody else, who will probably send us packing after someone else again. Where the hell is that going to get us?…

'And who's this hermit anyway? I never heard of a hermit round here before, did you?'

'No.' Edgar shook his head.

'I think *I've* heard of him,' Berry interjected.

'Have you?'

'Mmm… At least I heard there was someone living deep in the woods. An old man. A good man. I never heard him called a hermit, though.'

'That woods is probably *full* of weirdos.'

Edgar and Berry both laughed at that.

'You say the funniest things, Lee, you know that?' said Edgar, glad of his friend's sense of humour.

'Sure, if you didn't laugh, you'd cry.'

'That's true enough,' Berry agreed, a huge grin bisecting his face. 'You're the funniest person I've ever met, Lee. I wish I'd had you in the tower with me.'

'Oh, believe you me, there would have been no funny jokes in *there*. I'd've had the heebie-jeebies so bad you'd've got nothing out of me. Anyway,' he began, eyeing Edgar, 'it's high time I had a rest. Here, you. Take over from me and let me sit there for a while.' The boat lurched slightly when he stood up, leaning to one side when he turned to Berry and looked down at him. 'Unless *you* want a rest?'

He shook his head, staying his oar while Edgar clambered into place.

'I like doing this,' he told them.

He did, indeed. In fact, he was glorying in doing exactly what other boys did. It was heavenly to be rowing a boat. Not only had he gained his spurs, he had been crowned with a laurel wreath.

A gale blew up out of nowhere, the smooth swirling surface suddenly troubled by ripples. Their boat shook from side to side as dead leaves and twigs ripped across its path. The roar of the wind grew tremendous. One thunderous crack after another rent the air. The rowers turned to look ahead. A tree fell across the river. Another. Another!

'It's completely blocked!' exclaimed Lee.

'Anyone'd think it was done on purpose,' Edgar stated with awe.

'Maybe we can lift the boat out and carry it to the other side,' Berry suggested, still giddy after his exertions. Edgar doubted that.

'We'll give it a go, anyway,' said Lee steering towards the bank just below the trees.

He held on to tufts of grass to steady the boat while the others got out. They, in turn, bent down and gripped the gunwale for him. The instant he joined them, a freak current wrenched the boat from their grasp and out of reach. They watched helplessly as it was whisked back the way it had come.

'Well, that's that,' said Lee. 'It's out of our hands now. We'll just have to walk the rest of the way no matter *what* Buckrake said.'

'But... we've no wheelbarrow for Berry,' cried Edgar.

'I don't *need* a wheelbarrow.'

Berry was ruffled. He didn't want to be treated as an invalid any longer. Hadn't he rowed this far without being tired? A wheelbarrow would have been an insult.

'There goes our lunch too,' said Lee with a groan.

'The hermit's bound to have something,' Edgar remarked in a bid to cheer him up.

'If we ever get that far... If there *is* a hermit.'

'God, you can be so pessimistic sometimes.'

'Oh, that's nice! One minute I'm great for a laugh, the next I'm a pessimist.'

'Would you two stop fighting,' Berry sternly ordered.

Both turned to stare at him. The transformation coming over Berry was startling. They watched him as he walked ahead without waiting, Spike scurrying off ahead of him.

'Who's in charge *now*?' a sarcastic Lee asked.

'Yeah... From timid boy to commander-in-chief in the blink of an eye.'

29. Embarkation

'Hey, wait up!' shouted Lee.

Berry turned but kept on walking. 'Hurry up, then.'

'Yes, Sir!' Lee roared with a salute.

He winked at Edgar and ran ahead.

Edgar caught up and said,' We'd better keep as close to the river-bank as possible. Remember what Buckrake said.'

'Are you all right?' Lee asked Berry when he didn't respond.

'I'm fine.' He stopped and turned to face them. 'I don't like it when you two fight. I'd hate to see you fall out.'

'We're not going to fall *out*,' Lee gibed with derision. 'If you think *that* was fighting, you've never seen a real fight, has he, Ed?'

'Well, I'm not used to it. And I'm scared.'

'Scared of what?'

'That you'll stop being friends and give up and go home and leave me.'

Edgar and Lee stared at one another before answering.

'But we're *always* like this and *still* we're best friends. We're blowing off steam, is all,' Lee told him, putting an arm around his shoulders. 'There's nothing to get upset about, honest.'

'You've spent too much time on your own in that tower,' Edgar levelled at him as an explanation. 'We're not going back and we're never leaving *you*, got it?'

Berry smiled and nodded.

Edgar looked into the fast-flowing eddies of the river. 'I just hope Farmer Buckrake doesn't see the empty boat pass his place. He'll think we've drowned.'

'He'll think the Aetz grabbed us and gobbled us up,' Lee joked.

'Thanks, Lee,' Berry inserted with a cheeky smile. 'You always say just what we want to hear.'

'O-hoh. Just listen to *him*, will you? He's getting as bad as you, Ed. Well, you can shut up too, smartypants.' With that he gave Berry a bear-hug to prove that their banter meant nothing. 'You see? Still friends.'

— 30. Against the Tide —

An icy wind cut through their clothes. It blew stronger, carrying scant snowflakes towards them. Suddenly the air was white with crystals. A blizzard raged, a feather pillow emptied in their faces.

'What now?' Edgar murmured despondently.

They leaned into the wind while slush collected on their heads and shoulders. Soaking flakes clung to their clothes and seeped into their boots. The cold stung the skin of their hands and faces. The tips of their ears and fingers pained them dreadfully, the very marrow of their bones seemed frozen. Spike kept shaking himself, snorting and sneezing when he sank into the snow. He looked miserable but barked and swerved when Edgar tried to carry him. Berry smiled to himself in secret.

They couldn't see two yards ahead of them. Lee stumbled into a drift up to his neck. Chuckling, they stretched out their hands to haul him out.

'So you think it's funny, do you?'

With that he grabbed their arms and pulled them in. They floundered, laughing in the deep snow while Spike barked and whined and wagged his tail uncertainly. When they scrambled out the wind sliced into their flesh.

'We'll have to keep going,' a resolute Edgar announced. 'If we don't, we'll either die of cold or be buried alive.'

Berry's foot felt like a heavy block of ice roped to his leg. He kept that to himself, though, determined to keep up with them. He was never going back to those awful days when he was a subhuman castaway. Physical pain was nothing in comparison.

On they trudged and stumbled and slipped and fell. A ghostly, forbidding world hemmed them in. Its silence engulfed everything. They travelled in slow-motion, as if in a nightmare where they would never reach their destination. Now and again, contorted branches poked into their world - the craggy fingers of fell sentinels back from the grave.

I don't think I can go on much longer, thought Edgar, Lee's grunts and curses ringing in his ears. It was the sight of Berry struggling manfully onwards that kept them going.

Abruptly, as if they had walked through tall muslin drapes, the blizzard ended. Behind them stood a ghastly world devoid of colour. Ahead lay the green banks of the River Rudd which gurgled merrily in their ears.

'How weird,' Lee commented, staring at the wall of snow. 'It just cuts off without any reason. How can that be?'

'I have no idea,' Edgar responded, shaking his head. 'I'm just very, very glad it's over. I think we'd better sit down for a minute,' he added with a weary groan.

'At last,' Berry croaked, sinking onto the turf. 'I couldn't have gone on much longer.'

'I don't know how you made it this far,' Lee remarked in awe. 'You're what kept *me* going.'

'*And* me,' Edgar gladly admitted.

30. Against the Tide

Berry jerked up his head and gazed at them in sheer surprise. They both nodded and he beamed at them, floating milimetres above the turf. He was so proud of himself, for the first time in all of his life.

'Wow,' he breathed, more to himself than to anybody else.

Tears of gratitude welled up in his eyes. He brushed a tickling drop away and sniffed. Edgar and Lee squatted down beside him and patted his back. Spike nuzzled in between his knees.

'I will say one thing,' Edgar commenced... 'Someone or something doesn't want us to get to the hermit.'

Edgar leaped to his feet, scanning their surroundings.

'Best get going,' he insisted.

With a feigned whimper Lee stretched out his hand. Edgar smiled unsurely. Lee's whimper amplified, he frowned and nodded a pleading head. With a sigh Edgar grasped the nettle and was dragged to the ground.

'I *knew* you were going to do that!'

'Stupid for doing it, then. Give us a few more minutes, just a few more minutes. I'm on my last legs.'

Edgar gladly gave in. Lee had insisted because he could see how spent Berry was. He was pale and green by turns. Battling the fierce gusts and the drifts had required every atom of his will. At breaking-point, he had no strength left to draw on.

They were all gazing dreamily into the sky when the rustling began. Their heads popped up, expecting to see some creature emerge from the thicket. None did but the sound grew louder and angrier. With a scream, Lee was tugged from their midst, sliding helplessy across the grass. Edgar jumped up and was after him. Tentacles of ivy were entwined around his upper arms and shoulders. Eyes wide with alarm, Lee stared up at him beseechingly. For all he knew, the Aetz had grabbed him. He screamed again when, with a mighty wrench, he was hauled off faster than ever.

Brandishing his sword, Edgar caught up with him and hacked furiously at the ivy. There was a hissing sound when the vine was sliced in half. It reared up like a snake before slithering out of sight into the undergrowth. Those tendrils twined around Lee loosened their grip and fell to the ground, writhing in their death-throes. Black and slimey, they were sucked into the earth.

'God Almighty!' gasped Lee, wriggling with disgust and madly brushing his arms and shoulders. 'I wouldn't have believed it if I hadn't seen it with my own two eyes.'

All three loped forward half-heartedly, truly shaken by the experience. When ivy starts coming to life like that, you know you're in trouble. What on earth would they have to face next?

The question was hardly formed before it was answered. Myriad drumbeats crescendoed to a continuous roar as heavy droplets of torrential rain pounded the turf. They were wet through in seconds, bent double to avoid the stinging blows. They wanted to run to the edge of the copse for cover but remembered the ivy and kept well away. Soon they were splashing through sodden grass that was fast becoming a quagmire. The muddy, opaque waters of the Rudd had swollen to an unmanageable torrent rapidly bearing boughs and woodland litter past them. If they had been in the boat, assuredly they would have been swept to their deaths.

'We must be on the right track!' Edgar bellowed above the roar of the rain.

'I wish we'd never *heard* of the bloody hermit!' came Lee's angry reply. 'He'd better be worth it or I'll split his head open for him. For *free!*'

Edgar jutted a solicitous finger at Berry's back. He was slipping and sliding like a drunk. It was all too much for him. Spent beyond endurance, he sank to the ground, weeping uncontrollably.

'I can't go on!' he bawled, strings of saliva stretching between his parted teeth. 'You'll have to go on without me.'

Grim-faced, without saying a word, both boys gripped him under the arms, lifted him up and bore him along.

'No one's leaving anyone behind,' Edgar yelled above the roar of lashing rain.

As if sensing their heroic determination and the futility of further onslaught, the deluge eased and desisted. Single drops plopped here and there in the sudden calm. They panted, swallowed and brushed the hair plastered to their faces out of their eyes. All of them sat down in a puddle of water. Lee blew a drop off the end of his nose. Berry's legs were crumpled underneath him. He felt such a failure. His companions looked at him with pained expressions but didn't know what to say.

Everything glistened in emerging sunlight.

'Now, at last, *something* is on our side,' Edgar sighed with burgeoning hope.

They all stared up at the dazzling orb as steam rose from their clothing. A weight was lifting off their shoulders.

Once Berry'd had time to recover, they continued on their way. It was nice to feel the sun on their backs. But the heat and glare began to double and treble. They turned up their collars to protect their blistering necks. Barren dust rose with every footfall. They lay flat on their stomachs and drank long cool draughts from the river. When they got up, they stood in a desert.

All the grass had withered and died. The fissured soil resembled the scales of a lizard. Sweat poured down their foreheads and stung their eyes. Their lips were cracked and bleeding. Rivulets of perspiration trickled down their backs, saturating their clothes once more. The heat penetrated their boots and burned the soles of their feet. They felt as if they were in an oven and their heads throbbed unmercifully.

'This is unbearable,' gasped Lee, finger-rimming his collar to unstick it. 'It's like having all the seasons in one day!' He licked his scaly lips. 'I need another drink. Thank God for the river.'

He literally flung himself onto the hard ground and dragged his head over the edge. Without warning briars sprang from the earth and imprisoned him in a thorny chrysalis. He cried out in fear and pain as the thorns dug into his skin when he struggled to free himself. Tighter and tighter they wound, pressing him flat against the caked mud, making it more and more difficult to breathe. Edgar thought quickly. He couldn't hack away at them for fear he would harm his friend. Gingerly he eased the blade beneath the web of briars and cut upwards away from Lee's body, slicing the cocoon in half. The shoots writhed, coiling and uncoiling, immediately disappearing into the soil.

'What was that?' Lee grunted, sprawled there with his eyes shut tight.

'Briars.'

'But *how*?'

'I don't know… I don't understand half of what's happening to us.'

'But…'

Hoarse screams had them running towards Berry. More briars had tightened round his ankles and were creeping up his legs. Blood flowed from his cuts and scratches. He overbalanced and fell roughly backwards. This time Edgar raised his sword to hack at them where they emerged from the earth. Before the blade fell he was entangled and pulled to the ground. Briars shot out from the water's edge, wound round his head and neck and pulled him under. In a blind panic he fought to free himself, to resurface and breathe. Everything was green and murky and unfamiliar. Sounds were eerily muffled. His head was about to explode. His lungs were screaming for air. It took all his might not to open his mouth and inhale the water. He almost did with shock when something began to tug at his sword.

I'm going to drown… It's all over… I didn't think it would end like this but it's not so bad…

He drifted in and out of consciousness. There were bells ringing in his ears. Cool, bright light shone in and around and through him. He saw himself as he'd never seen himself before and he was beautiful to behold.

Faraway thoughts glanced off his mind, powerless to disturb the serenity welling up in his soul. They'll have to go on without me. Pity I can't give them the sword. I hope they'll...

Ineffable peace infiltrated his thoughts and ousted all concern for them.

I never knew it could be like this... I wish I could bring them with me...

He seemed to be floating downwards into himself, an unseen centre where real existence lay concealed and poised to embrace him. He was willing, oh, so willing...

Next he was slowly rising into the air, looking down at himself and Berry and Lee from a height. A fine mist began to condense between them, more and more difficult to penetrate. Then they were gone, out of sight, and he was bathed in a cool, unearthly light.

— 31. A Village Benighted —

Squire Trefoil sat erect at the breakfast-table, a powdered, bewigged footman behind him, another behind his consort. Shiftily he avoided her eyes, knowing full well she was trying to attract his attention. He munched his toast and hummed a tune to drown out anything she might care to say. At a swift, sly glance he could see she was frowning ominously. Hardly a morsel passed her grim lips. Yes, he knew what was on her mind. Yes, he knew he hadn't been hearing things last night. She was about to upbraid him and, yes, he'd heard it all before.

The Lady Squiress saw the colour mounting to his face.

'Sebastian, darling,' she crooned.

He started and choked on a crumb. The footman behind him leaped into action and patted his back for him. When that didn't work, he swung his arm back and brought it down on his master with a resounding thud. It stopped the coughing but convulsed Sebastian with ire.

'What do you mean by... by, by, by... by such familiarity? How *dare* you!'

'I was only trying to help, sir,' the hapless man explained.

'Help? *Help!*... If you haven't broken a rib or two, it's a bally miracle.'

The unfortunate footman sulked in silence.

'Get out this instant. No, come back!'

He remembered why he hadn't dismissed them. God… God be kind to the woman. It wouldn't do to curse a lady.

'Oh, Sebastian, dear…'

Confound the woman! Can't she see I'm at death's door?

'M'dear?' he responded, lace handkerchief to his streaming eyes.

'May I have a word with you in my sitting-room directly after breakfast?'

'Can't it wait?' he snapped like a petulant child.

'I'm afraid not, dearest.'

'Tell me now,' he whined in pleading tones.

'In… my… sitting-room.'

She annunciated each word with grim determination. Her spouse buried his face in his napkin and groaned aloud. The very next moment he leapt up from the table, overturning his chair, muttered something about having to see a man about a bull, and was gone in a whirl of swirling garments and a confusion of noise. The butler and the footmen stared at their mistress and she stared back at them. Her hand itched for a riding-whip.

Pius Hornswoggle woke early, grateful to be alive. Last night he had thought his end was nigh, had pleaded for forgiveness as was his wont. He was a parasite, living a youth denied him, loving himself and hating himself by turns. A tiny part of him, muzzled by infatuation, deplored his sins.

Out of danger, his thoughts fondly returned to Edgar. Edgar Falchion… A lovely name for a lovely boy. Growing up almost too fast. He smiled, feeling the excitement bloom within him, savouring it like a famine victim. He sincerely hoped he was alive and well, prayed that he hadn't been maimed.

A stern frown absorbed his smile. Lee Chetwood... Lee with the sharp tongue and the scowling eyes. Lee with his filthy suspicions, degrading and humiliating... But Lee was his friend. Lee was the one with him now, sharing his adventures, his fears, fighting alongside him, sleeping next to him under the stars. Envy rapidly ripened to hate. Curse him! Curse Lee Chetwood for getting in the way! Anything to get rid of him, to fight for Edgar. To save his life, oh, to save his life and have him eternally indebted to him.

Anger smote him. He ground his teeth and dug his nails into his palms. Fool! Last night was your chance! Instead of cowering under the bedclothes you should have gone to him! You should have been there to support him in his hour of need. Fool, fool, *fool!*... To give up your life for him... To die next to him, a hero at last. United in death and buried in the same grave. David and Jonathan... Achilles and Patroclus... Alexander and Hephaestion...

The school wouldn't open that day. Regret settled on his mind, of joy postponed. Then a bright idea overtook him. He smiled at his own ingeniousness.

'The way to a boy's heart... is through his *mother.* His parents are in difficulty. I shall go to them and offer my help. He shall hear of it. He will look kindly on me...'

Prickleback paced his library. The roar of last night had soured his palate, forcing him to quit the breakfast-table.

The pregnant silence was unnerving. He muttered under his breath, scowling at nothing in particular. Finally, as he was about to fling himself into his armchair, he caught sight of Racker Booth crossing the courtyard.

'Curse the man! I distinctly told Gannet to lower the portcullis first thing this morning. He shall suffer for disobeying my orders. And now this fool...'

He strode angrily to the door himself.

'How dare he knock so loudly... What is it?' he shouted as he flung the door wide.

At the sight of Racker's hives and bruises he couldn't surpress a smile. Was there a peculiar whiff about the man? Is that fear I smell?...

His smile broadened and Booth bristled. The reverend decided to be brusque with the creature.

'Well, what is it?'

'Watch yer tongue, Prickleback,' Booth growled.

'My dear fellow, what happened to you? You're all...' Fingers waggled and hands gestured at his face and neck and hands, more to infuriate him than show concern.

'None o' yer business, Prickleback.'

'Do you wish to enter?'

He stepped well back. Motioning him towards the library, he followed at a safe distance, determined the miscreant wouldn't foul his armchairs.

'Warm your seat at the fire, man. You look perished.'

''Tisn't the cold that...'

He stopped himself before admitting to being afraid. Too late. His sly confederate was too quick for him, he read it in his eyes. Booth determined to delve the cowardly depths of his opponent.

'Heard that noise last night, I warrant.'

'Noise? What noise? I slept like a baby.'

Rack knew by his face he was lying. There was a puffiness about the eyes and dark rings under them. He threw down the gauntlet.

'Ye lie, Prickleback.'

The reverend smiled crookedly. He saw he was caught out.

'I do, indeed… Yes, I did hear the noise.'

'Got the wind up ye, I can tell.'

'A noise, nothing more. Not in the habit of letting my imagination run away with me, Rack, my man. Hold a tight rein. God is my protector.'

'Kept ye awake, for all yer lyin'.'

'Did more than keep *you* awake,' he parried.

'Chetwood's gone.' He threw it at him like a live coal, hoping it would do damage.

'Gone? Gone where?'

'Dead and gone.'

'Don't be ridiculous.' The vague simper dissolved. He swallowed. 'How? Was it that Falchion brat?'

'Nay, Prickleback. 'Tweren't the cur. Drownded, so he was.'

'Drowned?'

'Aye. In the sea, or where the sea used to be. It's gone too.'

The reverend began to suspect something was amiss. Worry tightened his features and Rack chuckled inwardly.

The hypocrite has a yellow streak after all. He began to pour salt on the wound.

'And the tower… Can ye explain the tower?'

'What of the tower? Stop talking in riddles, man.'

He was becoming tetchy, wanting to hasten the interview to an end. The oaf was stinking out his library like an open sewer.

''Tis rebuilt, Prickleback.'

'Impossible… You've been dreaming.'

'No dream, Prickleback. Saw it with me own two eyes.'

'But it can't be.'

Fear was escalating and Booth was glad of it. Now I have ye, Prickleback. Where I want ye…

'Best come an' see for yerself. The village is in uproar.'

Impatiently he donned a heavy cloak and snatched up his cane, twitching it at Racker to lead the way. He glared vindictively at the back of the scurvy knave, saw himself bringing his cane down again and again and killing the reptile. He cast a furtive glance at the church on the hill. The heads of his two sentries were visible over the crumbling wall. He scowled at the creature ahead of him. You covet the mill, do you?… We'll see about that…

A straggling group of fearful villagers came down the hill and fell in behind them. They had caught sight of Booth making for the castle and waited by the church for developments. Now that their leader was abroad, they decided to follow him. It was safer with him than without him.

The Reverend Josiah Prickleback, blessed progeny of His Grace, Elbereth Jehosaphat Prickleback, Archbishop of

Dublin, brushed a low branch aside and stepped from the woods. He could see the tower, rebuilt to perfection. He crossed the intervening cabbage field, cursing the mud clinging to his shoes, despising his flock who had stepped back behind him. He stood, literally dancing with annoyance, waiting for someone to open the gate for him. Not one of them budged.

'Well?' he barked. 'Isn't anyone going to open the *gate*? Do I have to do *everything* myself?'

All eyes were trained on him but nobody moved. He could have waited till doomsday. In the end he climbed over and they clambered after him. He stopped so abruptly that the crowd stumbled into him. He proceeded so far and no further. He didn't dare approach the base of the hill. Stout trailers of ivy had leaves the size of rhubarb's, veins turgid with blood. Ravens circled over the tower like vultures. He heard whispering going on behind him.

However he derided their comments, he was powerless to stifle his fear. The tower *was* built, he couldn't deny the fact. To the very merlons and embrasures! But why did it appear inhabited…?… Had the roar last night come from within those four elevated walls?

Vaguely he recalled rumours from the past, too hazy to resuscitate. There was something about this place. An atmosphere had always lingered, emanating from the very stones themselves. But now… now that it thrust mightily into the sky and overshadowed the entire peninsula…

Their fear was infectious. He felt it simmering and rising within him, distorting his judgement, rendering him prey to all sorts of nightmares.

'What's 'e agoin' to do?' he heard from a bedraggled villager.

He wanted to scream and lash out at the brainless sheep. He felt exposed and vulnerable, sure they could sense his fear. To turn and upbraid them would be seen for what it was - cowardice. To continue forward and enter that yawning portal was utter madness. He refused to stare death in the face.

Strangled cries behind him had him focus on the tower anew. His heart turned to water. His bowels were loosened and he stood in his own degradation. A head and shoulders appeared above the battlements. Huge. Monstrous. His knees buckled, his legs gave way from under him and he fell to the ground, backing away, slipping and whimpering.

'Run for your lives!' he screamed, dragging himself to his feet. ''Tis Satan himself!'

He stumbled past the stricken crowd. With shrieks and shouts they followed him, the stench of his fear clogging their nostrils. But they couldn't keep up.

Their pastor had abandoned his flock.

A hideous roar, the roar of last night, filled the woods. He didn't stop running till he reached the church gate.

— 32. Cold Condemnation —

On tottering legs, with heaving chest, he fell against the door and pushed it open, slamming it to and locking it. He didn't care if they followed him, they weren't getting in. They could howl and hammer and beg forever. He staggered forward and gripped a pew for support. Fighting for air, he tried to swallow the phlegm lodged in his throat, sucking saliva from under his tongue to ease its passage.

He was alone at last, alone with his fears. Breathing becalmed, the silence of the place engulfed him. Dust lay thick on the window-sills. A cobweb stretched from the bishop's stony brow to the broken pediment. The odour of dampness swirled about him, making him shudder. A breeze outside rustled the dead leaves, swaying the spectral yews peering in at him. He felt cornered, a rat in a trap with a snake uncoiling next to him. The reek off his clothing filled the church, mingling with exhalations rising from the vaults beneath, redolent of death.

The impassive, sightless stare of the bishop's bust was no comfort at all.

'I am my father's son,' he murmured.

Never had he uttered a truer word.

Catching sight of the naked cross on the altar, he ran foward, clawing at the black wood, mumbling and whimpering and begging for mercy. He pulled it towards him, embraced it tightly and pressed his quivering lips to its cold, smooth surface. Sibilant whispers echoed about the damp and mildewed walls, crawling upwards towards an unseen and hitherto unheeded God.

He let go of the cross and slipped from the altar, biting his tongue as he hit the floor. Wracked by sobbing, he stared up at the ebony rood devoid of a Saviour. Tears coursed down his muddy cheeks.

'Please,' he begged. 'Help me.'

In vain the wolf pleaded with the Shepherd.

'Please! I am the issue of an archbishop. I am worthy of your help.'

He resorted to bribery.

'I'll give half of what I own to the poor… I'll… I'll… I'll love my *wife!*'

If he expected to hear a voice, he was sadly disappointed. His prayer was neither heard nor answered. Anger blinded him. He got to his feet, ignoring the ignominious stink from his clothing.

'Very well… I got down on my knees before you. I *begged!* Yet you heard me not… You closed your ears to a bishop's son. You don't know the meaning of love.'

Familiar lies and deluded fantasies bewitched him.

'I have built up your temple. I have called down your wrath on unbelievers. I took that whining mouse into my *home!*… You have never loved me as I have loved you. *Never…*

'But I can hate you more than you can ever hate me, do you *hear*?!'

He ground his teeth, turning this way and that. Spittle foamed at the corners of his mouth.

'I want a sign. I *demand* one. *Now*!...'

He waited, his heartbeat audible in the stolid silence...

He waited in vain.

'Very well, then... You would have answered that Falchion brat, I warrant... I *know* what to do.'

He spat at the figureless cross with all the venom he could muster. Spittle dribbled down the polished ebony to the altar. There were no tears now. It wasn't that he was resigned to fate. He took it in his hands and wrung it and tore it and stamped it underfoot.

For all his bitter disappointment, he felt he wasn't alone. He *had* sent the Falchion brat to the tower. *Before* knowing anything about it being rebuilt... How could he possibly have guessed?... Who was *inspiring* him?...

Somebody was.

But who?...

And how?...

†

— 33. Life-boy —

The delicious light began to waver. He didn't want it to, oh, how he didn't want it to. Fear of losing it inundated him but there was nothing he could do about it. Mists swirled before his eyes, thinning and slowly clearing until he could see himself again - his supine body, and Lee bending over him far below. Dim sounds began to register, a voice ringing in his ears. His skin came alive as somebody touched him.

Edgar was out of the water. He sucked in air, spluttering and hacking up his lungs. Strident, rasping sounds came from his throat. His whole system was fighting for oxygen but he still couldn't see. Numb, he lay on the hard ground, mind eclipsed...

Utterly stunned, Lee had watched helplessly at first, turning from Edgar to Berry and back again. With a shout of horror and rage, he'd run to Edgar, knowing there was little time left to him. Edgar would be dead in a matter of minutes if he didn't release him.

He fell upon the whiplike cords binding Edgar, tearing his hands to ribbons. Unable to break them, he screamed in terror and begun gnawing at them with his teeth. They yielded and he bit and sawed and tore at them until he got Edgar's head out of the water and dragged him ashore.

'Ed! Ed!' he yelled, tears falling on his friend's face.

He opened his mouth, removed a clod of weeds and breathed for him. Water flowed from Edgar's throat. He coughed. He inhaled and Lee cried for joy. With no time to lose, he grabbed the sword and ran to Berry buried beneath a thicket of brambles. He hacked away at them, but to no avail. Wielded by him, the sword was useless. There was nothing for it but to bite through the briars. His gums were raw and bleeding. The taste of the hideous sap mingling with his blood revolted him.

Berry was free, bloodied, terrified, but free. Lee staggered backwards and fell down exhausted.

They lay in silence for an age, unable to speak or think clearly. A merciless sun blazed down upon them but they barely noticed.

Eventually Lee heard his name being called by a weak, croaking voice. Edgar's voice.

'Over here,' he croaked himself.

'Are you safe?'

'Just about.'

'The sword is gone.'

'I have it.'

'Thank God for that.'

A prolonged and dazed silence ensued. Someone crawled over to him. He opened his eyes to see Edgar's face looking down at him.

'Is Berry all right?' he asked him.

He didn't have the energy to raise his head and check for himself. Edgar looked in his direction and nodded. Then he heard him stomping towards them. His smiling face appeared against the sky. Lee closed his eyes, at peace.

'We're safe…' he feebly murmured.

By the time they had regained their strength, their faces, arms and the backs of their hands were severely sunburnt.

'Where's Spike?' Edgar asked, suddenly remembering him.

'Spike! Spike!' they cried, but there was no response.

They searched the barren land for any more briar-traps. They ran to the river's edge and peered into the swirling waters.

'What could have happened to him?' Edgar asked with a groan.

Tears flooded his heart and welled up towards his eyes. It was awful to think of him gone, just awful.

'Where could he have got to?' Lee asked with exasperation.

'Something must have happened to him.'

'Maybe we'll catch up with him,' Berry said to comfort him. 'He could have run off in fright when he thought you were drowning.'

At intervals they called his name. Edgar prayed for his return. He wished he'd never heard of the goddamn hermit. To the devil with Buckrake and his boat and his cake and coffee!

Shortly after that there was no time to think of him for they were beset on all sides once more.

†

— 34. Flora and Fauna —

In the sweltering heat, thistles and nettles thrust forth from the scorched earth to hamper their progress. They darted forward to strike at their heels like vipers.

Edgar halted and rubbed his eyes. 'Am I seeing things or is the ground ahead moving?'

All Lee could do was groan in despair.

'Will we turn back?' Berry asked, certain he never, *ever* wanted to face anything out of the ordinary again.

'Best keep on where we are,' Edgar responded with a grimace. 'Buckrake did say not to leave the river. And Spike might be ahead of us.'

It *was* moving. Granules of soil appeared to be hopping up and down. A low humming reached their ears and their legs were soon covered in black particles.

'Oh, God!' Lee cried, stamping his feet. 'Fleas!'

The area was infested with fleas. They were crawling all over them. The boys slapped their arms and their legs, stamping their feet in a frenetic dance to be rid of them. With a roar of utter revulsion, Edgar tore off his clothes and dived into the river, Lee and Berry after him. Submerging themselves, they frantically ran fingers through their hair. Pin-pricks of blood appeared when the tiny clots on their skin dissolved. Resurfacing, they bored fingers into their ears and snorted down their noses.

'I think we should wade up river for the time being,' Edgar suggested.

'But what about our clothes?'

Edgar clicked his tongue with annoyance.

'I'll get them.'

He hopped out, grabbed his sword and clothes, skipped and danced to the next bundle and the next, groaning and shouting and stamping his feet. Lee chuckled at the sight of him.

'Look at them swing,' he quipped, laughing outright.

Berry blushed, then laughed along with him.

With an almighty roar Edgar leapt into the water again, letting go the clothes and madly washing off the fleas.

They knotted their shoe-laces together and hung their boots round their necks. They tied their clothes in a bundle leaving one sleeve free to drag the sodden masses through the water. All three of them waded forward, Berry finding it easier to advance in water than on land. The sun was fierce on their wet skin, they had to disentangle their shirts and place them on their heads to protect their necks and shoulders. Lee slung back a soggy sleeve, pretending to be a girl. The laughter waned in Edgar's eyes. Spike was out there alone somewhere, at the mercy of the scarecrows if not already dead.

Lee began to sing aloud but the tune soon faded from his lips. A peculiar black mist was skimming the surface of the river ahead and hastening their way.

'A mist? In *this* heat?'

34. Flora and Fauna

It was no mist. Gnats, in their droves, plastered their faces and necks and shoulders, gnawing at their inflamed and tender skin. They ducked below the surface, cheeks bulging with air. Lungs bursting, Edgar rose into the air fighting for breath. He splashed water onto his face to keep the midges off.

'It's no good,' he shouted when the other two resurfaced. 'We'll just have to keep splashing them off and wrap our shirts round our necks.'

Like translucent particles of light, the insects weaved back and forth in the air, alighting on the boys incessantly. Despite their best efforts, they were being eaten alive. Exhausted and close to tears, they gave up fighting. Berry tripped over something, lunged forward and disappeared. Lee watched him sink down into the green murky depths.

'No!' he roared, grabbing a fistful of hair and dragging him up again. 'We'll have to get him out of the water!' he shouted over his shoulder at Edgar. 'If we don't, he'll surely drown!' His voice rose in panic. 'Now, Ed. *Now!*"

Between them they got Berry onto dry land and crouched over him. While they busied themselves keeping the midges off him they were devoured themselves. The bugs got caught in their eyelashes. They crawled up their noses. It was just awful.

'What do we do now?' Lee sobbed.

'I don't know,' his friend replied, close to despair.

'We can't just give up and die,' Berry rasped, raising his head and letting it fall back again. 'I'm so thirsty,' he moaned.

Both boys collected water in the palms of their hands and poured it into his mouth. That done, they lay down on either side of him, faces pressed into the scorched earth, sun scalding the backs of their legs, their shoulders and buttocks.

'We're done for,' Edgar moaned into the dirt.

He drifted in and out of consciousness. He heard the moaning of his two companions but there was nothing he could do for them. The midges seemed to be dispersing and he found himself wondering whether they abandoned the dying like rats a sinking ship.

— 35. Straightforward and Downhill —

He began hallucinating. He had to be. Or was he dreaming?…

He lifted his numb cheek off the ground and listened. He blinked ever so slowly. Sounds were muffled. His eyes had glazed over and everything was out of focus. Every inch of him ached, a dull ache that reached to the very well-spring of his being. Pain filled his mind but something else was penetrating to the core of his thoughts. Insistent. Repetitive. Familiar. He blinked again and tried to swallow. His mouth was full of sawdust. He raised his head a little more. It throbbed agonisingly.

The noise grew sharper, more pronounced.

Yes… He knew it… He recognized it for what it was… Yes!

He licked his scaly lips and uttered a breathy sound.

'Spike…'

He could hear him barking. He sounded far away, as if he were at the end of a long tunnel. But it was Spike, all right. He'd recognize his bark anywhere.

Slowly, painfully, he rolled over and sat up, wiping dusty sweat from his brow, closing his eyes to concentrate. The grit was sharp daggers next his skin. He wasn't hallucinating. Spike was barking and coming closer.

Spike shot out between some leggy shrubs and bounded at his master. Edgar screamed when his paws pounded against his flaming skin. A startled Spike leapt back before jumping on him again and licking his face. Edgar held him at arm's length and tried to calm him down.

'Good boy, Spike. Yes, you're a great dog for finding us. Down, Spike. Down!'

'He's back,' Lee groaned, sitting up with a heart-rending moan.

Berry also stirred. 'Hello, Spikey,' was all he could manage.

Spike whined insistently, hopping backwards, coming forward and looking behind him.

'I think he wants us to follow him,' Edgar intoned.

Lee groaned viscerally. 'I don't think I can.'

'We've *got* to. We'll die if we stay here much longer.'

Still Spike skipped and barked in front of them.

'Oh, shut up, dog. *Please,*' Lee pleaded. 'My head's splitting, as it is.'

'He won't shut up until we follow him.'

They went to fetch their bundles of clothes and the sword.

'Where's mine?' Berry asked, looking about him.

'It must be still in the water,' said Edgar, looking to see if he could see it. 'The current must have borne it away.'

'You'll just have to make do without clothes,' Lee drily remarked with a smirk.

'But I *can't!*'

'We'll share out what we've got,' Edgar promised. 'Don't worry, Berry. He's only pulling your leg.'

They plodded along behind the excited and impatient mongrel, dragging their clothes by the sleeves through the dust. Every step was agony. Every movement redoubled the pounding in their heads.

'Would you look at that,' Edgar declared when Spike came to a halt.

He stood on the river-bank yapping, wagging his tail with pride. There was a boat moored right beside him.

'Who would have believed it?' Lee murmured with awe.

'Good old Spikey,' praised Berry. 'But can we take it?'

'Either we get into that boat right now or I'll just lie down and snuff it,' Lee growled, aghast at Berry's scruples.

Spike hopped into the boat, barking joyously. They eased themselves in for fear of scraping their ever-so-delicate skin.

'Thank God the oars are here,' said Edgar, dreading the prospect of rowing. 'What's this?' he cried, rummaging beneath them.

Three earthenware pots sealed with thick corks lay under the blades of the oars. Edgar slowly leaned forward and picked one up. He pulled out the cork and sniffed the contents. The intoxicating scent of herbs and balsam filled his nostrils, he breathed it in with pleasure. He dipped two fingers into the contents and scooped some out. A greenish, translucent ointment glistened in the sunlight.

'I wonder what it's for?'

He shrugged his shoulders and wiped his fingers clean on his thigh. His eyes opened wide with astonishment. He chuckled and stretched out his leg for Lee and Berry to see.

Two short lines of perfectly normal skin were clearly visible on his red and blistered thigh.

'It's healed!' Lee exclaimed.

They grabbed a pot each and all three were immediately rubbing the unguent into their skin, helping one another in the places they couldn't reach. Overjoyed, they lay back and sighed with relief. Not a blister or a red patch remained.

'It's magic!' Lee exclaimed exuberantly.

Edgar nodded. 'And it proves this boat was left here for us. And, if it wasn't for *this* little fella...'

He sat forward and pulled Spike onto his lap.

'Who's a great boy, Spikey. If it wasn't for you... You're the best dog a boy could ask for.'

He bent down and kissed the top of his head.

While Lee and Berry took the oars he busied himself laying their wet clothes in the bottom to dry, chuckling to himself when he remembered that Berry hadn't got any.

'What was *that*?' they asked, jerking the oars with fright and unsettling the boat.

The roar echoed off the trees and filled the entire woods. Even the leaves were shaken by it.

'We're fair whemmled here!' Lee shrieked before covering his ears.

The roar died down. It ceased as suddenly as it had begun.

'It's the Aetz,' Edgar whispered. 'It *has* to be.'

They sat still in the boat, taken by the current back the way they'd come. Edgar's hands rested on the oars. He stared into Lee's eyes.

'Sword or no sword, how could anyone fight such a thing?'

They were tempted to let the current take them out to sea. Resolutely, he gripped the oar handles and began to row again.

His hopes abruptly rose at the beautiful sight glimpsed through a gap in the trees. Two mute swans were curving round the perimeter of a meadow, dazzling white against the distant trees. The faint sighing of their wings came to him across the clearing. For the benefit of his companions he nodded in their direction.

'Over yonder,' he said.

They followed their course, smiling all the while. They were a flash of sunlight, uplifting because beauty still actually dwelt in Garten. If something so glorious could still exist in a world beset by horror, there had to be hope.

'I've never seen anything so beautiful,' Edgar breathed with delight.

The experience, almost spiritual, expunged the startling roar from their minds. They felt a deep longing blossom inside them, in a place they'd never been aware of before. This is as things should be, as they were meant to be. This is what we were born to, our true inheritance. And this is where we will end our days.

— 36. Another Country —

The River Rudd chuckled and gurgled, meandering through picturesque woodland. Pale, kindly sunlight filtered through fresh green leaves. The scent of spring filled the air, complemented by a riotous chorus of birdsong. The ache of longing stirred in their breasts - for what they had lost, for what they yearned to revive. They had returned to Eden, unexpectantly, unannounced, recapturing a youth stolen from them. Berry felt the joys of Spring thrilling every nerve. Like never before, he wished to be whole like his boon companions. To be able to kick out both legs in the water and swim against the current. To run barefoot between the trees unhindered. Excitement gaped his throat. It almost seemed possible.

'Please let me row now,' he begged, desperate to feel his muscles straining, to be fully alive, himself bearing his friends into this magical land.

Edgar gladly moved over to make room for him. He had forgotten about the Aetz. He had forgotten his parents. The love and joy of existence bathed every cell of his body, inundating his soul. He wanted to run and leap, to dance and fly, to jump out of his skin with a roar of triumph.

Lee too basked in prodigious happiness. All hurt and shame had been washed clean away. He loved the whole world, a world that returned his love. He accepted the fact at last. As his due.

Not for one moment did they sense they were unworthy trespassers. They too were beautiful and part of this place. Beauty shone from their faces – kindness and love, courage and fellowship, peace and serenity. The taint of sorrow was unknown here. No harm could befall them among the currents and eddies of the River Rudd, between its soft and gradient banks. It was a magical place, remote from the world whence they'd come.

Lush vegetation overhung the crystal waters. A blanket of bluebells was an azure mist wafting between the smooth grey boles of the beach trees. Bees droned merrily about their business. In the distance, tall, feathery bracken swayed in a gentle breeze. Stately foxgloves bowed their manifold heads to them, freckled throats on display. Psychedelic dragonflies flitted here and there, hovered out of curiosity and darted away while tiny insects trapped the sunlight and danced like fairies. A stream chattered into the river on their right, the nearest thing to extraneous laughter they had heard that lengthy day. The air was sweet with herbs – wild thyme, garlic, mint - sharp and flavoursome.

At first they thought the whispering they heard was the wind rustling the leaves. But the leaves were motionless. The trees seemed to be whispering among themselves, as if they were welcoming them and glad of their company. Lee plucked a leaf from an overhanging bough and placed it in the water, watching it hurtle into the distance. He smiled to himself. He liked being a boy, happy as he was, happy and proud.

'This is the life,' he said with a contented sigh.

'It *is* the life,' Berry agreed, a huge smile irradiating his features. 'I've never been so happy before.'

'Right you are, Berry, me lad.'

He hummed a tune, then tried to sing a song. He was woefully tone-deaf and laughter spluttered from both his listeners.

'You sound like a half-dead tom-cat,' Edgar teased him.

'A whole gang of them,' Berry added with glee.

'Shut up, the two of you. Anyone'd think you were the greatest singers in the world.'

'So we are compared to *you*.'

'Edgar Falchion, come down here and say that to my face.'

'Just you watch yourself,' Edgar joked, testing the blade of his sword.

'Oh! Oh! I'm scar-ared, so I am.'

The face he put on had Berry doubled up in kinks.

'You just watch it, young Berry, or we'll be back where we started. Keep rowing there, boy!'

Berry felt Edgar's hands on his shoulders before he sidled past him and stepped over the oar. Lee stood up. The boat began to see-saw when they locked arms. Laughter escaped them, water slopping over the sides when the wrestling grew more intense. With a roar both disappeared into the river. Shrill laughter filled the air as they splashed and tussled, one raised up out of the water as he pushed the other down. It was all too infectious and, heart in his mouth, with a drawn out cry, Berry leaped in on top of them. Wild excitement bubbled through his veins. One minute he was under, struggling in turbulent waters, the next he was coughing and spluttering and holding someone's head down. And all the while Spike barked furiously in the boat.

Laughing boisterously, screaming in his attempts to escape, Berry grabbed the edge of their craft and tried to haul himself in. He felt hands grip his legs and suddenly he was vaulted into the air and sprawling in the bottom of the boat with Spike hovering over him. It was he who had to haul the others in, slippery as eels.

They lay in the bottom of the boat, panting and smiling and immeasurably happy. The unseemly cares of their world were far behind them. They were three boys off on an adventure, squinting up at the treetops and the glorious sunshine.

Berry gripped an oar and pulled himself onto the seat. The second oar slipped into the river.

'Whooooa!' Edgar shouted, springing up and lunging out to save it. 'That would have been a disaster and a half. One oar lost and we'd be going round in circles for a month of Fridays.'

He fell silent, straining his ears.

'Shush!' he ordered Lee. 'I heard something.'

Both Lee and Edgar scrambled for their clothes. The worried look on Berry's face filled the woods with their mocking laughter.

'Just look at him!' snorted Lee. 'He thinks we're gonna *leave* him like that.'

'Sorry Berry,' muttered a half-chastened Edgar, peeling off his shirt and handed it across to him.

'Oh yeah,' Lee barked. '*Very* clever. And I have to give him my *pants,* I suppose.'

Edgar leaned back, both hands clasping one knee. He laughed long and heartily.

'Of course! He can't very well go round with a shirt on and everything hanging out!'

'But I suppose *I* can. Leaving nothing to the imagination.'

'All right. You give him *your* shirt and he can have my pants, I don't care.'

'Be careful you don't get a draught up there,' Lee cracked. 'Don't want a chill in your privates.'

'Shut up, you.'

They all started for they clearly had heard a man coughing. Slowly and quietly they rowed forward, keeping their eyes peeled. A grassy knoll topped by a crooked hazel appeared among the trees on their right. The branches swayed with sussurrating whispers, making it all the more eerie.

They approached with caution.

†

— 37. End of the Beginning —

'Let it drift in,' Edgar whispered.

The boat rocked when he stood up, took the coil of rope and tied the free end to the wooden jetty. He hopped out and steadied the boat while Berry stowed the oars, helping him out when he was ready. Lee wanted no assistance, springing from the gunwale to land on the platform. In his haste he had pushed the stern off so that Spike fell short and splashed into the river. Paddling furiously, he stretched his neck to keep his head above water.

'Trust you,' Edgar muttered, on his hunkers, lifting Spike out by the shoulders.

Water droplets sprayed in every direction while he shook himself dry. They gazed up at the grassy mound, a great shoulder of earth resembling a fallen giant conquered by grass. The noise had come from the far side of it.

'I didn't think of it before,' Edgar whispered, 'but these are the Garrow Woods.' A thought hit home and he half turned and thrust a forefinger at the landing-place. 'That boat *belongs* here.'

Both the others looked at the boat and the jetty and nodded.

Spike growled when a low, sonorous chant reached their ears, a sombre melody rising and falling effortlessly like wind in the willows. They all slunk forward and crept round the curve of the mound. The chant continued unabated. Putting a finger to his lips, Edgar gestured that he would go first and that they should follow in single file. Step by ponderous step, he edged forward and craned his neck. He put his finger to his lips again and beckoned. They all stood close together, watching in silence .

A squatting figure stooped low over a small fire and stirred something in a pot. It was obviously the hermit. His face was seamed and scored, it was impossible to age him. He might have slid down the space between the centuries and been forgotten. Beyond Time's power, he was older than the ages of man.

Without interrupting his chant he gestured at them to join him - as if he'd been expecting them for centuries. Huddled together, as if in a trance, they stole forward as one. He smiled to encourage them, beckoning with a forefinger. When they were close enough, still chanting, he spread out a hand and invited them to be seated round the fire. The melody faded to a drawling hum, then ceased when they were in place.

'Greetings!' His tone of address sounded ridiculously archaic. 'Well, well, well... Here at last.'

'You were expecting us!' Berry piped up.

Of the three, he was the one who felt completely at ease. Inexplicably, a sort of peace had descended upon him. When the hermit smiled at him he beamed back unruffled. Spike sniffed at the contents of the pot and licked his chops.

37. End of the Beginning

'And in the nick of time,' said the hermit. "Tis cooked to perfection.'

Aromatic steam rose from the pot to torment them.

'Hungry?' he finally asked with a mischievous smile.

'Starving,' Edgar murmured bashfully.

'Good. That's what I like to hear. Boys are born with an appetite. It never forsakes us.'

While he spooned the contents onto battered pewter plates they inspected their surroundings.

The clearing was full of sunlight. Golden rays slanted through the canopy like light in a cathedral. The grass was vibrant green, festooned with flowers of every colour. A wicker gate blocked the entrance of a shallow cave scooped out of the grassy knoll. To their left, a large clump of whin was in flower, filling their nostrils with the bitter-sharp scent of coconut. Holly trees, laden down by berries, rose behind it, a prickly dark fence to obstruct their view. The fire crackled and a thin reed of smoke rose into the air. Who wouldn't be a hermit in a place like this, they thought.

Their host handed round the plates and spoons and they fell to. It was delicious, a stew of fish and meat, vegetables and herbs. With a mournful whine, Spike sat down and stamped his paws impatiently. The hermit forked some of the contents of his own plate onto the ground and he wolfed it down.

While they were eating they cast shy glances at the man. Of the fact that he was old they were certain, but it was a young world he inhabited. He was bald, his pate and sloping forehead burnt brown as a nut. His was a calm and vigilant expression. Ageless, sapphire eyes were disconcertingly piercing, yet full of kindness. His lips were full and good-natured, fringed by a beard. He looked as if he laughed a lot. He was his own master. He needed no companions.

He wasn't good-looking. He wasn't ugly. Humour and mercy shone through, suffusing his features with a kindly light. What grey hair he had seemed to have been cut with a blunt knife. Tufts of it stuck out at odd angles. He went barefoot, the soles of his feet were thick and leathery. His tunic was of homespun wool, reminiscent of a monk's habit, gathered in the middle by a rope.

'Had enough?'

He startled them and they nodded self-consciously.

In the intervening silence the hermit looked into their eyes, one by one. They rested on Edgar last of all. He felt the man peering into the depths of his soul and turning all his secrets belly-up. A blush rose from his insteps.

'And so, Sabrehilt, we meet at last.'

All Edgar could do was gape. 'You know me?' he stammered.

'I do.'

'Buckrake told you,' Lee intervened, squinting at him with a sneery smile.

'I knew you long before Buckrake came into your life,' he still directed at Edgar.

'What's *my* name, then, if you're so clever?'

'Lee.'

'You could have heard him calling me that. What's my second name?'

'Chetwood.'

'Hmm...'

37. End of the Beginning

'Any further queries, my bold inquisitor?'

'Do I have another name, a special name like *he* does?' He pleaded it were so.

'Spalpeen. Rapscallion. Ragamuffin. Pert bobtail.'

'But they're insults, not names.'

'They fit.'

He fixed his serious gaze on Lee. He obviously came to a satisfactory conclusion for he smiled to himself.

'Would you like a special name?' he gently asked him.

Lee nodded eagerly.

'How about… Shieldbearer?'

'Shieldbearer? A bit of a mouthful, isn't it?'

'Fussy, aren't we?… Mmm… Buckler? Escutcheon?'

'Nothing like Sabrehilt?'

'That's his name, a name *you* gave him, I might add.'

'Did better than you, didn't I?'

The hermit sighed to himself, whispering under his breath.

'So it has to be one of them, does it?'

'It does, forsooth.'

'All right, then… Em… Let it be… Shieldbearer!'

'Shieldbearer, it is.'

'I think I prefer plain old Lee.'

'As you wish. But remember… There is no one greater than a trustworthy friend and you have proved your worth a hundredfold.'

Lee smiled in acknowledgement. 'Hey!' he ejaculated.

'Yes?' A different expression was stealing over the hermit's face.

'What about him?' he asked, pointing at Berry. 'Do you know *his* name?'

'Berry Blakelock. A boy who for his tender years has suffered more than anyone else I know. And has borne it like a man, I might add... I'm sure *you* never thought you'd be sitting here under such circumstances.'

Berry shook his head.

'Hmm.'

He studied Berry's features for quite some time. The boy never looked away, he had no secrets to hide. No spark had kindled his hopes or desires or made turbulent the blood in his veins. A little voice inside persisted in pleading to be normal, no different from anybody else.

'I suppose you don't require a special name, hmm?'

Why not, Berry thought. Why shouldn't I have one like the other two?

He began to nod in agreement, hiding his real feelings. But the words would out. The little voice asserted itself at last.

'I *would* like one, actually.'

'Would you? Hmm... That surprises me but I see your point of view. And, do you know... there's only one suitable name for you.'

'What's that?'

'Berry the Brave.'

'While we're on the subject of names, what's yours?' Lee asked, rather rattled that Berry's name was better than his.

'Houghton Miffler, that's my name.'

'Houghton Miffler?'

'Aye, indeed.'

'Does it have a meaning?' Lee asked.

'Not that I'm aware of.'

'Who cuts your hair?' he started off again.

Edgar was shocked. He had heard it said that a hermit riled was like unto the wrath of God. And here was his idiotic friend trying to prove it!

'*I* do,' replied the hermit, as if he didn't mind at all.

'But why cut it like that?'

'So I don't become the prisoner of Vanity.' To add weight to his admission, he struck his breast with a closed fist. 'And no water has touched this flesh in many a year. *That's* mortification for you.'

Mortification for *us*, you mean, Lee said to himself. I *thought* I got a strange whiff earlier on.

'Hah!'

The hermit smiled and chuckled, then broke into uproarious laughter. It echoed from the confines of his cave, bounced back at them from the surrounding trees, grew muffled in the verdant canopy overhead. Edgar couldn't for the life of him understand what was so funny. Lee and Berry began laughing at the sight of him and then he laughed too.

†

— 38. More End Than Beginning —

While Edgar laughed with the rest of them, inside he wasn't laughing at all. His heart was heavy and sinking fast. An old man dressed like a monk, living on his own in a cave, protected from reality… What can he do for us? Buckrake said that speaking to him might save our lives. Is he the one who remembers?… Even if he does remember, what difference will it make?

He looked at Lee and Berry, still laughing heartily. A deep sigh welled up from the depths of his despair. They can afford to laugh… I'm the one with the sword, I'm the one who has to fight… I'm alone in this and they can't help me… Nobody can.

The laughter of the hermit stalled and stuttered to a halt. The smile faded from his lips and he regarded Edgar closely.

'It's hard, isn't it?' he said.

Edgar nodded, sure he was about to start crying. But crying wasn't going to solve anything.

'Do you know the Aetz?' he asked the hermit to banish the levity getting on his nerves.

Lee and Berry fell silent and sombre.

'The Morgammeron Aetz...' the hermit drawled soberly. 'Aye, I know it.'

'What is it like?'

Deep searching eyes bored into his own from under brambly eyebrows. A rumble came up from the bottom of the hermit's lungs. His tone was solemn, his face grim.

'It is like nothing you have seen or heard of.'

'As bad as that?'

'Sore sorry am I to prove you right. If I am mistaken, may a wild stallion drag me to Mizen Head and back.'

Berry drew up his legs and clutched his knees. Lee twitched. Something like a woodlouse was crawling all over his spine.

'But,' the hermit said, raising a hand at the dumbstruck threesome, 'be not beguiled nor beflummed.'

They had no idea what he was saying. They had never heard of being beflummed before. It sounded like being smothered in lamb's-wool.

There was no point in sparing them, these three poor innocent boys. His task was to enlighten them, just that. Only then would they begin to plumb the murky depths of reality. They noticed that as he began to speak he appeared to be talking more to himself than to them. Perhaps that came from living alone so long.

'You seek a light in the darkness that besets you... I have no light. I am no torchbearer...'

'But what are we *here* for?' shouted Edgar in sheer exasperation. 'Why did we battle our way through so much if you can't even do *that* for us?'

The hermit held up a hand to quiet his anger.

'Patience, my lad,' he whispered in soothing tones. 'All will be revealed. My unique role is to interpret the way that opens before you... *All* of you.'

Lee and Berry shifted uncomfortably. Edgar wanted to fling the sword into the fire or stamp on it and grind it to dust. He cupped his chin in his hands and stared ahead in misery.

'What I say onto you, Sabrehilt, is... Knock and it shall be opened. Seek and you shall find.'

Edgar groaned inwardly. How often had he heard those selfsame words? It was mumbo-jumbo to him, Prickleback cant. He began to wonder if the old fool was laughing up his sleeve at them. He felt the urge to split his head open with his sword.

'So you want to split my head for me, Edgar Sabrehilt?'

He practically jumped out of his skin when he heard him.

'The trees have ears,' the hermit remarked with the gentlest of smiles. 'Hear what I have to say before judging me. Learn how I can help you...

'Your tragedy was to be born into this land, all three of you. Such a place invites the presence of the Aetz, how could it not? Prickleback, that so-called bearer of the wrath of God, has called that wrath down upon *all our heads!*...

'Is it surprising when man is sundered from man, husband from wife, father from son, mother from daughter? They gird themselves in evil, they invite it amongst them. Such an unwholesome stench rises from them into the air that the Aetz comes like a fly to dung.'

'Not all of us are bad!'

'Nay... Not all of you...'

'But that's not fair!' Lee remonstrated.

A scowl clouded the hermit's features. He glowered at the boy.

'Fair?! Of course, it's not fair!' The hermit's features relaxed and he looked kindly upon Lee – he was too young to understand. 'My dear, young boy, the Goddess of Justice was blinded by lawful man. She sees no more. And so mistrustful have men become that they hide their truth from themselves.'

'But look at *this* place,' Lee said in a plaintive voice, gazing up at the broad expanse of leaves, the smooth tree-trunks at their ease. 'It's so peaceful here. How do *you* escape?'

'The eaves of the wood bend low to stave off evil... This is a blessed place and blessed it shall remain... This haven is eternal, cut off from the rest of the world.'

'But couldn't we all come *here*? What's to *stop* us? We would be safe here and Edgar wouldn't have to fight.'

'Is this the place for you? Would you be happy here?'

'Yes!'

'You say that now. You would not have said so a short time ago.' He gave little shakes of his head, barely perceptible. 'Your land is under assault, that is the sole reason you wish to escape. But...' He held up a finger to forestall him. 'But there is another, more relevant question... Would *you* be a hermit?'

'I would... have to become a hermit to live here?'

'Oh, yes.'

Lee's thoughts immediately ran to Felicia Arnold and Dainty Lacey. No, he didn't want to become a hermit. But what if they all were to die? What if he never had a chance to know a girl?... It was worth fighting for. He didn't wish to exile himself from the human race. He couldn't.

Edgar had waited for him to answer long enough.

'Could the bad people come here if they knew about it?' he asked.

'No. Quite impossible. The portals wouldn't allow them entry.'

'But the Aetz tried to stop us getting here, didn't it?'

'It did.'

'How?… Can *it* get in here?'

'No. Its influence can only reach this far if I allow it.'

'You *let it* do that to us!' he shouted in horror. You *let* all those dreadful things *happen to us!*'

'I had no choice.'

'But you said you *let* them happen.'

'To prepare you for what lies ahead… To strengthen you. To test your courage and prove to you that you can do it… Now do you see?'

Edgar slowly nodded. 'That was only a taste of what's to come, wasn't it?'

'I dread to say yes but 'tis so.'

'Oh, God…'

'My child… Read the signs… Why do you think it tried to prevent you? Because it feared your reaching me. And here you are despite *all* it strewed in your path… The first skirmish is over and won… By *you*.'

'But it was only a skirmish!' He sounded desperate.

'Would you have expected to win if you had known?'

'No...'

'As I said… The first skirmish was won by you. As will the next and the next…'

'How can you be so sure?'

'I cannot. But you must believe... Finally light appears at the end of a long tunnel. A pin-prick, but light none the less. The shadow that long cast despair on our land, again and again, shifts... and may dissipate on the wind afore long.'

Doubt clogged Edgar's mind and dulled his features.

'Can't you help us?' he beseeched.

'I?... A mere hermit help you? Nay... I can guide and give counsel, no more. Mine is not to take up arms in combat. Besides, the fresh mind of the young is unjumbled by the clutter of age. Rejoice in your youth. Spring is far sweeter and resilient than Summer or Autumn.'

'But...'

'My child, what purpose does an anchor hold?'

'To keep the boat in place.'

'Exactly... *I* am such an anchor. The barque may be buffeted by winds, tug angrily at the hawser; it may whip around violently and creak and groan, but the anchor prevents it from drifting onto rocks and being smashed to pieces. If the *anchor* comes loose and moves, there is no hope for the ship. She is lost.'

'So... Does every place have a hermit?'

'There are fewer of us than there should be. Some places are without and suffer abominably.'

'Where are the hermits that should be there?'

'Those who answered the call?... Betrayers adrift. Sweeping across the seabed with the unfortunates they abandoned... And there are those who refused the call. They loved themselves more than their neighbours. They chose a different path to the one destined for them.'

'But that means that you *are* fighting.'

'A battle on a different plane. Without arms… I cannot retreat just as I cannot desert, not without taking you all down with me.'

'And what if *we* don't fight?'

'No one can take your place, of that I am as certain as your name is Edgar Sabrehilt. If you step back from the fray and flee, all will be crushed.'

Edgar's face became that of an heroic soldier before relapsing into that of a frightened boy again.

'Your courage has been tested in the fire and found sufficient… You all have a role to play…

'Time is an implacable continuum, a tightly wound spring released and slowing down as it uncoils. One day it will cease and rest will come to us all. *Until* that day, we must be vigilant and fight when we have to… The reward for fighting will be great…

'The tragedy of this life is not that people perish – mark what I say – but that they cease to love… If what you do is for love, it will stand in your stead and never betray you. You are safe if you follow your destiny.'

Lee spoke up in a shrill voice.

'In other words, it's all down to us. *Us?!*'

'Oh, there are others involved, my child.'

'Thank God for that,' Lee muttered under his breath.

— 39. What the Hermit Had to Tell —

'Tell us more about the Aetz,' Edgar requested, curiosity overmastering his dread.

'Is it a sort of *banshee*?' Lee butted in before the hermit could answer.

''Tis no banshee, my lad.'

'A goblin, then!'

'Nor a goblin... The seneschal of evil itself, it is the embodiment of all your fears. It is the shadow that stalks you, the dream that haunts you, the doubt that plagues your waking days.'

'How can I kill such a thing?' cried Edgar in dismay.

'No one said anything about killing. *I* certainly didn't.'

'What are we to *do*, then?'

'Banish it... Overturn its throne.'

The hermit's thoughts turned inwards. He seemed to be scanning the past, reliving ghoulish experiences.

'Where did it come from?' Berry intruded into the silence.

'Hmm?... Ah... There are those who claim some madcap fool of an alchemist began experimenting with things he shouldn't have and overthrew the bounds of nature. The Aetz is the terrific consequence of his toying with the very germs of life itself. He himself was destroyed, a fitting end for so fell a creature. If it be true, that is…'

'Don't you believe it?'

'Frankly, no. It is the spawn of malfeasance, of that I am sure. But how exactly it came to be, even I cannot delve the depths of Time to discover. Enough that it lives and dwells among us!… And that braying coxcomb, Prickleback, believed it errant fancy. But the blustering fool has seen his error. He and his kind, *they* are the alchemists! The darkness in their hearts summons it to the half-light they dwell in!'

'Does the tower belong to the Aetz?' Berry asked, sensing it was a personal question. 'Has it been there before?'

'Many times… Many times before and many times to come, if they will not mend their ways.'

'And other Falchions got rid of it,' a sombre Edgar stated.

The hermit gazed steadily at the sword lying on the ground beside him. A little powdery ash had blown across the blade. Edgar followed his eyes and brushed the ash away.

'You, Edgar Sabrehilt, of the line of Falchions,' he solemnly intoned, 'you are here because it *has* come. For every evil there is good, never forget that.'

'A great deal of evil and a tiny bit of good,' was his rueful response.

'We shall see… We shall see. Don't go destroying your eggs before they hatch, as the farmers' wives are so fond of saying.'

'But *you* said,' Lee piped up, 'that they brought it on themselves.'

'And so they did.'

'But if they had known…?'

'I doubt it would have made a whit of difference. Man has a knack of blindfolding himself when in the grip of avarice and lust. 'Tis a fraught situation, my friend…' He paused and dwelt inwardly, then spoke his thoughts aloud without meaning to. 'This could be the last winter. There may never be another spring.' He roused himself, realized what he had done and was angry with himself. 'That depends on *you,* Edgar Sabrehilt… Shieldbearer… Berry the Brave. I have every hope you shall succeed. *Every* hope.'

'At least someone has hope,' muttered a forlorn Edgar.

'Courage, man! *Believe* in yourself. You're not a Falchion for nothing.'

'And if we win, will you take over?' Lee excitedly asked.

'That would never do.'

'Why not? It would be perfect!'

'Halcyon days never last for long. Nothing is perfect in this fleeting world.'

'Why?'

'Because man, by nature, is an imperfect being. One imperfect leader after another,' he sighed. 'All we can hope for is one *less* imperfect.'

'Edgar?' Lee tentatively suggested.

'I would not burden his young shoulders with so heavy a load. He has enough to bear, as it is. You all have… Would you care for the task, Lee Chetwood?'

'Who, *me*? No way.'

The hermit grunted and jumped to his feet, clutching his thigh and grimacing. After a few minutes he sat down again, stretching his leg out before him.

'Old age,' he muttered. 'Brittle bones... Muscles like old rope…

'Now,' he declared brightly. 'There are a number of things I want to tell you - a series of instructions, scant warnings and an introduction or two. But before I do that, I want to carve some thoughts in your heads. So that you never forget. In your hour of need they will be your sustenance.'

The boys sat up straight and concentrated.

'The Aetz is here, but not for the first time. It has been gone an age, thanks to the last Sabrehilt. Another Sabrehilt is here to banish it yet again. That is so… That is *fact*… And you have emerged unscathed from the first of your skirmishes.

'Many will comment that Satan paces the echoing labyrinths of his anti-kingdom, but he has been doing that since time immemorial. You have nothing to worry about there. He was pacing them the day you were born, the first time you walked, the happiest days of your lives, today and tomorrow. What odds? He can't touch you if you don't want him to.

'But far more important than that, of *immense* importance, are the following truths. Drink you fill, inundate your souls, you cannot go wrong if you do so.

'Firstly, the Lord loves us and will always give us what we need, every last one of us without exception; whether we ask or not, whether we're aware of what to *ask* or not! What you require will be provided at the exact moment you require it. Remember Spike and the boat, the tree and the ring… What is there to be anxious about? You don't fall asleep worrying whether the sun will rise in the morning, you take it for granted. Just as you don't have to concentrate on making your heart beat. You are safe in God's hands.

'Secondly... What causes offence today will the the first crucial step in changing the events of tomorrow. A setback is never a setback seen in this, its proper perspective. The scarecrows were a horrible bunch, but out of their midst strode a friend who showed you how to use the ring.'

'Was it put there by the last Sabrehilt?' Edgar suddenly asked, trembling with excitement.

'No. That came by another route. You are the first to hold it in a very long time. But you will leave everything for the next, come what may...

'Keep gazing into the light. Ignore the darkness besetting you. It will fade.

'And lastly... One thing you must be sure about. Never doubt it... No matter how far you fall, and you may fall very far, you're never out of the reach of God's hand. And, I swear it by all I hold sacred, he *will* pick you up... I always feared loneliness, strange as it may seem. But I faced my fear and embraced it and grew to love it. How? Because I realized you are never alone. Not ever. There is no such thing as loneliness. It is a myth.

'Read the presages is all I have to say.'

'The what?' Lee asked, screwing up his face.

'The signs, lad. The *signs!*'

'How do we know we'll be able to read them?' Edgar timidly asked him.

'Open your eyes! They are there for you to see and no one else. All you have to do is look for them. Be vigilant, that's all that is required.'

'Yes...'

'Now, then... Has all that sunk into your thick skulls?'

The three of them nodded, Lee muttering under his breath something about his own thick skull before desisting.

'Good. Time for more material concerns...

'I have already avowed that I cannot go with you. That is so. But I did not say that no one or nothing can assist you.'

'Well, I'm glad to hear it... *Mighty* glad,' Lee quipped, nodding all round and smiling broadly.

The hermit cast him a disparaging glance but went on without commenting.

'How great or small that aid shall be, I cannot tell. And no, they won't take your place for you. They may offer advice – here Lee looked up to heaven – or material assistance, but there are certain assets within your reach. One I can give you. The others you must find for yourselves.'

'Such as?'

'I'm coming to that. You have an uncanny knack of getting under people's skin, do you know that?' he aimed at Lee.

'That's my charm.'

Lee cocked an eye at Berry who covered his mouth and sniggered. Edgar smiled, repressing a chuckle.

'Is that what they term it?... Odd... I can think of other words to describe it.'

Edgar frowned at Lee before he sank deeper into trouble and roused the dormant temper of their host.

'You said there are others who will help us?' he mentioned in order to ease the tension.

'May.'

'*May*?... In other words, they might not *want* to!'

'There is that, though I doubt it. The nitty-gritty is whether they *can* help and how much.'

Berry was about to burst into tears. Was he to lose his dearest friends so soon after finding them? He couldn't bear it. He wanted to grab that sword of Edgar's and rush headlong into the tower. Better to die first than be left alone and friendless again.

'Who are these people?' Edgar persisted.

'In a moment, in a moment. Give me time to gather my thoughts. I *will* get round to everything.'

The hermit rummaged in a deep pocket. With a grunt of satisfaction he finally drew something out in his fist. Unfurling his fingers one by one, he showed them what it was. They all craned their necks and looked at what appeared to be a red, polished pebble covering half his palm. Veins of translucent amber dissected its surface.

'This will summon the Great Deer.'

'The great dear? Who's *she* when she's at home?' Lee foolishly interrupted.

It was too much for the hermit. He lost the hold of himself. 'Flippant imbecile! Cease this mockery before I cast you into oblivion!' His eyes smouldered. He really was livid.

All right. Keep your hair on, thought Lee to himself. Realizing he had very little of it in the first place, he was seized with a fit of the giggles. His shoulders shook. His eyes streamed. Red-faced, he looked as if he was about to explode. Another glare from the hermit had him clearing his throat and adopting a serious expression.

Edgar felt fear and tension prickling uncomfortably beneath his skin. This man could be dangerous when he wanted to be, he was sure of it. Anyone who had power to prevent the Aetz from entering his domain was a figure to be reckoned with, certainly not somebody to be mocked at to his face.

'Lee. He's trying to help us,' he said. 'If he doesn't, where will we be?'

'Sorry,' Lee directed at the hermit.

The old man smiled and nodded. 'He who has the courage to say sorry and mean it will go far… And now I'll tell you what the Great Deer are. I'm sure you've heard of them.'

They all shook their heads.

'The Great Elk, does that ring a bell?'

'Oh, *elk*. Yes, we've heard of *them*.'

'Do you mean to say…' Lee began with bulging eyes, enthralled at last. 'But they're all dead. Last I heard, that is,' he added for fear of insulting the hermit yet again

'That is why I am giving this stone to you.'

'When you said *summon* them, did you mean bring them back to *life*?'

'That is exactly what I mean… *Megalocerus hibernicus*…' He slowly roamed over the syllables sotto voce. 'The Great Irish Elk… These majestic creatures trod the earth many moons ago. They traversed this island in great herds and woe to any man, *any* man, who disturbed their peace. But, like all great things, they came to an end…' He sighed mournfully before explaining. 'The people became treacherous, you see. They lost the right to commune with such beasts.'

'They could attack the Aetz, couldn't they?' Berry said.

The hermit beamed at him, eyes widening. He nodded. 'You *are* a bright spark, Berry Blakelock.'

39. What the Hermit Had to Tell

'And what do we do with this stone to get the elks to come to us?'

Not only the hermit was pleased at the change coming over him. The boys were too. They had seen him at his worst, cowering timidly in the grate of the tower. They had delighted in his laughter when he'd forgotten himself. They had sadly watched self-doubt creeping back into his eyes and seizing his mind. But they were unaware what a battle he was waging inside. His physical handicaps were only a part of it. The treatment meted out to him because of them had dragged him down, eroding his self-confidence, even his self-love. Here was a boy who had learned to dislike himself, conditioned to do so by a cruel and heartless world. The villagers deserved the coming of the Aetz for what they had done to Berry alone.

'Boys, oh boys, Berry Blakelock, you know all the answers.'

'Only the questions, Lee,' he rejoined, laughing freely.

'Same difference.'

'No, Berry,' Edgar interjected. 'Lee's right. I can't count the number of times you have said the most sensible thing of all three of us.'

'I don't doubt it,' the hermit declared. 'Keep it up, my boy. Your companions need you. And to answer your question…' he said, handing Berry the pebble.

'For me-e?' he stuttered in awe.

'And why not?… Why shouldn't you keep it safe? Put it in your pocket.'

'*Ed's* pocket.'

'Yours *now*… So *that's* how it came about.'

'The less said the better,' Edgar remarked, pulling his crossed ankles closer to him and making sure the tails of his shirt hung low.

'I won't ask...'

Edgar nodded his appreciation.

'Now for what you must do with the stone,' the hermit resumed. 'You know that area of bog t'other side of Tower Hill?'

'Yes,' they all said, nodding together like schoolboys in a classroom.

'Stand at the edge of that bog and throw the stone into the very centre. Then stand well back to either side.'

'What will happen?' Lee asked.

'You shall see for yourselves soon enough.'

'And?'

'Don't anticipate.'

'But can't you tell us something good to keep our shirts up? Spirits, I mean *spirits!*' Despite the smirk there was a note of desperation in Lee's voice. 'Will the elks kill it?'

'I have no crystal ball to gaze into, but I doubt it.'

'So what use is the stone, then?'

'They *may* rid Garten of its presence, isn't that worth a try?'

'And if they don't?' Edgar asked.

'You said there were other things that could help us,' Berry reminded them.

'And you have brought me directly to them, my lad.'

He leaned over and fondly patted him on the head. Berry felt he could up and float away with euphoria. He fingered the stone in his pocket. 'Elk-summoner,' he breathed to himself and exhaled all his doubts and fears and complexes.

'The white witch will come to your aid,' the hermit explained.

'Wi-itch?' Lee asked. 'I don't like the sound of that.'

'*White* witch. Friendly and good, on your side,' he spelt out. 'I believe you have seen her already.'

All three heads shot up.

'Yes, indeed.'

'When?' Edgar croaked.

'On your way here. You *did* catch sight of a beautiful swan, did you not?'

'Swans,' Lee emphasised.

'*Swans?*'

'Aye, two of them.'

'Two swans,' the hermit muttered to himself with a puzzled expression. 'How odd. Can there be two white witches…?…'

Edgar felt doubt and insecurity descending like a heavy, dark cloud. It was cold inside, and damp. Does he know as much as he thinks he knows?… He *must* know what he's talking about.

'What can the witch do for us?' he asked.

'White witch. Never witch. Don't forget the white. Isn't happy being addressed any other way.'

'White witch, then.'

'She's an ally. What more could you ask for?'

'And how do we contact her?'

'You don't. She'll appear on the scene when she's needed. She's here already for that purpose. *She* will contact *you* at the opportune time.

'But there are more pressing concerns than that. Three boys with one sword among them cannot do battle against a hebdomad.'

'Are we *all* going to have swords?!' Lee asked excitedly, forgetting all about the danger involved. 'I've always wanted a sword of my own. Edgar used to make me green with envy showing off with his.'

'There is a spear and a shield.'

'Where?! Have you got them *here*?'

He shook his head. 'Your task is to seek them.'

Lee groaned and let his shoulders droop.

'What do they say about faint hearts?' the hermit asked with a smile.

'Mmm… Where do we find them, then?'

'Among the dead.'

'Is that a riddle or something?'

'Nothing of the kind.'

'Among the dead?'

'You know the cairn?'

'Cairn? What's a cairn?'

'The burial mound.'

'On Prickleback's land?'

'There.'

'And how are we supposed to get in? It'd take *years* to dig.'

'Knock.'

'*Knock*?… And I suppose the folk inside will answer, will they?'

'They might.'

39. What the Hermit Had to Tell

Lee's expression said it all. Who could be expected to believe such rubbish?

'Anything else?' he asked, his tone dripping sarcasm.

The hermit glanced momentarily at Berry before responding.

'Something extremely important, I cannot stress this enough. The Salmail of the great Finn MacCumhal... It has many magical properties. Prithee, if all else fails, discover its whereabouts... It may cure even *this* brave fellow,' he directed at Berry.

'Is it to be found in the mound as well?' Edgar asked.

'No. I cannot put you right there. All I know is that it is secreted by the four-faced liar.'

'I've heard of two-faced, but *four-faced*? What's *that* supposed to mean?'

'Think and think again. I cannot help you more. But it is vital you discover it... You are familiar with the tale of how the Druid named Finegas caught the Salmon of Knowledge and set Finn to cook it, bidding him not to taste its flesh, and how he burnt his thumb turning it on the spit and sucked it. The flesh of the salmon imparted to him all the knowledge of the ages and he had the scales magically wrought into a coat of mail.'

The three began mumbling among themselves, retelling the tale, correcting one another, enlightening Berry.

'Whist. It grows late. You must be gone from here and home before dark.'

'Won't I have time to see my folks?'

'If you make haste. I shall finish now. There is little else to tell but told it must be. Then I have done my duty.'

They sat and listened, musing on the sheer insanity of turning their backs on such a place. They sighed to themselves for they knew it was impossible. Their wish would not be granted. Peace seemed the most important thing on earth, and yet, the most elusive.

A twinkle came into the hermit's eyes and a faint hint of mischief.

'One final thing and I'm done... There is somebody else you must meet. That person will introduce... em... themself.'

Edgar looked up. The hermit was definitely smiling, enjoying some private joke. 'Them-*self*?'

'Aye,' he jovially replied, rubbing his hands together. 'That person will assist you greatly... Because that person has arguably the greatest asset of all...'

He smiled knowingly, obviously seeing that person in his mind's eye. With a grunt the hermit struggled to his feet and gave a slight jump to settle his tunic.

'And now, my young soldiers, I must bid you depart.'

They reluctantly got to their feet. Spike struggled out of sleep and barked. Edgar bent down to pat him on the head and retrieve his sword.

'Oh! Before I forget... Beware the fool moon.'

'The full moon?'

'The *fool* moon...'

'The man in the moon's a fool,' muttered Lee with a grimace.

'It alters shadows and hides danger. Keep that constantly in mind...

'I bid you farewell, honoured guests. I bless your endeavours.'

He shook all their hands, Edgar's last, looking deep into his eyes. He mimed a knock and shaped the word with his lips.

'I am afraid you cannot take my boat this time. Follow the river back to the one stream flowing into it and follow that. It will take you near the church in Garten. Nothing shall hinder you this time. That battle is over. We shall not meet again this side of the divide.'

'You mean we'll never see you again?'

'There's a tree to remember me by,' he answered elliptically. 'God go with you, my children.'

They walked away with heavy hearts, looking up at the trees, inhaling the scents one last time. Soon they would step into a very different world. Too soon. Glancing back they saw a lone figure by a dead fire, in a clearing next his cave, raise his arm and wave.

'Gird your loins!' he shouted after them.

His voice seemed to echo far away – even sounds were reluctant to leave this place. They waved back at him.

By the time they'd reached the stream he was well out of sight. What did he mean we'll never see him again, they all asked themselves in the silence of their hearts. No one dared give answer.

— 40. The Vault —

'Gird your loins,' Lee repeated with a chuckle as they retraced their steps. 'I think he was laughing at you, Ed.'

'Maybe he was. He did see the funny side of things.'

'Do you think?' commented his friend with a doubtful shrug.

Early afternoon had seeped all the colour from the beautiful wood. The rich bouquet of scents was fading fast. Irritation pricked Lee at having to go. He beheaded a few wild flowers with the toe of his boot.

'We've as much chance as an icicle in hell!' he erupted.

He put into words what all of them were feeling. A huge weight hung over their heads, a pendulum strung on a cobweb and ready to drop.

'Fool moon, what the hell was he on about? *We're* the fools, leave the moon alone...

'Can you believe half the things he told us? White witches and spears and shields under cairns. I can imagine how happy Prickleback will be to see us traipsing across his land with picks and shovels. Oh, hullo, Reverend. You mean *these*? Oh, we're only going to dig up that mound of yours, you know. You don't mind, do you?...

'And that mail thing. As for the stone he gave to Berry, how do we know it'll do anything, let alone call up them elks.'

'We won't till we chuck it in.' said Edgar, trying to cool his ardour.

'Not so sure I trust elks... Ever notice how they all keep telling us what to do but never raise a finger to help? And if they know so much, why the *hell* didn't they tell us long ago what to expect?'

'Because they knew we'd have got out when the going was good.'

'Too bloody right!... Kept us here to do their dirty work for them, the cowards. I know what he meant by us not seeing him again. He's packed his bags and scarpered, so he has. And, sure as sure can be, Themself will pack us off somewhere else till there's no one left and the Aetz has our guts for garters...

'Od's-bodikins!' Lee muttered to himself, mimicking the hermit's accent. 'I'll od's-bodikins *him!*'

Both Edgar and Berry glanced at one another and began to chuckle while Lee boxed himself in with his own gloomy thoughts.

It was with surprise that they glanced up and found themselves close to the church. They had stepped from Spring into Winter. Goose-pimples erupted on Edgar's thighs and legs. They could just make out the crenellations of the bishop's palace in the distance. There was nobody about, not a living soul.

40. The Vault

They dropped to the ground and stealthily skirted the wall. The two guards were there. They heard one of them spit. Edgar put his mouth close to Lee's ear.

'I have an idea. This way. Pass it on to Berry.'

Edgar worked a stone loose from the wall and threw it over.

'What was that?' they heard. There was a ring of panic in the voice.

Edgar inhaled and let out a moan increasing to a snarl.

'Did ye 'ear that?!'

He lobbed a stone onto the roof and it clattered down the slates.

'Prickleback or no Prickleback, I'm out o' 'ere. He said nowt 'bout fightin' the divil with bare 'ands.'

Stamping feet were heard, then, 'Wait for me!'

Gates rattled angrily.

'Bloody cowards!'

It was the miller's voice.

Edgar clambered over the wall and ran through the tussocks between the tombstones. Spike ran after him, barking furiously.

'They thought it was Old Nick,' he explained over his shoulder as he ran.

Both boys examined the stump he pointed at and nodded with raised eyebrows. They were impressed.

Their friend was over the railings and down the steps as fast as his legs could carry him.

'Dad! It's *me!*'

'Ed, my boy! God ha' mercy on us!'

The miller clutched his son through the gates. Moll took one of Edgar's hands and pressed it to her lips, moistening it with her tears.

Spike whined miserably, unable to poke his head through the railings. He barked at the sound of the miller's voice and wagged his tail. Lee and Berry stayed aloft, respecting their privacy. It brought a terrible ache to Lee's heart and tears to his eyes to hear them. He turned away and sniffed. Why? Why can't it be like that for me?

'Ed! Where are your breeches, in God's name?!'

'It doesn't matter, Mam,' he gently chided. 'I had to give them to Berry. He lost his.'

'And couldn't this Berry have done without for being so foolish?'

'Ma-am… Shush.'

'You have to admit you do look odd, son, with no breeches to your name,' quipped his father.

Edgar smiled, almost overcome at hearing his voice again. In vain he rattled the gates. The heavy chain and huge padlock had him clicking his tongue with dismay.

'Are you all on your own?' asked his anxious mother.

'No, Mam. I've got Lee and Berry with me. They're up there,' he threw over his shoulder.

'Well, let's have a gawk at them,' barked his father.

Edgar called for them to appear.

'Hullo,' said Lee, waving down at them through the railings.

Berry nodded and waved sheepishly.

'Glory be to God, why it's the Blakelock chappy! Is it a ghost I'm seeing?'

'Mam!… His folks had to hide him in the tower, that's where we found him.'

'The poor cratur.'

She muttered something inaudible to her husband who nodded in silence. Berry flushed, certain they were commenting on his disability. Oh, if only the salmail would cure him…

'Is he looking after you, sonny?' she shouted up, and when he nodded with a smile said, "Tis no wonder if he's given you his breeches.'

'I told him not to!'

'What harm is it? Sure, hasn't he a fine pair o' legs?… Is he all right?' she asked Edgar in a loud whisper, eyes more probing and eloquent than her words.

'The best of us and the bravest,' he stated with decision.

'I'm glad of it. To think of him all alone in that terrible place. It's a mercy he's in his right mind.'

'And he has our boy to thank for it,' responded the miller, pride overspreading his features.

'Me *and* Lee.'

'I knew that ragamuffin'd come to good despite the hard knocking he's had. Pity I can't say as much about his father.'

'Shush, Dad. He'll hear you.'

'He knows in his heart I'm right.'

'Has anyone else been here?' he asked to rapidly veer off the subject.

'Aye,' growled his father before turning and spitting into the corner. 'That schoolmaster o' yourn were here. A pest on him and all like him.'

'Hornswoggle?'

'Aye, that's him… Pius the weathercock. Sins o' the flesh,' he muttered to himself. 'Flesh?! Sin through and through.'

Edgar frowned, not understanding fully.

'Came slithering round here like a snake… Asking if we needed anything. As if we couldn't see through him like water. A pity they don't burn *him* at the stake, God knows he deserves it. But his kind never get punished, do they?…'

'How did he get past the guards?'

'Paid them, the sly schemer. Bribes, that's all he knows. Be off, I ordered him. Be off, foul cur of hell. Get back where you belong and never let me set eyes on you again… Slunk away, he did, tail between his legs. Tarring and feathering's too good for him.'

He spat again. Moll shook her head at Edgar behind his back.

'Dad… Do you think the squire would help us?' Edgar asked, wondering if he could possibly be the Themself mystifying them all.

'*That* puffed up ninny?' was his father's response with a curl of his lip. He laughed as he thought of it. 'If pigs could fly… That type are all the same. Thieves who stole the land of their betters. All them notions… He goes outside to the closet like the rest of us, don't he? What comes out of him is no different…'

'No, but a lot more of it,' Edgar joked.

'Aye,' his father responded with a grin, 'a lot more… Don't look to him for help, lad. You'd be better off asking his ancestors in the leaden boxes here,' he said, jerking a thumb at the coffins behind him. 'Though his lady wife's a good 'un. Has a kind heart, so she does, but it's a fair-sized cross to carry being married to that clown... Don't trouble yourself about him, son. He'd set the dogs on you.'

'Has Prickleback been round?'

'Nay. But I can feel him lurking in the background as always. If he ain't in the ploy of the devil, nobody is. Keep well away from him.'

'I will. I just wish I could get you out of here!' he shouted, gripping the gates with his fists and shaking them. One of the copper leaves scratched the back of his hand and drew blood. He licked and massaged it.

'Never you mind about us, son. We're all right here, ain't we, Moll?'

'Yes... We are.' She didn't sound too convinced about it.

'What am I thinking of?!' Edgar exclaimed, slapping the palm of his hand down on his brow. 'The *sword!*'

He placed the blade against the metal chain and tried to cut through it. Not even a scratch did he make. He hacked at the padlock to no avail. Sparks flew but it held fast. With a groan he hung his head. For some reason it wasn't meant to be.

'Now, don't you be wearing yourself down, Ed,' admonished his father.

'But why doesn't it *work*?' he asked through gritted teeth. 'It's *supposed* to work.'

'Away home with you, son. Before it gets dark. Fill your bellies and have a good night's rest. God knows, you need it. Your eyes have sunk into the back of your head.'

Edgar nodded without looking up. His dad tousled his hair for him.

'Come here,' he said, pulling him forward and hugging him through the wrought-iron gates.

After hugging his mam, who sniffed and shed a tear, he climbed back up the stairs, scaled the railings and started for home with his pals, cursing their ill-fortune. I hate this place, was what he shouted in his head. I hate this place so *much!*

With weary, aching limbs they stumbled through the door. It did feel good to be home. A single light had shone out across the wasteland and puzzled them until Spike's barking filled the room.

'What are you *doing here?!*' Edgar roared at the top of his voice, incandescent with rage.

There, lounging in his grandpa's armchair as if he owned the place, was Racker Booth. A puff of smoke escaped his smirking lips but he never budged an inch. Slowly, provokingly, he turned his head and spat into the fire.

'Get *out,* I said!' Edgar screamed, red in the face.

Rack ignored the kid, puffing away, scornful eyes running up and down his bare legs.

'Get out or I'll *kill you!*'

'Will ye now, little maneen?' he sneered, spitting once again to drive home his point.

'And that's my *grandpa's pipe!*'

He slapped it from Racker's mouth. It flew from between his lips and struck the grate. Racked leapt to his feet, knocking over the mug of cider by his side. He massaged his cheek, red as a beetroot. He raised a fist to strike the boy but Edgar swung back his sword.

'I said I'd kill you,' he breathed, menace in every taut line of his body.

Rack lowered his arm.

'Nothin' but a squirt in a skirt,' he scoffed. 'Ye have to go back to the tower, Missy,' he jeered, 'an' none who venture there ever return. *Then* I'll be back...'

'You'll never set foot in this place again, so help me God.'

'*Will* he help ye?... I wonder about that... I wonder...'

'I said get *out!*'

Booth slowly swaggered past him, smiling to himself to prove he wasn't frightened. Spike growled and went for his leg. He kicked him in the mouth and he rolled over with a vicious snarl–cum-yelp. Rack almost took the door off its hinges before striding across the mill yard. Spike ran to the threshold but never made after him.

Edgar knelt down in the grate and picked up his grandpa's pipe. Lovingly, he turned it over in his hands.

'It's cracked,' he sobbed in dismay.

He fought the rising tears but his energies were spent. A whimper trawled upwards and exploded as a wail. Tears coursed down his cheeks. He shook with grief. Lee ran to him, knelt down by his side and put his arms around him.

'No one would have blamed you if you *had* killed him,' he muttered, hugging him tight.

'I'm never going to be able to do this, Lee. *Never!*'

'Yes, you will. When all hope is lost, we have no choice but to do it ourselves. We're being forced to do it, Ed. It's our destiny.'

He remained there with Edgar in his arms, sobbing and sniffling, wracked by despair. Fear was a tiny larva feeding off his courage, piecemeal; bite by bite, morsel by morsel, the "devilish miner" his grandpa had spoken of.

Berry went to the door and shut out the night. In silence he twirled Spike's ears with his fingers, feeling an intruder spying on the greatest friends in the world.

— PART III —

RITES OF PASSAGE

— 41. Beginning of the End —

A hush lay over Garten. In less than twenty-four hours, it resembled a ghost town. The fool moon guttered, casting monstrous, flailing shadows in all directions. Night didn't settle on the village. It engulfed it, plunging it into unfathomable darkness. Clouds dispersed and an advancing line of frost resembled a marching army. An exaggerated, ominous silence embalmed everything like a shroud. Garten was a strange place that night, an alien land ruled by terror. No lamps shone through the windows. No wisps of smoke belched from the chimneys. Not a single soul was abroad.

Drapes were drawn and shutters barred. Doors were locked and bolted. People cowered in their homes, banishing all thoughts of the outdoors from their minds. Children hid beneath their beds or buried themselves under the blankets. Babies were distracted by all means possible. Noise had to be stifled at all costs. They started at the slightest sound outside, straining their ears in terror. Let tragedy befall anyone but us, that was their prayer.

A lone wolf howled, a plangent note expanding to fill the void, ringing in every ear. More joined in, a chorus to set their teeth on edge. They had cornered themselves in their own homes, that's what they had done! They should have fled the peninsula when they'd had the chance. What did possessions and property count for now?

Legions of scarecrows strode purposely across the fields, breaking gaps in the hedges. Their silhouettes jerked forward between the trees of the woods. All were approaching the wide-awake, prick-eared village. They lumbered down the main road over the bridge, descended the knoll behind the inn and waded across rivers and ponds. It was an invasion never to be forgotten. Factions broke away to investigate every laneway and homestead, every barn and stable. An empty face pressed against every door and window and listened. And heard. And set up a low moan, waxing louder and louder, more deafening, more intimidating than the howl of the wolves.

Silence fell like an axe onto velvet. The people inside wanted to scream, but their throats constricted. Sweating and trembling, they were glued to their seats, paralysed in their beds. Muffled sounds could be heard as their enemies brushed against the walls of their dwelling-places. The creaking and groaning of wooden frames turned their bowels to water.

Children and babies began to whimper and cry. The sickening crack of splitting wood silenced them all.

Vengeance took a strangely inhuman form.

Tender shoots of ivy fingered their way between slits in the doors and the window-frames. Delicate tendrils gripped the wood and thickened. Jambs bent and buckled, panes cracked, screws loosened and hinges gave. Sashes rose by unseen hands. Emasculated fathers and fainting mothers leaned against walls and mantels while the ivy crept across the floor and twined round their offspring, dragging them screaming and howling away. Back they slithered with their prey, through woods and hedges and fields to the foot of the tower. A cacophany rose from the gargoyles as the unconscious innocents were drawn into the fortress, never to see daylight again.

— 42. Contrasts —

Day no longer chased night into corners and hunted it down. Light had joined forces with the darkness. A numb silence lay over everything like a pall of ash. Death and bloodshed had come home to roost, from its hiding-place at the base of the cliffs. Every family in Garten was in mourning. Their wailing rose to the padlocked gates of heaven.

Farmer Buckrake stared at his untasted breakfast. He had no appetite for food.

'Wha-at? Not hungry?'

'How could I be, Grace?... I saw the remains of my boat swept by this morning. I sent them to their deaths, Grace... May God forgive me.'

'You did all you could, no one can ask more than that. You don't even know for certain if they *be* dead. Get a spoonful of that porridge inside you and you'll feel a lot better.'

He put the spoon to his lips and retched. With a mournful sigh he replaced it in the bowl.

'Heaven help us... Who will fight for us now? Who is brave and foolish enough to take up a lost cause? We're *done for!*'

Turlough Grindlewick listened to the faint snoring in the pitch blackness.

'Gladys, lass, wake up.'

He whispered into the gloom, reluctant to light the lamp next to him or raise his voice. Something had happened last night, something frightful. Whoever they were, they had been in the inn. He'd heard them upstairs, turning over the tables and chairs, smashing the tumblers and bottles. For all he knew, they were still there. Waiting for two fools to emerge from the cellar.

'Glad, how can you sleep so?'

He stretched out a hand, found her soft shoulder and shook it. She snorted and came to.

'Is that *you*, Grindle?'

'Shush… Who else, lass?'

'For a moment I thought they'd got in. Are they gone?'

'Can't tell. There's no sound above but that could be a trap. Something brushed against the door last night. They know we're in here.'

'Any sound from the childer?'

She asked, not out of maternal concern but in another frame of mind altogether: if they were alive it would be safe to leave their refuge.

'Not a peep.'

'We'll wait a little longer before stirring.'

'We will.'

Isolda Trefoil slammed the flat of her hand onto his pillow and he rose in the bed what-whatting.

'All night it was a ghost town,' she informed him. 'Till the shrieking started. Now it resembles a commune of banshees.'

'What does?'

'The *village!*'

'What *happened* in the village, woman?'

'Something perfectly horrid.'

'Humph,' he muttered before lying down again. 'Fortunately we live out here. It's no concern of ours.'

Racker Booth lay stiff in his bed. If it weren't for the shallow breaths flaring his nostrils he might have been dead. He'd met the ivy on his way home from the mill. It had tickled his ankle as he'd stood in the road. He'd watched diminutive leaves on a supple stalk curl round his boot and climb his leg. Kicking wildly, he'd freed himself and fled across a field, throwing himself down when strange silhouettes stalked through the grass ahead of him. They resembled men, with heads and limbs, but walked so oddly, lurching forward in fits and starts. He'd had to stuff a fist into his mouth to avoid screaming at the dreadful moans coming from them - the sound of a deaf mute, thickened and cavernous and terrifying.

All night he had waited for them. All blessed night. That tongueless, lipless moaning, it still rang in his ears... Why don't they come?... What's *stoppin'* them?... Stale sweat filled his nostrils while he listened to the screaming swell and swell and swell that morning. Screams of horror. Screams of fear. Screams of the broken-hearted. They too died down and he lay on in the silence, awaiting the inevitable.

But nothing happened. No one came.

A sob of relief escaped him. He breathed more easily.

He smiled.

'Rack, old boy, yev done it again. Yer a cat with nine lives.'

Prickleback had heard nothing and fallen asleep making plans. Such plans...

Miller Falchion woke with Moll in his arms. They had both seen the scarecrows pass the railings but never look down. They had heard the cries of the unwary guards who had slunk back after Edgar and the boys had gone home. Then dawn had brought the village chorus to further alarm them. He kept his thoughts to himself. He was fearful of driving her out of her wits.

What in God's name had happened to Ed? Could he possibly be still alive?

The smiling face of Racker Booth broke in on his thoughts.

'Rack. Rack! You're alive! How's my *boy?*'

'Dead, I 'ope,' he sneered maliciously.

Moll broke down and he clutched her to himself.

'Go to the devil!' he growled. 'If I ever get out of here…'

'That, ye never will. Yer finished, Falchion. You and yers. An' just to get things straight… Ye'll be with the divil long before I will, remember that, Falchion. When that son o' yourn is done away with I'll garrotte the pair o' yis. That's a promise, mind…

'Who do ye think'll be the next miller o' Garten, eh?' he chuckled as he walked away.

Oaf's head poked out, tentative as a tortoise, warily poised to dart back in again at the slightest hint of danger. He breathed a sigh of relief, returned to the huddle of his brothers and sisters and nestled back down among them. He hadn't even bothered to shuffle them down the steps to the cellar, he'd known better this time. Bundling them instead into the stable, all he could think of was his recent success with the burning straw. He'd heaped a mound of it against the half-door and gathered them about him in the far corner.

They had buried their heads in his jerkin when the scarecrow's head had appeared at the door. He himself couldn't take his eyes off it. Twiggy fingers had gripped the top of the door and wrenched it off its hinges. The creature had stood there moaning while it listened for the approaching ivy. Oaf had flung the oil lamp onto the pile of straw. The glass had shattered and a flame had reared up to the limestone lintel. With a loud 'whumph' the scarecrow was alight. To Oaf's horror it had just stood there, neither shrieking nor thrashing about. The face and body were gone in seconds. The branches tumbled to the ground with the smouldering rags on top of them. Blackening, the straw had begun to curl. Singed tendrils of ivy had jerked back from the heat and retreated. The tips of charred straw had glowed in the dark and clinked as they were extinguished. All that remained was the scorched, blackened stone at the door.

Like a mother hen, he'd clutched his brood beneath his arms and lulled them back to sleep.

†

— 43. Out of the Ordinary —

The boys had heard nothing, seen nothing and slept through it all. They woke, in their crumpled clothes, in the chairs round the fireplace. Spike was sprawled on the rug at their feet. He whimpered and snarled and paddled in his sleep.

Edgar struggled from his seat, stretched, emitted a loud, drawling yawn and stumbled through the doorway. Outside, he stuck his head into the trough and, spluttering loudly, shook the cold water from his hair. Lee and Berry followed suit. Wide-awake, they squinted and peered into the sky.

'We'll have something to eat and head off to Prickleback's. The sooner we get there, the better.'

'Here we go again,' Lee murmured while stretching. 'I could do with another eight hours.'

Berry chuckled fluidly. He wanted to leap and skip and do a somersault, though anchored to the ground by his leaden foot. His spirits were so buoyant that they bubbled to the surface and made him giddy. This was the adventure of a lifetime. No longer was he the pathetic child who'd cowered in the shadows of the tower. He felt he could march straight down into that village and knock the block off any sneering idiot who dared to mock him. He'd show them what Cripple and Peg Leg could do. The names of those bullies were ingrained in his psyche. They weren't strong or tough. They only picked on those who couldn't fight back, were more handicapped inside than he had ever been.

They approached Prickleback's land from the West, avoiding the village. They turned often as they went, walking backwards, on the lookout constantly. A party of crows flew overhead and descended noisily into a clump of trees. They didn't give the impression that they were spies. Nothing out of the ordinary took place.

'You don't think they might have gone away?' Lee ventured.

'What, the Aetz as well?' Edgar scoffed. 'The hermit said nothing about them disappearing overnight.'

'What the hell does *he* know?' Lee angrily murmured.

It was horrible having his hopes constantly dashed to pieces. It made him so irritable. Isn't there anything good in this life, he asked himself. If there is, when am *I* going to see it?

'There it is,' Edgar pronounced, pointing at the burial mound.

They came to a halt and gazed at a grass-covered knuckle of land in the middle of an outlying field. Two massive stones stood solidly before it, portals to the Kingdom of the Dead. Ancient trees grew atop the mound, leaning this way and that, unable to gain a proper purchase.

They just stood there, the wind stirring their hair. There was an aura about the place, a solemnity echoed by the purple clouds tinged with ochre overhead. The cairn might hold a spear and a shield but what else was in there?... They swallowed the lumps in their throats and stole forward, keeping the mound between them and the castle.

In venerable silence they passed between the granite monoliths, remnants of the great circle once guarding the precints of the tomb. The wind died. A funereal quiet settled on the place. Were those interred within listening?...

'They sent us round the living,' Lee whispered, 'now they're sending us to the dead. God help us.'

Nobody reacted. They continued forward, their gaze fixed on the huge stone right ahead, carved with scrolls and circles, diamonds and zigzags and ripples. This lay before the entrance and blocked their way. They stood in front of it, eyes wandering over the geometrical patterns. Was there a meaning to them? Were they warnings to keep away?

Edgar went round it, shouting back at them, 'There's a sort of door the other side and an opening above it.'

'Can you fit through it?' asked Lee.

'No. Not a chance.'

Lee and Berry came round and all three of them gazed at the doorway, a flat slab of stone positioned between two granite lintels. They placed their shoulders against it, straining with the effort.

'Not an inch,' Edgar gasped. He stood, arms hanging, shaking his head. 'It's hopeless. We'll never get in.'

'No point hanging round here, then, is there?' Lee chimed, making to leave.

'But we need the weapons!' exclaimed Edgar, frustrated at Lee's short-sightedness. 'Don't you *see*? We need all the help we can *get!*'

'You haven't said how we're going to get *in* yet.'

'Let me think for a minute, would you?'

Lee raised his eyes to heaven, flexing his knees impatiently. In his mind, Edgar referred back to their time with the hermit. He remembered him miming and repeating one word emphatically.

'Of course!' He slapped his hand over his pocket and groaned. 'Oh, no…'

'What?'

'Oh, *no*… I've lost it!'

Berry smiled. Wordlessly he held out the ring to him.

'Thank God,' Edgar exhaled with relief, taking it from him. 'Knock!' he explained. 'He said to knock and it would open, remember?'

They watched intently while Edgar held the ring to the door. The silver hand came to life immediately, the delicate fingers fusing with the stone. Edgar gripped the ring and leaned back with all his weight.

'It's no use!' he wailed.

'Aren't you forgetting something?' Lee asked in a sarcastic voice. 'Knock…' he intoned.

Edgar clicked his tongue. He took the ring again and rapped it against the stone door. Echoes could be heard deep inside, reaching across the chasms of time. They died away and nothing happened.

'No one home,' joked Lee.

Berry sniggered. Edgar didn't seem to hear. With a frown of annoyance he knocked again, harder and louder this time. Once more the echoes faded to nothingness. He stamped his foot with annoyance. He was about to rap one final time when there was a sudden sharp grating of stone on stone. The door jerked open a fraction. They stood there, too afraid to move – for fear something was peering out at them. The stone slab jerked once more and opened fully. A cautious Spike stretched forward and sniffed. They stood on the threshold of a long narrow passageway lined by tall, tapering stones. It continued past two heavier ones leaning towards one another and was lost in the gloom.

'We should have brought candles,' Edgar whispered.

He placed one foot inside. As soon as he did so, a ray of amber light seemed to follow him, coming through the opening above the door. It preceded him step by step. A slight slope led them to the leaning stones and they squeezed on through. The second part of the passage continued ahead with a noticeable incline. Here and there, scrolls were carved on the stones they passed. They imagined they could hear the sharp tap-tap of stone on stone, the heavy breathing echoing off the roof, the scraping of leather on grit. Where was this passage taking them, into the past or the future?

They spilled out into a circular, domed chamber bathed in golden light. The very stones themselves seemed to be glowing from within. Slabs of granite overlapped in decreasing circles overhead till topped by a capstone. This was a work of reverence and love. Whoever was laid here to rest must have been very, very important.

A sharp intake of breath escaped all three of them. With awe and respect they retreated a step. A shallow basin stone lay at their feet. On it was lying the occupant of the chamber. For some time they stood there, looking down at the remains, transported and engrossed. Uneasiness crept over them. They felt they were intruding, trespassing on the dead when they had no right to. But they had been sent. They were expected.

A tall skeleton lay stretched on the stone before them. No flesh remained but long yellow hair still covered the skull and reached to his shoulders, held in place by a thin band of gold round his temples. About his neck hung a golden torc, beaten as thin as air. Tapering skeletal fingers were wrapped round the shaft of a long spear laid by his side. A circular shield of gold and silver inlay was placed over his midriff and solid gold bracelets encircled his wrists and ankles.

Edgar knelt down, Lee and Berry did too.

'He must have been a great man when he was alive,' Edgar whispered.

'I bet he was afraid of no one,' Berry concluded.

'I wish we had someone like that on our side,' ruminated a forlorn Edgar aloud.

'Do you think it's right to take the spear and the shield?' Lee faltered. 'It seems disrespectful to me.'

'Not if it's meant to be,' Berry propounded with conviction.

'Berry's right,' Edgar said.

'*You'd* better take them,' Lee suggested.

Edgar stretched out his hand towards the shaft of the spear. Gently, with profound reverence, he made to unfurl the bony digits.

With cries of alarm they sprawled on the ground while Spike raced down the passageway, barking hysterically.

A sonorous, sibillating whisper echoed round the chamber.

'Who dares disturb the peace of the Dead?'

'If you p-please...' Edgar stuttered, ' the *hermit* sent us!'

'Who dares disturb the *peace of the Dead*?'

The voice had grown in volume and menace.

'He's *Sabrehilt*!' Berry bellowed.

'Sabrehilt?...' The voice returned to normal. 'Long have I expected thee.'

'You...You *know* me?'

'The creature has returned...'

'Yes. The Aetz is back and we need your help!' Lee shouted in desperation.

'My deeds were accomplished long ago, little one.'

'Will you lend us your spear and your shield? We'll bring them back when we're finished with them, honest we will.'

Lee fell instantly silent, realizing they might never be able to keep such a promise. In an instant, he forgot what the future might hold. He smiled and panted in awe as he watched the fingers loosen their grip. Edgar leaned forward.

'No... Let the little one take them for himself.'

Lee gaped in wonder. Never in his life had an adult shown him the respect he deserved. With trembling hands he picked up the spear. It was heavy, so heavy. Gingerly he laid it across his knees and stretched out for the shield. Gently he slipped the loop along the length of the forearm and disengaged it.

'Fight well, little one, and bravely too.'

'I wi-ill. I promise.'

'Fare thee well.'

The words echoed hollowly and faded as a breathy whisper on the air.

'Farewell to you too. And thank you.'

He took up the spear and the shield and got to his feet. They bowed, all three of them, and set off down the passageway.

After closing the door, they scrambled past the entrance stone and orthostats before anyone broke the silence. Lee clutched the shield to his chest and held the spear horizontally with difficulty.

'I don't know if I'll be able to do much good with this. It weighs a ton.'

'He wouldn't have given it to you if he'd known you wouldn't be able to use it.'

'That's right, Ed,' he replied, grinning and aiming the spear more easily. 'All in the mind, eh?… You've got your sword. I've got these. And Berry will soon have his salmail.'

'If we ever find out where it is.'

'We'll find out when we need to.'

Lee felt optimistic now that he was armed. Shieldbearer… It *did* have a certain ring to it… He saw himself as a mighty warrior, testing the weight of the spear, holding the shield next his chest. He was delighted with himself.

Edgar, on the other hand, was feeling dejected.

'There's still so much to find out and do.'

'Cheer up, Ed, me lad. We'll get there,' he said, aiming the spear, drawing it back to hurl it. 'Hey! Wait for *me*, you two!!'

'Well, hurry up, then, and stop lagging behind.'

'Where's the respect due to Shieldbearer?'

'You'll get it when you've earned it.'

Edgar sniggered. Berry did too. Lee wasn't the slightest bit amused. Then, realizing the honour that had been bestowed on him, he chuckled and ran after them. They could rag him as much as they wanted to, for now he was somebody to be reckoned with.

— 44. Night-Watch —

While they lay fast asleep, sword and ring, spear and shield well within reach, dust was falling on Garten. It fell to earth and rose into the sky. The tension in the air fell with the dust, growing heavier and heavier. The moon became a red disc casting no shadows. And through the dust crawled the ivy. Yet Lee's romantic dreams didn't forsake him. He was a great knight doing battle with evil. He smiled into his pillow and muttered brave words in his sleep.

Meanwhile, the villagers cowered in their homes, behind boarded-up windows and doors. They knew the scarecrows would be back and, with them, the ivy. But where else had they to betake themselves? Some said that the ghosts of the shipwrecked dead were guarding the road out of Garten. They didn't dare face them.

One young mother had beaten herself senseless against the leg of her kitchen table, laid low by a grief so immense that it unhinged her. Her baby had gone missing during the day. Calling and weeping, she had hurried to her neighbours and searched the adjacent fields, stumbling home only when dusk was falling. Her husband was still out there, probably never to return. All she wished for was that they would come and put her out of her misery. She never heard the nails loosening in the boards and dropping to the floor, deaf to everything but the sounds of her missing baby. Her senseless body was dragged through the door into the night, limp arms stretched out above her head.

A slatternly crone crouched by the corner of her window, whiskers twitching on her prominent chin as her toothless mouth kept working. In the gloom she could just make out the bundle outside. The little baby lay there, weak after a day without milk, cries stifled by a dirty rag stuffed into its mouth. Barren herself, she took some perverted pleasure in watching it. Betty Stegwold had taken the child as an offering for the ivy, to save her own leathery hide. Tender, succulent baby-flesh had to be more appetising than her own. Her eyes widened, she rocked back and forth at the sound of rustling leaves. Intent on her offering, she smiled and mumbled to herself, sucking her breath in when twirling tendrils twined themselves round the pudgy legs and arms, the swollen belly and softly-fissured head. She imagined the strangely blue eyes starting, the gagged scream unable to escape its throat, clutching at an existence it hardly had had time to be aware of. A guttural squeak of curiosity escaped her. She craned her neck as the bundle jerked and slid slowly through the undergrowth and out of sight. Blinded, in the grip of self-preservation, the full horror of what she had done hadn't dawned on her yet.

— 45. Themself —

Edgar submerged his head in the trough, withdrew it, and vigorously shook water from his hair. It dribbled down his bare torso. The shock of the cold banished the last veils of sleep from his mind. A bunched fist lightly hammered his shoulder and made him jump. He turned his head, expecting to see Lee or Berry. A frown puckered his brow. His eyes became mean slits of hostility.

'What do *you* want?' he asked with a curl of his lip.

He felt a shiver run down his spine. They all knew her for what she was. Dressed like a tramp, with her mop of wiry, grey hair. Definitely not someone to be trusted.

Gerty Mallock ignored his rudeness, suppressing the sharp retort on her smiling lips. Her eyes twinkled with mischief.

'And top of the morning to you *too,* Master Edgar Falchion, Squire-in-the-making.'

His hackles were rising. She had expressly come out here to scoff at him, wasn't that just like her? He turned his back on her and made for the door. His skin tingled where her eyes rested on him. He forced himself to walk at a leisurely pace.

'Is that how you treat a lady, Edgar Falchion?'

He stopped involuntarily. *Some* lady...

'Where are your manners? I'm sure your parents would be ashamed if they saw you.'

He turned round with a grimace.

'What have they got to do with you?'

'Oh, you'd be amazed.'

'Yeah, I'm sure I would.'

'Sabrehilt is armed. So is Shieldbearer. But where, oh, *where* is the Salmail of Finn MacCumhal?'

He stalled in amazement. 'You know about that?'

Her eyes bored into his. 'You'd be astonished at how much I know.'

'Who told you?'

'No one. I know without being told.'

'There,' he muttered under his breath, 'you *are* a witch.'

'Am I, now?'

There was no point pretending. 'How else *could* you know?'

'How else, indeed...? Are the others still asleep?'

'Should know that too without me having to tell you.'

She smiled to herself. 'You're not there yet,' he thought he heard her say.

'What do you want with me?' he brusquely asked her.

'It's what *you* want with *me*, young man, that's more to the point.'

'With *you*...?... What would I want with you?'

The riddles were getting to him. Scorn was written all over his face and he turned away once more.

'I have come to introduce Themself.'

He whipped around, eyes searching the yard.

45. Themself

'Where is he?... I don't see him.'

'Him? Who said anything about a him?... 'Tis Themself you are *speaking* to... *I* am Themself... who happens to be a she.'

'*You?*'

'Aye.'

'Why themself?'

'A little ruse of the hermit's, I shouldn't wonder. Effective, don't you think? Besides, you wouldn't have come to me if he'd told you.'

'You'd better come in, then.'

He said it, though his tone was far from welcoming. He still didn't trust her.

Both her hands gripped his shoulders from behind. 'My, oh my, Edgar Falchion, you're a tough nut to crack.'

His spine tingled, he didn't like her that close. With a sigh she lowered herself into one of the armchairs and tapped her heels on the hearth-rug.

'Go along, then. Wake them up!' she playfully barked.

A sleepy voice was heard upstairs. Lee's bare feet and legs appeared. He yawned and scratched his scalp. He saw her and stopped.

'What's *she* doing here?'

'She's come to see us.'

'Well, get rid of her. Enough to put you off your breakfast.'

Edgar suddenly began to feel ashamed of himself. That's how he had sounded only moments ago - uncouth and nasty.

Berry hove into view close behind Lee, rubbing sleep out of his eyes. He saw Gerty and recognized her. He said nothing, too familiar with the glancing blows and razor-sharp stabs of taunts and insults. He pitied her, though he didn't blame Lee, couldn't blame Lee. He felt her eyes on him and looked her full in the face. There was something there that he alone, of the three of them, could discern. They were kindred spirits in many ways.

'Berry Blakelock,' she announced with a bow, a kindly smile kindling on her lips. 'I am honoured to make your acquaintance.'

He smiled back somewhat timidly. 'Hello.'

'And hello to you too. At least *someone* here knows how to address a lady.'

Lee snorted with derision. Lady, my ass. In *that* get-up?

'Yes. I say it again and I'll always say it – a lady… And how is Berry Blakelock this morning?'

'Leave him alone, you witch,' Lee sternly admonished. 'If you touch a hair of his head…'

'Pipe down, malapert!' she yelled back at him. 'Though, give you your due,' she soothingly added, 'you *are* defending your friend.'

'Lee,' Edgar interjected, 'she's *Themself*.'

'*She* is? I don't believe it.'

'I believe her,' Berry spoke up.

'*Do* you?' Lee asked him over his shoulder. 'Mmm,' he nodded. 'If Berry says so… I believe her too.'

'Good man, yourself,' Gerty saluted him. 'This fine figure of a boy truly is the Shieldbearer.'

Lee couldn't help beaming with pleasure. She had won him over, won him easily.

'Once you have broken your fast, you must all accompany me to Ferny Deep.'

'Ferny Deep? Where's that?'

'My home.'

Snorting and sneezing, Spike eventually emerged from under the blankets once he'd noticed they all had left him. On seeing Gerty he bounded down the stairs, barking madly. He ran up to her, sniffed her proffered hand and wagged his tail. Edgar began to relax. If Berry and Spike trusted her, so did he.

Acting on Gerty's instructions, they gave the village a wide berth.

'It wouldn't do for you three to be seen in *my* company,' she humorously quipped. 'We'd all be lumped together under one banner – rotten to the core: witch and budding warlocks under instruction...

'Don't be afeared if we *do* meet anyone, boys. I can screech and fight like a wildcat when pressed. I may be only a woman – I can see it in your eyes, oh yes – but we women fight dirty. We have teeth and claws like any self-respecting moggie.'

Lee and Edgar simpered out of politeness, acutely embarrassed. They were wondering what it felt like to be shunned and stigmatized by a whole community. *This* was the woman who had been held up to them as a threat when they'd misbehaved as children. "If you don't stop that whining, *Gerty* will come for you." "I'll tell *Gerty* on you if you're not a good boy." "Shush! Are those *Gerty's* footsteps I hear outside?"... Next time it *will* be Gerty, if you're not careful."

They had mobbed her as children when she'd entered the village precints, running off screaming once she'd turned to look at them. Adults had hissed and crossed themselves at her approach... And all the while it was she who was going to help them, she who was smiling and telling them jokes as they walked along, as if none of it had ever happened.

Gerty ushered them through a squeaky, rusty gate in need of a coat of paint and a drop of oil or two. They were on the other side of the very fence they had never dared climb over, through which they had spied on her house, only to scarper if a shadow appeared in a window. They crossed a wild garden, expertly tended, growing up to the very door and, very surprisingly, in bloom – a more than sufficient excuse to have her burnt at the stake in Garten. It was lush and green and musical with the bourdon of insects, reminding them of the Garrow Woods. They had never noticed before, too hell-bent on catching a glimpse of the "witch" inside. To them, it had always seemed an overgrown, derelict dump, mirroring the dishevelled creature who lived therein. Clumps of nettles stood here and there.

'For the caterpillars,' she explained with a smile. 'We must look after the butterflies.'

Her arms swung gaily as she walked. This was her home, her castle, her paradise. Here, she was out of reach of senseless taunts. And her garden grew fresh and bountiful around her. They wondered if she were married with children of her own, now that they'd begun to regard her as normal.

Gerty groped under a terracotta flowerpot for the key to the house, opened the door and gestured them in. A strong smell of tobacco smoke punctuated the atmosphere; a manly, homely smell reminding Edgar of his dad and his grandpa. They thought it might imply the presence of a Mister Gerty till they remembered that she smoked a pipe. They stood in silence and looked about them, going from room to room once she gave them the nod.

She certainly had stamped her personality on the place. Her home showed a whole new side to her. The beams of the ceiling, the wooden panelling, all were richly carved. The rooms were dark, festooned with rich brocades. Persian rugs were oceans of gorgeous colour beneath their feet. The glint of gold bounced back at them from costly antiques. In many ways, she seemed more grubby housekeeper than elegant chatelaine. Perhaps she dressed like that to be different, to irritate the short-sighted, hidebound villagers, though she would have looked odd in satin and lace.

On peering closer they saw things more in keeping with the Gerty Mallock before them. A crispy bluebottle hung lifeless in a dusty cobweb in one corner of the last room they visited. Further brittle bodies lay scattered on the window-sills. The glass panes were ancient, smoky and wavy, distorting the view of the garden outside. It was a most peculiar room. For one thing, there were two fireplaces. The faces carved in marble would have been gargoyles if it weren't for their pleasant expressions. The fenders were so elaborate as to take your breath away. Brass figures marched two-by-two from either corner. On meeting in the middle they saluted one another. Commodious armchairs were grouped here and there. In the centre of the room was a large circular table. She gave them all the time they needed. Then she took a plate of home-made toffees from the table and offered them round.

'I made them myself... Put those down first, why don't you?'

Reluctantly, with a loud clattering, they laid their weapons on the floor. For a moment, to their consternation, they were reminded of the cunning ruse of witches. Quickly, with a smile, they accepted the toffees to hide their confusion. They were delicious, the warm, sweet liquid flowing thickly over their tongues and down their throats. She threw one to Spike who squatted on the rug, jaws locked together, and drooling profusely.

Edgar greedily stole a glance at the plate. His eyes were drawn beyond it and he frowned in bafflement. On the same table was what appeared to be a chessboard. Though the figures... the figures...

Fantastic, phantasmagorical chessmen!

Edgar stared, incredulous, awestruck.

Scarecrows!!... Elks!!... A boy with a sword!!... Trees!! Other boys!!... Castles!!... A woman who looked like a queen!!... A hideous creature!!... The church and the vault!!!...

The tower stood squarely in the centre of the board.

It's *us*! he exclaimed in his head.

He began to question the spectacle before him once his awe had partially evaporated.

Does she move them?... Does it all depend on her, the final outcome?... Is this a trap?...

Lee and Berry were distracted by the offer of more toffee and never noticed. Edgar accepted another piece and made no comment. He hoped it wasn't poisoned.

'Now that your curisoity is whetted,' Gerty said, 'there is something I have to show you.'

Was it the chessboard? Were they, to some degree, in control of their own destiny?

But she made no allusion to the gameboard. Instead, she went to one of the mantelpieces and touched some hidden spring. There was an audible click and the entire structure swung outwards.

Was it a trap? A dungeon? A cell they'd rot in where nobody would hear them or find them?

'This way,' she airily chimed.

Edgar didn't know whether to shout a warning, snatch up his sword and run for the hall-door. Would they follow or would they just stare after him? Would there be time to explain? How is it possible to escape the clutches of a witch after coming so far?... He wanted to roar at himself for being so blind and so stupid.

†

— 46. Scapegoat —

Prickleback leapt from his bed and dived into his clothes. There was no time for breakfast. There was work to do… Serious work.

'Come on!' he roughly shouted. 'Get up!'

Repeatedly he punched the soft flesh at the back of her arm. Finally, in exasperation, he pushed her out of the bed onto the floor.

'Lazy good-for-nothing! When I tell you to get up, you bloody well *get up!*'

There was a wildness about his eyes. His voice rose to an insane pitch. She was terrified of him. He hadn't been the same since the night before. Still on the floor, trembling hands clutched at her clothing and she fumbled to get into them. He kicked her haunches because she was too slow for him.

'Get a move on!… By God, you'll regret your snivelling ways, madam.'

Silent tears trickled down her face. Her heart was broken. She didn't hate the man, too downtrodden to hate anyone. Once dressed, he gripped her bruised arm and dragged her from the room. She cried out in pain and he shook her pitilessly. She stumbled after him, down the staircase and out the door, onto the grit and stones where she slipped and grazed her knees. Viciously, he tugged her to her feet and, with a wrench of her arm, had her struggling to keep up with him.

— 47. Behind the Fireplace —

Gerty held out an arm to encompass them and usher them through. Her smile was sweet, *too sweet,* Edgar thought. His legs automatically followed his comrades through the gap behind the mantelpiece, as if he were in a trance. Instantly they were plunged into impenetrable darkness. A dry, musky smell reminded him of something he couldn't put his finger on. He expected to hear shrill, cackling laughter coming from the other side of the false door.

But there was no cackling laughter. She had come too and sealed the room after her. It was dry and warm and stuffy in there. She struck a light and lit a candle. By its pale luminescence he made her out and his friends' wan faces turned towards her. They were all at her mercy now. He anticipated a blinding flash, wreaths of smoke and her fell transmutation into an evil, cackling crone.

Nothing of the sort occurred. Slowly, shielding the candle flame, she walked around the room and lit a series of oil lamps on stands. Light increased as from a rising sun and the secret chamber came fully to life.

They were in a library. That was what had jogged the mothballs of his memory, the musty smell of old leather-bound books. It reminded him of the small collection belonging to his grandpa, the scent wafting up his nostrils while he sat on his knee and was read a story. But this was no small collection. They had never seen so many books. Ancient, scuffed spines rose from floor to ceiling. Gilded lettering glinted in the lamplight, highlighting titles and authors. One almost expected the dust of the library to be thick on her shoulders and greying her hair.

'Now…' whispered Gerty. 'For the greatest secret of all…'

Edgar still half expected her to whip out a wand and turn all three of them into moths or spiders or woodlice.

'You are exceedingly privileged boys to be about to see what you are about to see,' she informed them.

With that, she bent down and, finger on the spine of a tall, thin volume, drew it towards her. There was a whirring noise and a whole section of shelves swung inwards. Taking up an oil lamp she beckoned them through.

What if…? Oh, my God, what if this is a secret way to the tower and she's taking us to the Aetz herself?! Edgar felt a scream bubble in his throat, just on the verge of escaping. The bubble burst but no sound emerged.

By the swaying lamplight they could see they were in a small, cubical room with bare, yellowing walls. A small square table was all the furniture there was. On it lay a book of immense proportions.

'There she is…' breathed Gerty reverentially. 'The Ancient Tome of Mallock. Or, to give it its full title, The Ancient Tome of Hildenstock-Brackenfiled-Mallock.'

'Is that your real name?' Lee asked her.

'Gertrude Hildenstock-Brackenfield-Mallock,' she responded.

'Why don't they call you that?'

'Too thick to get their tongues around it. They can just about manage Gerty Mallock and that sticks in their throats. But enough of that… This is far more important,' she whispered in a deferential tone, tenderly patting the cover.

The tome was bound in metallic scales of a bluish hue, into which golden hinges were embedded, top and bottom. An ornate clasp and lock shut out prying eyes. Into this Gerty inserted a plain gold key she took from her pocket. Lovingly, she unhooked the clasp and raised the uppermost cover. An exquisite scent rose from the vellum pages she turned.

'That's the leaves of the Tutsan you can smell,' she explained. 'They have no scent when fresh, but dry them for a few days and they're reminiscent of ambergris. It lasts for years.'

She turned to the back of the book.

'Come and see,' she whispered.

Edgar suspected it was her book of spells. She'd soon get to the right page for turning adolescent boys into toads or eels or frog spawn. Or a shadowy wraith would loom up out of the book and wreathe them in death. Though he hated himself for doing it, he stepped back behind his companions. Lee evidently harboured no doubts whatsoever. He leapt forward eagerly.

'Try this one for size,' Gerty quipped with a wide grin, finger holding down a page.

Lee stepped into her place and lowered his head. He started and bent closer to the book, staring eyes darting all over the page.

'It's me,' he murmured. 'I can't believe it. It's *me!*' A finger followed the text, his lips moved. 'It's definitely me,' he whispered in astonishment. 'Bloody hell, I'm in a book. I'm in a *book!*... Oh... my... *God.*'

He looked over his shoulder at his friends, discomfited, and slapped an open palm onto the page.

'Careful,' Gerty reprimanded with a frown of displeasure.

'No one's to read this page,' he commanded. 'And I mean *no one.*'

A faint blush suffused his cheeks.

What he saw, in black and white, before his protruding eyes, were his words, his feelings, his thoughts - his very actions! All there, plain to see, with nothing left to the imagination. Things he'd never believed would reach the light of day.

'Oh, my God... Please don't read it,' he pleaded.

He'd never get over it, never be able to look Edgar in the face again. They'd be sworn enemies forever! This was the most embarrassing, most shameful, most humiliating thing possible. All there in indelible ink, in a flowing, attractive hand. What he'd thought about Felicia Arnold. *And* Rhoda Barrows. And *done!* Oh, my God... He was so horrified it never dawned on him that Edgar's thoughts and deeds were also inscribed in the book. He quickly turned a leaf, another, *another,* and stepped back from the table.

Gerty looked to Edgar who made no effort to approach.

'Aren't you curious?' she asked.

'Curiosity killed the cat,' he muttered.

'Yes, but cats have nine lives, and curiosity also revealed to you your birthright, did it not?'

Dumbly he shrugged his shoulders.

'Here it is,' she said, leafing backwards. 'Come.'

Edgar timidly came forward and read the paragraph indicated.

Simultaneously he was transported back to that midsummer eve when he'd sneaked the sword out of the house. He read it exactly as it had happened. In every detail. He smiled to himself when he saw what had gone through the minds of his friends. He blushed even. They held him in such high esteem.

'You're not reading the bit about me, sure you're not?' Lee asked with trepidation.

Edgar slowly shook his head. He flicked back through a wad of leaves till he came upon his grandpa. Pride and joy blossomed and swelled his breast as he plumbed the depths of his fondness for him.

I love you too, he silently formed with moving lips.

His eyes rose from the book, deep in thought. He let the pages fall back into place and turned to face Gerty.

'Did you write this?'

'No.'

'Who, then?'

'Anon… The book writes itself.'

'What? On its *own*?' Lee guffawed in derision.

'Take another look. Go to the last page.'

'God almighty! Edgar, look!! It's writing *now*!!!'

All three leaned over the book and read their own astonishment leaning over the book watching the words form and Edgar reading about his grandpa and Lee's reactions before that.

'Can we read into the future?' Edgar eagerly asked.

'I'm afraid not,' Gerty answered. 'Probably for the best, don't you think? Each day is enough in itself to keep us occupied without the rest of our lives before us...'

'But this is the last page. Does that mean it's the end of the world?'

'Look again. More closely.'

They did and ceased breathing. Blank pages shimmered into existence from the back cover, as if they were floating to the surface from a bottomless lake.

'Now go to the front,' she instructed them.

There, pages were being absorbed into the cover, sinking into the depths. All you had to do to retrieve one was to catch the edge of it with you forefinger and ease it back into being.

'How far does it go back?' Edgar asked.

'To the Beginning of Time.'

'Is this the Book of Life Prickleback's always going on about?'

'No. That's another book entirely. This is the History of The World in the making.'

'How did you get hold of it?'

'We, the first daughters of Mallock, have been the Guardians of the Great Tome since the beginning.'

'But you have no children.'

'I have a brother who has a daughter. She takes over from me.'

'When?'

'When she has to. As I said already, you cannot read the Future, no one can. It does not yet exist. This is purely a book of the Past.'

'And the present,' Lee wise-cracked.

'The Present as it becomes the Past.'

Edgar turned back to the book and flicked to another page at random.

'The scarecrows have no thoughts,' he commented.

'No. They are fully under the control of another.'

'The Aetz, you mean?'

She gave a solemn nod of her head, sobering in the extreme.

'We could read *its* thoughts.'

'No, you won't,' she admonished with a hint of anger brought on by fear. 'Would you really be so foolish?'

'What's behind the Aetz? Who controls *it*?'

'No one we know. It seems an entity onto itself. Evil inspires it. Evil informs it. Evil sustains it...'

'Can evil be destroyed?'

'Ah, there you strike the nail on the head. Just as good cannot be destroyed, neither can evil.'

'But isn't evil the destruction of good?' Berry cleverly asked.

'The negation of good,' she replied with a laudatory smile. 'The absence of Good... Evil can be diminished or circumvented, it has been before... only to flare and wax strong again and again...' Her gaze lost focus and faded far away. She whispered to herself, audibly. 'The shadow of Death lies over us, blotting out light and hope. His legions advance. The Legions of the Grim Reaper advance. Death calls to us as the sea calls to the mountainous spring...'

They shifted uncomfortably. Sensing their perturbation, Spike curled up in a tighter ball and groaned. By now they were used to this. The Aetz and the times upon them had that effect. They could smell the fear on her breath, see its cold mist in her eyes, feel its weight settle on her mind. It was a horrible sensation, enough to make their blood run cold.

With a shudder Edgar flicked through a wad of pages, glancing here and there.

'You're not in it,' he declared, somewhat accusingly.

'Am I not?'

She mused with a knowing smile but didn't enlighten him. He considered that suspicious. Perhaps the whole book thing was witchcraft. She didn't want him to read about the Aetz because he'd discover they were one and the same. No wonder she'd smiled at the sword. It might as well have been a brittle, dry stick full of woodworm.

'I wonder will we survive or be killed?' he speculated aloud.

'The book will note it the moment you know, not before.'

So dry. So unfeeling, it seemed to him. As if she couldn't wait. He failed to notice that his every thought was being recorded as he formed it.

'It's not a crystal ball,' she went on. 'Nor a soothsayer. It's nothing but a true and historical account, the truest there is.'

'Written by itself. So you say.'

'Written by itself,' she hollowly echoed.

Half-heartedly, he acknowledged her and abstractedly turned a page. A chance name caught his eye and he read on. Betty Stegwold conjured up a living, repellant image, making him grimace with disgust. He started as he continued reading.

'Look at this,' he called to the other two in a startled voice.

They moved in and all three of them took up reading the account.

'This must have happened just before we woke up,' Edgar murmured.

Berry and Lee were struck dumb by horror.

Briars lash the roof and walls and door of Betty's house while she cowers in a dark corner, mumbling incoherently.

'I did it for you... 'Twas for you!' she screams.

What had she done? They didn't understand.

'Spare an old woman without bairn to solace her in her old age. Haven't...'

The whiplashes drum more violently, drowning out her voice. Her mumblings cease and her mind goes blank with fear.

Her thoughts clarified and they read her deed of horror. They knew the mother. Often had they seen her dandling her baby on her knee. To think that that hell-hag had...

Betty shrieks when the door burst inwards. On her knees she falls to muttering shrill pleas of desperation.

'No, please! I did it for you. I can do the same again. I promise! Spare an old woman without bairn of her own...'

The moan they hated above all else echoed from the pages.

A scarecrow stands framed in the doorway. She hears scratching behind her and slews round her head. There's another in the corner. She whimpers to herself. She screams but there's nowhere to flee to. She rushes into the adjoining room and throws her meagre weight against the door. The drumming begins once more, louder than ever, the hammers of hell.

'They've come to fetch me!'

She is almost glad of it. The terrific suspense will be over. Yet a thin heart-string clings feebly to life and she leans more heavily against the door. Buffeted by one of the scarecrows, it bursts open but bangs shut again. She moans as a huge bruise swells on her head. The creature on the other side raises a twiggy fist and smites the door.

It disintegrates into smithereens beneath the impact. The crone screeches and falls back, pierced by a thousand splinters. She crawls away from the plodding monster, whimpering balefully, shielding her eyes with a withered forearm. Stolidly the scarecrows advance in her wake, flecks of her blood staining the floorboards.

The avid readers wanted to but couldn't tear their eyes from the text…

Pressed against the hard uneven plaster of the far wall, Betty Stegwold throws back her head and screams. A creature stands over her, moaning lasciviously. Slowly, deliberately, it holds out a hand, crooks its middle finger and slashes downwards.

She hardly feels a thing. No searing pain takes her breath away. Her head shoots down when something tickles her belly. Her shabby dress is torn from collar to waist. Blood trickles over her skin from a gaping wound in her abdomen. A sharp intake of breath has the wound bulge. Loops of glistening intestine, marbled by fat and by veins, plop onto her knees and slowly uncoil onto the floor. Frantically she fights the dehiscence, but the loops churn in her hands, heaving against her efforts to contain them.

Her glance darts from her entrails to the two stooping figures above her. Eyes widen and a moan of despair escapes her when their hands take hold of the coils and draw them out, length by length. She is aghast at the furlongs she contains. It seems neverending. Finally, one massive loop stretches round the perimeter of the room, her two assailants in opposite corners. She feels the two ends tug at her body, above and below. A dull, excruciating pain alternates with waspish pangs. The sharp edge of a russet-brown lobe of liver protrudes through the opening.

An ear-piercing screech rends the air when both ends snap. Thick red blood fills the cavity and pours from the swelling belly. Her last meal gloops out like vomit. Tiny gasps shake her frame. The death-rattle gurgles in her throat. Betty Stegwold lies dying in a crimson lake of her own making.

Edgar, Lee and Berry fell back from the book and turned away, gagging. Such a ghastly way to die. Quickly Edgar flipped over a page. What came next arrested his attention and made him completely forget the disembowelled crone.

'I don't believe it!' he ejaculated. 'Oh my God, look what he's *doing!!*'

Lee craned his neck and gasped as he followed the forming words.

'We've got to go,' cried a breathless Edgar. 'Berry, you stay here. There's no time to lose. We might be too late already.'

Spike whirled about barking, desperate to go with him.

'Can you please let us out!' Edgar pleaded from the library.

Gerty went and released the mantel. They were gone in an instant.

— 48. Human Sacrifice —

They did arrive too late. Much too late. Prickleback was hurtling towards them. Alone. Horribly alone. He stood in the dogcart, wild as a madman, lashing at the horse with his whip. He never even saw the boys. They had to dive into the ditch to escape being crushed.

They clambered up the grassy bank and stood gazing after him. The wheels of the dogcart rattled furiously. The whip cracked. Prickleback hollered. The equipage took a bend and was lost to sight.

'Too late,' Edgar sobbed, drawing a sleeve across his eyes.

'We couldn't have made it in time, Ed. Too far to run.'

'Damn him! Damn him to hell!... How could he have done such a thing?'

'He's Prickleback, isn't he? I reckon he can do anything, he's *that* bad.'

'If only that damn book would write in the future.'

The now familiar roar of the Aetz rent the atmosphere. The ground shook seismically and flung them down. They lay there stunned. Eventually they raised their heads, looked cautiously about them and got to their feet. Mercifully, the woods shielded them from the creature's gaze. They pushed its existence to the back of their minds and trotted back to Gerty's.

While the boys were speeding towards the tower, Berry had followed their thoughts and words and actions, and Prickleback's too, as they'd unfolded in the book. Gerty stood by him, hand on his shoulder, and together they'd read. What they witnessed was as bad, if not worse, than the incident involving the Stegwold woman.

Hurling her against the dogcart once the horse is between the shafts, he forces her to clamber into the seat.

'Don't you dare move,' he growls through gritted teeth and goads the horse with the reins.

They skid out of the stable yard and soon are hurtling along the road. Are we fleeing for our lives, she wonders. Timidly she glances up at the grim face, the set mouth, the truculent eyes. I have failed him and he hates me... Tears distort his image. She sniffs. He turns and almost spits at her.

'Aye, you'll cry now, won't you? All these years you have thwarted me. Not any more, madam. Not any more!'

A frightful guffaw escapes him when he realizes that there will be no need of a tombstone. He lets a roar at the horse and curls the whip round its shoulders. It jolts the cart and gallops faster than ever, foam at the corners of its mouth, nostrils flaring.

She's sick with fear and foreboding. He's insane, driven that way by guilt, she can find no other excuse for him. She has no conception of the depths evil plunges to in his heart, no idea of where he's taking her. If she had only borne him a son...

At the edge of the woods he pulls on the reins and brings the horse to a neck-breaking standstill.

48. Human Sacrifice

'Get out!' he shouts, spittle flying like venom.

He grabs her wrist and drags her through the undergrowth. His is a grip of iron, hurting her grievously.

'Hurry up, woman!'

Gasping and sobbing, briars tearing at her bare arms and legs, she stumbles after him.

'Where are you taking me?' she finally asks in high-pitched terror.

'Well may you ask, you strumpet...' Without turning round, he continues with a demonic grin, 'I'm taking you home... Where you belong... I'm returning you to your kin!'

The grin he graces her with startles her.

'Let go of me!' she cries, struggling to free herself.

His grip only tightens and she groans in pain. He yanks her forward with a curse and, when she falls, drags her prone body through the brushwood, lacerating her fair skin. She strives to get to her feet and blunders after him. Dashing her head against the bole of a tree, she's momentarily stunned. Blood courses down the side of her face, she tastes it in the corner of her mouth. He is rougher than ever, ordering her to keep up and be damned.

They emerge from the woods. Across the intervening fields they tear at a terrific rate, she has no time to take stock of where she is. They come to an abrupt halt beneath the shadow of the tower. He stands, holding her at arm's length.

Panting, gaping like a frightened bird, her gaze of blank amazement follows the entire length of the wall upwards.

'It cannot be,' she murmurs.

A shiver accompanies a tremulous exhalation at the sight of what is strewn about the base of the structure. Evil sweats from its very walls and proof of evil surrounds it on all sides. The gargoyles seem to be watching her, out of the corners of their eyes.

'Why have you brought me here?' she asks in trepidation.

Foreboding makes the hair on her head stand on end.

'Why? WHY?!' he roars. 'I'll show you why.'

With that, he shakes her so violently he almost pulls her arm out of its socket. With a curse he flings her to the ground, squinting up at the roof and shouting at the top of his voice.

'Here she is! Take her! Accept her as my tribute. Take her in lieu, I beseech thee!!'

Panic scatters her thoughts helter-skelter. What does he mean? Whom is he addressing? Who can live in such a place? She gasps, words stricken from her mind.

The heads of the gargoyles move. They look down on her and mutter and hum and grin avariciously. Saliva drools from the gaps in their teeth. Pink tongues flicker and protrude between parted lips. Is she imagining things or are clouds of insects really coming from their maws?... A guttural growl begins deep in their throats and swells as it emerges. She claps her hands over her ears to shield them. Then, she sees a shadow moving round the battlements. A fit of trembling takes hold of her.

'Take her!' her husband shrieks. 'I've brought her for you! Spare me and take her!'

So this is what he intends... It all makes sense now... What else am I good for?... She understands at last. On this ghastly hill her life is to be forfeit... She recalls her own father who had beaten her black and blue. She remembers Mort and his ill-usage. She glances at Prickleback and all sense of hope and justice leaves her. The thing leans over the parapet and stares straight into her eyes.

'Yes! Yes! Take her!' He is breathless. 'I bring her as my offering to you!' With a grimace he looks down at her and spits, muttering, 'That barren jinnet has cost me more than a rib. Let the creature gnaw at her bones.'

She loses consciousness before her husband flees the vicinity. Her lustreless gaze fixed on nothing, she is dead before the monster gets to her.

48. Human Sacrifice

Mercy has been shown her in the end, at her time of greatest need. What is left for the Aetz is a mere shell. It cannot defile her for she has escaped its clutches. It slobbers and slavers, crunching bone and gristle between its teeth while the gargoyles screech and thick phlegm rattles in their throats. 'Tis a fitting accompaniment, though her ears hear them not. She has been spared. Peace envelopes her after a life of turmoil and grief.

†

— 49. Ferny Deep —

Lee and Edgar fell silent as they pushed their way through the gate. They entered the house and walked through the rooms to the gaping chimneypiece. Sheepishly they tiptoed into the hidden chamber, knowing that both Gerty and Berry had followed their every step in that book of hers, their every thought and word. Spike staggered through the door, tongue out a mile, and collapsed on the floor.

'Ah' she said, wheeling round. 'Hard luck, you two.'

'If only we'd been a few minutes earlier,' Edgar moaned.

'Don't be too harsh on yourselves.'

'How could he do such a thing?'

Berry looked up for that, then returned to the text.

'Prickleback?' Gerty said. 'How, indeed,' she added with a prolonged sigh. 'He does not know it yet, but he has started the avalanche. He couldn't contain it now even if he wished to.'

'But his own *wife*.'

'In name only... By force. He had her poison her husband, told her he'd denounce her if she didn't marry him.'

'But why isn't something done about it?'

'He's only the tip of the iceberg. A grasping, small-minded man. Blinded by his own passions.'

'He's only getting started,' Berry interjected over his shoulder.

They all hastened to the book and crowded round him…

Prickleback was home, heaving and panting, shut in his library.

Bloodshot eyes roam round the laden shelves. He hacks, then laughs aloud, a vicious laugh full of hatred that soon dies on his parted lips.

He has seen it… Like his cohorts he has seen the Aetz, and seen his reflection there. Each and every one of them has recognized a part of himself, as if they were the building-blocks, the cells, the organs that sustain this interloper from hell. Horror strikes him broadside like a thunderbolt, suffused with a certain ill-defined relief. He has seen power there, unimaginable power. Can it be harnessed, though…?… Why plead with an unknown, unseen God when this is so close?…

He leaps into action as if from a dream, runs to his bureau and bustles about for paper, quill and ink.

'I know what I'll do and I'll do it now,' he says to himself with an evil grin.

He produces a scroll of ancient paper. On this he begins to scratch with his quill a false prophecy in florid characters.

'Not too obvious,' he mutters to himself. 'We don't want suspicions fluttering in the wrong direction… A hint of a riddle will convince the wooly-headed knaves of its veracity. A vague reference to the water-wheel, that should do it.'

He chuckles to himself at his own ingeniousness while he racks his brain for suitable-sounding words.

In thou, ancient village of Garten, there liveth a ruddy youth. Water doth provide his family with bread to eat.

This aforesaid youngling doth possess a cutlass which wieldeth powers supernatural in his gripe. He alone shalt destroy the monster that ravageth thy land, invadeth thy homes and destroyeth thy crops.

However, this youth is loath to fulfil his destiny. Coerce him by fair means or foul, that unto battle he mayeth go. If he doth fail, thou all shalt perisheth and the fair village of Garten shalt be laid waste. Know ye that 'tis imperative that the youth lay seige to this denizen of hell and rid the land of its evil.

He holds the parchment at arm's length, nodding and humming with satisfaction. It is rough and inaccurate but what does that matter? The majority of his flock are illiterate. Anything that sounds grandiose to them will do. As for the few who won't believe it...

'To the devil with them.'

He rattles the manuscript and places it on the desk, smoothing it flat with a forearm.

'Now... for the final effect...'

With a smile of pleasure he sets to cutting pieces of red ribbon, melting wax and pressing any ring or small coin to hand into it.

'Perfect... Let us hope and pray that the creature devours the brat... The mill shall be mine in a trice,' he murmurs with contentment. 'To hell with Booth.'

'But I don't even *want* the mill!' Edgar cried with astonishment.

'That's neither here nor there, my friend,' Gerty responded, massaging his shoulder. 'He wants it to appear all above-board. You're one of the fortunate ones, in fact, for others have been done to death so he could lay his filthy hands on their property. It's all in here…

'Look at him… Why he's even ordering that straw be strewn in the yard.'

'What's that for?' Lee interjected. 'Is he going to set fire to the place?'

'His bishop's *castle*?!… His pride and *joy*?!… Not a bit of it. The straw is to silence the carriage wheels – so as not to disturb the chief mourner.'

'God, he's such a hypocrite. He makes me want to throw up.'

'You're not the only one,' she said with a smile. 'Just listen to him weeping about his love, his darling wife snatched from him by the devil incarnate. How does he keep it up? How does he not erupt into peals of laughter?'

'I'm surprised he's not struck by lightning,' Lee growled.

'Yes, indeed. The scar goes too deep ever to heal. All it can do is fester and poison more flesh, his own and other's.

'But what's he got his clutches in the mill for?' Edgar asked, trying to understand his motive.

'Lucre, my boy. Nothing but filthy lucre, though he's after your skin as well.'

'But *why*?'

'You're dangerous. You're a rival with that sword of yours. One thing he can't stand is a rival. That's why he redoubles his efforts to grind you under his heel. See how he uses your sword against you, the very instrument of your power.'

'He's mad.'

'Nay. Take not his responsibility from him. He is who he is, he knows and accepts it. He has deformed his soul wilfully... There stands a depraved man indifferent to probity, rotten to the core. He is the evil at the very heart of this village. He is the abscess, the filth that draws the scavengers, the bloodsuckers, all that is unseemly.'

'Then if we kill him, all will be well.'

'No. Do not attempt to usurp his throne. Leave him to Providence...

'Always remember that this book is a corkscrew in his heart boring ever inwards and drawing the truth to the surface for all to see. He detests its very existence because he abhors the truth. He deals in subterfuge, you see. Yet this tome is the Mirror of Truth. He cannot alter it. He cannot hide from it. He cannot destroy it. Between these covers he is unearthed, the foul burrowing creature that he is, and unmasked.

'The fool is blissfully unaware that he plays into the hands of providence. You wield the sword for that very purpose. And while he imagines he is cornering you, all he does is assist you to fulfil your destiny and his own.'

There was a profound, impassioned earnestness in her voice that made it tremble. It impressed them that they could see no anger in her eyes, no desire for revenge. Love of truth and justice prevailed, nothing more.

'What does your life matter to him?' she went on, a hard edge to her tone. 'What does any life but his own and the son's he's denied? You are grit in his eye, the sharp stone in his boot, the pretender to his throne. Suspicious minds always pick on someone. But you, my boy, are the pearl and he is the sand-flea. He knows it and it infuriates him. He hates you because of it and means to steal your birthright, to…'

She drew back from the full truth with a sharp intake of breath emitted as a dolorous sigh. Why tell him now that the man meant to orphan him?

Berry felt invisible wings gently fanning his face. It wasn't the first time. He couldn't explain it, referring to it as a fit or a daydream. The initial "startlement" gave way to happy peacefulness, a resignation almost joyful. It usually lasted a matter of seconds and left him pleasantly dazed. Gerty regarded him intently but held her peace. Things were better left unsaid until the book said them for them.

Edgar grew excited as a thought struck him.

'Maybe if we go back far enough we will be able to see how the last Sabrehilt did it!'

He feverishly turned the pages. Calmly she laid a hand on the book to stop him.

'That's not the way,' she gently admonished. 'A different person, a different time. Choose your own way.'

'I don't know how to choose,' he glumly responded.

'You have two doughty companions. He was alone. You *have* made choices, good ones.'

'But I just wish I could see into the future.'

'You really wish that, do you?'

'It's better than not knowing, isn't it?'

'I wonder…' She clasped his arm to emphasise what she was about to say. 'Imagine a breathtakingly tall stairs you have to climb. You stare up at the top step and lose hope. You say you cannot do it. Cast your eyes down and regard the bottom step, your first. It's easy. So is the next and the next... Before you know it, that final step is as easy as the first. You understand?'

He shrugged his shoulders despondently.

'Step by easy step,' she explained. 'It's a tough climb, though not impossible, but it is better not to see *how* tough at the very beginning. The time to mop your brow is afterwards. Never forget that.'

'But we will have help?' he asked, intent on clutching at straws. 'Where is the white witch? Show me her in the book.'

'She doesn't appear in the book.'

'Won't they burn her when she comes?'

'There's no fear of that. They burn innocent old ladies. They would never dare lay hands on a real witch.'

'I'm surprised they haven't burnt *you*.'

'Prickleback knows of the book, that is my hold over him.'

Lee laughed aloud. 'No wonder he looks frightened when he sees you.'

'But if he killed you,' Berry stated, 'he'd be out of danger.'

'Others besides myself know of the book and its whereabouts. It's too great a risk to take.'

'But why don't you show it to everyone and be done with it?' Edgar asked in earnest.

'You cannot alter history, my young friend.'

Edgar looked away without saying a word.

'You still doubt me, Edgar Falchion,' she remarked, making him start and blush. 'You still ask yourself why I didn't knock on your door and introduce myself. But you would have shut it in my face, oh, yes, don't you dare deny it… I had to bring you to me by this roundabout route, from your friend, the billy-can man, to Farmer Buckrake, to Houghton Miffler. You would never have listened to me if I hadn't.'

Edgar nodded, lips compressed. 'Sorry,' he croaked.

'Don't bother apologising. I understand. But please… please trust me. I'm your only chance.'

He nodded, casting her a wan smile of recognition.

'Now… Where was I?… Ah, yes… Unfortunately for all of us, Prickleback and his ilk have released a power greater than themselves. That, in essence, is the problem of evil. They have formed an allegiance with evil and evil will devour them in the end. For evil knows no allies.'

'But what about those of us who *aren't* evil?' Edgar stressed complainingly.

'Like a forest fire, evil consumes everything in its path. But *they* are the ones who unleashed it, not you.'

'Some comfort that is,' Lee muttered.

'You must fight it, all of us must… Good can flow from evil because good cannot be vanquished. Take the storm. It toppled the elm for a purpose, did it not? The bats drove the fools to force you to act, the one person who *can* act.'

'But why?'

'Ah… there you have it. Good never solves its own riddles to our satisfaction. We should be grateful it solves them at all. Evil can sprout and bud but evil invariably fades. Of course, 'tis better if it be expunged early than late… Good brought Lee to your side and led you both to Berry. Good was waiting, dormant in the cairn, under the tree, in the sword, waiting for evil to emerge and manifest itself. You, all three of you, are good, and Good is on your side. Be glad of that.'

'We are.'

He sounded terribly alone, in a desert of good which seemed overwhelmingly remote.

'Good hasn't finished yet,' she declared with a smile. 'Come, let us seek the salmail.'

They returned to the book while she flipped through the pages. They followed her forefinger as it glided over the words.

'The squire has it!' Lee exclaimed.

'You must go to him.'

'Well, according to my dad, he's no use,' Edgar grumbled. 'What if he won't give it to us?'

'Cross that bridge if you come to it.'

Edgar turned the pages. The name Pius caught his eye. He wanted to read more, to discover what his dad had been on about. She wouldn't let him, stopping him with a shake of the head.

'Don't delve into evil,' she advised. 'Protect and defend your innocence as long as you may. It is a most precious thing. The book has no more to reveal to you.'

She closed it, locked the clasp, and took them back to the room beyond the library, sealing the secret chambers behind her.

'Remember, Edgar... Believe in the power of Good. Believe in yourself.'

'That's the difficult part,' he commented with baleful eyes.

'Fear not. It will come in time.'

'Will it?'

'In the end it will. When it's called for…'

Lee glanced over his shoulder at the table as they left the room.

'E-em,' he stammered.

'Well, Lee?'

'Can we take the rest of that?'

'The toffee? Go right ahead. I'm glad you liked it.'

She emptied the plate onto a sheet of brown paper, twisted it up and handed it to him. With that, he skipped out the front door and waved a cheery good-bye.

'We'll tell you if we get the salmail!' he shouted.

'Aren't you forgetting something?'

'Oh, yeah! You'll know right away!'

Gerty stood on the threshold looking after them.

'Poor boys,' she murmured. 'Poor innocent babies…'

— 50. Evil Recoils —

Neither the straw nor the reverend's grief fooled anyone. Too many had seen him hurtling past with his wife cowering beside him. They shuddered at first, but soon it made sense to them. An eye for an eye, a tooth for a tooth, how often had he bellowed it from the pulpit? The exact meaning hadn't been clear until now. And now that it was...

'Oaf, my lad,' Grindlewick crooned with a cunning smile, having cajoled his son into the bar, ''ave a sup o' somethin'.'

Oaf was wary. He cast rapid glances at his father, certain he was up to no good.

'I don't want no drink!' His voice rose in alarm.

'Suit yourself, son. Only askin'...You don't mind if *I* 'ave one?'

He watched while the innkeeper filled a glass and tossed the contents back. Black eyes regarded the boy, giving nothing away. He had something on his mind and he seemed to toy with it in his mouth, his tongue twirling back and forth behind his teeth. Finally he broke the brooding silence.

'Your mother and me, we've been thinkin'.' He looked along the length of the bar before pouring himself another drink. 'You see, lad... We've a big family to protect, 'aven't we?'

Oaf nodded, wondering what he meant by protect, considering how they were abandoned the moment danger loomed.

'That thing out there,... well, there's no love lost between us, is there?... What we was thinkin' was... How about you, bein' the eldest an' all, give yourself up to spare your brothers and sisters, eh? *I* would, only I 'ave to run the business. They need a mam about the house so there's no point in *her* goin', is there?... How about it, son?'

Oaf gaped at him, stunned by so wicked a suggestion. He wasn't as stupid as his father imagined. Eventually he mustered the energy to stagger backwards, slowling shaking his head in disbelief.

'No-o,' he faltered. 'No! Go *yourself!!*' he yelled before fleeing his father's presence, his sole objective to take his siblings away from there before another was harried into self-sacrifice.

'Curse the boy,' Grindlewick growled, spitting on the floor.

Other sons, more quick-witted than Oaf, *did* obey. Their better feelings were plucked like strings, their idealism exploited until they felt it their duty to die for their families. After all, if their reverend leader's *wife* had done so, who were they to object? The beast would accept their offering and spare their nearest and dearest. No man hath greater love than to lay down his life for his friends, wasn't that what

Prickleback had told them with tears in his eyes? He *knew* what he was talking about.

Stark figures in the landscape, they slowly, inexorably, approached the tower, never looking back, never faltering, buoyed by love for their families, convinced that they did the right thing. They never even cried out when they were snatched up by the Morgammeron Aetz and taken into its slavering maw. A grotesque pilgrimage of the youth of the village further blackened the name of Garten.

— 51. The Salmail of Finn MacCumhal —

She opened her eyes and remained perfectly still. He was in the throes of a good mood. He usually was when he sat bolt upright and bounced up and down, humming cheerfully to himself. The tassel of his nightcap bobbed about frantically, making a mockery of him. Normally when he was high as a kite he was in for a fall, a harsh one at that.

Oh, I can't stand this any more, she said to herself, sitting up.

'Ah, at last... Morning m'dear.'

'Is it morning?' she grumbled.

'Indeed, it is. And *what* a morning! The sun is up. The birds are singing...'

'I don't hear them.'

'Metaphorically, m'dear. Metaphorically. But, what's more to the point...' he paused for dramatic effect, 'I am bright-eyed and bushy-tailed!'

'I never would have guessed.'

'Come, dearest.' He nudged her playfully. 'Rejoice with me.'

'I'd rather not,' she rejoined with a groan as she slipped from the sheets.

'Tarry, rash wanton,' he quoted. 'Am I not thy lord?'

'You can forget the Shakespeare. You are *no* Oberon.'

'More a Puck, do you think, m'dear?'

She sat down on the edge of the bed and regarded him over her shoulder.

'Puck?... You!... Titania, I'd say.'

'And you're the buskin'd mistress, I suppose.'

'Cease thy braying.'

'Oh, very drole. Very drole, indeed. Quite the comedi*enne*.' He sulked, bobbing slightly with annoyance, head turned away from her. 'You can be horrible at times. Quite the trollop,' he murmured with a sullen pout.

'I thought I was supposed to be Titania.'

'And so you could have been if you'd played your cards right.'

'We never do seem to hit it off,' she sighed before leaving him for her dressing-room.

She was mildly surprised to find him at breakfast, expecting him to be sulking in bed still. He certainly was more bubbly than usual. He never even grumbled when the toast shattered while he was buttering it, tossing a piece over his shoulder and sucking his fingers.

'Butter-fingers!' he ejaculated, as if inspired, with that awful falsetto laugh of his.

Isolda deliberately sat down, eyes fixed on the tablecloth.

'Eat up, m'dear! Hale and hearty and full of *joie de vivre*, what?'

There was a knock at the dining-room door. A footman entered and went to the butler. Her eyes followed him. They whispered together. The butler frowned and bent lower.

While the footman went out again Gannet whispered in his master's ear. The asinine humming ceased.

'What?' he snapped, cocking his ear. 'Who?!'

Crash. Isolda formed the word with her lips, bringing her teeth together.

'What the devil do they mean by coming here? Get rid of them this instant.'

Garbled shouting came from the hall, followed by rapid footsteps. The door burst inwards, the footman stumbled. His wig shot across the floor with a puff of powder. Sebastian rose instantly to his feet.

'What is the meaning of this rude intrusion?' he bellowed, purple in the face.

Three boys she did not know and a dog stood inside the door. One had a sword, another a shield and a spear far too big for him. The third was clearly disabled. The dog darted at the prone footman, growling and barking, then worried his wig. Even the impassive butler flickered momentarily to life before getting a grip on himself. Meanwhile his lordship was working himself into a frenzy.

'How dare you!' he shrieked. 'Disturbing your betters at their breakfast… Don't just lie there like a mouse!' he directed at the unlucky footman. 'Get up, man! Defend your master and mistress! Our home has been *violated!!*'

Bloodshot eyes bulged out of their sockets like hard-boiled eggs.

'Do something!' he ordered, slapping the butler full in the chest.

His eyes almost popped with shock and indignation. Roaring at a mere footman was one thing, but striking a butler was quite another. He felt he should instantly quit his position, had there been anybody else to employ him. The thought of truckling to that upstart, Prickleback, sent a shiver down his spine. Anything had to be better than that.

'Contain yourself, Sebastian,' Isolda exhorted.

'Contain myself?… Con-*tain* my-*self*?!!!'

'Shut up, then.'

The three boys from the village snorted at that. He staggered towards them, clenching his napkin.

'Get out!… Get out, you urchins!!'

'Sebastian… Sit down… *Sit!!!!*'

He sat, purpler than ever.

'How dare they soil my precious rugs with their dirty boots,' he muttered with chagrin.

Isolda ignored him. Gracefully, she rose to her feet. His bluff attempt at bravery had truly irritated her. If they'd been grown men, they wouldn't have heard a squeak from him. She smiled at their unexpected visitors. She had an inkling why they were here and dismissed the servants accordingly.

'Now,' Isolda began, once the door closed, 'what may we do for you?'

Huffing and snuffling came from the opposite end of the table. She pretended not to hear him, signing at them to ignore him too.

'If you please,' Edgar commenced. 'We're sorry for butting in so rudely,' – the others nodded – 'but it *is* a sort of emergency.'

More spluttering. Loud sighing. Noisy creaking of his chair.

'That's quite all right,' she assured them. 'How can we help you?'

'Hah!'

She took a deep breath and held her head high.

'How can *I* help you?'

'We need the Salmail of Finn MacCumhal,' tumbled from Edgar's lips.

'Good God! The sheer effrontery of the brat. Who told you, you impish lout?'

'Shush, dear.'

'It's nothing short of a gross outrage. To break their way into my home and churlishly demand my property, why it's beyond the *beyonds!*'

'Sebastian… shush.'

'I will not be shushed in my own home, I tell you! The *audacity* of the brat.'

Her eyes were steel-grey flint to pierce his heart with.

'Please be quiet, my dear.' She ground the words between her teeth.

'I shall be nothing of the kind.'

'Then I shall have to resort to more persuasive tactics.'

He humphed and huffed and folded his arms histrionically.

'In my own home…' they all heard. 'Is nothing sacred these days?'

'But we *need* it!' Edgar pleaded on deaf ears.

'It belongs to me and my family and, so help me, God, it shall remain in my family for evermore.'

Isolda held up a hand.

'I forbid you, woman, to tamper in affairs that do not concern you. As your lord and master, I utterly forbid you to give anything of mine to those, those… that *riffraff*… The idea! To hand such a precious article to such scum of the earth would be to cast pearls before swine. Unthinkable!'

The boys looked at one another and sniggered. Soon they were trembling with suppressed laughter.

Her ladyship ushered the three lads out of the dining-room and across the hall. At the front door Edgar turned to remonstrate with her.

'But we really do *need* it, milady. We can't fight the Aetz without it.'

'The Aetz?'

'The creature in the tower.'

'My God… So that's what that frightful noise was. It's far worse than I thought… But *he* has no intention of parting with it…'

'Couldn't *you* give it to us, milady?'

'Yes, please do,' Lee whined after him. 'It's supposed to cure Berry!'

She smiled fondly at the invalid, musing aloud. 'I'd never live it down, not that that overly concerns me.'

She cocked a mischievous eye at them.

'You'll just have to steal it.'

'*Steal it?!*'

'Come back tonight,' she instructed in a conspiratorial whisper. 'I shall leave the door open. You'll find it in the museum. In through that door there. You may have to break some glass but don't let that bother you.'

'Thank you, milady.'

'And please drop the formalities. I'm no more a milady than you are. My husband is not a milord, though he'd dearly love to be.'

'Yes, milady.'

She laughed at that, a merry ripple of laughter that appealed to them all - a beam of moonlight on a crisp winter's night.

'How did *he* end up with it, your husband, I mean?'

'You would never guess to look at him that he was a descendant of the great Finn MacCumhal, would you?' They slowly shook their heads while she nodded and grimaced at them. 'Oh, yes,' she sighed. 'How far a family can fall…'

She watched them walking down the avenue away from the house, three boys and their dog off to face unimaginable horrors, before returning to her husband and slamming the dining-room door behind her.

'I'm most disappointed in you, Sebastian.'

'Not half as much disappointed as I am in *you*.'

'Do be quiet. There goes a band of stalwart warriors. Don't you feel the slightest twinge of shame?'

'Not a bit of it.'

'I sincerely hope that Daniel shall be like them.'

'Great God Almighty! Next you'll be sending him to live amongst them in the cottages!!'

'He'd learn more about bravery *there* than he ever would *here!*'

'Stuff and nonsense. Now you're gabbling.'

She smiled to herself at the thought of the next crash hurtling towards him, more so as she was a party to the crime.

†

— 52. Thieves in the Night —

Carefully, as noislessly as possible, they let themselves in through the hall-door. The house had an unmistakable smell all of its own, rather pleasant, redolent of past history.

'Should we leave it open?' Lee breathed in Edgar's ear.

He shook his head in response. 'In case it bangs shut in a draught.'

Their leader beckoned and they crept across the floor to the museum door. He gripped and ever-so-slowly turned the brass doorknob. Gradually, inch by inch, he swung the door inwards. Not a creak or a groan was to be heard. Obviously she had oiled the hinges. The room they were entering was bathed in sombre light. A dim lamp cast pale yellow hues on all about it.

'She thinks of everything,' he mumbled appreciatively.

She lay awake in bed, listening intently, trying to catch the slightest sound. *His* soft snores and splutterings were profoundly irritating. She couldn't sleep, on tenter-hooks as to whether they'd succeed or not. How she yearned to be a girl their age again.

'Sabrehilt, that's what they call him,' she whispered to herself. 'Sabrehilt…' She savoured the word, repeating it silently with her lips. 'Sabrehilt will make some girl a fine husband… They remind me of my brothers…'

Edgar signed for Berry to close the door. The pale shaft of light slicing into the darkness would undoubtedly arouse suspicion. In silent awe all three of them wandered around the museum, leaning over glass-topped exhibition cases, peering into display cabinets, gaping at polished suits of armour.

Edgar put a forefinger to his lips. They all stopped what they were doing, raised their eyes to the ceiling and listened. Not a sound could be heard. After a few moments they settled and recommenced examining the treasures on every side. They forgot what they were about until a glimpse of the central glass case took their breath away. Berry reached for the lamp with his good hand and held it high. Yes, it was breathtakingly beautiful, one of the most beautiful things they had ever set eyes on.

Hanging on what resembled a wooden dressmaker's dummy, was the Salmail of Finn MacCumhal.

A sussurating whisper had them leap out of their skins. Berry almost dropped the lamp. Spike rumbled, baring his teeth.

A ghost-like figure in a white nightdress stood in the cleft made by the partly open door.

'I couldn't resist coming down,' she confessed. 'It's exquisite, isn't it?'

They turned and gazed at the coat of mail before them, nodding dumbly.

52. Thieves in the Night

It might have been a diamond whose facets glistened in the artificial light. The scales fit perfectly together, shimmering pink and silver and white and green and sapphire. Sparkles of light dazzled them when they moved. In awed silence they stood around the case staring at the incredible cuirass. To think it was made of the scales of the Salmon of Knowledge.

'Break the glass,' Isolda whispered.

'It's not necessary to break the glass,' Edgar told her.

'It's magic, you see,' Lee vaguely explained.

She didn't see at all. Rapt in astonishment, she watched Edgar literally slice the glass off the frame. He instructed Lee and Berry to support the pane and gently lower it to the floor.

'Truly amazing,' she whispered in wonderment. 'Whoever would have guessed?'

Edgar stretched in and lifted out the dummy. He seemed almost afraid to touch the coat of mail.

'Go on,' she encouraged him.

Gingerly, reverentially, he lifted it off the wooden shoulders and held it out. It was so incredibly light. Lighter than air.

'Try it on,' she requested.

'It's not meant for me.'

'Oh, but it is. Please try it on,' she cajoled.

He assented, put one arm through one sleeve and hooked the other arm to negotiate it through the second. He couldn't. It was too small for him.

Edgar held it up for Berry. It fit like a glove.

'So it *is* meant for you, my strange little warrior,' Isolda crooned while keeping her thoughts to herself. The coat had shrunk to fit him. It had been far larger the last time she'd seen it.

Berry was very pleased with himself. He looked down at the coat with pride, stretched out his arms and examined it more fully, forgetful of his withered hand.

'Fits you perfectly,' Lee gurgled with delight. 'All that time ago Finn MacCumhal must have been thinking of you when he made it!'

Suddenly Berry winced and went pale. He crouched and cringed. He cried out in pain, writhing on the floor.

'Quick, take it off him. It's some trick of Gerty's!' Edgar shrieked.

He bent down to help but Lee dragged him off.

'Don't be so bloody stupid, Ed. Still don't trust her, do you?'

Berry was stretched out on the floor now. A burning sensation travelled down his arm and his leg. It grew so hot that he felt he was beginning to swoon. Until he held up his hand in wonder. As a dragonfly's wings unfold and are pumped to life, so Berry's frozen fingers gently unfurled and straightened to form a perfect hand. Using it to prop himself up, he pulled off his shoe and watched his foot reshape itself. He bent it this way and that to admire the beautiful curves. Getting to his feet, he twirled on his heel, hopping and skipping and laughing out loud.

Lee whooped and held out his hand. Berry gripped it with his cured hand and almost shook it out of its socket.

'Another man to fight our corner,' Edgar stated, shaking his hand in turn.

They laughed as they looked at one another, three miniature warriors against the whole damn world. Isolda could say nothing, too close to tears. She was doubly angry with her husband now. He would have prevented all of this.

In the heat of the moment Lee forgot himself. Crowing with elation, he swung his spear in an arc. It clattered into a suit of armour which heaved over giddily and smashed into the glass case. The noise was deafening. They froze on the spot. Nor was it long before they heard shouts and footsteps descending the stairs. The only reason he'd come down was because his wife was missing and he'd guessed where she was. He caught sight of them skidding through the front door, his greedy eyes glued to the sparkling salmail.

'Come back with that, you thieving rascals!' he roared at the top of his voice, shaking his fists at them. 'I'll have you *flogged* for this. Within an inch of your *lives!!*'

Their laughter drifted back to him, driving him into a frenzy.

'Come back here!' he shrieked, purple wattles juddering with fury. 'That belongs to me and my family!'

He turned and ran into the museum.

'*You* did this!' he screeched, trembling with ire. 'This is *your* doing, madam.'

'Don't madam me,' she retorted in anger.

'Madam you?! You're fortunate I don't flog you within an inch of your *life!*'

She took up a mace from among the heap of dismantled armour and swung it with all her might. He shrieked, grabbed the hem of his nightshirt, skipped up the stairs two at a time and locked himself in the bedroom.

Isolda dropped the mace and began to laugh till she was doubled up with merriment. The spectacle he'd made of himself. In that nightshirt and that cap with its tassel, roaring like a toothless lion!

She took a deep breath, calmed herself and went to the front door.

'Use it wisely, my brave little men,' she whispered in the direction the boys had gone. 'How I wish I could join you,' she sighed, closing the door.

†

— 53. Hiatus, Too Brief at That —

The three jogged along side by side. No more did they have to wait for Berry to catch up with them. He could run faster than both of them, as fast as the wind. He raced ahead, a greyhound doubling back to laugh at them before speeding off again. Spike followed, barking at his heels, jumping up to playfully grab his sleeve. Berry lifted him off the ground, teeth clenched, and swung him through the air with his right arm. His *right* arm!

He hooted with elation and leapt high into the air, a fledgling which had stretched its wings at last and thrown itself out of the nest. He knew that Prickleback and his cronies would scowl and mutter words like witchcraft and Beelzebub but what did that matter to him now? He would laugh in their miserable faces, soaring high above them into the sun-drenched sky.

His two companions watched him as he scurried and slalomed ahead of them, arms outstretched, whooping with sheer delight.

'I wonder if the salmail can cure other people,' Lee mused aloud.

'It *might*.'

'Let's try it on poor old Tomothy.'

Through the chinks in their boarded-up windows, people stared after them as they strode purposely through the village, unafraid, unencumbered, light-hearted even. At the sight of Berry cured they were as awestruck as the crowd seeing Lazarus walk from his grave untangling his bandages.

'There he is,' said Lee, pointing to a sorry figure perched on a fence, his favourite roosting-place. He had no home to go to.

It was time to make amends for all the occasions they had jeered like the rest of them and chased him into the bog, lampooning his slack mouth and the loud incoherent sounds emanating from it.

He moaned loudly when he saw them coming and scrambled from his perch. He lurched away on unsteady legs, glancing over his shoulder till he tripped and sprawled in the dust. In seconds they were on top of him. He thrashed wildly in self-defence.

'Hold still,' Lee ordered. 'We mean you no harm. Hold *still*, I say!'

All three of them literally had to sit on him, pinning his arms and legs to the ground. Edgar was forced to slap him in the face. He lay still then, a tear rolling down his sorry face.

'Forgive me,' Edgar pleaded. 'But, please, we want to help you. If we let you go, will you promise not to run off?'

Tomothy nodded and slowly, braced to grip his wrists and ankles again if necessary, they let him go. He just lay there staring up at them, eyes wandering from one to the other.

Berry smiled his kindest smile. 'Here, put this on,' he told him in the gentlest of voices. 'I was a cripple, remember? Now look at me. All thanks to this.'

Tomothy sat up and accepted the coat of mail. Without understanding, he did as bidden. After a few moments his expression changed. He lost that vacant look mingled with fear and sorrow. His eyes brightened with an inward light. His Adam's apple bobbed up and down as if he were having difficulty swallowing. His tongue flexed itself behind his parted teeth. He looked them full in the eyes, unflinching, an equal for the first time in his life.

'I can talk.'

He uttered the words as if he were too astonished to rejoice.

'I can talk at last. I can make myself understood.'

With horror and shame Lee and Edgar realized that he had never been an idiot. He had understood their taunts all this time. Tongue knotted, he hadn't been able to tell them that there was nothing the matter with him. They had treated Tomothy as a freak when all the while he wasn't one.

'We're so sorry,' they muttered with burning shame before moving off.

'Wait!' he shouted. 'Can't I come with you?'

'You've been through enough already,' Lee rejoined. 'You don't want to get mixed up with us. Just make sure not to go anywhere near that tower and stay indoors at night. Better still... Go out to the mill and wait for us there.'

They waved at him and went on their way.

'The same could be said about you, Berry,' Lee began.

'Don't you dare,' was the growl of a reply he got for his trouble. 'Don't you bloody dare.'

'What about giving poor *Oaf* a go of it?' Edgar pronounced to dodge a nasty development.

They rapped on the door of The Slaughtered Ox. The ugly head of Gladrag Grindlewick appeared behind a window for an instant and was gone. All of a sudden the landlord wrenched the door open and scowled down at the three of them.

'What might ye be wantin'?' he snarled, spitting out of the corner of his mouth.

'We're looking for Oaf,' Edgar stuttered.

'*Oaf,* if ye don't mind…'

He knew the miller brat and the fatherless waif. He thought he recognized the other. It sure did look like the crock but his hand and his foot weren't all twisted and, so far as he knew, there was no twin brother. Nay, it couldn't be Clubby.

'Be off with ye or I'll knock yer blocks off in a trice.'

'But we're only looking for Oaf,' Lee exclaimed in exasperation.

'Oaf's gone to the devil and good riddance to 'im.'

'Gone to the devil? You don't mean…'

'Aye, I mean what I mean.'

'But…'

'Clear off, the lot o' ye!'

He swung his huge arm at them and they backed away. Then he slammed the door in their faces.

'Rotten bully,' Lee murmured with disgust.

'I hope the Aetz didn't get him.' Berry worriedly declared.

'Wouldn't surprise me if they'd served him up on a platter.'

'There are lots of poor people in this bloody place,' grumbled Edgar with a pang of guilt, 'who get the short end of the straw. All because they stick out like Bert did.'

They walked home in silence, each busy with his own reflections. Edgar and Lee were feeling bad about themselves. Berry was elated. Intuiting the gist of their thoughts, he held his peace. To him, they were without fault. They could do no wrong.

'Don't be hard on yourselves,' he eventually said to comfort them. 'We all do things we don't mean to and feel bad about them afterwards, but we wouldn't do them again.'

'Berry, you're a brick,' Lee stated with admiration. 'A ruddy *brick*,' and left it at that.

They curved in through the mill gates and drew up abruptly. The hair on Spike's shoulders and spine bristled. A growl rumbled deep in his throat.

Racker Booth was leaning nonchalantly against the well, feet crossed, for all the world at ease with himself. He smiled and snorted at his companion, not really caring whether he succeeded or not. Turlough Grindlewick was hammering with his fists on the barn-door, shouting at the top of his voice. He was so purple in the face that he was about to burst a blood-vessel.

'I know yer in there, ye miserable git!' he roared. 'You come out o' there before I break this door down, d'ye *hear*?!'

'Go away!' came a timid, though determined voice from within. Oaf's voice. 'Leave us be! We're never coming out. I know what you're after and you'll never get your hands on any of us!'

Grindlewick stood there listening, head hanging while one hand leaned against the barn-door.

'Rack,' he swung over his shoulder, 'get me an axe.'

'Do no such thing!'

Both men turned on a sudden and glared at the trio. Contempt and amusement began to replace the surprise in their eyes.

'Get off my property.'

'*Yours*?' Rack mocked.

'I warned you before...'

'An' I warned *ye*, ye little tike.'

Rack drew a knife from his pocket and braced himself. With a roar he rushed forward once Grindlewick moved in.

The innkeeper let out a shriek and gripped his wrist. Four of his fingers lay in the dust, in a pool of blood drip-dripping from the four raw stumps. Rack fell back when the blade of his knife shattered on the salmail. Coward that he was, he had purposely set upon the weakest of them. Or so he'd thought. He bolted, leaving a whimpering Grindlewick fumbling to pick up his fingers.

'Don't ever come back,' growled Edgar. 'The next time I see you here it won't be your fingers. It'll be your *head*... Oaf can stay here as long as he likes and if you ever bother him again... you know what I'll do.'

Off loped the innkeeper, casting frightened glances over his shoulder.

53. Hiatus, Too Brief at That

They lounged before a blazing turf fire. Oaf's young siblings were seated on the hearth-rug clasping their knees. They had tried the salmail round Oaf's shoulders but nothing had happened apart from his eye being cured.

'You're fine,' declared Edgar at the time. 'There's nothing wrong with you, Oaf. Don't believe a word they say.'

Oaf had told them, with tears in his voice, what his dastardly father had suggested and they in turn recounted what had happened to the late Mrs. Prickleback.

'Don't be surprised, Oaf,' Lee commented. 'They'd do anything to save their ugly skins, my father included.'

'He's dead, Lee... Sank in the sand off the cliffs.'

'I didn't know.'

Lee felt sorrowful. Sorrowful that there was no father to mourn. He was untouched by his death, just as he'd been untouched by his heart when alive. I wanted to be a son to him but he never let me...

Tomothy stood there regarding him, somewhat unsure of himself, distrustful of his new-found voice. He plucked up the courage to say what was on his mind.

'I'm sorry to hear about your father, Lee.'

Lee smiled at him with tears brimming in his eyes. 'Yours wasn't much of a father either,' he croaked, swallowing his grief while Tomothy grimaced and shook his head.

The young ones slept where they were, before the clinking grate, while the older boys lolled in the armchairs, heads falling forward and jerking back with the odd snort or snore, dreaming of exploding bladders.

Except for Edgar.

Sabrehilt had his sword.
Lee was equipped with his spear and his shield.
Berry wore the salmail.

That meant one thing and one thing only...

Tomorrow was the day.

TOMORROW!!

The sun inexorably climbed above the horizon. It rose faster than ever before, skimming across the firmament. Light flooded the room and sharply delineated the sleeping forms all around him. How he envied them. How he yearned for that wonderful feeling he'd never appreciated till now, a smile on his face as he snuggled down, closing his eyes on impertinent daylight. He willed them to sleep forever. As he did so they began to stir and mutter and smack their lips and open their eyes and smile at him before remembering.

†

— PART IV —

MALESTROM

— 54. The Stench of Death —

They stood there, three boys and a dog, at the base of the hill in a land despoiled. The tower seemed to soar into the sky. Oaf had gladly stayed behind to protect his brothers and sisters. No one blamed him. Setting a scarecrow alight was one thing, facing the Aetz quite another. Tomothy, to his eternal credit, had had to be forced to remain. They'd left the pair of them looking after them, the kids still asleep on the rug.

And now, here they were. Where destiny had brought them.

What they had had to wade through to get here was seared into their subconscious forever.

A scene of desolation stretched all about them. A world grisailled, sapped of colour. Twilight settled on their minds. They forgot about love and joy and youthful vigour, their blanched senses as pale as their surroundings. But one colour predominated.

Red.

Red for blood.

The buzzing of flies was tremendous. Mounds of maggots seethed in waves, making their own marshmallow sound. Great masses of them filled rotting ribcages. Gorged on filth, they plopped to the ground, heavy as pine-cones.

They had stumbled over half-eaten arms and legs while crossing the field. Limbs torn out at the sockets, knees twisted and pulled apart, were strewn about in the trampled grass. Smooth laminae of cartilage glistened in what light there was.

In disbelief they stared about them at tangled coils of steaming entrails, cupped hooves, hollow horns, longbones sucked dry of marrow. A skinned head lay on its side like a discarded football, bulging eyes staring at nothing. Strips of matted sheepskin resembled torn mats and rugs thrown here and there. They trod in the stinking stools of the Morgammeron Aetz, pulling out their boots with grimaces of revulsion. Hairballs, skulls, shards of bone and teeth were clearly recognizable. It had fouled the fields, fouled the landscape, fouled the peninsula – fouled their world.

The unforgettable stench of an abbatoir filled their nostrils. Their arms and legs and faces were smeared with blood and slime. The noisome stink of detritus rose from everywhere into the air, clogging their airways and filling their lungs. They felt sick and giddy. The world about them lurched and swayed drunkenly before misting over. Lee staggered and vomited. If there was one thing Berry couldn't stand it was vomiting – he puked as well. Edgar retched, spewing more than anyone when Spike sniffed at Lee's.

54. The Stench of Death

They looked up at the tower and lingered momentarily. They began to climb the hill as one.

†

— 55. Into the Wasps' Nest —

The tower seemed to be shrinking, stooping down to meet them. And the hill was a hill no more - a bump they could leap over had they wished to.

'We should form a plan,' croaked Edgar.

'It's a bit late now,' rasped a despondent Lee.

'But what are we to do?'

'Go on, I suppose… Fight.'

'To the death,' Berry interposed like a pessimistic soothsayer.

The atmosphere was charged with expectation. A bleak wind moaned and made them shiver. Ugly, sibilant whispers wound themselves round the walls and pierced their eardrums. Sounds crashed back and forth like angry waves. They quailed and covered their ears, eyes fixed on the tower.

The gargoyles had been watching their approach from the corners of their eyes. They twitched and suddenly turned their heads. Those out of view craned their necks to curve round the corners like pythons. They stared viciously and fixedly, the stench of boy tingling in their nostrils. All together, as one, they squawked, they shrieked, they growled, they screamed. The hideous sound was hurled against them and knocked them down. It swept over them into the woods, bending bough and tree-trunk on its way to the village. Every man, woman, child and beast froze with terror.

As for the boys, they lay flat on their backs staring dazedly upwards. Their eyes widened. Their hearts beat a riotous tattoo on their ribs. Their hair stood on end.

Something was up there.

On the roof.

And that something knew they were down below.

A head shot out over the parapet. A low growl reached their ears, thick with saliva. It gripped two merlons and swung itself out. The gargoyles fell silent and stiff-necked. A foot rested on one. A second foot stretched out to reach another. Pus and clots of blood spurted from their open mouths. Huge fists grasped the solid heads and down it came towards them. There was no denying what it was.

The Morgammeron Aetz was approaching.

It sprang from the face of the wall and the ground shuddered beneath it. The gargoyles screeched with bloodthirsty glee. It turned and faced them, more hideous than anything they had ever imagined.

This was their enemy, seen at last. This was Nemesis incarnate, not something to send little boys to do battle with. Still they lay stretched on the ground, pinioned to the earth by terror. Sabrehilt was forgotten, Shieldbearer eclipsed. Berry was no brave.

Their eyes travelled up the length and breadth of the monster, a colossus to separate earth and sky. It was hideous to behold. With hardly any neck, its enormous head seemed propped on its massive shoulders. Its arms were gigantic. So were its legs, bowed under the weight of its torso. Those mammoth fists could pulverize a meteor, a comet, *all* of planet Earth.

The most awful stench filled their nostrils and seemed to flow in their veins. Of potato-blight, rotting cabbage and cauliflower. Of tom-cat pee and sweaty socks and cheesy toes. Of filthy barns and stables and styes. The sharp reek of ammonia stung their sinuses. As for its breath – warm blasts of slurry struck their faces every time it exhaled.

The Aetz' lungs sounded like a gigantic bellows. With every breath, dense black clouds of flies exited from its mouth - bluebottles and dung-flies and many, many more. Swarms of the vile insects rose into the air and started for the village. A few remained to circle the creature's head as a diabolical halo. Sounds emanated from between its lips. For every dissonant syllable, wasps emerged.

Its skin was dark brown, leathery and cracked, great patches of it scaling in places. Longish, crinkly hairs poked sparsely from its hide, rendering it uglier still. Stuggy fingers ended in dirty, broken claws, clotted blood and guano caked beneath them. Slab-like toes were filthier than its fingers, nails frayed and riddled with canker.

Their eyes rose to its swollen belly, a mat of hairs in the centre. A long tubule of rotting flesh protruded from its navel and hung down over its groin. Flies swarmed about it. Maggots crawled from the recesses and plumped to the ground. The creature bent down, took a juicy specimen between finger and thumb and sucked it into its mouth.

Tufts of hair resembled patches of dirt over its chest. Crusty nodules encircled its nipples. A small swelling moved about under the skin, their eyes followed it mesmerized. A nipple bulged, opened, and out wriggled a huge yellow grub. Its dirty black head latched onto the nipple and dangled there. Their empty stomachs knotted and they retched loudly.

Its gargantuan head towered above them, a monstrous boulder on the edge of a precipice. Muscles like taut rope stretched from its shoulders and prevented it toppling over. The scalp was horribly scarified, the skull exposed in places. Worms fed at the livid edges of broken skin. Pustules and open sores covered its face. Thick lips were fissured and scarred. Bristles poked from wide nostrils at the end of a flattened nose. Scaly insects parted the hairs of its bushy eyebrows and moved on through them. One fell and a lightning tongue caught it, crushing it between sharp, yellow teeth. Clumps of hair and clots of blood were lodged in the spaces between them. The thick, muscular tongue was caked in a heavy layer of scum. Hooked spines poked through it.

The badness was oozing out everywhere, like magma through the earth's crust. But all this was nothing compared to its eyes – black, empty, merciless wells of hate and destruction. The lids were transparent membranes so that it never stopped watching you.

A thing of menacing power, it was neither goblin nor ogre. They had lied, the lot of them. No one had said anything about a creature like this. It was the personification of all the evil and greed of the villagers. It was their own neighbours they were fighting. Edgar almost cursed his grandpa for saving their lives. But this thing was all too real for that, more lethal than a mob of yokels with a hypocrite at their head. *They* couldn't resist the sword but could *this...?*... Bony plates thick as the tower's walls protected its evil brain. Above its left temple was a small dent caused by a slingshot in a forgotten time. It had done no more damage than a pebble.

This was the monster that had killed the last Sabrehilt...

The creature's eyes glazed over. It grimaced and grunted. Loose balls of dung dropped between its legs to steam on the ground. Hot, foetid air exploded from its innards and relief relaxed its features. To their horror, these balls broke open to reveal the hairless embryos of mice curled up inside them. Rapidly they grew in size, as hair covered their delicate pink skin. They crawled from their revolting cradles and scurried towards the woods and the village.

Urine suddenly dribbled from an impenetrable thicket of hairs, quickening to a sturdy stream. The liquid arc widened and its voidings frothed on the earth before their feet. They could feel droplets splash onto their faces and arms, crawling backwards to avoid it.

Their look of unmistakeable repugnance amused the creature. But it was amusement which quickly turned to anger. A harsh glint shone in its eyes. A rumble started in its belly and became a full-bodied roar of malediction which the gargoyles amplified immediately. Its teeth were clearly visible in its gaping, bony head, the back of its cavernous throat, the swinging uvula. They felt they were being sucked into the chasms of hell.

— 56. Pius Ecorché —

At that precise moment, who should appear round the corner of the tower but Pius Hornswoggle. He strolled towards them as if completely oblivious of danger. Unbelievably, there was a flicker of a smile on his face. The boys gaped in astonishment, certain he was out of his mind. Sensing there was something behind it, the Aetz ceased roaring and looked over its shoulder. It liked what it saw. A grunt of appreciation escaped it and it lumbered round to face the schoolmaster who looked through it to amicably nod at Edgar.

'Hullo, Edgar.'

'He *is* mad,' Lee managed to whisper between his teeth.

Edgar acknowledged him with a frown of utter confusion. What did he think he was doing? Didn't he *see* it? Had he any idea what it could *do* to a person?!

But Pius only had eyes for Edgar. Demented by failure, he had come to save his life – to become a hero in his eyes. It was such a wonderful dream that he couldn't help acting on it. So there he stood, that spindly body, those sad, haunted eyes, the bubble of spittle in the centre of his lower lip.

Chuckling sounds shook the Aetz' mighty frame. Edgar felt his hair stand on end. He knew what was coming.

'Get out of here,' he shot at the schoolmaster.

'I've come to help you. Nobody else has.'

A pang of pity stabbbed at Edgar's breast. This fool, this poor, poor, deluded fool has come out against the Morgammeron Aetz for *my* sake.

'Go home, Mister Hornswoggle,' he gently admonished.

'You need me here.' A desperate man, his voice was rising shrilly.

'No, I don't. There's nothing you can do for me.'

'But...'

Self-pity, victimization and melancholia ran to addictive proportions. He could not imagine life without them, his identity stolen from him. His one consolation was that he suffered and suffered cruelly. It set him apart. Happiness was an alien attribute possessed by lesser mortals. If the boy refused him, he wished to die in his presence – so that the ungrateful wretch would spend the rest of his life tortured by guilt.

'Please go away,' Edgar pleaded.

Pius only flashed him a wry smile and shook his head.

'Before you're *hurt!*'

He was in earnest and Pius was glad of that. It meant he cared.

'Leave him,' Lee snarled out of the side of his mouth. 'The fool's off his rocker.'

'I used to think you were a good lad, Lee Chetwold. I was sadly mistaken.'

He wallowed in self-imposed affliction, avid for more suffering in Edgar's presence. Drunk with vicarious love and triumph, he hadn't even glanced at the monstrosity before him to figure out how on earth he could rescue Edgar.

A shritch shrivelled the flesh on their backs. The creature snatched up the schoolmaster in its hand and roared in his face. Pius screamed in terror at his folly. Too late. Delusions had blinded him to danger. He knew he was lost, forgot even Edgar in his panic. Fingers and claws tore at his clothing and he was dropped to the ground, naked as the day he was born. Lee almost spluttered at the concave chest, the bony legs, the putty-coloured skin. The pathetic figure was snatched up again before a smile stretched his lips. The Aetz took delight in playing with the man, a cat with a mouse. It dropped him, seizing an ankle before he got away.

Pius clutched vainly at the dead grass, uprooted in tufts by his fists. He swung through the air over the boys' heads before being released. With a sickening thud he fell flat on his face from a height. Sad, despairing eyes glanced Edgar full in the face. But what was the boy to do? He'd warned him. He'd shouted at him to get away. The schoolmaster shrieked and sprawled in the dust as a huge foot was planted in the small of his back. The Aetz stooped and gripped one of his hands, tugging at his arm till he wailed in agony.

It grew bored with its plaything. An ominous frown darkened its features. In an instant Pius was flung high into the air, his cry waning in the distance. The Aetz caught him as he fell and shook him. They thought his head would tear off his neck it wobbled so violently.

Done with preliminaries, the creature gripped a sliver of skin at the nape of his neck and tore it off, exposing his spine. Pius' agonized screams were bloodcurdling. Strips of skin fell all about the boys. Dropped onto the ground, the unfortunate schoolmaster writhed in agony, every muscle and sinew and ligament exposed. Unhooded, unblinking eyes stared up at his adversary. He whimpered as it bent down. He screeched when it gripped him round the ankles and calves like a doll. He roared while he approached its slavering mouth and an arm was bitten off at the shoulder. It chewed and swallowed while he wailed in its face.

His shrieks became muffled when rubbery lips closed on his neck, amplifying again when they opened. They saw his head between its teeth. There was a sickening crunch and silence. A headless, armless torso was held out for inspection before being flipped down that hideous throat.

The Aetz smacked its lips. It belched unceremoniously.

He had been right about one thing, Pius had. They would never forget him. Because they had never witnessed death at close quarters before, nor seen such an end as his. They were harrowed to the depths of their souls.

A huge bony face appeared hovering over the grass before their eyes. It grimaced, tongue working in its mouth as if something were lodged between its teeth. Its lips bulged and it spat. A bloody foot flopped onto the ground before them. They started, cried out and clawed their way backwards. Somehow they got to their feet but one stamp of its foot had them sprawling on the earth again. The ground shook as if rent by an earthquake. They stared at the foot, all that was left of the schoolmaster. The Aetz picked up the grisly remnant and waved it before their faces while they arched their necks to avoid it. It grunted, popped it into its mouth and swallowed.

Pius was no more.

— 57. Reinforcements, Fleeting at Best —

A white speck distracted Edgar out of the corner of his eye. He gasped as his heart did a leap in his breast. A magnificent swan, grace bewinged, slowly descended in a decreasing circle. As it glided to the ground behind the Aetz, its feathers ruffled and it became a lady of dazzling beauty. She gently set foot on the brow of the hill.

'It's the witch,' Lee whispered through barely parted lips.

'It's got to be,' Edgar breathed.

'*She'll* get rid of it,' Berry murmured with relief, mesmerized by her loveliness.

Her garment seemed to be of earth and sky, shimmering like silver-backed leaves in a breeze, morning sunlight on a saltwater marsh penetrating to the greenery below. Soft, dark hair cascaded over her shoulders. Topaz eyes smiled at them and warmed their hearts. She was real, yet unreal, a nymph, a sprite, denizen of a city of golden light.

No sound reached their ears, but they heard her velvety voice echoing in the labyrinths of their minds. Her dulcet tones dispelled their fears. Their worries floated away. They heard each other's thoughts addressed to her and the replies she gave.

'Can you help us?'

'I have come for that.'

'Are you quick enough?'

'As quick as time.'

'It can't harm you, can it?'

They all yearned for an answer, though none was forthcoming.

She looked up at the towering bulk of the Aetz and smiled. Not a smile of despair or of triumph, impossible to decipher. Then she smiled at them and they forgot their concerns but briefly.

'You're not going to *die*?'

She laughed, crystals in the wind.

'Is death so dreadful?'

'Don't do it!'

'You too must follow your path.'

'But...'

'Do not fear. Hope derives from the birth pangs of despair.'

All this occurred in a matter of seconds. The Aetz let out a grunt of surprise at the fact that there was somebody else behind it. Looking over its shoulder, it squinted down at her while she continued to talk with the boys. It made a peculiar guttural sound in the back of its throat. Slowly, fearlessly, she looked up into its eyes. The Aetz showed no signs of fear but it didn't chuckle as it had at Pius.

A rustling sound reached their ears. They looked down to see hordes of scarecrows surrounding the hill. The Aetz had obviously summoned them. Their vacant eyes stared upwards, transfixed and waiting for a signal. Each and every one of them had a hoodie on its shoulder.

57. Reinforcements, Fleeting at Best

Edgar realised with a sharp pang of fear that there was no need for a Sabrehilt if the witch was going to destroy the Aetz

'Don't do it!' he shouted at the top of his voice.

She chose not to hear him. Rising into the air, her garment drifted in her wake like a a mist. As she gained height she once again adopted the form of a beautiful swan. Slow, muscular wingbeats took her higher and higher till she soared above them, dazzling white.

An impatient flick of the Aetz' wrist had an impenetrable pall of crows surging towards her, cackling and squawking till they were deafened below. She was blotted out entirely from their sight but they knew she was coming off best by the clouds of black feathers floating down, the corpses thumping the turf all around them. Then she was free, in a wide circle of sky while the crows kept their distance. A surly growl had them plummeting to earth to perch on their scarecrows' shoulders.

A peculiar whistle emerged from between the Aetz' teeth.

Cloud upon cloud of raucous bats erupted from the roof of the tower. Leathery wings savagely beat the air in discordant rhythm. This time no flittered bodies fell to earth. No circle of sky opened in the lowering cloud. There was a high-pitched scream. The white form battered through the dark mass and struck the ground full force. Her shattered body relaxed in death. Before their eyes she turned into a beautiful woman again and vanished.

'Quick,' Edgar whispered while the thing pondered her disappearance. 'Run!'

Fast as lightning they reached the base of the hill. Edgar hacked a way through for them, Spike hot on their heels.

The Aetz turned, saw them and roared. The scarecrows immediately shook and rattled and let out that hair-raising moan of theirs.

'The elks!' Edgar roared. 'Make for the bog!'

They sped through the crowd, Spike barking jubilantly as the sea of staring faces separated to either side of them. The earth shook and they almost fell on their faces. It shook again. Over their shoulders they saw the Aetz descending the hill and coming after them. They ran faster than ever.

'We've got to get there before it catches up with us!' Edgar shrieked with alarm.

They redoubled their efforts and reached the edge of the bog moments afterwards.

'Berry, throw it in. Quick!'

Berry frantically fished in his pocket and withdrew the polished stone, throwing it far into the murky morass.

They waited...

An age passed...

Dread and panic fizzled in their veins, effervescing in their groins. A ripple disturbed the black viscid water, but they couldn't be sure. Then bubbles rose from impenetrable depths and broke the surface. They began to rise with fury, the water hissing and boiling. The black spongy soil rippled and bulged. Sharp spurs emerged at intervals.

57. Reinforcements, Fleeting at Best

Antlers!

Four of them!

They were gigantic, dwarfing the two skulls that bore them aloft. The vertebrae of their necks appeared, then their backbones and ribcages. These majestic beasts waded through bog water to reach solid ground. Giant forelimbs struck the earth a shudder and they drew themselves onto dry land. Water ran down huge skeletons the colour of ebony. They swayed slightly before steadying themselves, towering above their summoners. They stretched their necks. Empty sockets surveyed the landscape and fastened on the Aetz.

'*Now* who's for it?' Lee mumbled to himself with satisfaction.

The boys stepped back in expectation. The elks bucked and thundered across the field to meet their adversary. As they closed on it, one galloped forward and lowered its head. The Aetz ran before them towards the woods.

'It's running away!' Edgar shouted with glee.

The foremost elk's antlers skimmed the ground as it approached the creature. They waited for the impact, but the Aetz swung out of the way and uprooted a tree. With this it struck the beast a resounding blow. Bones flew in all directions.

The second elk pawed the ground and flew at it next. They connected. The Aetz lost its balance and fell. The boys held their breath while the elk stabbed it with its antlers. Thousands of crows swooped on the animal. It resembled something tarred and feathered but kept up its pounding and prodding. The Aetz let out a roar and jumped to its feet. It gripped the two antlers and grappled the elk to the ground. There came a loud snap and the skeleton collapsed in a heap. It held the head and antlers high above its own head and roared and roared. One after the other it pounded the bones to dust, ordering the crows to fetch the rest. Never again would the elks be recalled from the bog. It had made sure of that.

The boys groaned as one and sagged in despair.

'Will nothing stop it?' sobbed Edgar. 'Everything sent to help us is killed.'

Lee grimaced wryly. Berry was lost for words. Edgar just glanced at his sword and shuddered.

— 58. Lost Without It —

Edgar felt his ribs constricting round his heart. It hurt so much to breathe. The Aetz had pounded the last of the elks' bones to powder and now turned its thoughts to them. It growled menacingly, mephitic vapours reaching them on the wind. Slowly they sank to their knees.

'Now we're for it,' Lee murmured despondently.

Things were happening too quickly. There was no time to think.

Edgar had a very bad feeling, a premonition... Could Gerty be reading the book and shouting at him to get the hell out of there?... But what chance had they got of escaping? That thing could run, could vault over entire fields if it wanted to.

'God has forgotten us,' he moaned with a sinking heart.

Refusing to give in to morbid thoughts, the flat of his palm felt about until it came in contact with the hilt of his sword. He lifted it and tensed every muscle, training every nerve on the task before him.

With a roar he leapt to his feet. Holding his sword high in the air, he ran at the Aetz with a high-sounding battle-cry. Lee and Berry scrambled after him, echoing his clarion call.

A breathy gasp escaped the astonished scarecrows. The Aetz stalled, stunned by their temerity. It was laughable, in-*sane.*

It was time to finish them off.

It shook its head angrily, disturbing the halo of flies. A frightful roar drowned out the boys' voices.

Edgar accelerated, drawing his sword back as far as he could. With a roar to match the creature's, he swung it upwards and forwards.

He stopped dead in his tracks.

Hyperalert senses plunged everything into slow-motion.

His arm was being held up before him. Four fingers and a thumb. The crook of his elbow. The torn skin and muscle. The creamy knob of bone which should have been fixed to his shoulder-blade. . . The white sliver of a nerve dangling free like a huge worm... He took it all in so slowly and rapidly. It was hard to believe. He should have been writhing in agony. And yet...

He turned to examine his shoulder, a mess of bloody pulp. A fine spray pulsed into the air and fell in an arc. His blood stained the earth. He began to feel faint as a dull throbbing became a sharp, insistent pain screeching to be recognized. It throbbed in rhythm to his pounding heart. He seemed to be alone with his pain, in a mist absorbing all sound, all colour, all reality outside of himself. Muffled noises vaguely penetrated to his ears but he knew not what they signified. He sank to his knees, weak from the loss of blood.

With a riotous, baritone roar, Lee sprang forward to be swept aside like a gnat. He tumbled and rolled and lay behind the Aetz, stunned momentarily. He looked up at the granite shoulders, the lower back and legs solid as a building. For some unknown reason he was reminded of the schoolmaster. The thought jogged his memory, reminding him of Achilles.

Achilles!

Lee staggered to his feet and grabbed his spear. He hurled it with all his might. It hit the massive tendon and penetrated the bone, shivering on impact. The Aetz dropped Edgar's arm immediately, emitting a roar of pain and surprise. It lifted its foot and plucked the spear from its ankle. Flinging it down, it heaved round to destroy the culprit. But Lee was too quick for it. He shouted at Edgar to get the hell out of there and snatched up his spear and his sword. Berry rushed in to pick up his arm. He ran to Edgar who was still in a daze, shaking him vigorously, bawling in his face.

'We've got to get away *now*! It's our only *chance*!'

Edgar finally stood up, tottered and ran for his life. Lee checked over his shoulder.

'He's not following! He's just staring at us… *Edgar*!'

His best friend crumpled and collapsed on the ground.

'He's bleeding to death!' Lee cried out in horror.

Berry had a flash of inspiration.

'Lee!' he ordered. 'Hold the arm up to his shoulder. Just do it!'

Lee jammed the arm into place, apologising when Edgar screamed in agony.

Berry threw the salmail over his shoulders.

The bleeding stopped. The tissues began to knit together. The torn ends of the arteries and veins and nerves fused to perfection. The fingers twitched and jolted to life. And finally, there, before their very eyes, the broken skin seemed to melt and merge into a flawless covering.

With no time to lose, they gripped Edgar's wrists and hauled him to his feet, dragging him after them. A breathy moan escaped the scarecrows scattering to either side of them.

But the Aetz had seen.

And the Aetz wouldn't forget.

Back home, they sprawled in armchairs. Still in a daze, Edgar held up his arm and gazed intently at it. He moved his fingers, watching the ligaments glide smoothly beneath his skin. Probing the groove behind his thumb, he felt his pulse. If it weren't for the salmail...

He massaged his neck, slowling revolving it from side to side. For the briefest of moments he felt invincible.

Lee had woken up and was watching him in silence.

'It's only starting,' he leaned forward and whispered to bring him back down to earth.

†

— 59. Fury Unleashed —

The Aetz was fain to vent its anger on the populace at large. The brats had escaped. Their leader had had his arm restored by that magical coat of mail. A deplorable outcome, it stank too much of good fortune. Incensed, the creature stomped through the army of scarecrows, flattening those in its path underfoot, dashing some more into the adjoining fields with the back of its fist. The flies round its head flew in frenzied circles. Those that alighted on its scalp were snatched by the jaws of worm-like creatures boring and burrowing beneath its skin.

It huffed and it puffed and it blew clouds of bluebottles into the air. It growled and grunted and spat swarms of wasps and hornets from its maw. Prodigious amounts of dung was voided to release hordes of mice which streaked across the fields towards the village. When it reached the tower it yanked the head of a gargoyle from out of the wall and threw it high into the air. It fell to earth on the village green, grinning and baring its fangs.

The Aetz climbed to the roof and vaulted over the battlements. The hoarse whistling began in its throat again and a world of bats burst forth from every window and door, swirling and corkscrewing, ascending and scattering. A few, in their eagerness to obey, emerged from the mouths of the gargoyles who snapped at their heels. A subtle roar had a host of crows leap into the air from scarecrow shoulders, chattering and chuckling and cawing sweet death threats. It threw back its head, opened wide its mouth, and howled. Wolves danced on their hindlegs and howled in unison before galloping off into the woods.

Once the moon rose the Aetz straddled the jagged merlons and rocked to and fro. More than anything else it wanted to see and hear what those three boys were up to... Why did they preoccupy it so? Why didn't it descend the tower and hunt them down?... Was it afraid? Did it recognize him with the sword? It denied any such thing, grunting and snarling until the moon reached its zenith.

The truth of the matter was that it was powerless to leave the precincts of the tower. It knew that somewhere close by, hidden by the trees, was a presence. *He* placed a limit on where it could go. *He* spelt Fear and Loathing, a Power it could not engage. Yet this binding force had its limits... The creature chuckled, a guttural ruffle of phlegm. The wickedness of the villagers, that was his stumbling-block. The Aetz drew its strength from their vices. Without them, it wouldn't have been there at all.

In the silence that suceeded its fall, the gargoyle rocked and tilted on the grass of the green. Gagging sounds came from its throat. A dark mass began to emerge from its mouth. But this was no pulpy mess of vomit. This was alive. It tapered towards a tail and was free. Immediately it was exposed to the air, its skin hardened. Small fissures then appeared in the brittle surface. They widened to cracks. The front end burst open and a head protruded. Legs appeared and it began to draw itself forth, until it was free of its shell.

A giant millipede, black as coal, quivered in the midst of the village. Armour-plate segments glinted in the moon-light, midnight scales reflecting her mournful face in facets. A hundred feet of tensile muscle under impenetrable chitin, it savoured the atmosphere with its flickering antennae. It wriggled. It curled on itself. It set off in the direction of the hill and the bridge, legs working so quickly that it appeared to glide through the air.

At the same time hordes of scarecrows broke down stiles, smashed through hedges and strode across fields. In silence they proceeded through the undergrowth and congregated next the perimeter of the woods. Waiting...

Without one solitary squeak, clouds of bats had pitched down to hang from gutters and rafters. Waiting...

Mice were banked up in the ditches, wolves grouped in packs in the shadows. Waiting...

Mute gangs of crows balanced on every twig on every treetop. Waiting... Waiting... Waiting...

The atmosphere was pregnant with portent. An intense hush lay over the entire peninsula. The air was charged with electricity and heavy with moisture as before a tremendous storm. The very stones seemed to hum and tremble. People sat or stood in their barricaded houses, ears straining for the slightest sound, willing it and wishing it away. The ten-sion was agony. Children curled up and pretended to be elsewhere.

Waiting...

Turlough Grindlewick nursed his damaged hand, staring at his severed fingers pickling in a jar of brandy. Under his breath he swore he'd lop off Edgar's fingers one by one and then he'd start on his toes and his ears. Gladrag stood in the shadows massaging a split lip. He had caught her smirking and struck her full in the face. Secretly, she was glad the boy had hurt him, so angry that she wished it had been his head that had bitten the dust. But that would have to wait. It was high time they descended to the cellar...

Rack hid at home, fermenting. His thoughts too were focused on the boy. He knew he'd have to kill the brat to get his clutches on the mill. A knife in the back before he knew anything about it would be best. He was good at that. But now was not the time. Alone, free from the pressure of prying eyes, he could cower under his bed unknown...

Prickleback slouched in an armchair in his library, before a roaring fire. He sipped from a pint glass of sherry and chuckled to himself, excitement, astonishment and a tiny atom of guilt bubbling in his veins. He had done it... He had finally got rid of the barren, mewling jade. More wondrous still, his peace-offering had been accepted, rendering him immune from danger. He was safe. The whole village could go to the devil. He threw back his head and guffawed at a ceiling ornamented by mitres and croziers. He would be archbishop one day. God wanted it so. Why else had he been spared?

59. Fury Unleashed

While the rest of the villagers were cowering behind barricaded doors and windows, there were many who were gone. Their homes had been invaded and emptied of all who lived there. The wind stirred the dust on the floor. A broken jug rocked back and forth on bloodstained floorboards. A mug fell from a table and burst asunder. But nobody was there to see or hear save the ghosts of earlier times, ghosts who also had barricaded themselves indoors against a common foe...

Waiting...

Then, its army in battle array, the Aetz jerked up its head and roared that montrous roar. A dull throaty rumble rose to a shrill yawp that set the molecules of air vibrating. The entire peninsula was engulfed in sound, as if had been torn from the earth by those encrusted teeth and wobbled on the back of its tongue. Uppermost in every mind was the insatiable gullet making that hideous noise.

The army cast no shadow in the village that night. Scarecrows stalked from the fringe of the woods. Mice scampered after them. Wolves loped from the shadows and cantered to a gallop. Bats and crows rose into the air. All descended as one on the cottages. There was a face in every window, a wolf at every door. Bats and crows tumbled down every chimney. Mice crept over every threshold.

The screams that erupted in the houses vied with the roar of the Aetz - a harmony of terror and hate. Crazed by fear, they broke through their barricades and ran helter-skelter. Man abandoned wife. Mother abandoned children. Brothers and sisters who clung to one another perished.

Doors and windows were smashed to smithereens. Shards of crockery littered the floors. Rent curtains blew through empty panes, soaked by the rain. Blood dripped onto bare floorboards and left an indelible stain. Not a body remained. Not a corpse was to be seen.

Those who had escaped fled to the bishop's palace and pounded on its reinforced door. A casement opened overhead and a rude voice barked down at them.

'Who is it? What do you want?'

The pale face of the reverend leaned out above them.

'Reverend Prickleback, 'tis us!'

'Who's us?' he testily questioned them.

'What remains of yer flock, man!'

'The village is beseiged!'

'We're undone!'

'What nonsense is this? Get thee hence to thy beds!'

'We've nowhere to go!'

'Let us in, we beseech thee!'

'Certainly not… Go home… No, wait!… Go to the mill and find the Falchion brat!.

'He's dead.'

'Are you certain?'

'Aye. Him and his cronies… They were seen at the tower, they couldn't have escaped.'

'Are you sure, man?'

'Aye. They haven't been seen since.'

'And Booth? Racker *Booth*?'

'Dead too, for all we know.'

'Go home,' he admonished and shut the window.

They lingered below, close to the walls for comfort, drenched to the skin, starting at every sound and fearful of what daylight would bring. While Prickleback, their Shepherd, skipped jubilantly back to bed.

†

— 60. A Close Call Closing —

The millipede darted across the green and up the hill. It cornered an old woman in her cottage, too feeble to barricade herself in. It coiled around her unconscious body, gripping her tightly with its feet. Sharp fangs pierced her temples, injecting venom into her brain. Her eyes shot open. Her body went rigid as steel. She threw convulsions and frothed at the mouth. A squeal escaped her as the air was forced from her lungs. Death clouded her eyes and she entered the realm of indifferent shades.

Grindlewick and his woman stood in the hall between entrance and stairs, about to descend to the cellar when something without struck the doors a heavy blow. They strained under the weight and bulged inwards. His initial reaction was to hurl the bulk of his wife against the doors and fly upstairs. The doors gave way, fortuitously shielding Gladrag next the wall. Unseen by her, the head of the millipede jutted into the inn and the myriad segments ascended the stairs. She heard another door open and a cry of horror from her mate.

Turlough cowered in the corner of an empty room, arms splayed against the wall, eyes peeled on the sight before him. But the millipede drew no closer. He watched in disbelief as it reversed through the door, down the staircase and out of the inn. He threw back his head and crowed with laughter. Remembering his wife, he peered down the stairs. She was nowhere to be seen. Had it devoured her? Was it too full of her lard to eat him as well? What did it matter when he lived to tell the tale?

Unless…

His eyes dilated in alarm. He rushed headlong down the stairs to the cellar.

The door was shut fast.

She had locked herself in. He knew she wouldn't open it up for him.

'Gla-ad?' he cooed in wheedling tones. 'Are ye in there?'

He rattled the handle and pounded on the door.

'Glad! Open up, there, Glad!… Please, Glad.'

She sat in the dark and listened.

'First cooin' like a dove,' she murmured under her breath. 'Then a little panicky, oh, dear. After that comes the commandin' 'usband who must be obeyed till death do us part. An' now… now the little boy who's afraid o' the dark.' Her features convulsed in a glare of malice. 'Ye can stay where ye are, ye cowardly ape. I 'ope it comes back for ye!'

He gasped and trembled at the howl of a wolf.

'Glad, open up… I *beg* thee, Glad!'

She heard him pound his way upstairs, dash across the taproom and out the back door. She heard no more.

Grindlewick locked himself in a stable and climbed to the second floor where he knelt by the window, peering out.

60. A Close Call Closing

His breath came in shallow bursts, turbulent in hairy nostrils. So scared was he that he would have welcomed Oaf as company. But Oaf was far away, driven off by his own father.

It was so quiet out there. Too quiet. He slid down the wall and slumped beneath the window, a solid heavy heap of misery. He shook his head and clicked his tongue in self-pity at the thought of Gladrag safe and sound in the cellar.

''Ow could she do that to me?' he murmured to himself. 'Tomorrow mornin' I'll pay 'er back, the strumpet. I'll beat the livin' daylights out of 'er, so I will…'

A decrescendo moaning had the hairs on his neck stand on end. His ears strained painfully, following the sound till it faded away. He heard the wind stir in the bare branches of the oak. He felt a desperate need to reinforce his possession of the inn and its environs.

'What's gittin' into me?…'

He doused his fears with anger, fanning it till it flared and consumed all else.

'I'll teach 'er a lesson for disobeyin' me, if it's the last thing I do. She needn't be sittin' too pretty down in that black 'ole of 'ers.'

Turlough opened his eyes with a start and got to his feet. Squinting against the daylight, he peered through the lattice. The sun was up. His bladder ached with the fears of the night before. He went outside to relieve himself.

'Nothin' to worry about, after all… She's up, I see,' he said to himself, noticing the open curtains at the back of the inn. 'So she's safe too... Not for long, my lovely… Not for long.'

Smirking, he squinted up at the brightening sky. The smile was instantly wiped from his face. The colour was struck from his cheeks. He looked this way and that for a means of escape. There wasn't one. The gate was locked. He hadn't the key. He strained his eyes to see if he could make her out through any of the windows.

'Where are ye, gir-il?' he breathed to himself.

He swallowed hard. Feigning nonchalance, he sauntered across the yard, never once looking up. He reached the back door and thumped it.

'Glad,' he `burred. 'Are ye in there, girl?'

He thought he heard the shuffle of feet but it came to nothing.

'Now's not the time, Glad. Let me in. I promise not to 'urt ye. I swear it, Glad!... Please, Glad,' he pleaded in a whine. 'So 'elp me God, Glad, if ye don't let me in I'm finished! *Glad!!*'

Tight fists remained in contact with the door. He leaned his head against the wood and sobbed.

His back went rigid. He'd heard a ruffling and a rustling on the roof. Slowly he edged backwards and looked up. He gulped. There they were peering over the gutter at him. He knocked once more, words stuck in his throat. He put his shoulder to the door in desperation.

All in vain.

He flung himself across the yard into the stable opposite and quickly bolted the bottom door. The top wouldn't budge. He leaned against it but the hinges had seized. For want of a few drops of oil… He cursed Oaf with every atom of spite in his body.

He floundered up the stairs and slammed the door. Chest heaving, he stood in the middle of the room waiting. It didn't take long for the fluttering to begin. A shadow crossed the window and had his heart in his mouth. He bit the edge of it. The pain down his left arm into his ring-finger was searing. He gulped air and began panting, thick mucus plugging his throat. One of them lighted on the window-ledge and stared in at him. He knew those pale blue eyes, oh, so well he knew them.

The room went dark. They crowded the sill. Unflinching, they stared in at him. He read cold, calculating determination in those horrible eyes. They examined the lattice, heads cocked on one side. They picked at the wood to see if it was rotten. Three of them tumbled into the grate.

Jackdaws!

Their cackling was insane laughter in his ears.

'No-oo,' he whimpered, curling up on the floor.

More and more spilled down the chimney and filled the room. They launched themselves at him. They pecked his exposed skin while his arms thrashed about to shield himself. He knew what they were trying to force him to do. He knew he would have to do it.

With a shriek he darted to the door and tumbled down the stairs. An explosion of chattering erupted in the stable, the space was alive with them. He staggered out into the yard, every inch of him covered by a fluttering, pecking jackdaw. He whirled about, arms akimbo, but they held on fast, digging their claws into his skin and hair and clothing. His screams were muffled by the millions upon millions of feathers. He rushed across the yard and plastered himself against one of the lattice windows.

From the gloom inside, all Gladrag could see was a single eye peering out at her from a mass of feathers. She was relieved when a wing drooped in front of it. She never moved a muscle to help him, indifferent to the guttural scream filling her ears when the mass began to rise into the air. Craning her neck, she watched them ascend, silhouetted against the pale blue sky. She hurried to another window to keep him in view.

A cloud of jackdaws burst outwards away from him. He came hurtling down at breakneck speed, head first, arms flailing, mouth a black hole of silence. She blinked when he hit the cobbles - awkwardly, skull crushed, neck snapped like a twig. He literally bounced before her, arms and legs giving one last convulsive jerk before lying still. She stared out at the corpse, eyes dancing in her head. The ties that had bound them together had been dashed to pieces with him.

The ragged cloud descended, pounced on him and drew him aloft once more. Again he struck the ground - limply, nothing more than a dead-weight. Her eyes were wild with glee, on the verge of madness while she stood on tiptoe to catch a final glimpse of the body borne away over the chimney-pots till the mighty oak hid him from view. This time he was gone. Gone for good.

She staggered towards the bar and leaned against it, pouring herself a tumblerful of brandy. Shaking hands held it to her lips while she gulped and spluttered and coughed. Another. And another. She exhaled and dragged her feet to a settle into which she fell heavily. There she sat, shocked and shaken.

'Thank the Lord 'twere 'im an' not me.'

Once again she followed him in her mind, high into the sky and over the oak.

'*My* oak now,' she whispered.

She emptied her glass and rose stiffly to her feet.

'My inn now,' she directed at the settles and bar and bottles, at the ring of brandy on the table below her. 'All mine.'

Revived, she scurried from room to room, to all their hiding-places. She carried the bags of gold and silver in her apron to the cellar, hiding them all in a dark corner, dragging over barrels to shield them from prying eyes. That done, she went and wiped the table and replaced the bottle of brandy, curling stray wisps of hair behind her ears. She looked about her, checked the back door was secure, went and fastened the front doors as best she could. Satisfied, she sat in her window. *Her* window. She looked out on an empty roadway and fell to musing.

She was alone in the inn. With no man to protect her. She shivered at the thought that that thing might return. The place suddenly appeared gloomy to her, too eerie for words. Trembling sleeves wiped the perspiration from her forehead. She swallowed and patted her breast. Her heart was pounding in there, she feared it would stop. In her mind's eye she saw him, Turlough with his crushed skull and broken neck. Turlough bouncing off the cobbles. That wide-open mouth coming closer and closer to swallow her whole. She dared not look round, certain his ghost was framed in the doorway, hands outstretched to strangle her. Seized by an importunate desire to flee the place, she stumbled over a table and chairs and fell with a cry. Scrambling to her feet, she rushed to the door and flung herself out in the open.

'They can 'ave a roof o'er their 'eads, but it's *my* 'ome…' she mumbled as she knocked.

Edgar opened the door and gazed impassively at her.

'Is 'e 'ere?' she asked.

He nodded and went to fetch him. While she waited on the doorstep she examined the room. A cosy room, she thought. Warm and 'omely. Would be nice to rest 'ere awhile.

Oaf stood before her, one hand clutching the open door. She nodded and flashed him what passed for a smile. He stood there, unmelting.

'Yer daddy, 'e's dead, son.'

Oaf's eyes widened. She never even noticed that the bad one was cured.

'There's no reason for ye to stay 'ere now. Ye or the little 'uns.'

Oaf swung the door a fraction but made no answer. She wanted to snap at him and cudgel that empty skull of his. Her fingers itched to tear a wad of hair from his head.

''Tis all ours, son,' she said as a huge concession. 'All *ours*.'

Greed lit up her features. He felt she was almost glad his father was dead.

'Come 'ome, lad, an' I'll give ye 'alf.'

'I don't want nothin' to do with it!' he finally shouted at her.

'Nothin' to do with it?' she asked incredulously. 'Don't be a fool, lad.'

'Nothing! Not me *or* the others.'

'Ye *are* soft in the 'ead... Ye've got to be.'

'You're a monster!' he bellowed.

'That's right, Oaf,' came Lee's harsh-sounding voice from idoors. 'Nothing but a monster. Only a monster'd want to throw her own son to the Aetz.'

'What are ye on about, ye 'alf-wit?' she snapped. 'Throw 'im *where*?'

'Lock him out, it's the same thing.'

'Lock 'im *out*?'

'Yeah. The other night, don't you remember?... You and him snug and safe in the cellar and Oaf and his little brothers and sisters locked out. You didn't even listen when he *begged* you to let them in.'

Light began to dawn. Hastily she proffered an excuse.

''Twas yer father, Oaf, not me.'

'Yes it *was* you,' Oaf vehemently retorted. 'You never said a word to stop him. And when he asked me to go out there to the tower, you knew about that *too*!'

She didn't deny it.

''Ave it yer own way,' she growled, turning her back on him.

Gladrag wiped her nose on her sleeve and turned tail for the inn.

'All mine,' she muttered with a gloating smile.

She'd be safe in the cellar all alone. Determined to survive, her fears were forgotten. The glint of gold had erased them.

— 61. Early Bird Too Early —

Oaf stepped in, hair standing on end. Mumbling incoherently, he pointed out the door.

'She's back, is she?' asked Lee, jumping up. 'I'll settle her. Leave her to me.'

He skipped to the door and came to a standstill. Gladrag Grindlewick was nowhere to be seen. A mob of villagers was crowding through the gate, Prickleback at their head. They had followed him as he briskly stepped out that morning to take possession of what was rightfully his, swinging the bishop's cane, humming a low tune and smiling to himself. He was a man in a hurry. If Rack were alive, he wasn't to know that the brat was dead. He would get there first and stake his claim.

Lee whistled through his teeth. 'We're in for it now,' he said.

'Out of my way, boy,' Prickleback ordered, pushing him aside.

'You!' he cried, pulled up suddenly by the unwelcome sight of Edgar in an armchair. 'You're supposed to be dead… How *dare* you be alive!'

Edgar was speechless. Prickleback wondered if he should just throttle him and take over. But the mob outside might begin to put two and two together. There was also the insurmountable inconvenience of that cursed book. His eyes wandered from Edgar to Berry and widened.

'*You!*' he gasped 'How did you get here?… Who…'

His words trailed away and fear clouded his brow. There was more to this than met the eye. Perspiration moistened his features. The hand that held the handkerchief trembled, though a sly smile appeared from behind it.

'I have your parents in my grasp,' he whispered for Edgar's ears alone. 'Go back and destroy that thing!' he shouted for the benefit of the mob outside. 'If it doesn't despatch you, I'll have you burnt at the stake as a warlock. There's more than enough evidence here… You either save the village or you'll never set eyes on your parents again.'

Prickleback leered at Edgar, cast a disparaging glance at Berry and turned on his heels. Slewing round in the yard, he pointed at the quartet crowding the door.

'I warn you!' he shouted. 'I…'

A shadow crossed their path. The blown-out carcase of Grindlewick smashed onto the cobbles between them. Gas hissed from the open mouth. Bloated limbs stretched the seams of his garments. Holes were pecked in his face and hands. An eye was missing. The other lay on the ground next to him.

They only recognized him by his clothes. They stared in blank amazement till a cry arose from one of them.

''Tis Grindlewick!'

61. Early Bird Too Early

Spell broken, they scrambled shrieking through the gate and scarpered. Prickleback shot a terrified glance at the remains and scuttled after them, looking over his shoulder now and again till he turned a corner.

— 62. Eye for an Eye —

'Oaf,' Edgar murmured, 'make sure the little ones go upstairs and keep them there.'

Oaf nodded and disappeared inside. He took them up to Tomothy who had been cowering in a bedroom ever since Prickleback had arrived.

Edgar began to say something but the fluttering of numerous wings drowned out his voice. Hundreds of jackdaws descended on the corpse and bore it away over the crooked, pointing digits of the trees. The single eye remained, staring them out of countenance, lying there on a cobblestone like the setting in a ring.

'Oh, God,' Edgar moaned, a lump rising in his throat.

Berry and Lee held hands to their mouths. No one wanted to kick that thing into the river, watching it roll over and over, seeing and unseeing. There was the fear that Spike would snatch it up and swallow it, with Grindlewick spying on them from his insides forever. But how to get rid of it without having to go *near* the awful thing?

With a shudder Lee slammed the door on it.

'Ugh,' he groaned, shaking the horror off him like a dog shakes off water.

They ran to their armchairs and clutched their knees in dismay. It was still out there... Watching them... Peeping under the door. Staring through the window. Would they ever have the courage to walk past it?

Edgar shot up out of his chair. 'I've got to get rid of it,' he said with grim determination. 'Imagine if one of the kids saw it!'

Before he could change his mind he strode to the door and flung it open. It hit the wall, making the latch rattle. Edgar heard it as if it were miles away. He stood there transfixed, fear creeping through the hairs on his head.

The leader of the scarecrows was framed in the doorway. Behind him crowded his army, filling the yard, spilling through the gate and still thronging the road. They surrounded the mill and the house. The eyeball dangled on its stalk from his hand. He held it out to Edgar like a conker. A chuckling sound emerged from the gaping hole of a mouth of his. His minions hustled closer. Swinging it on its cord, he slung it high into the air. A lone jackdaw swooped out of nowhere, snatched the gruesome object and made away with it. The leader jerked back his head and gargled a croak of displeasure. He had been robbed of his trophy.

'Ed, what the hell is keeping you out there?'

Lee's breathing was audible directly behind him. He murmured the worst swear-word he could muster. Neither moved a muscle, eyes homed on the creature.

'Ed...' It was air in his ear, no more. 'Close the door.'

They were halfway up the stairs, and Berry right behind them. Deafening bangs struck the door and shook the house.

62. Eye for an Eye

There was a tinkle of glass. Spike barked from the top of the landing, his hair a brush up his back, his tail between his legs. They thundered into the bedroom and slammed the door behind them.

'Don't ask!' Lee shouted, flat palms held out to the young ones.

'Oaf!' Edgar roared. 'Help us push the bed against the door! You too, Tomothy!'

All five of them shoved it into place before the children had a chance to remove themselves. Their fear was infectious. One little boy began to cry. Armchairs moaned across the floorboards downstairs. Something broke in pieces.

The bottom step creaked.

The fourth step moaned.

'The ring!' Berry screeched.

'We're *upstairs!*' Edgar screamed back at him in a panic.

'Try it anyway!'

The bedroom door rattled on its hinges. The bed began to move. Edgar grabbed the ring off the window-sill, merely glancing at the crowd outside. While he placed it on the floor and watched the silver hand come to life, Berry and Lee gathered up his sword, the spear and the shield. One of Oaf's little sisters was wearing the salmail, unable to resist its jewelly glitter. Edgar raised the trapdoor and ushered in the children while the others threw their weight against the bed and held the door.

'Hurry,' Lee pleaded over his shoulder.

With his head he motioned for Oaf and Berry and Tomothy to follow, waiting for Edgar to lower himself inside before sliding across the floorboards and in.

Not a moment too soon.

The four feet of the bed grumbled across the floor and the door burst inwards. The tramping and angry booming overhead was ear-splitting. Silence fell all of a sudden. A command was given, a shot in the dark. Something swift and light bounded up the stairs and scratched across the boards. A wolf. Sniffing, furiously. Then the horrible moaning recommenced. Echoes of it crashed against the walls and floor and ceiling, vibrating through the joists and beams, assailing their eardrums mercilessly. Nails rattled in the boards. Dust fell from the gaps. They held the children tight, whispering in their ears, begging them not to cry or whimper or scream.

'Just a little bit longer.'

'Shush, they can't see us. They don't know we're in here.'

'Listen… They're going.'

'We're safe.'

†

— 63. From out the Petticoats —

Sebastian Trefoil was still reeling. His wife's treachery had thrown his whole world into disarray. A great rent had been torn in their marriage-contract.

'That coat of mail has been in my family for generations,' he sniffed. 'But to give it to three dirty-faced urchins!... Execrable behaviour,' he muttered under his breath as his toast turned to ash in his mouth.

He had hoped to drape the salmail over his own shoulders if the worst came to the worst. Now that hope was dashed, as his brains would have been if he hadn't fled to his bedroom that night.

'She's mad,' he murmured disconsolately. 'Quite mad. Thank God my son isn't here to witness this.... His mother in the act of assisting thieves and whirling a mace around her head. Abominable.

'I think I shall go away... Yes... There's danger out there. *She* doesn't need me, doesn't *want* me.'

Vivid forebodings haunted him. He was terrified for his safety. He would sneak away without her knowing.

'Let *her* pretend to be squire for a change. If you wish to remain and expose yourself to danger, so be it... I am not abandoning you, Madam. If you value your life as little as you do, I cannot dissuade you. But *I* choose to put a greater store on *my* life.'

He clutched at straws, scraping the very bottom of the barrel to justify his flight. His conscience was easily muzzled.

'Best go before sunset,' he determined with a shudder. 'I shall give Longman his orders immediately.'

A weak smile wavered upon his lips as he thought how sorry she'd be. He imagined her beating her breast and wailing. Oh, what have I done? How I have wronged him!

'She'll be a different woman when I return,' he sniggered. ''Tis meet that I go.'

— 64. Grist —

Rumour had it that the scarecrows hadn't vacated the village at sunrise. Those inhabitants who had tried to flee the peninsula were driven back by flocks of angry crows and ravening wolves. Stumbling home, they caught sight of blank staring faces in lightless corners.

Wasps were building nests under the eaves of their homes. Hornets droned in the hollows of trees, at the same task. Hoodies were perched on the chimneys and roofs, shuffling together and conferring at the sight of the villagers. It boded ill.

A scream had them slewing round to face a terrified neighbour tottering towards them. She had found, in her quest for booty, the corpse of the crone killed by the millipede. Others began to speak of the monstrosity, claiming they too had seen it cross the green. It grew bigger and bigger in their widening orbs till they all chattered wildly. Sanctuary was their only hope, but where?

'Them cottages out at church. They're still standin',' an old man croaked.

En masse they ran, the strongest of them hauling the poor inhabitants from their dwelling-places before boarding themselves in.

'There ain't enough room for us all!' they snarled.

'The inn!' shrieked one of the evicted. 'There's a cellar at the inn!'

The febrile group tumbled back to the village and up the hill to The Slaughtered Ox. In vain they threw themselves against the double doors. They couldn't budge the kegs inside. In the end they smashed the windows.

Glad heard them from her safehouse, shuffling outside the door. She lowered the wick of her oil lamp and waited.

'Mistress Grindlewick, are ye in there?'

She smiled at that. Aaah… Appealing to me womanly tenderness now, she thought with amusement that quickly turned to hatred. They're after me gold… She glanced over her shoulder, to reassure herself all was safe. It raised her spirits.

'Let us in!'

Fists hammered on the metal door to no avail.

'Let us in or we'll burn the place down!'

She glanced up, studied the ceiling and smirked. Stone, not rafters. No flame would penetrate.

'Burn it, ye fools,' she breathed. 'I 'ave all I need down 'ere.'

'Ye'll be burnt at the stake if ye don't open up,' came growling through the door at her.

She shook her fist at the door.

'I know ye, Col Lickspittle,' she breathed. "D know yer voice anywhere. An' ye won't be burnin' *me* as a witch… I'll strangle ye with me bare 'ands first! I'll 'ave yer guts for garters.'

64. Grist

Once they were gone she turned up the flame of the oil lamp and took a swig of brandy. A shiver raced through her. She felt alone in a lonesome place in a lonely world. She missed her Grindle. He had been company, despite his growling and his fierce bouts of temper. Oaf she disowned as an idiotic lump not worth his salt. She sniffed. Two tears strolled down her ruddy cheeks. For herself.

Miller Falchion was endeavouring, unsuccessfully, to reassure his sorely troubled wife. No one had brought them breakfast. Their guards were missing.

'Edgar's in dreadful danger, I *know* he is. He could be *killed!*'

'There, lass,' he crooned, placing an arm about her shoulders.

She shook off his kindness. 'Don't you hear me?' she screamed at him in anger.

'*I* hear you.'

She gripped his lapels while he looked sadly into her eyes.

'I hear you,' he softly repeated.

'What are we to do, Ben?'

'What *can* we do, Moll?... I can't get out!' he bellowed in exasperation, gripping the bars and shaking the gates till they rattled. 'I can't get out,' he sobbed, slipping to the floor and burying his head in his hands.

'Oh, Benjamin,' she soothed, kneeling beside him and planting both hands on his shoulders. They shook uncontrollably, convulsed by the sobs that rent him. 'I didn't mean it, Ben. Not like that.'

'But I'm no good to him,' he cried through welling tears. 'He's out there on his own and I'm stuck in this *accursed place.*'

Tears streamed down his face. There was no consoling him.

'I'm useless,' he repeated. 'A useless father to my son.'

'No, Ben. You're a good father. He loves you more than I can say.'

'What use am I to him now?' he wailed through gritted teeth, sniffling loudly.

'More than you realize… You taught him to be brave, to stand up for himself. You taught him to weigh the odds and act on them. That's true wisdom. That will see him through.'

'Will it?…'

'We can only hope and pray it will.'

The miller nodded and sighed, steeping himself in misery.

Brad trudged warily along the lane to the mill. He was running away from home. Piper was holed up in one of the paupers' cottages with his parents who refused to let him out. Sam was missing and nobody wanted to think about what might have happened to him. As for Nico, his folks had sent him to the tower. Which was precisely what Brad's wanted to do. He wasn't fooled by their coaxing smiles. All that talk about Christ dying on the cross, they didn't believe a word of it. If they had, wouldn't *they* have been willing to go?

His dad had smacked him in the face when he'd refused.

'Get out if ye won't do it. Let the scarecrows get ye!'

He would never forget those words. And then to shove him out the door and slam it in his face. To have to hear the bolts being driven home... The finality of it, that's what hurt the most.

Brad's heart missed a beat every time he heard a rustle in the undergrowth. He walked faster, heading for the mill because there was nowhere else to go to. He skidded to a halt, turned and looked back the way he'd come. He had completely forgotten about Edgar's parents. Now that he was gone, there was no one else to feed them. Should he go back, he wondered. He shook his head.

'I've nowhere to get them breakfast even if I do.'

He sighed and continued onwards. He'd never felt as sad in all his life. It didn't seem worth living any more. So much had changed in such a short time. It was as if he'd never really known these people before, his parents included. They did nothing but snarl and fight. Hadn't they heard of clubbing together, as he and his friends were wont to do when there was trouble? It seemed the most natural thing to do. But they never learned anything, did they?

'I'll be glad when I get to the mill,' he murmured to himself.

— 65. The Bald Facts —

'They've gone mad out there,' Brad solemnly declared, chest heaving after that final dash for the mill. 'My own dad kicked me out and told me he hoped the scarecrows would get me… Because I wouldn't go to the tower and give myself up.' He nodded to confirm the horror of it. 'Hard to believe, eh? My own dad…'

'What's coming over everyone?' Edgar whispered in shock.

'They were always like that,' Berry flatly stated, coming down the stairs.

Lee nodded in agreement. 'Pity the Aetz wouldn't get rid of them all and leave us in peace.'

They all watched Berry drawing the salmail over his shoulders.

'Don't you worry,' he directed up at Oaf leaning on the top newel, 'I'll find her.'

'Find who?' Edgar asked.

'The little one. She's gone missing.'

'But where can she be?' Edgar sounded alarmed.

'I'll find her. Probably went out to the yard when nobody was looking and wandered off.'

'You're not going on your *own*.'

'Of course, I am… I'm only going out to the yard. I'll shout if I need you.'

'Make sure you do,' Edgar ordered. 'But don't *you* go wandering off… How are my folks?' he asked Brad when Berry was gone.

'They're fine… At least, they were fine yesterday. I didn't get a chance to bring them any breakfast this morning, but your dad always keeps some by.'

'I'd better go see them today.'

'Wait till Berry comes back,' Lee told him.

'I'll wait, don't you worry.'

'As for the village,' Brad stated, 'it's bedlam… I don't know how many are dead.'

'I bet Rack isn't one of them,' Lee interrupted. '*Or* Prickleback.'

Brad shook his head.

'Doesn't surprise me. Nothing ever happens to the bad ones. They go on living forever.'

'How bad is it?' asked Edgar, rerailing the conversation.

'Just about as bad as it could be... Bodies all over the place. People missing. Homes wrecked. Mice and flies and wasps and crows everywhere. And them scarecrows lurking and ready to hop out at you. Not forgetting the wolves and bats and hornets… All waiting… as if to start a war…'

They all remained in silence after hearing him.

'We've got to do something,' Edgar finally whispered.

'What *can* we do?' Brad asked, sure it was hopeless.

'*We've* got to,' Edgar solemnly rejoined. 'Me and Lee… and Berry.'

'Are you mad? That thing will *kill* you!'

Edgar shrugged and grimaced. 'We've still got to try.'
'You *are* mad.' Brad breathed barely above a whisper.
'We'd be madder not to do anything.'

— 66. Flight —

He leaned out the window and bellowed at the coachman.

'Faster, damn you. Faster!'

The pair of horses thundered over the road, covered in lather, foaming at the mouth. And still the driver lashed his whip. Those left in the village stared after the strange equipage disappearing in a cloud of dust.

The squire of Garten was quitting his people and his duties. But not his precious possessions. Portraits of himself, most of his wife's jewels – which had belonged to his mother anyway – and his favourite outfits were crammed in beside and before and above him.

He was spooked, by a daydream he'd had while packing. Out of the wardrobe there burst a creature, half-bird, half-reptile. It dug its talons into the flesh of his back and crunched the bones of his neck between its powerful jaws. The clocks in every room, along the corridors, on the stairs, in the bedrooms, outside in the stable-yard, chimed a mournful dirge while he lay dying, the flag on the roof torn to ribbons by a hurricane.

He shivered, banishing the image from his thoughts.

'What the…'

He started and stared through the window at a ridiculous sight. A scarecrow by a gate. At the edge of the road and not propped in the middle of the field.

'Good God!' he croaked.

The empty, soulless face was following the progress of the carriage! Holding up an arm!! Pointing at him!!!

He fell back in his seat, sweat starting from his pores. Trembling hands in leather gloves had difficulty gripping his cane and pounding the roof.

He croaked, then shrieked, 'Faster! Fly as the wind!'

The coachman heard the stifled scream and pulled a face. He cracked his whip over the horses' heads, beginning to feel sorry for them.

'Where's the hurry?' he growled.

His hair stood on end. Through a gap in the hedge he caught sight of the looming silhouette of the tower. Those on the estate had been cut off from the appalling truth until now.

'God 'a' mercy on us,' he prayed, lashing the horses into a frenzy.

He let out a cry and swerved to the left. The carriage veered over on two wheels before righting itself. Great, muscular vines of ivy had plunged through the hedge and tried to trip the horses. Wild-eyed, they neighed and reared up, jolting the carriage and throwing the squire about inside. He saw the writhing tendrils and screeched in his turn. The drumming of his cane was relentless.

'Go, go, go, go go!'

66. Flight

Out of sight, a lone scarecrow pointed imperiously towards the woods screening the village. His hoodie launched into the air and sped over the intervening fields. A black cloud rose above the treetops, growing larger and larger the closer it came. Hornets, in their millions, swooped on the coach, covering the haunches of the unfortunate beasts and stinging them mercilessly. They neighed hysterically, kicking, stamping and plunging till they broke the shafts and galloped free. Inside, the squire was helplessly flung about. Diamond pendants and pearl necklaces raised weals on his face and hands. The corners of picture-frames grazed his temples and bruised his ribs and thighs. A welter of clothing engulfed and almost smothered him. He lay sprawled on the carriage floor, panting and sobbing.

Slowly, feebly, he pushed the mound off him. He got to his knees and leaned out the shattered window. What he saw froze him to the spot. The horses were nowhere to be seen. On the driver's seat was a seething hulk of hornets. They hung from the coachman's arms. They delved into his boots. They burrowed beneath his greatcoat and wormed their way under his eyelids. When he opened his mouth to scream they hurried in and filled it, covering his tongue, stuffing his throat.

Then, all together, they unsheathed their stings and thrust them deep. The body went rigid and fell to the ground.

With a cry the squire opened the door and made to descend. A cloud rose from the corpse and drove him back. He mopped his brow and wished he'd never left home. Isolda was instantly transformed into the dearest, most loveable wife on earth. How he yearned to be beside her. Married life had become all it had promised to be.

His hair stood on end. A terrible moan assailed his ears on all sides. He covered his eyes and whimpered. Gaping faces stared in at him through the windows. Twiggy fingers wrenched the doors off their hinges. Branch-like arms entered and drew him out kicking and screaming.

'My possessions!' he screeched.

He clutched at a diamond necklace. His fingernails clawed down a portrait of himself. He was lifted onto the scarecrows' shoulders and borne across the field. A second black cloud loomed closer against the twilight sky. He squeezed his eyes shut, imagining what it felt like to be stung to death. He opened them again in a vortex of leathery wings. Spindly fingers lifted him up and bore him away. Head hanging, it took time to orientate himself and recognize the terrain far below.

There was the inn with its kingly oak, the river winding below the bridge next to it. There the church, the bishop's palace, a black bastion in shadow. There his home. Was that a figure on the lawn? Isolda, perchance? He made to wave but little hands clutched his arm tight. He swung upwards in a arc, to a dizzying view of clouds, of land and sea at a confusing angle.

He was swept away from his home, his life, everything that made sense of it. They held a steady course over the village, the woods and the cabbage field. Where are they taking me, he wondered in a detached sort of way. It was a surreal experience. He had never heard of a person being kidnapped by bats before, half expected to wake any second and find

Isolda reading by his side and scolding him for shouting in his sleep. I'll miss that scowl, he thought with a wan smile. I *have* been silly... She was right all along...

His mind stalled mid-sentence. They were plummeting towards a tower, loftier than anything he'd ever seen on the peninsula.

His mouth stretched wide. His eyes bulged. His heart jolted in his chest.

'Nooooooooooooooooooooooooo!'

The gargoyles took up his wail and spat it back in his face, croaking and shrieking with laughter. The bats skimmed so close over the ground that he almost smashed into it. Suddenly, he soared up the sheer wall of the tower and spun over the parapet. Free, he began to flail and claw at the air as he hurtled towards the earth. They caught him up again and spiralled into the sky at giddying speed.

They swooped towards the roof-top and let him go. He plunged downwards, helter-skelter, his clothes beating a painful tattoo on his ribs. That was when he saw it, hurtling nearer and nearer, bigger and bigger. Monstrous!

He screamed as brawny arms extended to catch him and a hideous face leered up at him. The spade-like hands disappeared only to reappear with a sharp spike gripped between them. He received an almighty thump in the chest and wriggled like a skewered beetle.

The thing held him up to examine him at leisure. A strange lethargy and peace came over him. He was drained of all fear and all hope of escape. This was the end and he knew it. He had done wrong to flee. Closing his eyes, he waited for death, hoping it would be sudden and merciful.

His final thought was of Isolda and his son. How he wished he had done better by them.

— 67. Missing, Presumed Innocent —

'Where can he be?' asked Edgar, clicking his tongue impatiently. 'He said he was only going out to the yard.'

'Mustn't have found her,' Lee suggested.

'Yes, but I told him not to go anywhere without us.'

'Don't be too hard on him, Ed. It's the first time he's been able to do anything on his own.'

'I know that,' he snapped, 'but that doesn't make it any the wiser to wander off without any back-up.'

'It's the little *girl*. He's *worried* about her.'

'Supposing she's *dead*?'

At that precise moment there came a feeble knocking at the door. It was Oaf's little sister, but there was no sign of Berry. They called his name. Over and over they called it, peering into the barn and stable, checking the ditches, running to the mill.

'Ed! E-ed!'

It was Oaf's voice and they ran to him. He was inside, down on his hunkers, gripping his sister's shoulders and peering into her eyes.

'Listen to this,' he said, glancing up at them. 'Say it again, Ell. Tell them what you told me.'

Ell just clasped her hands in front of her and squirmed.

'Go on, Ell. Be a good girl,' cajoled her brother. 'You saw that nice boy, didn't you? The one who gave you a loan of his shiny coat.'

She nodded, lips clamped together.

'Did he say anything to you?'

A shake of her head, a definite one.

'Why didn't he come back with you? Did he go somewhere else?'

A nod.

'Where?'

Nothing.

'Did he go with somebody else?'

'People,' she faintly uttered.

'What people?' Edgar butted in anxiously.

Oaf held up his hand to stall him. 'Did you know those people, Ell?'

Another shake of her head.

'Were they friendly people?'

'No.'

Oaf looked up at Edgar. He too was beginning to fear the worst.

'Which way did they go?' Lee shouted. 'Ask her, Oaf!'

Her brother grimaced at him. Because of the shouting she was now pouting her lips and close to tears. Edgar squatted down and questioned her, in gentler, coaxing tones.

'You're a great girl for telling us so much, Ell.'

She made a brave attempt at a smile beneath her eyebrows.

'Did they go off down the road?'

'Trees.'

'The woods, you mean?'

A nod sufficed. Edgar ran to retrieve his sword while Lee grabbed his shield and spear. They dashed through the door and were gone.

'I'm really scared for him,' Edgar panted as they jogged along. 'We should never have let him out of our sight. I'll never forgive myself if anything's happened to him.'

'Not after him being cured and all.' Lee swore aloud and kicked viciously at a heap of pebbles. 'If anything's happened to him I'll kill that Aetz stone-dead! With my *bare hands!!*'

They heard a yelp of a bark and Spike came tearing up the road after them.

'I thought I told them to keep him in,' Edgar growled. 'Can't they do anything I ask them?!'

'Be reasonable, Ed. As if anyone could keep you and Spike apart. I bet he bit Brad good an' proper. And Oaf as well, if I know Spike.'

They skidded to a halt, Spike growling feebly behind them.

'It's them,' Edgar whispered.

'Aye,' Lee whispered back. 'They must be the people Ell was talking about. No wonder she was tongue-tied.'

The two of them crouched down, crossed a ditch and crawled through the undergrowth. Spike reluctantly followed them. The scarecrows were in a circle, with their backs to them. The boys couldn't make out what they were doing. Edgar signalled that he was going to make for the wide bole of a tree to their left. He peeped round the trunk but still could see nothing. He motioned for Lee to spring onto his shoulders.

'They've got Berry, right enough,' he breathed into Edgar's ear once he'd climbed down again.

Something moved through the undergrowth. The circle was breached and the moaning began in earnest. The scarecrows stamped their feet, never had they seen them so animated.

Berry cried out in fear, piercing the din.

That was more than sufficient. The two friends leapt from behind the tree. Lee smashed his shield into the nearest scarecrow and pinioned it to the ground with his spear. Spike tore its hair off and worried its head. Edgar slashed to right and to left. Bits of scarecrow flew in all directions. The dog pounced upon a crawling hand and chewed the fingers off, spitting fragments out of the corners of his mouth. Those who were still intact thrashed about with high-pitched moans and edged away into the depths of the forest, merging with the shadows.

The boys stood still, panting and shuddering with horror. Never had they seen anything like it, never had they dreamed it possible. The gigantic millipede was coiled around Berry, clattering its poisonous fangs off the salmail, unable to penetrate the magical scales.

'What are you waiting for?'

Edgar started at Lee's question and nodded. What *was* he waiting for?

He strode forward, raised his sword in the air and smote the loathsome insect. The blade clanged off the brittle plates. He struck again with greater force. A plate cracked down the centre and gaped. He thrust the point into the soft membrane beneath. Out glooped a yellowish ooze. Again and again he shattered the rows of armour-plating. The creature reared up, shuddered and fell back across Berry. Edgar drove the point home between the head and the body. All the legs wriggled for an instant and then hung limp and lifeless.

'Help me!' he shouted at Lee.

Together they pushed the monstrosity off the prone boy and pulled him free. Edgar clutched Berry's head between his hands.

'Berry!' he shouted, patting his cheeks. 'Can you *hear* me?'

The eyelids quivered and he breathed a sigh of relief.

'He's alive! He's all right!'

He sat him up, supporting his shoulders in the crook of his arm. Lee rubbed one of his hands and smiled at him.

Berry let out a cry and looked wildly about him.

'It's dead,' Lee crooned. 'Ed killed it.'

'What was it?'

'Looked like a giant centipede to me. Thank God for that salmail of yours. That's the second time it's saved your skin for you.'

Berry nodded and sank back against Edgar. Feebly he held out a hand to Spike who was wagging his tail like there was no tomorrow.

'We'll have to carry him home. He's not fit to walk.'

Lee nodded in agreement. 'He's not that heavy.'

Between them they raised him to his feet, crouching to get in under his armpits. With the force of the impact they dropped him and collapsed in a heap. Spike let out a yelp and bolted.

Droves of bats plummeted from the sky and fell on them. They grasped and bit their ear lobes. They hung from their bleeding lips. Wings flapped madly in their faces as they scratched at their eyes. When they tried to ward them off they nipped their fingers. Edgar attempted to raise his sword-arm but too many bodies weighed it down. Lee's shield seemed to have come to life. He was sinking beneath it. So frenzied was the onslaught that it was impossible to see anything. They were driven to the edge of the woods and back down the laneway. The bats only left them when they'd hounded them through the door of the house.

— 68. Bolt from the Blue —

'What happened?' asked a startled Brad while they leaned, breathless, against the door.

Edgar gulped. 'Bats,' he said.

'You didn't find Berry, then?' called Oaf while trying to force his brothers and sisters back into the bedroom.

'Berry!' Lee and Edgar cried at once. 'Isn't he *here*?'

Desperation shone in their eyes. Brad and Oaf slowly shook their heads. Edgar fought with the door latch and the two of them plunged outside. They were off towards the woods while the others stood on the threshold, wondering should they follow or not.

It wasn't long before they returned, crumpled and forlorn. Lee had fought with Edgar back in the woods, he sported a bruise on his cheek to prove it.

Edgar had been determined to reach the tower.

'Don't be a fool,' Lee had shouted. 'What if it's a trick?'

'So what if it's a bloody trick? What about *Berry*?'

'What can you do for Berry now?'

'You don't know whether he's dead or not.' Edgar's face was contorted by rage and contempt.

'Do you think for one minute that anyone is alive up there?!'

'If it's using him as bait, he *could* be alive.'

'You saw what it did to Eelman. You think it's gonna have mercy on Berry? He got away once already, remember?'

Lee was eroding Edgar's fury. Fear was sapping his courage and he hated Lee for it, hated Lee and hated himself.

'You just want to save your own skin,' he growled with loathing. 'You don't give a ha'penny damn about Berry.'

'Who are you to say that?'

With that he slapped Edgar in the face, who head-butted him in retaliation. They tusseled and rolled in the dry leaves, directing punches anywhere they could. Edgar lost all self-control, roared like a madman and jumped to his feet. In no time the point of his sword was quivering before Lee's throat.

Lee looked up into his glaring eyes and flaring nostrils. 'Do it,' he spat. 'I'm not afraid... You'd save Berry but you'd kill me.'

Edgar dropped his sword as if it were white-hot. He turned away and spat into the thicket. He just stood there, hands on his hips, heaving for air. After reflecting for a minute he turned back to Lee and held out his hand.

'I hate all this,' he said. 'I wish I'd never set eyes on that damn sword. I wish everything was normal again... I don't know what came over me.'

'Forget it.'

'We'd best be getting back. If we ever had a chance of helping Berry, it's too late now. God damn the Aetz! God *damn* the village!!'

'He already has, Ed.'

— 69. Requiem —

A heavy weight struck the roof, rolled down the slope and fell to the ground. With Berry's name reverberating in his head, Edgar ran outside. He heard faint bat squeaks fading in the distance and all hope failed him.

'Oh, Berry, it can't be true. They can't have...'

A prone figure was a silhouette in the gloaming. He was reluctant to approach, afraid to discover it was his friend and that there was nothing he could do for him.

'But it can't be!' he exclaimed, hope resurfacing. 'The salmail won't *allow* him to die. The salmail will protect him at all *times*!'

Warily he approached the body, apprehensive that it might spring up in ambush. He sobbed and fell upon it once he recognized his friend.

'Berry! *Speak* to me, Berry!'

He made no answer. Edgar stared up at the roof and searched the ground, hoping against hope that it had come off in the fall or was hanging from the gutter. Not a sign of the salmail could he see.

'Help me!' he screamed. 'Lee,' he shouted once they had lain him on the hearth-rug, 'run out and see if you can find the salmail. *All* of you!'

Alone with Berry, he patted his pallid cheeks and raised his head.

'Oh, please be alive,' he groaned.

A hint of colour enlivened blue lips. They parted slightly. Vacantly he looked up into Edgar's eyes. A calm, resigned smile lit up his face when he recognized him.

'Ed,' he breathed, scarcely audible.

'You're safe now, Berry. You'll be fine.'

Desperation quaked in his words. By his faint smile it was obvious that Berry knew better.

'Oh, Berry,' Edgar moaned, 'it can't happen like this. There must be something we can do.'

The wry smile said it all. You can do nothing for me.

'Don't be sad,' he croaked. 'I've had the best time of my life these past few days. It's been great...' He heaved, then continued. 'I was cursed, you know. Those who cursed me had no right to but they did it all the same and I believed them. Till I met the two of you.' He smiled with profound gratitude. 'Now I'm free. And all because you and Lee came through that door and found me.'

'This wouldn't have happened if we hadn't met you,' Edgar said, grinding his teeth with annoyance.

'Worse would have happened, you know that... Don't worry, Ed. I'm not scared...' He struggled to breathe. 'Look after Spike,' he added with a smile.

'I will. Of course, I will.'

Edgar sobbed and hung his head. Great tears plopped onto the rug.

Berry went rigid, scowled, then relaxed. The pain contorting his features melted away. Something akin to music reached his ears from a distance. Notes mingled, fused imperceptively and drifted apart only to merge again. He saw his friend before him but couldn't make himself heard or understood – a gulf was widening between them. With supreme effort he picked at Edgar's sleeve.

'Lee,' he croaked. 'Get Lee for me.'

Edgar instantly rose and ran outside, calling Lee's name.

Berry did it to spare him. He had wanted to tell him that this was real life, fuller and better, but Edgar had begun to fade like a mist and he was surrounded by other beings. Had he ever truly been a part of this world? His life was a thread, a cobweb that had been stretching and weakening since the day he was born. It would snap and recoil whence it had come, taking him with it... There were those wings again, only stronger, ever gentler. He smiled and felt he was sinking into down.

Both boys dashed into the room. Wordless, they stood there. Berry looked so unbelievably peaceful. A tiny insect lit on his face and he noticed it not.

He was gone.

'I never got a chance to say good-bye,' Lee murmured in sorrow.

Edgar felt such anger rising at such a waste of a life. To die when he was well and everything was going right for him. So unfair... So *wrong!*

Their grief became calm and peaceful like the boy before them. As if his essence were being dispelled on the wind and touched them both. Tears flooded their eyes and they wept for a friend whose life had been cut short, a good friend, a great friend.

'I *will* kill it now,' Edgar growled darkly.

— 70. Milestone —

The loss had rendered his rage elemental. His expression bore that grim readiness for strife and suffering – for death, if necessary. He had put it off too long. If it wasn't for his cowardice, Berry would still be alive, not that cold lifeless image of him lying on the rug before him – cold no matter how roaring a fire licked up the chimney.

Spike was sniffing his face and whimpering. A paw darted at a rigid arm, beseechingly. He stepped back, crouched, and barked, tail wagging expectantly. He whimpered and gazed up at Edgar.

'Come here, Spikey.' He knelt down, pulled him next to him and wrapped an arm around his neck. 'He's gone, Spike… and he's not coming back. He was a good friend to you, wasn't he?'

As if understanding, Spike whined and pulled away.

'You don't want to believe it either.'

Spike slunk into the farthest corner where he sat and stared at the body. Edgar remained on his knees where he was, head hanging. It was so hard to believe that he had been alive and well only a few hours ago. Such a lovely person. Such a quiet and kind person. And brave. So brave…

Dead because I didn't fight when I should have...

Went out looking for the little girl and never came back. Always thinking of others when he had every right only to think of himself... And those bloody *cowards* in the village forced him out of his own home and into that tower. I wish the Aetz would take *them all*!

Why should I fight to save them? Why should I risk my neck for people like that? Don't they deserve the Aetz, to spend the rest of their rotten lives in the tower with it?...

I'll kill it. But not for them.

For Berry...

An' I'll kill Prickleback and Racker Booth while I'm at it. I'd kill Lee's dad if he was alive, and anyone else who gets in our way. I'll hack them all to pieces. A quick death is too good for them. They deserve to suffer and scream and crawl and beg for mercy and see their own life's blood spurting onto the floor and know they've only a few more minutes to live. I'll sneer into their faces. You're dying... You're dying and you know it and there's nothing anyone can do to save you. Of course, I'm going to kill you. You killed *Berry*! You didn't lay a finger on him, is that what you say?... You didn't have to, but you did it all the same.

And then... just before they die...

I'll stick the sword into the soft part under their chins and lean on it and listen to them squealing like stuck pigs till it turns to a gurgle and they die.

70. Milestone

Let the rats gnaw at their bones. Burying's too good for them.

— 71. Silent Vigil —

He sniffed.

He hadn't noticed Brad and Oaf and the children approaching. They crowded round the body in silence. Tomothy held back, so upset that they worried he'd lose his mind again. He burst out crying and Edgar hastened to his side to comfort him.

'He was my best friend,' Tomothy howled. 'He was special, wasn't he?'

'Yes,' Edgar replied. 'So special…'

'Why?… Why did he have to die?'

Edgar hung his head. He'd put off fighting the Aetz too long, *that's* why.

'Poor Berry,' he said in a low voice.

They all nodded in silence.

'We'll have to bury him, won't we?' Lee cautiously suggested.

Edgar turned and looked fixedly at him. Bury him… That drove the dagger in deep. A searing pain gripped his heart. With a long, melancholy sigh he shook his head.

'I have something else to do first,' he murmured. 'I'd like to do that before we bury him.' His words trailed away, hoarsely, falteringly. 'Let's get some candles,' he said, rousing himself.

He took four candlesticks from a table in a far corner of the room, screwed candles into them and placed them on the rug by Berry, two at his head, two at his feet. He lit them with a taper from the fire.

Some of them knelt down awkwardly. They felt it was expected of them, what was done in church. Edgar remained standing. To kneel stank of Prickleback on his knees pretending to be holy and God-fearing.

Damn them, he shouted in his head. Damn them all to *hell!*

He fidgeted. He couldn't just stand here above the heads of the kneelers and gaze into the dead boy's face. He had something to *do*. He lunged towards his sword and snatched it up.

Lee laid a restraining hand on his arm. 'Not now, Ed... Wait till morning.'

'But...'

'Your head'll be clearer in the morning. If you dash off blind with anger you won't be able to fight it. Because you won't be thinking straight. Don't you go to your death as well.'

Edgar laid the sword on the rug and sobbed. He too knelt down and buried his face in his hands. Lee patted his back and placed an arm around him.

His head jerked up and he said, 'We'll have to tell his mam and dad.'

'Tomorrow,' Lee whispered. 'It's too dangerous to go out there now.'

71. Silent Vigil

Nobody wanted to leave the body. Eventually Edgar sent them all to bed, intent on maintaining a solitary vigil.

'You go to bed too, Ed,' Lee crooned. 'You'll need to rest for tomorrow. I'll stay up.'

'But...'

'Of course, I'm going with you. No way in hell am I staying behind. But I don't need to rest as much as you do.'

They heard a creak on the stairs and both looked up. Brad crept down, frowning because of the noise he'd made.

'Both of you get some sleep,' he whispered in earnest. '*I'll* stay with him.'

They gave in and crept upstairs. Neither thought they would, but both slept soundly, too drained emotionally and physically to dwell on what awaited them on the morrow, on the corpse of their friend belowstairs.

†

— 72. Death March —

'Do you think we're going to die?' Lee asked as they strode purposely down the laneway.

'Dunno... It's possible.'

The same thought had entered both their heads while they stood over Berry before leaving. Edgar had promised to avenge him. Boyhood wrestled with manhood in his frame. His shoulders had broadened to bear the burden. His will had hardened, proved like steel, sharp and as dangerous as the blade of his sword. Sabrehilt was truly born from the forge's flames. Perhaps he would be robbed of his youth in the encounter, that was a risk he was willing to take. He might close his eyes on life, but he would die a man, as much a man as his dad and his grandpa.

Images of the past flashed through his mind, as ephemeral as tissue-paper in a candle's flame, gone before fully realized. If we *do* die, he thought, all this will still exist. Just like it did after the last Sabrehilt. Maybe *because* he died...

What did his life amount to?... Not much as yet. And now, on the brink of being extinguished? What then? Glory? Myths and legends?... God?...

Did the last Sabrehilt know he was going to die? Was he as scared as I am?

He shivered and drew his coat tighter about him. It was getting chilly. It also seemed to be getting darker instead of brighter. He turned to Lee.

'I thought I was imagining it at first but it *is* getting darker, isn't it?'

'I thought so too. Look! The *moon's* coming up over there!'

'Beware the fool moon,' Edgar muttered.

'Should we turn back, do you think?'

'What's the point? It'll only happen again. And again and again till we face up to it. Till *I* do...'

The moon was a sharp sickle well above the horizon, radiant with the cold glint of steel. But the constellation, Orion - the hunter, the protector, the avenger - dominated the black dome of the sky. Sure-footed, sword removed from its scabbard, he strode across the firmament to engage the enemy.

Edgar hoped it was a sign. His heartbeat seemed to him to fill the universe, thumping off the planets and stars and galaxies. Soon, very soon, it would either dissolve in that immense void or resettle in his breast.

Every now and then a pang of terror pierced his entrails, followed by calm as the inevitability of it all came back to him. He vividly recalled the seasonal smells and rhythmical sounds of his world. Blackbirds trebling at dusk. Clucking hens warm in the coop. The bark of a dog in the night. The harsh, jarring notes of a pheasant at daybreak. Cows mooing. Horses nodding over doors. Gaggling geese. Clacking herons. The sudden warmth of the sun emerging from a cloud. Invisible larks gabbling on high. A solitary corncrake...

All replaced by … the Aetz.

The past thirteen years had led him inexorably to this. It was now or never…

They reached the edge of the woods and a path lay bare before them. No cunning briars tripped them up this time. No craggy branches scratched their faces or snared their clothes. It was as if a way were opening up for them.

Scarecrows dotted the muddy fields, heads tilted in expectation. Vacuous faces stared in their direction from all four points of the compass.

'I hope I don't turn coward,' mumbled Edgar.

'I don't think a coward would have got this far.'

'It's what lies ahead…'

They strode forwards, nearer and nearer to the tower and the Aetz. Their destiny loomed large in their minds.

I wonder if it'll be like that time I was drowning, Edgar mused. As if I'd fallen off the edge of the world but wasn't falling at all. As if someone was holding me up, someone who loved me and would never, ever, let me fall and hurt myself again.

†

— 73. Fool Moon Ascendant —

Crows wheeled about the roof of the tower like flies above a cowpat. The moon had risen high, waxing as it did so, full face pitted by unfamiliar craters.

'I don't like the look of that.' Lee's voice trembled.

Noises behind them made them start and turn. The branches of the trees were weaving together, gnarled fingers interlocking to form an impassible barrier, blocking any retreat they might have contemplated.

'It knows we're here,' Lee whispered.

'Come on... Before we get cold feet.'

They walked across the field, careful not to slip in the ooze. The ugly face of the moon glared up at them from filthy puddles. Sucking noises caught their attention. Scarecrows were congregating behind them and following. With a cry Lee jumped to one side, almost toppling face first into the mire. The head of a scarecrow was rising up out of the mud.

'*That's* where they come from... They were here all along!'

'The sooner this is over, the better,' Edgar growled, angry at his own waning courage.

The unsettled question of life and death hung directly over their two young heads, pushing them bodily into the mud. Who was to live?… Who to die…?… Not even Gerty's book knew the answer to that.

Poor Spike, Edgar thought with a sigh from the depths of his heart. How he'll miss me.

Unless the light was playing tricks on them, shadows were flickering back and forth across their path, faster and faster till their entire world was spiralling out of control. They felt giddy, peering into the night sky to see if the bats were responsible.

'Look!' Edgar gasped, pointing at the moon.

Its expression was changing before their very eyes. The craters were actually moving!

A living face was leering down at them. A cruel smile contorted its features, savouring their fear. Edgar shook a fist at it and the smile became a grimace of hatred.

A warm wind blew dust in their faces, they coughed and spluttered. Splayed fingers shielded their eyes while they edged forward with difficulty. They passed through a gap in the hedge and stood in the tower field. Lee pulled at his lower lip. It quivered, either from fear or obduracy. He pulled at it again and it curved into a wry smile. He stepped upon a fallen bough which collapsed to powder beneath his weight. Mounds of woodlice scurried out of his path. He swore. He smiled one-sidedly, patting his spear arm. For some inexplicable reason his confidence was rising. Edgar watched him pick up a pebble and throw it into the air. He caught it and threw it up again and again.

It was such a normal, such a boyish thing to do. Seeing him do it brought a smile to his face and plucked up his courage. Something had to be all right for Lee to be able to do that. It wasn't all death and gloom in the world. For the Aetz, there was nothing else. It seemed to wield death like a weapon. But the Aetz didn't control their world *yet*...

Yes, death lay over the peninsula like a yawning tomb. Everything was tainted by it. It was something he could not scrub off, something in the very cells of his skin and his organs, tattooed there forever. Yet, for all that, he felt comforted and consoled. There was good out there still, Lee had shown him that. All they had to do was tap into it. The sword and the spear belonged to good. What was there to fear?... Relinquished of the dread of combat, he was bathed in ineffable peace.

— 74. Briefer Than Brief —

They passed between jagged bones, inhaling the stench of rotting flesh.

'Soon *we* might look like that,' Lee grumbled, hurling the pebble from him.

It clattered in a ribcage over yonder.

A hissing sound made them glance upwards. The gargoyles were staring down at them. They gurgled and spat plugs of filth from their throats. It splatted into the mud about them, steaming and stinking to high heaven. Chuckling began in those disgusting throats of theirs, and rose to chill, sneering laughter.

'I'd love to lop a few of their heads off their scrawny necks,' Edgar snarled.

'Ed! Look!! The salmail!!!'

It was stretched across the battlements, glinting in the moonlight.

'It's a trophy… The rotten maggoty creep,' Edgar growled venomously.

An icy blast struck them full force in the chest. They winced as sleety particles bit into their faces.

'Come down, you filthy maggot!' Edgar roared at the top of his voice. 'Are you afraid of us?!' he shouted when nothing appeared.

That set the gargoyles screeching in a frenzy. They lusted after their blood, yearning desperately to see them torn to pieces.

'Now you've done it,' Lee moaned. 'Why make it worse than it is already?'

'Because I want to have done with it,' Edgar angrily barked at him. 'I'm sick to death of being scared. Berry'd be alive now if it wasn't for me.'

'That's stupid.'

'If I'd come over earlier and killed that thing, it wouldn't have got its clutches on him!' he shouted, stabbing his fingers at the roof. 'Go back if you want to!' he spat at his friend.

'Drop dead. I'm not going nowhere!'

Edgar chuckled. It was so close to the bone that it had to be funny. But the smile was wiped clean from his face when a massive head and shoulders appeared over the parapet.

The Aetz had heard his challenge.

Edgar opened his mouth to insult it but was struck dumb by the sight of a gargoyle's neck stretching so far that its repulsive face was next to its master's. It whispered in its ear. The creature started and growled with fury. It muttered something and a posse of bats soared into the air. It snatched up the salmail, waving it above its head like a victory flag.

'Let it fall. Please make it let go of it,' Lee pleaded in a whisper. 'It could be the saving of us.'

But the creature's grip was sure and it flung the salmail onto the roof behind it.

We're history, he wailed internally.

74. Briefer Than Brief

The boys watched as the thing descended the wall from gargoyle to gargoyle. Evil-smelling slime spurted from their mouths and nostrils. Everything seemed to be happening in slow-motion. Edgar thought of David and Goliath, Samson and the Philistines. If only he were strong and brave like them… If only he were older… David had been a boy, hadn't he? But this thing bearing down on them was far bigger than any Goliath.

Time had forsaken them.

The ground shook as the Aetz leapt onto it. The vibrations travelled up their legs, jarring their bones. The gargoyles fell instantly silent, awaiting the inevitable. The hush was unbearable.

This was it, then.
Their moment had come.

'Can't we use the ring?' Lee whimpered.

Edgar never even heard him.

They stood their ground in silence, knuckles white around shaft and hilt.

'I'm not afraid of you,' Edgar growled, clenching his teeth defiantly. 'Not any more.'

— 75. Morgammeron Undone —

The Aetz made one fatal mistake. In a bid to goad them to the very end, to see fear and suffering etched in their faces, it had sent the bats on a devilish mission. It waited, anticipating the shock, the horror, the insult and humiliation. This waif with his sword deserved to have his suffering heightened to the utmost.

Its cruelty backfired.

The living cloud returned. The malicious face of the moon crept from behind the tower for a better look. A dark shape suddenly broke free of the posse and smashed against the wall. Berry's limp body rebounded onto the earth below. His left arm snapped. A sharp splinter of bone broke through the skin. Part of his face was crushed.

With a cry of utter dismay, both boys ran and knelt down beside him. The disfigurement would haunt them till the end of their days. Delicately, with love, they straightened Berry's arm, trying to manoeuvre the bone under the skin. Edgar smoothed his face to conceal the concavity and pulled the flesh of his nose into place.

A hideous chuckling sound finally registered on their ears. Anger bubbled in Edgar's veins like lava.

Like lava it erupted.

He leapt to his feet and literally danced in his rage.

'I'll kill you!' he screeched, veins like ropes in his neck, blood practically starting from the pores of his forehead. 'You'll wish you'd never been born when I'm finished with you!'

But there was no Aetz to be seen.

Beware the fool moon...

Both boys were bathed in cold light, their stark shadows stretching out far behind them. The Aetz, in contrast, was veiled by shadowy night. A glint of light, reflected back from Edgar's sword, illuminated it but briefly. For an instant the moon was forced to reveal its fugleman.

'The moon,' Lee whispered to himself. 'The fool moon... We can't fight it if we can't *see* it!'

He stared up at the face mocking them, willing them to be crushed to pulp. He didn't know why - never in later life was he able to explain it - but he raised his right arm, jerked the shaft of the spear backwards till he was gripping it midway, steadied it, took aim and hurled it with all his might. The blade cleaved the night sky, unwavering in its course. It glinted in the treacherous light, as if guided to its target.

The yellow face shuddered when the point buried itself deep in its cheek. The mouth formed a round O of surprise and the hideous face was extinguished in an instant. Simultaneously the Aetz reappeared. Unshackled at last, the true moon battled her way to her zenith. Orion leapt over the horizon once more.

Doubt flooded the creatures eyes. It grunted uncertainly, unable to decide whether to attack or retreat. A stupid grin distorted its features. It made its final mistake, the blunder of all blunders.

The Aetz smashed its foot down on Berry's body and roared.

The roar became a scream of pain for Edgar's sword had pierced the leathery skin of its shin and notched the bone. It drew up the leg and massaged it, aghast at the temerity of the boy.

A blast of icy wind struck Edgar full in the chest. He fought back, leaning into it and forging forward. Nothing was about to stop him now, nothing but death, and death he no longer feared. He would relinquish life for the memory of his lost friend. He was hell-bent on avenging him. Spittle splashed on his face. He retched at the stench of its foul breath. A gargantuan fist came down and struck the earth beside him and he hardly noticed it.

A cloud mass swirled at a great height above Garten, twisting itself into a knot. What little colour there was faded from everything in that accursed field. The sea grew restless, waves jostling and buffeting one another. They hurled themselves against the cliffs in a vain attempt to escape the fury of the deep. A brassy glare suffused everything. Monstrous thunderheads rose miles into the sky, waiting to unleash their pent-up violence. And yet it seemed to drain from them, inhaled by the apex of the tower.

The gargoyles exhaled and the wind became a solid mass driving Edgar backwards. Bones half-buried in the mud rattled together. A skeletal hand struck him full in the face. Still he battled forwards. What was pain to him now? The gale knocked him down, prevented him from rising. He crawled nearer on all fours. Because he had to. Because duty lay before him and he held on to it like a rope leading him home, to the light, to survival. The gargoyles poured stagnant water from their mouths and spat hail in his face. The tower swayed in the hurricane, the noise of the wind breathtaking round its battlements. Lightning tore through the firmament. Thunder rumbled, crashed, then shook the universe. This was no ordinary storm. This was Nature perverted grappling with a single boy trying at last to fight his corner, to take on the elements for the sake of a fallen humanity.

Chaos reigned. An invisible fist squeezed the gray sponge and rain fell in torrents. His sodden clothes clung to him and hindered him further, weighing him down, making it difficult to move his arm.

The arm.

Arm of the sword.

He slapped his wet hair out of his eyes, smearing it back from his forehead. He raised his head and screeched into the wind.

'Are you done yet?… Is this the best you can do?… Because, if it is, I'm not *impressed!*'

75. Morgammeron Undone

Meteors spilled from outer space, bouncing off the atmosphere, puncturing the blackness in a final burst of light. A glorious death, Edgar thought, hijacking the spectacle. Fire of the Avenging Angel.

Orion!

He struggled to his feet and dashed forward, ran headlong into the creature and jumped back. A huge spongy clot filled the wound he'd inflicted. Worms wriggled, trapped in the mass of congealing blood.

He was fear, living fear. It possessed him, towered within him, commanding the creature to die. Thoughts of Berry filled his mind; his bluing lips, that faraway gaze, his sightless eyes, his loyal concern for Spike when he had so much more to worry about. But that was Berry all over, wasn't it? Selfless, to the very end.

His own blood boiled as he remembered. With a roar of a growl of a scream Edgar hacked and hacked, barely aware of what he was doing, knowing he had to and couldn't give in. The tower surged upwards before him. The screams of the gargoyles faltered, clotted blood stuffing their throats and filling their mouths and nostrils.

Numbed by exhaustion, he let his arm drop.

He could do no more.

†

PART V

WATERSHED

— 76. All That Glittered... —

Silence.

Absolute silence prevailed.

Not a breeze. Not a raindrop. Only his heartbeat drumming in his ears and his lungs inflating and deflating. They too calmed and he heard nothing at all. He was alone in dark quietude, wandering the labyrinths of an exhausted mind.

He opened his eyes, unsure what he was about to see, too tired to care. Lee was standing next to him, frozen to the spot, staring in blank astonishment.

'You did it,' he whispered. 'Ed, you *did* it!'

Fingers closed tightly round his forearm and he nodded.

He *had* done it.

The hideous evidence lay all around him. Pieces of the Aetz were all over the place. Blood covered the ground and spattered the walls to a height of ten feet. Viscid, black, putrid blood coated the blade of his sword.

'You've really done it, Ed. I can hardly believe it myself.'

'Not without you're help, I wouldn't.'

'Rubbish. What did I do?'

'If it weren't for you tossing that spear at the moon, I would never have seen it... We'd both be dead now if it wasn't for you.'

Lee tore himself away from the remains of the creature and smiled at his friend.

'My God... What we've been through together!... It's past describing.'

They both turned back to the aftermath and studied the debris in silence. The heads of the gargoyles hung heavy on limp necks, their leathery eyelids closed. The ivy had wilted, leaves blackened and torn. As for the tower, it leaned over at an angle. At the very top, rows upon rows of bats clung to the battlements and covered the roof. They were alive, staring down at the two boys and what lay scattered about them.

Together, all at once, they launched into the air and plummeted downwards. Edgar and Lee crouched and covered their heads. Nothing came of it. Opening their eyes, they found themselves in a vortex of winged bodies, whirling, stooping, soaring away. Each and every one of them was gathering a piece of the monster in its claws and carrying it off. Edgar's sword was knocked from his grasp. They licked the blood off it where it fell. Scores of them covered the saturated wall and cleaned it. Done, they flew to the roof, busy accounting for all the pieces. Satisfied at last, they rose into the air en masse and disappeared.

The necks of the gargoyles craned upwards after them. Unable to follow, they screamed and howled in self-pity, the noise rising to fever pitch when the ivy slid rapidly down the walls and began to sink into the mud. Tendrils attached themselves to the crazed scarecrows and dragged them down with them. The mud seethed and bubbled. The strewn bones sank out of sight.

The ground began to shake. A shudder went through the tower. Large cracks appeared in its walls. The roof blew off and the walls exploded outwards. Great lumps of rock smashed into the earth, huge projectiles hurled by a giant.

They lay where they fell.

Nothing remained but the ruin of the past, the stump of their youth.

A fresh breeze stirred in their hair. The woodland trees sighed in the pale dawn light. Edgar and Lee looked over their shoulders in surprise. The branches of the trees were no longer knotted together. They stretched wide in welcome. An unseen bird warbled in the undergrowth, serenading a new world born through strife. It was as if it had never happened.

The two warriors surveyed the scene of devastation.

'Who would have thought we could have created such havoc,' Lee stated with a lop-sided grin.

Edgar grunted and smiled.

'And this time Sabrehilt *did* survive, Ed, I'm mighty glad to say.'

'So am I, you won't be surprised to hear.'

'Let's go and rescue your mam and dad,' Lee sang and skipped ahead.

They ran across the field, chattering and guffawing, pushing and tumbling, carefree boys once more.

— 77. The Day That Was in It —

A cock crowed to wake the sun and bid him rise. It pierced the clouds and spilled liquid gold upon a scarified earth. Blood drained from the woolen fibres in the sky. A gentle breeze dispersed them. A dome of azure once more curved above them, clean and translucent. Light rain bathed the landscape, pouring through the mouths of the petrified gargoyles, cleansing their gullets and the tower walls below them. It sealed away the cloying dust and freshened the atmosphere.

A bird twittered. Another answered. Owls, hunting by daylight, swooped over the rim of the field to rid the peninsula of vermin. Swallows tumbled like acrobats, intent on every insect. A lone curlew flew in a low arc across the field, its warbling wail triumphant - not a cry of despair but of hope rekindled. It reminded them of the witch. Who could fortell what Fate had in store…?

The bell of the church awoke, its lyrical peal revived. The sun, now warm on their skin, dispelled the terrors of nightmares, the pall of death. The world was alive again. The rhymes and rhythms of Spring coursed through the roots and the branches with a surge of glee. Clover thrust its way through the bare soil and covered the desolate landscape, soft and sweet to look upon. Sap rose relentlessly. Fresh green buds swelled and burst into leaf. A wild rose nodded boldly at the end of an elastic briar, face fully open to the sunlight. A single rose, it sang of midsummer. Nature's cycle had recovered, silent, insistent, inexorable. Life and joy were rearing their heads and their spirits climbed high.

Smoke from a few early fires rose into the still, morning air. As if nothing had ever happened. As if winter had never been. A cloaked and hooded figure stepped from the edge of the woods and waited for them. The hermit! They ran to him, proud and relieved. Both his hands went to the rim of his hood and lowered it. A stranger he was. Their hearts sank in their breasts.

'Who are *you*?' Lee demanded. 'Where's... *our* hermit?'

The stranger smiled fondly before answering.

'I am another... To replace him.'

A babbling brook of a voice, over polished granite boulders. They could have listened to him always, sighing and straining after the sound. He was a young man, with golden curls encircling his tonsure. His habit was of a lighter colour, less soiled, less course. Was he a hermit at all, they wondered.

'What happened to him?' Edgar finally asked him.

In reply he held up his arms, wide sleeves slipping back and baring them. A wind blew through the trees, stirring the new leaves, disturbing the dead ones, eddying them into currents and heaping them against boulders and tree-trunks. That which they covered was revealed: ancient warriors in stone cast down, half buried in the mulch. A pathway appeared as a clearing and they saw the tree their old friend had mentioned. And there, carved into the gnarled bark, they recognized his likeness.

'He had been here since the last Sabrehilt was born,' the new hermit explained.

'And you'll be here till the next,' Edgar finished for him.

He gave a solemn nod in answer.

'Everything comes in time to him who knows how to wait.'

'Death,' Edgar murmured.

'*Life*,' the monk stressed with an emphatic whisper, eyes alight with merriment.

Edgar nodded, understanding at last.

Slowly he replaced his hood, bowed to them both and turned. They watched his figure recede into the wood, bracken fronds meeting behind him. Delicious peace wafted in his wake. The birds began to sing the dawn chorus. The boys tore themselves away and strode purposely through the woods in the direction of the church.

Prickleback and Booth were at the rear of the building. The reverend stood at the top of the steps by the open gate. Racker was below, keys rattling while he struggled to undo the lock. Prickleback turned sharply and stared at Edgar.

'You!' he rasped in fear and loathing.

'Were you expecting him to be dead, Prickleback?' Lee asked with a sneer.

'Shut your filthy mouth, urchin. Is that a becoming way to address your betters?'

Lee's lip curled. He shrugged his shoulders. The man didn't frighten him any more.

Edgar made to push past the preacher but he grabbed him by the collar and held on tight.

'Perhaps you arrive too late,' he snarled.

'Ed!' his father exclaimed on seeing him. 'Moll, it's Ed. He's *alive!*'

She ran to his side, peering up. Booth cursed and rattled the keys impatiently.

'This is no fairy tale, you fool,' Prickleback snarled with derision. 'No happy ending for *you*.'

'It's a *real* fairy tale,' Edgar rejoined with a wry smile.

He shook off the reverend's grip and slowly descended the steps.

'Out of my way, Rack,' he growled.

The fool guffawed, then fell to snarling. 'Just you try and stop me,' he spat.

'I warn you, Prickleback,' Edgar shouted. 'Either control your henchman or pay the consequences.'

'What consequences, pray?'

'We're witnesses.'

'Who would believe you?' he scoffed.

'It's all recorded in the Book, remember?'

His wicked smile waxed, then waned. The scornful resolve in his eyes wavered.

'Gerty has it safe,' Lee mocked at him. 'Don't pretend you don't know about it... You'll never escape, Prickleback. All we have to do is show everyone the book.'

The reverend's lip quivered. 'Booth, step back,' he feebly muttered. 'Step back, I say!' he shouted when Booth ignored him.

77. The Day That Was in It

'Damn you, Prickleback. Damn you to hell! You may be a dastard but *I'm* not.'

With that he turned the key in the lock. Drawing a dagger from beneath his jerkin he stepped into the vault.

'Now then, miller,' he quipped. 'Prepare to meet thy Maker.'

The miller's wife screamed. Her husband shielded her behind him.

'Booth!' Edgar roared in warning, lunging through the entrance and nicking his arm.

Furious at the humiliation of being wounded by a stripling, Racker swung his blade to cut the boy's throat. Edgar sprang out of the way just in time.

The two adversaries stood staring at one another, nostrils flared, breath coming in short, rasping gasps. Rack envied the boy his power and hated him all the more. In his jealousy he forgot the mill, determined to kill Edgar's parents and torture him for the rest of his life.

'I'm warning you, Rack!' Edgar stormed in anxiety. 'One step closer and I'll…'

'You'll what, ridgling?… You haven't got it in you.'

He gripped his knife and made for the miller.

It was the very last step he took.

Rack's head toppled off his shoulders and rolled under a shelf. Averting their eyes, Edgar's mother and father stepped over the body and through the gate. Their son stood staring down at the corpse in a trance.

'I killed him,' he muttered. 'I killed a man when I could have cut off his arm and spared his life.'

'That wouldn't have stopped the likes of him,' his dad said to console him. 'He deserved to die, that 'un. It was him or us, son. You had no choice... 'Twas a demon in man's form, Ed. Your conscience is easy. He paid the price of his wickedness.'

Edgar nodded mutely.

'You're a man, Ed. A fully-fledged man. You've earned your stripes far earlier than most. There are few out there like you. Your grandpa'd'ev been proud of you.'

That brought a smile to Edgar's face. To hear such words from his father's lips made it all worthwhile. He embraced him and the miller hugged him tight, patting his back with his big, strong hands. He hugged his mother too while she sobbed with relief.

'Thank God you're safe.'

'A hero, Moll. Your son's a *hero!*'

Edgar felt the keen edge of discomfort at the tone of his father's voice. He didn't want to be a hero and have his dad looking up to him. He wanted to remain a son hoping to grow up like his father, nothing more. They made to ascend the steep steps together. Prickleback stood at the top with the darkest of expressions. Around him were grouped a goodly number of villagers. His plans were uncoiling, the mill no longer a distant promise. He couldn't bear that. Edgar read his thoughts and stopped in his tracks.

'Let us go. I did what you asked.'

All he got in answer was a glare of absolute hatred.

'Let us go or I'll separate your head from your shoulders like I did his.'

A hiss went up from the motley group. The reverend had an idea.

'I *will* allow you to go,' he deigned. 'But you must leave this place forever. If you, *any* of you, dare to return, I shall strike you down. I shall leave no stone unturned, I promise you...'

'We'll take our things and be gone by tomorrow,' the miller gruffly told him.

'If by nightfall tomorrow you remain, your lives shall be forfeit.'

The group separated to let them pass, murmuring and grimacing.

Prickleback had to be rid of them, above all the boy. He was too powerful to remain, a threat he couldn't deal with. There can be only one shepherd to one flock.

'No good will come of their staying,' he whispered to the crowd who nodded in agreement. 'Black magic,' he intimated and they hissed and growled.

'Come on, son,' muttered the miller. 'Who'd want to stay here anyways?'

The strangest thing of all was that Edgar felt pity for these people. They had not grasped the meaning of life, its simplicity, its joy, all of which had been rudely thrust upon him. It was enough to live and let live, not to hate or envy, to covet or possess. To live from day to day, gratefully, gladly, happily, such was the mystery of life. Such pleasures could not be stolen away or broken. Such happiness lasted a lifetime. The mill would have been enough, after all, he thought with a wry smile. Heroics were for lesser mortals.

— 78. Eve of Departure —

The harsh winter thawed in their hearts while they warmed themselves before a roaring fire. They were home, really home. Edgar was plied with questions from every angle. Everyone wanted to know how he had killed the Aetz. Lee was shouting his head off, words tripping over themselves as he tried to describe everything in detail. Oaf and his siblings jumped up and down on the rug, eyes starting from their heads.

It was good to talk of fear when horror was banished forever. Spike groaned contentedly in Edgar's lap. It was a rare concession, but he had been so excited on his return. It would have been cruel not to. A blur of hands slapped Edgar's back, patted his shoulders, tousled his hair. He smiled vaguely, barely able to take it all in. Somewhere, deep inside him, mists swirled before his eyes while sunlight shone in his soul. He was happy, at peace.

He lay in his bed that night, alone with Spike. His father's voice still rang in his ears. 'Now, now, leave the hero be. He needs his rest. You can sleep wherever you like but not with Ed.' This above the clamour of pleading voices, begging to share his room, to lie on the floor, it didn't matter where as long as they were with the boy who had killed the Aetz. But the miller was adamant. They knew they wouldn't sway him.

In awe of himself he lay there. A short while ago he had been a boy bolting the barn-door for his mam, sharing a joke with his dad, shuddering at the sight of those toads. Now he was… What exactly was he? Surely the same boy as before… Sabrehilt, the name had overtaken and crowned him.

Did he feel sad at leaving his home?… Was he capable of feeling anything at all?

Gerty and Farmer Buckrake had come for Berry's body. They had taken him to his mother and father. Where would they bury him? Not it the churchyard, surely! Not surrounded by all those hypocrites. All that had happened hadn't changed them one whit.

No, he wouldn't miss his old haunts. Garten would never be the same again. The soil was polluted. The trees and grass had taken it up through their roots and he would always remember. It was a sickness of the heart, weighing as heavy as the burden he'd relinquished. But hearts that are young can grow tender and soft. Away from this place.

He sighed and turned over. Spike gave a groan of self-pity. He was tempted to kick him through the covers and tumble him off the bed in fun but was too tired to do so. There was a knock at the door downstairs. It opened and closed. He heard whispers but was beyond caring. They could deal with their own problems now. He had done more than his fair share.

†

— 79. Lest They Turn Back —

It had all been arranged overnight. Many of the children were coming with them. *They* heeded the warning, if their parents hadn't. As he were leaving, Edgar noticed the green shoots of a sapling piercing the soil next the gate.

'Lem!'

He bent down and gently dug it up with his hands. Wherever they settled he would plant it with the ring once again. Why leave it behind when no Falchion was returning to the mill and Garten? He looked back at the familiar place and couldn't suppress a sigh. Buckrake was to send their possessions after them. He was staying put. Someone had to keep a wary eye on these people.

Round a corner they ran into Prickleback and his mob, coming to see whether they had left or not. Among them Lee spotted the Arnold girl and ran to her. It was now or never. He swallowed his heart, blind to the antipathy in her eyes.

'Will you come with us?' he blurted.

She cast him a scornful look. 'My daddy says you're evil.'

It was the straw that broke the camel's back.

'He'd know all about it, wouldn't he?' he shot back at her.

'I prefer Jeremy to you. Always did.'

'You're welcome to him. I wish I could say that he'd had a lucky escape like *I* have.'

'You're nothing but a bunch of hypocrites, the whole lot of you.'

'Your daddy said that too, I bet… Who the hell cares what he says?' He was simmering nicely now and let her have it. 'Having a daughter like you says more than enough about him.'

'Shut your face, Lee Chetwood.'

'Oh, go milk yourself, you silly cow.'

'And you're an old bull, so *there*.'

'That's for sure, but there are plenty of heifers where I'm headed.'

'Get out of here.'

'Oh, I'm going, all right, but I won't be back…'

Words stalled and failed him. He'd caught sight of his mother. They looked into one another's eyes, Lee nervously flexing and unflexing his fingers. If she had said one word about coming home he would have run straight into her arms.

She never opened her mouth. A cold stare met his tentative smile, fading when she turned deliberately away. Lee hung his head and sobbed.

She never loved me, did she?…

Edgar watched in sympathy, his heart bleeding for his friend. He patted his shoulder when he returned.

'She didn't even speak to me, Ed… Never said a word.'

'You're one of us now, Lee. Part of our family.'

'I'd like that… That cow, Felicia Arnold, told me to hump off.'

'Doesn't surprise me.'

'How about Rhoda?'

'She's coming with us.'

'She *is*?… Lucky you.'

'Forget Felicia, Lee. I told you she was a rag-bag.'

Lee flared up. 'I can think of better words than rag-bag,' he growled. A mischievous smile glinted in his eyes. 'I called her a cow to her face. Told her to go milk herself.'

'You didn't.'

'Yep. I sure did.'

'You know, you don't need the likes of her. Sure, half the girls here can't keep their eyes off you.'

'They *can't*?!' He straightened himself up and pushed back his shoulders. 'In that case she can have her Jeremy Hildersmiths. And you know what?'

'What?'

'She'll be sorry one day.'

'Really sorry, Lee. Really, really sorry.'

Lee beamed with gratitude. 'You're some friend, Edgar Falchion.'

'So are you. It goes without saying.'

— 80. Dust Off Their Feet —

They avoided the village, turning left off the road and making diagonally for the river. A number of long-boats fitted with sails were moored there. The miller and the other men rowed, letting them drift in the current now and then. In silence they glimpsed the gable-end of The Slaughtered Ox. That was the last they'd see of the inn, the last they'd see of Garten.

Garten… Had it ever been a decent place to live in? A curse hung over it, periodically embodied by the Aetz, and men like Snake and Booth. What else could such a village nurture in its bosom? An involuntary shiver crept down their spines as they passed under the bridge. They wondered how they had stayed so long. Gasps of horror and stifled cries were heard and everyone stared into the field sloping down to the river on their right. Dumbstruck, their eyes were fixed on the dreadful sight as the boats drifted seawards.

A decomposing figure was staked upright with its arms outstretched, a human scarecrow to frighten children and adults away. Flesh had been torn from one side of the head to reveal the white skull underneath. Hands hung limply from lifeless wrists. Both eyes were missing from their lidless sockets. The mouth sagged open in an eternal, noiseless yell.

Wisps of blood-clotted hair stirred in the wind, the whole body shook. They recognized him by his clothes, soiled by guano. Grindlewick. A lone jackdaw pecked viciously at the top of his head and cackled with glee. A turn in the river snatched him from sight. They shuddered and breathed a sigh of relief, eyes intent on the mouth of the Mead and the sea beyond.

Edgar and Lee sat side by side. They stood up to wave to Oaf and his brothers and sisters in the second boat before they realized that it was their father they had just passed.

'Boy, was that a close shave,' Lee whispered.

'Whew. Just as well we remembered in time.'

'I completely forgot he was their father. Not that he deserved to be called one, like someone *else* I could mention.'

'You've a new father now, Lee, who'll treat you like a father should.'

'But what does *he* think about it, Ed? And how about your *mam*?'

'They're both delighted. Why wouldn't they be? I get the brother I always wanted and they get a second son.'

'Yeah, but me? *Me*.'

'That's the reason we're delighted. We wouldn't have anybody else.'

'Thanks.'

'I'm not saying it to be nice. I mean it.'

'I know… Always wanted to be your brother.'

'Did you?'

'Uh huh.'

Edgar smiled with delight. 'That's that, then,' he murmured.

'Hey, would you look at that,' Lee gestured, nudging him with his elbow.

Tomothy Brindleshanks was surrounded by girls. He was the wittiest person in the village and they loved him for it. No one made them laugh as much as he did. Lee and Edgar smiled at the sight. Good had come of their endeavours.

'He earned it,' Lee declared with conviction.

'Oh, yes… A hundred times over.'

'Who would ever have believed it?… What the hell. We *all* bloody well deserve it!'

Edgar laughed long and low. Was he glad Lee had survived alongside him. What would he have done without such a friend? Someone *had* been looking after them.

He surveyed the familiar landscape slipping away with tears in his eyes. This was his home he was leaving. Where he had grown up. Where his grandpa had played as a boy. Where he had had his adventures alongside his friends, some of whom he was leaving behind – innocent, boyish adventures before… Before he really knew the people he shared the village with. Before the Aetz came to destroy everything…

No… He hated the place, abhorred and feared it. Blood had been spilt there, innocent blood mingling with the not-so-innocent. Blood and evil… suffering and death. He had to get away. They would start another life, all of them together. He hoped a new land and new experiences would replace the memories, where they could laugh and smile and be happy. And forget. More than anything else, forget.

Gerty lurched along the boat and squeezed between the two of them.

'Move over, you two,' she said with a smile of greeting.

'Where are we going?' Lee asked her.

'Over there,' she replied, pointing her finger.

'The island?'

'Isle of the Guillemots.'

'But is it safe?'

'Of course, it's safe. I wouldn't take you there otherwise. Not after what you two have been through.'

While she spoke with Edgar, Lee struck up a conversation with the girl on his right. He'd been aware of her for some time. They emerged from the mouth of the River Mead and were in the open sea. A flash of silver sped across their bows and had all the children talking excitedly and craning their necks. The wail of sea-mews filled their ears, sound of salt-air and freedom. The sails were unfurled and Garten diminished behind them.

'How are you, young man?' Gerty cheerily asked Edgar, searching his face.

'So-so.'

'Only that?'

He nodded. 'Have you got the book?' he asked with unfeigned indifference.

'Of course. I'm hardly likely to forget it, now, am I? We Mallock girls don't shirk our responsibility. Not that we're on a par with you Falchion boys.'

He stared out to sea, carrying the pain of losing his home, the pain of all the wickedness that had unfolded before him, the pain of acting too late. That pain would never leave him, despite being a hero in so many eyes. Tears rolled down his cheeks and Gerty clasped his knee.

'I left it too late,' he sobbed. 'If I'd done it sooner, Berry'd be alive today.'

'Edgar, you cannot blame yourself for those who died.'

'I can blame myself for Berry.'

'Not even Berry… Yours was a tremendous task, daunting for a boy your age. You were not prepared for what was to come and the Aetz returned early to destroy you. It failed because of your courage, far beyond your years. If it weren't for you there'd be none of us alive here today, dwell on that.'

'It can come back again?'

'Oh, yes. If they don't learn by their mistakes.'

He almost hoped it would, but that wouldn't bring Berry back.

'If it comes back and I'm not there?'

'They forced you out. Let *them* deal with it.'

'… What about Berry's folks?'

'They're already on the island. They went across to bury him.'

'I'm glad they didn't leave him there… But what about the people on the island? What'll they say about all of us?'

'It's my island.'

'It's *yours*?'

'Yes… They're good, honest folk. They won't complain.'

'You knew this would happen.'

'To a certain extent.'

'Are you a witch, Gerty?' he asked, thinking of the second swan.

'Some say I am. Have been calling me one for years.'

'I don't mean like that. A *white* witch.'

'Maybe I am. Maybe I'm not,' she responded with an arch smile.

'They wanted to burn you at the stake, didn't they?… We used to think you were bad as well. How could we have done that? How can people *be* like that?'

'By having their empty minds filled by hate when they're young and impressionable. Ignorance is a dangerous thing in the wrong hands because you can be moulded almost to anything. The unscrupulous exploit it to gain power.'

'Prickleback, you mean. And he gets away with it.'

'So far... He's like a fish leaping from the water to escape a predator, seeking to do so in another element. He cannot, at least not for long. He falls back or he dies. Unknown to himself, he has tried to live in both elements at once. He is bound to fail.'

'Still and all, I wish we hadn't been horrible to you when we were younger.'

'You're a good lad, Edgar Falchion. You weren't fully responsible. But we all can change when we're older. *You* did.'

'I think you *are* a white witch.'

'Best be getting back,' she said with a smirk.

Getting to her feet, she squeezed his shoulder and returned to her place in the prow. He sat in silence, watching the island come nearer, leaving Lee chatter away with the girl beside him. At least *he* was happy. But Lee had that knack of always looking on the bright side. As he once had. Once…

The island did look peaceful and welcoming, but would it be home to them?... Maybe. Just maybe.

— 81. Horizons —

Edgar sat on the cliff top on the far side of the island staring out to sea, lulled by the hiss and gasp of the waves crashing against the black walls, sending up spray from below to sprinkle his face. He felt great peace, a peace amplified by nothing to prey on his mind. Peace before him. Peace within him. Peace everywhere around him. It was explosive, addictive.

Puffins waddled into burrows in the turf all about him. Guillemots and razorbills crowded the ledges, incubating their eggs while their mates wheeled over the waters or dived to catch fish for them. Soon they both would be working endlessly to satisfy their ravenous broods.

The new arrivals had had time to settle in, building cottages and doubling the size of the village. Gerty had had the school enlarged to accommodate so sudden an influx of pupils. The islanders had been kind to them once they'd realized that they weren't those puritanical types Garten was famous for.

He heard his name blowing faintly on the wind and turned to see Lee coming towards him. He waved, turned back to the sea and waited.

'I've been looking for you *everywhere*. The teacher missed you and wondered where you were. I should have guessed you'd be up here.'

'Are you supposed to come and fetch me?'

'She never said. Actually, I skipped out before she could say anything… You spend a lot of time up here, don't you?'

'I like it up here. I like being able to look out to sea and see nothing. I like the muffled roar of the waves below. It makes me feel good.'

Lee sat down beside him, locking his arms round his knees. 'It is nice up here,' he mused aloud. 'Must come more often myself.'

'You're way too busy with Stiggy Gilright to bother coming here,' Edgar ragged him.

'Could always bring *her* up here, couldn't I?' he answered with a mischievous grin.

He raised his eyebrows up and down, making Edgar laugh at the implication.

'She's lovely, is Stiggy,' Edgar complimented him.

'Yeah, but I do wish she was called something other than Stiggy.'

'What's wrong with Stiggy?'

Lee grimaced. 'It's sort of peculiar.'

'Better than Felicia, I would have said.'

'Miles better! Miles, miles, *miles*…' He looked out to sea before saying, 'I like it here on the island, do you?'

'Sure, I do.'

'It's way better than Garten. I don't miss it any more.'

'Neither do I.'

'I think I'll stay here,' he said with a languid sigh, lying back and dangling his legs over the cliff edge, 'and marry Stiggy.'

'Whoa! Who's getting ahead of himself *now*?'

Lee sat up and gave his friend a shove. Edgar's eyes dilated in shock as he felt himself overbalance.

'For God's sake, you nearly sent me over the edge!'

Lee lay back again and crowed laughter into the air, above the resounding waves.

'That'd be rich, wouldn't it? The Aetz couldn't do it but Lee Chetwood did away with him in seconds. Lee Chetwood, Shieldbearer, hero of the Gartenites! Poor old Sabrehilt… Still, I'd better be getting back. Stiggy might be missing me.'

He jumped to his feet, slammed his open palm into Edgar's back and ran off hollering.

'I'll tell her I couldn't find you,' he shouted from a distance.

Edgar nodded and held a hand up without turning.

The waves pounded the cliffs below, tumbling over one another to reach the shore. Endlessly. A new wave every time. Never the same one twice. A surge, a crash, gone and forgotten. Like Time. The past had become a dull ache and even that had been replaced by a vague, painless memory. He found it difficult now to form a sharp image of Berry's features. He remembered more or less what he'd looked like. He could still hear his voice, though. But he smiled now, fondly, glad he had befriended him when he'd had the chance, glad he had been in on the adventure with them and bitten off a chunk of life. It *had* been an adventure, hadn't it?… Despite all the danger and horror…

Spike was getting old now, prematurely, it seemed. White hairs faded the markings on his head. He couldn't skip and run as he had, or he just didn't want to, preferring to stretch out by the range and snore. Now and then he got it into his head to race ahead of Edgar and chase the grumbling puffins down their burrows. He panted more than ever, pink tongue lolling out the side of his mouth. But he enjoyed himself. He was happy.

The ocean heaved. What if some huge monster lay on the bottom, so big that when its chest expanded and contracted in breathing, it shifted all the waters of the world? Something so big that the Aetz was smaller than its fingernail. Something which lay in its mightiness between them. At first he'd regarded the horizon as a trip-wire to catch them unawares. Not any more. It was a tight-rope stretched between day and night, hallmark of the relentless but comforting passage of time. Berry was out there. On the tight-rope. Night and day no longer affected him. The sun remained high in the sky, reducing the shadow of the tower to nothing. One day he would come over the ocean smiling at him, at *them,* and all three of them would be reunited forever. He got to his feet, took a deep breath and smiled to himself. Time for a quick visit to Berry's grave before nipping round to Rhoda.

'The truth shall set you free,' he murmured before breaking into a canter.

Joy, like sunlight, searched the hidden chambers of his heart, warmed his thoughts and set fire to his words. Those soft lips… so soft that it had startled him the first time.

'The truth shall set you free!' he shouted, jumping into the air.

— Epilogue —

Da capo

The Gargoyles unstiffened, stretched their necks and raised their stony heads. Slowly, their eyelids opened, their tongues curled and they yawned. Delight gleamed in their cold, cruel eyes. They swallowed, opened their mouths and began blowing.

The wind rose and moaned ominously in the casements. It heaved its shoulders against gable-ends and sucked smoke and flames up chimneys. It roared and screamed through the woods, tearing boughs from trunks and toppling trees. Rooks and hooded crows hung suspended in an angry sky while they battled to reach the precincts of the tower. Women and children cowered before fires, bolting doors and shutters after their menfolk had left them. They had hastened to the inn at the first inkling of danger, to hold a meeting and decide what to do. With the boy and his sword elsewhere, only one course was left open to them. The flock had a shepherd. They would go to him.

With fear they watched the black cloud spread from the horizon, impenetrable as a cloak, while they stumbled and ran to the bishop's palace. The fury of the wind was increasing, they bawled to be heard above it.

'The Reverend will have to do it!'

'There's nobody else!'

'He should have done it in the first place!'

'Wouldn't be back if he had!'

'God's on his side!'

While they approached, Prickleback sat in his library listening to the frenzy unleashed outdoors. He rose and stood in the cavernous mouth of the fireplace. Flames licked the coals, some stretching towards him, recoiling and murmuring sourly. He turned his back and creeping hair on the murky shadows looming on the walls. Was that his wife stretching out her hands and pleading for mercy?! Did he see himself raising his arms to protect himself? Was that *he* falling in the dirt? And now... the Thing!... it's huge arms pounding the brickwork. Pounding... Pounding...

At the door!

With trepidation he took up a candlestick and crept to the hall.

'Reverend Prickleback, are you there?! Let us in!'

'Save us, we beseech thee!'

'The monster has returned, there's no one else to protect us!'

His hair stood on end. A whimper escaped him. He ran across the marble squares and fled upstairs. Seeing the light they hammered all the louder.

'Reverend, 'tis thy flock. Save us!'

'We have no one else to turn to!'

They were kicking the door now. Some of them were screeching in terror.

Locking himself in his bedroom, he drowned out all noise save the rumbling of his heart, the air quivering in his nostrils, the terror pounding in his head. Outside, in the dark, a single row of scarecrows circled the castle in the periphery woods. Prickleback heard their moans and bit his clenched fist to stifle a scream that would have given him away. The cries of the rabble reached him and a louder more insistent battering seemed to shake the entire castle to its foundations. Some of them had got axes and sledgehammers from the outhouses. They were breaking in! Splinters of wood skated across the marble floor. Their feet thundered up the stairs.

With a mewling whine he threw himself upon the floor and crawled in under the bed. Beads of sweat trickled down his forehead. Salt stung in the corners of his eyes.

They're at the door. Oh, my God, they're at the door!!

His heart was in his mouth, it was difficult to breathe. How did they know of his whereabouts? Who had shown them his bedroom? Those blasted servants. *Curse* them!

Flight was impossible. The blade of an axe came through a panel of the door, stuck fast, was dislodged and smashed through again. He caught a glimpse of faces. Grim, vicious, pitiless faces.

'Come out and save us!' erupted through the splintered gap, more a threat than a plea.

Prickleback hid his face in his forearms.

'Leave me alone,' he whimpered.

'Come forth, damn you!'

'No,' he pleaded with a sob. 'Please leave me be.'

'Prickleback!!... We know you're in there!'

'You can't do this to me,' he tearfully spluttered, phlegm gathering in his throat. 'This is my home. I am a bishop's son. You can't come in here... I made a pact. I am to be bishop. My day has not yet come. I...'

The sundered door crashed into the room followed by the angry mob.

He buried his head in his hands, pretending they weren't there.

'Why did I let him go?' he whined hysterically. 'Why did I ever send the boy away? What possessed me to *do* such a thing?'

The massive bed above him seemed to weigh heavily on his shoulders, the lid of his coffin bearing down to entomb him.

†

In memory of
Grouse,
an extraordinary dog,
a wonderful pet,
a great blessing.

14th April, 2001 – 20th May, 2011

Made in the USA
Charleston, SC
21 June 2011